"An engrossing portrait of a legendary period as well as a brain teaser of startling perplexity . . . In Tallis' sure hands, the story evolves with grace and excitement. . . . A perfect combination of the hysterical past and the cooler—but probably more dangerous—present."

—*Chicago Tribune*

"Holmes meets Freud in this enjoyable . . . whodunit."

—*The Guardian* (London)

Also by Frank Tallis

A Death in Vienna
Vienna Blood

Fatal Lies

Fatal Lies

A Novel

FRANK TALLIS

VOLUME THREE OF THE
LIEBERMANN PAPERS

RANDOM HOUSE TRADE PAPERBACKS

NEW YORK

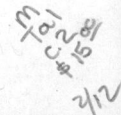

A Random House Trade Paperback Original

Copyright © 2008 by Frank Tallis
Dossier copyright © 2009 by Random House, Inc.

Published in the United States by Random House Trade Paperbacks, an imprint of The Random House Publishing Group, a division of Random House, Inc., New York.

RANDOM HOUSE TRADE PAPERBACKS and colophon are registered trademarks of Random House, Inc. MORTALIS and colophon are trademarks of Random House, Inc.

Originally published in the United Kingdom by Arrow Books, an imprint of The Random House Group, Ltd., in 2008.

LIBRARY OF CONGRESS CATALOGING-IN-PUBLICATION DATA
Tallis, Frank.
Fatal lies : a novel / Frank Tallis.
p.   cm.
ISBN 978-0-8129-7777-6 (trade pbk.)
1. Liebermann, Max (Fictitious character)—Fiction.   2. Psychoanalysts—Fiction.
3. Police—Austria—Vienna—Fiction.   4. Vienna (Austria)—Fiction.   I. Title.
PR6120.A44F38 2009
823'.92—dc22   2008023474

Printed in the United States of America

www.mortalis-books.com

2 4 6 8 9 7 5 3

Part One

The Saint Florian Mystery

I

THE BAROQUE BALLROOM was filled with flowers. Beneath three radiant chandeliers more than a hundred couples were rotating in near-perfect synchrony. The men were dressed in black tails, piqué shirts, and white gloves, the women in gowns of tulle and crêpe de chine. On a raised platform a small orchestra was playing Strauss's *Rosen aus dem Süden,* and when the waltz king's famous heartwarming melody was reprised, a number of onlookers began a sympathetic humming chorus—smiling with recognition and benign sentimentality.

Liebermann felt Amelia Lydgate's right hand tighten with anxiety in his left. A vertical line appeared on her forehead as she struggled to follow his lead.

"I do apologize, Dr. Liebermann. I am such a poor dancer."

She was wearing a skirted décolleté gown of green velvet, and her flaming red hair was tied up in silver ribbons. The pale unblemished planes of her shoulders reminded the young doctor of polished Italian marble.

"Not at all," said Liebermann. "You are doing very well for a novice. Might I suggest, however, that you listen more carefully to the music. The beat."

The Englishwoman returned a puzzled expression. "The beat," she repeated.

"Yes, can you not"—Liebermann paused, and made an effort to conceal his disbelief—"*feel* it?"

Liebermann's right hand pressed gently against Amelia's back, emphasizing the first accented beat in each bar. However, his guidance had no noticeable effect on her performance.

"Very well, then," said Liebermann. "Perhaps you will find the following useful: the *natural turn* consists of three steps in which you move forward and rotate clockwise by one hundred and eighty degrees, followed by three steps in which you move backward and rotate again by one hundred and eighty degrees. For the *forward turn* you move forward on your right foot, rotating it to the right by ninety degrees, followed by your left foot, rotated another ninety degrees so that it is now facing backward. . . ."

Amelia stopped, tilted her head to one side, and considered these instructions. Then, looking directly into Liebermann's eyes, she said plainly: "Thank you, Dr. Liebermann, that is an altogether superior explanation. Let us proceed."

Remarkably, when they began to dance again, Amelia's movements were considerably more fluid.

"Excellent," said Liebermann. "Now, if you lean back a little, we will be able to go faster." Amelia did as she was instructed, and they began to revolve more rapidly. "I believe," continued Liebermann, "that the optimal speed of the Viennese waltz is said to be approximately thirty revolutions per minute." He saw Amelia glance at his exposed wristwatch. "However, I do not think it will be necessary for us to gauge our performance against this nominal ideal."

As they swung by the orchestra, they were overtaken by a portly couple who—in spite of their ample physiques—danced with a nimbleness and grace that seemed to defy gravity.

"Good heavens," said Amelia, unable to conceal her amazement. "Is that Inspector Rheinhardt?"

"It is," said Liebermann, raising an eyebrow.

"He and his wife are very . . . accomplished."

"They are indeed," said Liebermann. "However, it is my understanding that Inspector Rheinhardt and his wife are more practiced than most. During Fasching not only do they attend *this*—the detectives' ball—but they are also regular patrons of the waiters' ball, the hatmakers' ball, the philharmonic ball, and, as one would expect"—Liebermann smiled mischievously—"the good inspector has a particular fondness for the pastry makers' ball."

As they wheeled past a pair of carved gilt double doors, Liebermann saw a police constable enter the ballroom. His plain blue uniform and spiked helmet made him conspicuous among the elegant tailcoats and gowns. His cheeks were flushed and he looked as though he had been running. The young man marched directly over to Commissioner Brügel, who was standing next to the impeccably dressed Inspector Victor von Bulow and a party of guests from the Hungarian security office.

Earlier in the evening, Liebermann had tried to engage the Hungarians in some polite conversation but had found them rather laconic. He had ascribed their reserve to Magyar melancholy, a medical peculiarity with which he, and most of his colleagues in Vienna, were well acquainted.

Liebermann lost sight of the group as Amelia and he continued their circumnavigation of the ballroom. When they had completed another circuit, he was surprised to see Else Rheinhardt standing on her own and looking toward her husband—who was now talking to Commissioner Brügel and the breathless young constable. Liebermann's observation coincided with the brassy fanfares that brought the waltz to its clamorous conclusion. The revelers cheered and applauded the orchestra. Liebermann bowed, pressed Amelia's fingers to his lips, and, taking her hand, led her toward Else Rheinhardt.

"I think something's happened," said Else.

Manfred Brügel was a stocky man with a large, blockish head and oversize muttonchop whiskers. He was addressing Rheinhardt, while occasionally questioning the young constable. Rheinhardt was listening intently. In due course, Rheinhardt clicked his heels and turned to find his wife and friends.

"My dear," said Rheinhardt, affectionately squeezing Else's arm, "I am so very sorry . . . but there has been an *incident.*" He glanced briefly at Liebermann, tacitly communicating that the matter was serious. "I am afraid I must leave at once."

"Isn't there anyone on duty at Schottenring?" asked Else.

"Koltschinsky has developed a bronchial illness, and Storfer—on being informed of the said incident—rushed from the station, slipped on some ice, and cracked his head on the pavement."

"What extraordinary bad luck," said Liebermann.

"Why is it always *you*?" said Else. "Can't somebody else go? What about von Bulow?"

"I believe he has some important business to discuss with our Hungarian friends." The air suddenly filled with the shimmering of tremolando violins, against which two French horns climbed a simple major triad. Nothing in the whole of music was so artless, yet *so* distinctive. "Ah," said Rheinhardt, "what a shame . . . *The Blue Danube.*" He looked at his wife and his eyes filled with regret.

"Oskar," said Liebermann. "Can I be of any assistance? Would you like me to come with you?"

Rheinhardt shook his head.

"I would much rather you kept my dear wife and Miss Lydgate entertained. Now, where's Haussmann?" The Inspector looked around the ballroom and discovered his assistant standing with a group of cavalrymen, gazing wistfully at a pretty young debutante in white. Heavy blond coils bounced against her cheeks. Haussmann, having clearly been engaged in a protracted surveillance operation, was about to reveal himself. He was clutching a single red rose. "Oh, no," said Rheinhardt under his breath.

The inspector kissed his wife, apologized to Amelia, and clasped Liebermann's hand. Then, moving quickly, he managed to intercept the rose just before Haussmann had reached his quarry.

2

THE INNKEEPER AT AUFKIRCHEN had been pleasant enough. Knocking a dottle of tobacco from the bowl of his clay pipe, he had warned Rheinhardt of a fallen tree: *It's blocking the road—you'll have to go the long way around.* The directions the man had given were full of local detail and were difficult to follow. When the little Romanesque church with its distinctive onion dome and spire vanished in the darkness, Rheinhardt doubted whether the exercise had been very successful.

The interior of the carriage was illuminated by a single electric bulb, the glowing arc of which was reflected in Haussmann's eyes. Rheinhardt fancied that this flickering scintilla of light was connected with the young man's thoughts—the fading memory, perhaps, of the pretty blond debutante.

Their ascent was becoming extremely uncomfortable. The narrow track that they had chosen was riddled with potholes, causing the carriage to pitch and roll. Rheinhardt pulled the curtain aside and pressed his face against the glass. He could see nothing. Releasing the catch, he opened the window and leaned out. The air was cold and dank. Ahead, the carriage lamps shone against descending blankets of thick fog.

Rheinhardt looked anxiously at his pocket watch and called out to the driver.

"Stop, will you? We should have arrived by now!"

The carriage came to a shuddering halt.

"God in heaven, Haussmann," said the inspector. "At this rate we'll never get there!"

He opened the carriage door and jumped out. His feet sank into the muddy ground, and he felt his best patent leather shoes filling up with freezing ditch water. Cursing loudly, he squelched up the road, grimacing as the sludge sucked at his heels. One of the horses snorted and shook its bridle. Rheinhardt peered into the opaque distance.

"Where on earth are we?"

"Left by the turnstile and left again at the old well," said the driver gruffly. "That's what you said, sir—and that's what I did. Turned left." Then he mumbled under his breath: "I knew it should have been right."

"Then why didn't you say so?"

The driver had not intended his final remark to be heard. He concealed his embarrassment by soothing the horses.

They were in the middle of a dense forest. An owl hooted, and something rustled in the undergrowth. Rheinhardt knew that they were only a short distance from Vienna, but the capital—with its theaters, coffeehouses, and glittering ballrooms—felt strangely remote.

The trees looked tormented: thick, twisted boles and bare branches that terminated in desperate, arthritic claws. There was something about a deep, dark wood that held unspeakable terrors for the Teutonic imagination. *Hansel and Gretel, Little Red Riding Hood, Rapunzel.* Within every German-speaking adult was a child who, from infancy, had cultivated—under the tutelage of the Brothers Grimm—a healthy respect for the natural habitat of wolves and witches.

Rheinhardt shuddered.

"Sir?"

Haussmann's head had emerged from the carriage window.

"Yes?"

"What's that?"

"What's what?"

"*There* . . . Oh, it's gone. No, there it is again. Can't you see it, sir?"

An indistinct luminescence was floating among the trees—a pale glow that seemed to vanish and then reappear.

"Yes, Haussmann," said Rheinhardt, consciously modulating his voice to achieve an even delivery. "Yes, I can."

The light was becoming brighter.

Rheinhardt heard the carriage door opening, a splash, and his assistant struggling through the adhesive mud.

"What is it?" Haussmann repeated his question.

"I don't know," said Rheinhardt. "But it is my impression that we will find out very soon."

"Do you have your revolver, sir?"

"No, Haussmann," Rheinhardt replied. "This may come as a surprise to you, but when dancing, I very rarely carry a firearm. The unequal distribution of weight about my person would make the performance of a perfect turn almost impossible."

"Of course, sir," said Haussmann, noting the appearance of a sly smile on his superior's face.

The advancing light was surrounded by an indistinct shadowy aura, the dimensions of which suggested the approach of something very large. The vague outline was lumbering, ursine. Rheinhardt wondered if the mist might be creating an optical illusion. Nobody could be that big! Yet twigs were snapping beneath a ponderous tread. The horses began to whicker.

"Gentlemen," said the driver nervously, "perhaps you'd like to get back inside. Shouldn't we be on our way?"

Rheinhardt did not reply.

The footsteps became louder and the light grew more distinct.

"Well, Haussmann," said Rheinhardt, "I suspect that in a few moments all will be revealed."

The thick curtains of fog parted and a huge figure stepped out of the darkness, the glow of the flickering candle in his lamp preceding him like a spirit emissary. Rheinhardt heard his young companion gasp.

"Steady, Haussmann," Rheinhardt whispered.

The man was well over six feet tall but appeared even more massive on account of his clothing. He was wearing a Russian hat, with the flaps released over his ears, and a long fur coat pulled in at the waist with a thick leather belt. Hanging from it was a cleaver. In one hand he held a tin lamp suspended at the end of a whittled staff, and in the other the hind legs of a brace of bloody animal carcasses that were slung over his shoulder. Almost all of his face was concealed behind a wild, wiry black beard.

"Good evening," said Rheinhardt. "We are looking for the Aufkirchen *oberrealschule*." The mysterious woodman remained silent. Rheinhardt tried again: "The military academy? Saint Florian's?"

At last, something in the big man's eyes showed recognition. He grunted an affirmative and began to speak.

"Back down the hill." The sound he produced was low and sonorous. "Take the right fork."

"Right fork?" Rheinhardt echoed.

The giant grunted again. Then, turning abruptly, he trudged back into the woods.

"Thank you," Rheinhardt called out. "Much obliged."

Rheinhardt and Haussmann stood very still, watching, as the mist closed around the giant's shoulders and the shimmering flame faded into obscurity.

"You see, Haussmann," said Rheinhardt, straightening his bow tie and adjusting the studs on his cuffs. "Country folk: full of stolid virtues, I'm sure. But their conversation always errs on the side of brevity, don't you think?" Rheinhardt turned to address the driver.

"Well, did you hear what our friend from the forest said?"

"Down the hill—right fork."

"Exactly."

"And you want us to follow his directions?"

"What else would you suggest?"

"*Himmel*, he was a strange one."

"True, but I dare say we looked a little strange to him too."

3

THE DORMITORY WAS PITCH-BLACK but alive with sounds: snoring, rustling, mumbling, and the occasional terrified cry as one of the boys surfaced from a nightmare.

Kiefer Wolf listened to the breathing darkness. It had an orchestral quality—a heaving, restless depth.

"Drexler?" He reached out across the narrow space separating his bed from the next, and poked his fingers into the warm eiderdown.

"Drexler, wake up!"

His neighbor moaned.

"Drexler, wake up, will you!"

"Wolf?"

"Wake up, Drexler. I can't sleep."

"Oh, for God's sake, Wolf," said Martin Drexler.

"I'm going for a smoke. Are you coming?"

The boy sleeping in the bed on the other side of Wolf began to stir. "What . . ." His voice was thick with sleep. "What's happening?"

Wolf's fist swung out with ruthless ferocity, slamming into the boy's stomach. The youngster let out an agonized cry.

"Shut up, Knackfuss!" Wolf hissed. "Just shut up!"

The boy began to whimper.

"Oh, for God's sake, Wolf!" It was Drexler again. "What's the matter with you!"

"I'm going *upstairs*. I'm going to the *lost room*."

Wolf got out of bed, felt for his clothes, and slipped on his jacket and trousers. He did not bother with his shoes.

"Well, Drexler? Are you coming or not?"

Wolf heard Drexler turn over, grumbling into his pillow.

"Sleep, then!" said Wolf angrily. "You . . . you baby!"

Wolf groped his way into the central aisle and—orienting himself by touching the bedsteads—took short steps toward the door. Turning the handle very slowly, he pushed it open and peered through the narrow gap. The corridor was empty. Slipping out of the dormitory and closing the door quietly behind him, Wolf took one of the paraffin lamps from the wall and tiptoed off into the shadows. He had not gone very far when he heard something: footsteps, rushing up the stairs, and voices.

Damn! Damn! Damn!

Wolf sprinted to the end of the corridor and, skillfully negotiating a sharp corner, pressed his back against the wall. He held his breath and listened. He could hear a man's voice (speaking very quietly) and then a woman's voice.

Nurse Funke?

He had no intention of waiting there long enough to find out. He hurried off.

On one side of the corridor were windows overlooking a courtyard, and on the other side was a row of empty classrooms. At the end of the corridor was a wooden staircase that rose in a series of right angles and small landings. A further staircase ascended to a locked iron door.

Wolf paused—and listened.

Apart from the sound of tiny claws behind the baseboard, there was silence.

The upper level of the school had—over a period of many years—been subject to a series of eccentric modifications and revisions. Thus, the partitioning of spaces around the attic had led to the creation of many architectural anomalies: redundant corners, blind alleys, pointless niches, and steps that led nowhere at all. Among these architectural anomalies was the *lost room*—a neglected cavity that existed between the attic and the third story of the building.

Wolf crept underneath the final staircase and, crouching down, ran his hand over the floorboards. The tips of his fingers soon found the edge of a trapdoor, which he lifted gently. He sat on the edge of the hole, dangling his legs in the cold emptiness. Then, lowering himself, he eventually found support on a crate that had been positioned there especially for the purpose. Reaching up, he grabbed the paraffin lamp and then leaped down. He landed with a hollow, dusty thud. Wolf hung up the lamp on an overhead beam and made his way to an old leather suitcase in which he (and his small circle of associates) retained a cache of recreational aids: cigarettes, matches, brandy, some games, and a modest collection of pornographic postcards.

Wolf immediately lit a cigarette and began pacing around the room. He was annoyed with Drexler. Why hadn't he come? He wasn't the same, these days. Something in his character had changed. He was becoming more contrary, obstructive, less willing to go along with things. . . .

Wolf sucked on his cigarette and blew the smoke out through his nostrils.

He didn't really want to confront Drexler; however, if he had to, he would. Wolf slumped down on a pile of cushions, and dragged a blanket over himself. Then, reaching into the suitcase, he pulled out a volume of philosophy that Professor Gärtner had given him. It was titled *Beyond Good and Evil*, and it contained a passage that had played on his mind. He didn't quite understand it, but he felt that repeated readings might reveal its secret—some special truth that resided just beyond the literal meaning of the printed words.

Wolf lengthened the wick of the paraffin lamp and opened the book at the correct page. He read the passage aloud: "*There are no moral phenomena at all, only a moral interpretation of phenomena. . . .*"

Wolf stubbed the cigarette out on the floor.

Yes, this was true—and so, by implication, one could never really go too far.

4

RHEINHARDT WONDERED WHETHER HE had treated the driver's remarks too flippantly. The woodman was indeed *a strange one*. Might such a man purposely instruct strangers to follow a dangerous road? Were they—at that very moment—blithely rolling toward some fatal precipice?

Again, he was reminded of the old stories: wolves, witches, and supernatural beings whose appearance invariably presaged death. To dispel his unease, he began humming *Rosen aus dem Süden*. His thoughts returned to the ball. What would the orchestra be playing now? *Künstlerleben*, perhaps—or *Wein, Weib und Gesang*?

After some time had passed, the driver let out a cry. "Inspector! Inspector! This must be it!"

Rheinhardt opened the window. They were passing between two cast-iron gates set in a crumbling high wall. The fog was less thick, and in the distance, across a flat expanse of land, he could see illuminated windows. Rheinhardt sighed with relief.

The carriage rattled down a long drive and finally stopped. The inspector and his assistant jumped out and took stock of their surroundings. They were standing next to a weather-beaten statue, the features of which had been worn smooth; however, it was still possible to identify a bearded warrior holding a lance, with one foot raised on what appeared to be a tub.

"Saint Florian," said Rheinhardt.

"He looks more like a Roman soldier," said Haussmann.

"Well, that's because he *was* a Roman soldier—a military administrator, posted here, in Austria. But that, alas, is the limit of my knowledge."

Rheinhardt faced the school.

The building was Gothic in design, possessing three rows of triple lancet windows and four octahedral spires. A cloistered courtyard could be seen through a central stone arch. Rheinhardt and Haussmann entered the courtyard, and as they did so, a door opened through which an elderly man appeared. He was clearly a servant, but he wore a military decoration on his jacket.

"Gentlemen!" the old man cried.

Rheinhardt and Haussmann stepped forward, but as they did, the veteran's expression changed from eagerness to disappointment.

"Oh dear—very sorry—I mistook you for someone else."

"I beg your pardon?" asked Rheinhardt.

"The headmaster is expecting two gentlemen from the security office."

"Indeed. I am Inspector Rheinhardt and this is my assistant, Haussmann." The old man narrowed his eyes. "Yes," Rheinhardt continued, recognizing that their appearance might require an explanation. "We *are* somewhat overdressed, but it was our misfortune to be called here directly from a ball."

"Ball, you say?"

"Yes," said Rheinhardt, adding emphatically, "The *detectives'* ball."

The old soldier mumbled something to himself and then, pulling himself up, said: "Humbly report—this way, please."

He guided them to a door beneath the cloisters, and they entered a long, shadowy corridor. At its end, in a pool of blue light cast by suspended paraffin lamps, stood two men in academic gowns.

"Headmaster," the old man called out. "They're here, sir. The gentlemen from the security office. Inspector Rheinhardt and his assistant."

"Thank you, Albert," said one of the men. "Dismissed."

The old soldier stamped his feet, saluted, and shuffled away. Catching Rheinhardt's eye, the headmaster whispered. "A good fellow— saw action in '48. The Budapest siege."

The headmaster was a man in his late fifties, with gray, almost white, hair. A snowy thatch had been raked over his head to conceal a thinning crown. Although his cheeks were ruddy and plump, he possessed an alert, severe face, with high, arched eyebrows. A small triangle of hair curled outward from his chin. He executed a perfunctory bow. "Professor Julius Eichmann, school superintendent." He gestured toward his companion. "And my deputy, Dr. Bernhard Becker."

The deputy headmaster inclined his head.

"Thank you for coming, Inspector," Eichmann continued. "And from a social engagement, it seems." He scrutinized the policeman from head to toe, his expression souring slightly at the sight of Rheinhardt's muddy shoes and splashed trousers.

"An accident," said Rheinhardt.

The headmaster nodded sharply and said: "Well, Inspector, this is a most unusual circumstance. We are entirely in your hands. How do you wish to proceed?"

"I would like to see the . . ." He hesitated before choosing to say "boy" instead of "body."

"Very well. We will take you to the infirmary."

Rheinhardt frowned. "What? He's been moved?"

"Yes," said the headmaster.

"Why?"

"Why?" repeated the headmaster. "Why?" His voice suddenly changed, climbing in pitch and volume. "What was I supposed to do? Leave him in the laboratory?" His rhetorical sarcasm revealed years of experience in the classroom. He glanced at his deputy, and something passed between them. When the headmaster resumed, his voice was more steady. "I feared the worst, but was reluctant to pronounce the boy dead. I am not a medical man, Inspector. I thought it best to get him to the infirmary and send for Nurse Funke; however, as I suspected, she could do nothing for him."

Rheinhardt automatically reached for his notebook but then, suddenly remembering that he was wearing his tails, allowed his hand to drop. The headmaster's expression declared—quite clearly—that he believed Rheinhardt was an idiot. The inspector took a deep breath and continued his questioning.

"And after sending for Nurse Funke?"

"I telephoned Dr. Kessler and the police. Some constables arrived within the hour. They are still here—one is standing outside the infirmary; the other is in the laboratory. I have no idea where Kessler is!"

"Kessler is the school doctor?"

"Yes."

"Where did he set off from, do you know?"

"His apartment in the sixteenth district."

"The main road above Aufkirchen is impassable—a fallen tree, apparently. He may have been delayed, as we were."

The headmaster tutted, almost as if Rheinhardt were a schoolboy presenting a weak excuse for not having completed his homework.

"The infirmary is upstairs, Inspector," said the headmaster. He then walked off at a brisk pace, calling back, "This way."

Rheinhardt and Haussmann followed the headmaster and his deputy down an adjoining corridor. They began ascending a narrow staircase. When Rheinhardt caught up with the headmaster, Eichmann proceeded to give an account of the evening's events.

"The deputy headmaster and I were in my office. We had barely begun our meeting when Professor Gärtner appeared at the door. He was evidently distressed. He had seen a light on in the laboratory and had entered, expecting to find the deputy headmaster."

"Science is my discipline," Becker interjected.

"Gärtner," the headmaster continued, "had found the boy, Zelenka, slumped over a workbench."

"At what time?"

"It must have been . . ." The headmaster glanced at his deputy for confirmation. "Just before seven?"

Becker agreed.

"What was Zelenka doing in the laboratory?" asked Rheinhardt.

"An assignment," said Becker.

"Which, presumably, *you* had set him?"

"Yes," Becker replied. "A simple inquiry into the effects of vinegar on certain compounds."

Rheinhardt studied Becker more carefully. He was Eichmann's junior by a decade or so. His hair was relatively long, but receding, which had the effect of increasing the salience of his high, domed forehead. This feature, taken together with his perceptive eyes and gold-rimmed spectacles, conveyed a strong impression of superior intellectual endowment. His mustache was stiff and straight, projecting outward beyond his jawline, and his thick beard was unusually styled, the tip having been clipped to achieve a forked extremity.

"Why was he doing this assignment on his own? Was he being punished?"

"No," said Becker, "not at all. Zelenka was one of our keener students. He was always requesting additional work."

"The deputy headmaster and I . . ." Eichmann resumed his story with renewed firmness of purpose, and his raised voice suggested he was a little piqued that Rheinhardt's attention had shifted to his junior. "The deputy headmaster and I hurried down to the laboratory, accompanied by Professor Gärtner. We tried to rouse the boy . . . but our ministrations had no effect. I returned to my office and made the telephone calls I referred to earlier, to the police and Herr Dr. Kessler. The deputy headmaster went to get Nurse Funke—she lives in one of the lodges."

"The lodges?"

"Accommodation for the staff: built on our grounds and mostly occupied by masters. Nurse Funke has rooms in the building nearest the school."

"And what did Professor Gärtner do?"

"He organized the transfer of Zelenka from the laboratory to the infirmary with the help of Albert and two prefects."

The mention of prefects made Rheinhardt ask: "Where *are* the boys? I haven't seen one of them."

"Asleep, of course," said the headmaster. "In the dormitories. They have to get up early for drill."

"And Professor Gärtner? Where is he?"

"I believe he is resting in the common room. I suggested he retire there with a brandy. He was very upset."

As they ascended the staircase, Rheinhardt noticed that the walls were very bare: blank expanses of grubby whitewash, no regimental photographs, trophies, or flags—in fact, nothing to please the eye. He also noticed the smell. A musty institutional smell—redolent of boiled vegetables, poor ventilation, and latrines. It was a smell that permeated virtually all official buildings in Austria, and had attracted its own special appellation: the "treasury" smell. It was one that had followed Rheinhardt throughout his life. Sometimes, even outside on a cold, clear day, he could smell that distinctive cloying odor in his nostrils.

They arrived at the top floor and the infirmary. A constable was standing outside.

"Security office?" asked the constable.

"Yes, yes," said the inspector, now becoming rather irritated by the effect of his clothes. "Detective Inspector Oskar Rheinhardt— and my assistant, Haussmann. You will kindly open the door, please."

The constable, detecting both tetchiness and authority in Rheinhardt's voice, clicked his heels and meekly did as he was told.

Rheinhardt entered a stark, featureless room, painted over in the same monotonous whitewash. The ceiling was low, and four beds occupied most of the space. A tin sink was fixed to the wall, into which a dripping tap was reproducing the rataplan of a snare drum. On one of the beds was the body of the boy, Zelenka. A sheet had been thrown over him.

Sitting at a small desk, next to the door, was a middle-aged woman in a nurse's uniform. She stood up as the men entered. The headmaster thanked her for waiting, and introduced Rheinhardt and his assistant. She then went to the nearest bed and gently pulled at the cover. It slipped away, revealing the face of a young boy.

"Thomas Zelenka," said the nurse.

"How old was he?"

"Fifteen."

"I see."

As far as Rheinhardt could make out, the boy was of medium build. He had a handsome, stoic face: a square chin and full, sensuous lips. His light brown hair—which originally must have been closely cropped—had grown out a little, producing a covering of dense bristles.

"What happened?" Rheinhardt asked, puzzled.

"I don't know," said the nurse, shaking her head. "He was already dead when I arrived. I tried to resuscitate him—but there was little point in trying."

"And the cause of death?"

"I am afraid you will have to ask Dr. Kessler when he arrives. I have no idea."

Rheinhardt leaned forward and examined Zelenka's head. As he did so, he registered a light dappling of juvenile freckles on the boy's cheeks.

"No bleeding? No signs of the boy having been struck?"

"No," said the nurse, sounding a sudden note of surprise.

Rheinhardt looked into her eyes. They were gray and watery.

"Did you know the boy?" he asked.

"Yes," Nurse Funke replied. "I knew Thomas Zelenka very well." She blinked a tear from her eye. "He was always catching colds. . . . I used to give him a balsam inhalation to help him breathe."

"Did he suffer from any serious ailments?"

"No—not to my knowledge. Although you had better ask Dr. Kessler."

Rheinhardt turned to face the headmaster.

"I would be most grateful if you would allow my assistant to call for a mortuary van. There will have to be an autopsy, and it is my preference that this be conducted at the Physiological Institute." He then turned to Haussmann. "See if you can speak to Professor Mathias. I'd like him to perform an autopsy as soon as possible."

"Tonight, sir?"

"Yes. Why not? Professor Mathias is a famous insomniac and is always happy to assist. And while you're at it, see if you can get a photographer . . . but tell him to get a driver who is familiar with the woods around Aufkirchen. Otherwise they'll never get here!"

"Yes, sir."

"You will then meet me in the laboratory, equipped with pencils, paper, a notebook, and . . ." He broke off to address Eichmann. "Is art taught in this school, headmaster?"

"Yes," Eichmann replied. "We have a drawing and calligraphy master—Herr Lang."

"Good," said Rheinhardt, before continuing to address Haussmann: "Some clean paintbrushes—preferably unused—and about twenty stiff isinglass envelopes. I am sure that the deputy headmaster will help you to find these items. You, headmaster, will kindly escort me to the laboratory."

For the first time, the headmaster and his deputy were looking at Rheinhardt with something approaching respect.

"Well?" said Rheinhardt, his voice rising in a fair imitation of the headmaster's earlier reproach. "What am I supposed to do—find it myself?"

5

LIEBERMANN HAD HAILED A CAB for Else Rheinhardt and was about to do the same for Amelia when she surprised him by saying:

"No, Dr. Liebermann. I would very much like to walk home. I am still excited and will not sleep. A walk will do me good."

"Very well," said Liebermann. "You will, of course, permit me to escort you?"

Amelia offered the young doctor her arm, and they set off in the direction of Alsergrund. At first, their conversation was given over entirely to the subject of Fasching. Amelia showed a keen interest in the historical origins of the ball season; however, in due course, Liebermann inquired how her studies at the university were progressing and she began to speak of more serious matters: microscopy, anatomy, diseases of the blood. She had also chosen to attend a course of philosophy lectures and had become very interested in the writings of Friedrich Nietzsche.

"Are you familiar with his works, Dr. Liebermann?"

"No, I'm afraid not."

"A pity. As a devotee of Professor Freud, you would appreciate his thoughts on the importance of unconscious mental processes. I have been somewhat preoccupied of late by his notion of eternal recurrence."

"Oh? And what is *that*, exactly?"

"The idea that we are destined to repeat our lives again and again—in perpetuity."

Liebermann was taken aback by Amelia's comment. She possessed a very logical mind, and he could not understand why such a whimsical notion had captured her attention.

"As in reincarnation?" said Liebermann disdainfully. "The transmigration of souls?"

Amelia shook her head.

"No, Herr Doctor—not at all. Nietzsche's proposal is rather different, and should not be confused with Pythagorean or Hindu doctrines."

She had turned her face toward him. Beneath the brim of her feathered hat, Amelia's expression was typically intense. A silver ribbon had loosened and was dangling past her ear.

"If my understanding of Nietzsche is correct," continued Amelia, "then he is suggesting something much more plausible . . . something that—unlike comparable religious ideas—does not contradict science. Perhaps this is why I have been so preoccupied. I have had to reevaluate a notion that I had previously rejected. Nietzsche seems to have provided a perfectly rational explanation for a supposedly metaphysical phenomenon."

"But how?"

Amelia's forehead creased.

"If time is infinite and there is also a limited amount of matter in the universe, then past configurations of matter must eventually recur. Is that not so?"

As Liebermann considered the argument, Amelia pressed on: "Imagine, if you will, that the world in which we live is analogous to a game of chess. Because of physical limitations—for example, the number of pieces, the number of squares, and so forth—there are only *so many* games possible. Therefore, if two immortal adversaries were locked in competition forever, at some point the precise sequence of moves that constituted a previous game must necessarily be repeated. And so it must be with atoms and the universe."

"Well," said Liebermann, slightly perplexed. "That is indeed a fascinating argument. If one accepts that time has no end and that matter exists in only finite quantities, then one is also bound to agree with Nietzsche; however, I find the idea of my own personal reconstitution vaguely depressing. It makes me think of all the mistakes I have made."

"Nietzsche hoped," Amelia continued, "that contemplation of eternal recurrence would inspire humanity to make wiser choices. If we are trapped in an infinitely repeating cycle of existence, then we should make every effort to live our lives to the full."

Their destination came into view: a substantial town house, where Amelia occupied rooms on the top floor.

Liebermann had been so absorbed by Amelia's conversation that their walk across the city seemed to have taken no time at all. Reluctantly, he released her arm.

"Thank you so much for inviting me to the detectives' ball," said Amelia.

"I am delighted you enjoyed it."

"It is such a shame that Inspector Rheinhardt was called away."

"An occupational hazard, I fear."

"And thank you also for your invaluable guidance on the dance floor."

"It was my pleasure."

Neither of them moved. The subsequent silence became awkward, and they both began to speak at once. Liebermann gestured that Amelia should continue.

"If I am to stay in Vienna, I must take lessons. Can you recommend a teacher?"

"Herr Janowsky. He instructs my younger sister. But you must not judge yourself unkindly. You did very well . . . considering."

They were still standing close together. Amelia's face was tilted upward—the silver ribbon reflecting the yellow lamplight.

Liebermann's fingertips were troubled by memories of the ball. The warmth of Amelia's body—flesh, shifting beneath velvet. There had been so many accidental brushes, touches, inadvertent intimacies. Now these memories were crowding back, accompanied by turbulent feelings that he had hitherto sucessfully repressed.

"Dr. Liebermann." Amelia said his name softly—so softly that it was as though she had merely inflected a sigh. The exhalation carried a faint note of inquiry.

He could smell her perfume—a heavy, soporific lavender.

He felt curiously dissociated—*Too much champagne?*—and became aware that he was leaning forward.

He stopped himself.

The moment passed.

Amelia was raising her hand.

He continued moving forward, bending low until his lips were pressed against the silk of her glove.

"Good night, Dr. Liebermann."

"Good night." His voice was strained. "Good night, Miss Lydgate."

The Englishwoman found her keys and opened the door. She paused for a moment on the threshold, and then stepped into darkness.

Liebermann did not go home. He felt far too agitated. Instead, he walked to the Josephinum, where he paused to gaze at the statue of Hygeia—the goddess of healing. He lit a cigarette, and addressed the deity directly: "Well, if old Nietzsche was right, I've just missed an opportunity: an opportunity that I shall continue to miss for all of eternity."

6

RHEINHARDT, THE HEADMASTER, and Professor Klodwig Gärtner were standing together in the laboratory. It was an ugly, dilapidated room. Exposed water pipes followed the wall just below the ceiling, and from these oversize conduits brownish stains of varying intensity dribbled to the floor. A constant hissing sound filled the air.

"I thought he'd fallen asleep," said Gärtner. " 'Wake up, Zelenka,' I said. 'Wake up, boy!' But he didn't stir, so I said it again 'Come on, boy, wake up!' And I clapped my hands, loudly. Still—nothing. So I walked over and shook him."

Gärtner was an old master—almost completely bald, except for two tufts of silver hair that sprouted above his ears. His eyebrows had the consistency of wire wool and curled up at the ends, giving his face a curious, demonic cast. This effect was assisted by a sharp pointed beard and a thin mustache. His nose was long and bent slightly to one side, suggesting that he might have been a pugilist in his youth.

"Was he breathing?" asked Rheinhardt.

"I don't know—I don't think so."

Rheinhardt could smell alcohol on Gärtner's breath. He had clearly drunk more than was strictly necessary to steady his nerves.

"To be honest, Inspector," Gärtner continued, "I didn't think to check. I simply ran to get the headmaster."

Rheinhardt peered into one of several large glass-fronted display cabinets. It contained geological exhibits. Most of the collection was uninspiring. He studied the labels: *slate with pyrites, basalt, flint, red sandstone.* The only thing that captured his interest was a shiny black trilobite with large protruding eyes.

"Go on," said Rheinhardt, "I'm listening."

"We laid him out on the floor," Gärtner continued, "but it was obvious something very bad had happened."

Rheinhardt turned. "Where did you lay him out, exactly?"

"There, Inspector," interrupted the headmaster, pointing between the two front benches where the high wooden stools had been pushed aside to accommodate a supine body.

The surface of the first bench was scattered with the paraphernalia of experimentation: labeled bottles with glass stoppers, small dishes filled with powders, a pipette, a rack of test tubes, a small burner, and a flask of brown liquid. Rheinhardt lifted the flask and swirled it under his nose. It was vinegar.

Zelenka's notebook was still open. Various chemical formulae were scrawled across the page, some supplemented with modest observations: *bubbling, unpleasant smell, evaporation.*

Gärtner addressed the headmaster: "You examined the boy with Becker, and then you told Becker to fetch Nurse Funke."

"Thank you, Professor Gärtner," said Eichmann. The sharpness of his tone indicated that such assistance was unwelcome. He could remember perfectly well what had happened—and did not need Gärtner to remind him.

Next to the notebook was a small pastry on a plate. It was untouched. Rheinhardt felt a sudden pang of pity—a tightening in his chest. He imagined Zelenka purchasing the cake from the canteen, saving it as a special treat to be consumed at the end of the day. It seemed unjust that the boy should have been deprived of this one last innocent indulgence.

On the floor were some fragments of glass and scattered white granules.

"Do you see that broken dish, Professor Gärtner?"

"Yes."

"Was it there when you arrived?"

Gärtner looked at the headmaster. "I suppose it must have been. We didn't knock it off the bench when we were moving Zelenka, did we?"

"No," said the headmaster.

At that moment, the deputy headmaster returned with Haussmann.

"Ahh . . . there you are, Haussmann," called Rheinhardt. "Everything in hand?"

"Yes, sir."

"Good. Now, I would like a sheet of paper, an envelope, and a clean brush, please."

Rheinhardt squatted on the floor and gently swept some white granules onto the paper. He then folded the sheet into a flat packet and slipped it into the envelope, which he sealed. Haussmann handed him a pencil, and the inspector wrote on the upper right-hand corner: *Sample* 1. *Saint Florian's—Contents of broken dish. Laboratory floor. Fri, 16th Jan,* 1903.

"Inspector," said the headmaster. "Would I be correct in assuming that you are treating Zelenka's death as suspicious?"

Rheinhardt looked at Haussmann, whose usually impassive face showed the ghost of a smile.

"Yes, Headmaster," said Rheinhardt. "That would be a very reasonable assumption."

7

PROFESSOR MATHIAS was seated on a wooden stool, staring at the corpse of a young woman. An incision had been made from her larynx to her abdomen, and the skin and superficial layers of tissue had been peeled back. The expression of concentration on the professor's face, and the peculiarity of the woman's condition, suggested to the onlooker the more familiar sight of an avid reader poring over the pages of an open book. Above the body was an electric light, the beam of which shone down into the raw, empty cavity of the woman's torso. A collection of glistening organs—heart, liver, lungs—were strewn across a nearby table. The stench was overwhelming.

Haussmann covered his mouth and looked beseechingly at his superior.

"All right," said Rheinhardt, "go outside and have a cigarette. I'll join you shortly." His assistant nodded and made an undignified exit.

"Professor?"

Mathias's gaze seemed to be fixed on the woman's pudendum.

"Professor?" Rheinhardt called more loudly.

Mathias cleared his throat. "A man who had lost his axe suspected his neighbor's son of stealing it. Observing the boy, the man discovered that everything about him—his gait, narrow features, speech, et cetera—declared the boy a thief; however, the following day the man discovered his axe beneath a sack in his own cellar. When he encountered his neighbor's son again, he no longer saw anything unusual about the boy's appearance." The professor paused for a few moments. Then he added: "Well, Rheinhardt?"

"I really have no idea," said the inspector.

"No, I didn't think you would. It is by an ancient Chinese author. I have been making a study of their literature—and very interesting it is too."

Mathias stood up and rolled a mortuary sheet up to the dead woman's neck. Before covering her face, he gently touched her hair.

"So very beautiful," he said softly.

"Yes," Rheinhardt agreed. "How did she die?"

"Natural causes—a congenital defect of the pulmonary semilunar valve." Mathias wiped his hands down the front of his brown apron. "We are advised," he continued, "to be cautious in our judgments. Yet . . . yet . . ."

He suddenly fell silent.

"Yet what?" asked Rheinhardt.

"I strongly suspect that the last time this woman *received* her husband, she had already been dead for some time."

"I beg your pardon?"

"The gentleman exercised his conjugal privilege post-mortem."

"Dear God," gasped Rheinhardt.

Mathias shrugged. "I cannot share your disgust, Inspector. It is my understanding that what passes for sexual relations in most Viennese marriages is essentially necrophilic." The old man began to chuckle. "Only joking, Rheinhardt. Now, who have we here?"

Professor Mathias shuffled past a metal bucket in which a length of colon was coiled like a sleeping serpent.

"Thomas Zelenka," said Rheinhardt.

The boy was laid out—like the eviscerated and misused hausfrau—on a brightly illuminated table. The brilliance of the electric light beam showed his freckles more clearly. They were more numerous than Rheinhardt remembered, and their ginger dappling had the effect of making Zelenka look much younger than his fifteen years.

A child, thought Rheinhardt. *Still only a child.*

"Inspector?" Mathias's voice sounded querulous.

"Yes?"

"Why are you wearing tails?"

Rheinhardt sighed. He gave an account of the evening's events while Mathias pulled a cart of surgical tools over to Zelenka's table.

"Help me get his clothes off, will you?"

Rheinhardt baulked.

"Oh, come now, Inspector!" Mathias reprimanded. "Your coyness with the dead is becoming quite tiresome!"

The old man tutted and began to undo the buttons on Zelenka's woolen shirt. Rheinhardt reluctantly manipulated the boy's stiffening arms, and the shirt came off without too much difficulty. He then removed the boy's vest. Rheinhardt placed each article of clothing in a paper bag and sealed it. When he turned to assist Professor Mathias again, he found that the old pathologist was standing very still, staring at the body with intense interest.

"The trousers, Professor?"

Mathias grunted—but it was evident that the meaning of Rheinhardt's words had not registered.

"The trousers?" Rheinhardt repeated.

"Shh," said the pathologist, waving his hand in the air. He then moved forward, his stealthy gait and purposeful gaze reminding Rheinhardt of a predatory animal. Suddenly, Mathias pounced. He lowered his head—his nose almost touching Zelenka's body. He then snatched a magnifying glass from the cart and began to examine the boy's chest.

"Professor?"

"Extraordinary."

"What is?"

"Come here. Take a look at this."

Rheinhardt could not see anything at first. But as he drew closer he saw that there was something unusual about the boy's skin: a patch, about the size of a five-krone coin, just above the right nipple, that seemed to be reflecting the light differently. As Rheinhardt lowered his head, he detected a lattice of faint white lines.

"Here," said Mathias, handing Rheinhardt the magnifying glass.

The lens showed that the white lines were in fact tiny weals: raised ridges of pale flesh.

"What is it? A dermatological disease?"

"No, Rheinhardt. It's scar tissue. The skin has been slashed with a razor. The wounds have healed over now—but the manner in which they have healed suggests they were repeatedly reopened." Mathias's magnified finger appeared beneath the glass. "The uppermost incision was once infected."

"Could these cuts have been self-inflicted? I have heard of prisoners injuring themselves to relieve boredom."

"Only if he is left-handed—a right-handed person would instinctively cut contralaterally, thus inflicting wounds on the left pectoralis major."

"I'm afraid I do not know which was his preferred hand."

Mathias examined the boy's thumbs and then squeezed Zelenka's upper arms.

"He was right-handed," Mathias said with absolute certainty. "His right thumb is slightly larger than the left, and his right biceps is more developed."

"Very impressive, Herr Professor."

Mathias did not acknowledge Rheinhardt's compliment, and his expression suddenly changed from one of confidence to one of perplexity. He lifted Zelenka's left arm and allowed it to swing out over the edge of the table.

"I thought I could feel something odd."

A few centimeters below the boy's armpit was a square of bloody gauze. Mathias eased the dressing away, revealing another network of cuts. Unlike those on Zelenka's chest, these had not healed. The lines of the crisscross pattern were black and scabby. Mathias closed his eyes and explored the wounds with his fingertips. They trembled over each crusty laceration, like those of a blind man reading braille. He then pressed the flesh until one of the cuts opened.

"Quite deep," he said softly.

Rheinhardt scratched his head. "Have you seen wounds like this before?"

"No," said Mathias, "I haven't."

Rheinhardt puffed out his cheeks and let the air escape slowly.

"Is there some connection between these wounds and the boy's death?"

"There could be. For example, his blood might have become poisoned. But we must proceed further with the autopsy to find out."

"Of course."

"Hold him down, will you?"

Rheinhardt grimaced and gripped Zelenka's cold, waxy shoulders.

Mathias removed the boy's shoes and socks. He then loosened the youngster's belt and pulled off his trousers. Beneath these, Zelenka was wearing knee-length drawers with a button overlap and drawstring waist.

"Excuse me," said Mathias to the corpse, tugging at the undergarment and exposing the boy's genitals.

"God in heaven!" cried Rheinhardt.

Another square of bloody gauze was stuck to the boy's upper thigh.

The two men looked at each other.

"Haussmann!" Rheinhardt called.

The door opened and his assistant stepped over the threshold. "Sir?"

"We shall be needing the services of a photographer again."

8

THEY HAD PERFORMED SOME POPULAR songs by Carl Loewe—
Edward, Prinz Eugen, Archibald Douglas—and were tackling his setting of Goethe's *Erlkönig*. It was a competent piece of lieder writing,
although somewhat melodramatic. Even so, the two friends surrendered their musical sensitivities to the spirit of the work, and
Liebermann was pleasantly surprised. Rheinhardt's baritone was particularly expressive, finding qualities in Loewe's arrangement that
had previously escaped the young doctor's notice. When the final
chords descended over a mysterious, rumbling bass, Liebermann was
thrilled by the effect.

"Bravo, Oskar," said Liebermann, clapping his hands together.
"Exceptional. I haven't heard a better performance on the concert
platform."

Rheinhardt considered feigning modesty, but decided that this
would be ungracious.

"Yes, it *was* rather good. The *Heimlich* passage in particular."

"Indeed—I was utterly convinced. Chilling. Chilling!"

Rheinhardt rifled through the music books and found a volume of
Schubert: *Der Doppelgänger?*

"Yes, why not?"

Rheinhardt placed the book on the music stand—but it was not
open at the right page. Instead of *Der Doppelgänger*, the song title
was—once again—*Erlkönig*.

Liebermann smiled at his friend and pointed out the error.

"Oh, I'm so sorry," said Rheinhardt. But the inspector did not correct his mistake. Instead, he looked mischievously at his companion and said, "What do you think?"

Schubert's setting of Goethe's *Erlkönig* had a notoriously taxing part for the pianist: relentless octaves and chords played by the right hand and executed at breakneck speed.

Liebermann flexed his fingers.

"My wrist feels a little tired, but I think I can get through it."

"Excellent."

Liebermann launched into the torturous triplets of the introduction. Immediately the atmosphere in the room altered, a musical spell was cast, and they were both transported.

Storm clouds and the descent of darkness.

Merciless cold.

A galloping horse—its frantic hooves throwing up clods of turf.

"*Wer reitet so spät durch Nacht und Wind?*"

Who rides so late through night and wind?

A father and his son.

The boy buries his face in his father's cloak. When the father asks him what is wrong, the child replies that he has seen the elf king.

Liebermann attacked the keys of the Bösendorfer, manipulating the pedals to create an expansive—almost orchestral—sound.

The father tells the boy that he is seeing mist, but the elf king is calling— and the boy clutches even more tightly at his father's cloak.

"*Sei ruhig, bleibe ruhig, mein Kind.*"

Be calm, keep calm, my child.

Rheinhardt's voice shook with authentic terror. Liebermann glanced up to see his friend gazing into the distance—his eyes searching for a spectral crown and train. Inhabiting the skin of the doomed child, Rheinhardt cried out: "The elf king has hurt me!"

Liebermann imagined an icy, clenched fist squeezing the child's heart. He struck a pianissimo chord—and, holding it, waited for the last, devastating line of the song to be delivered.

But it did not come.

Rheinhardt was still gazing into the distance, now seemingly insensible of his actual surroundings.

Liebermann waited patiently until the inspector started again and finally produced the delayed recitativo.

"In seinen Armen das Kind war tot."

In his arms the child was dead . . .

The words were half-spoken, loosely timed, and heavy with despair. The sound that Rheinhardt produced was hollow—empty and croaking. Thus released, Liebermann played the forceful two-chord cadence that brought Schubert's *Erlkönig* to a precipitate end. Its abruptness left a bleak silence—as if the music had been snatched away like the boy's life in Goethe's poem.

"I do apologize," said Rheinhardt. "I think my last entry was a little late."

"A little," said Liebermann, "but your performance was . . ." He paused to select an appropriate superlative. "Operatic!"

As was their custom, the two men retired to the smoking room for brandy and cigars. After enjoying a few moments of quiet contemplation, Liebermann said: "This evening, you will—of course—be wishing to present me with the facts relating to the mysterious death of a young boy."

Rheinhardt coughed into his drink. He had never quite got used to his friend's habit of telling him what he was about to say.

"Your performance of Loewe's *Erlkönig*," Liebermann continued, "was curiously committed, given that it is not great music. This suggested to me the presence of a memory—or memories—finding a sympathetic correspondence in Goethe's poetry. My suspicions were confirmed when you placed Schubert's *Erlkönig* on the music stand instead of *Der Doppelgänger*. As Professor Freud has explained, such bungled actions often have a deeper significance.

"Once again, your performance was compelling; however, by the time you had reached the final bars, the contents of your unconscious—stirred by Schubert's genius—were rising from the depths. . . . You became distracted, and subsequently missed your entry. Indeed, you were so preoccupied that your silence lasted for two whole measures!"

"Two?" said Rheinhardt, skeptically.

"At least!" Liebermann insisted. "The *Erlkönig* describes the unnatural death of a child. One does not have to be a very great psychologist to connect the subject of Goethe's ballad with events that might have transpired in the real world. I simply supposed that your premature departure from the ball on Friday evening was for the purpose of investigating a child's death—and most likely under mysterious circumstances."

Rheinhardt produced a smoke ring, through which he observed the flames of the fire.

"Well, Herr Doctor—you are absolutely correct. On Friday evening I did investigate the death of a child. A fifteen-year-old boarder at Saint Florian's military school."

"Saint Florian's? Where's that?"

"Up in the woods."

"Ah," said Liebermann, showing evident signs of satisfaction. "That makes perfect sense."

"I beg your pardon?"

"The *Erlkönig*. The father and son ride through a wood."

Rheinhardt stubbed out his cigar.

"Please, do continue," Liebermann added.

"Saint Florian's is situated close to the small village of Aufkirchen—built on the site of a religious foundation of the same name. Some of the original building still survives behind the new Gothic façade—old cloisters, a chapel, and so forth. I've been told that the school attracts the less academically gifted sons of well-heeled families."

Liebermann filled Rheinhardt's empty glass. The inspector thanked him, and recounted the general facts of the investigation. He summarized the statements of Nurse Funke and the three masters: Eichmann, Becker, and Gärtner. He then opened his case and removed a thick brown envelope. Inside were photographs, which he passed to his friend.

The boy, Thomas Zelenka, lying on the infirmary bed.

A school laboratory.

The surface of a bench covered with bottles, dishes, and test tubes.

They were not particularly clear photographs. Most were dark and grainy.

A notebook and an untouched pastry.

"What kind of experiments was the boy doing?" Liebermann asked.

"He was looking at the effects of mixing vinegar with certain chemical compounds. We took samples and had them analyzed. The findings were unremarkable."

"And what did the school doctor have to say?"

"Nothing. He arrived after the boy's body had been removed. A tree was blocking the main road, and his driver—like ours—got lost."

The next image showed Zelenka's naked body in the morgue. Under the bright electric light, his features and physique were more clearly defined.

"So, how did he die—exactly?"

Rheinhardt shook his head. "We don't know. Professor Mathias couldn't find anything wrong with him."

"He just . . . died?"

"Yes."

"In which case, I would have expected Professor Mathias to assume the presence of a subtle pathological process and ascribe the boy's death to natural causes."

"Which is precisely what Professor Mathias did."

"Then why are you treating the boy's death as suspicious?"

Rheinhardt grimaced. "Natural causes! Can a boy of fifteen really die of *natural causes*?"

"It is unusual, but *yes*, it can happen. One can speculate—tiny hemorrhages, deep in the brain, for example. They are exceedingly difficult to identify. A thorough microscopic analysis of transverse sections might reveal something—though one can never be sure. Then there are pulmonary anomalies . . ."

"Look at the next photograph."

Liebermann picked up the image and tilted it in the lamplight.

A metal ruler showed the lengths of several faint white lines.

"What is it?"

"Scar tissue. About here." Rheinhardt indicated the location by touching his chest. "According to Mathias, the wounds have been repeatedly reopened with a razor."

The following photograph was equally puzzling: a crisscross pattern of darker lines.

"Cuts," said Rheinhardt. "Found on the boy's torso, under his left arm."

Liebermann considered the image for a few moments before examining the final photograph, which showed the boy's genitals—pulled to one side by the pathologist's hand. The displacement of these organs revealed three deep incisions in the pale flesh of Zelenka's upper thigh.

"Were any of the wounds infected?"

"Mathias said that the scarring on the boy's chest showed signs of past infection, but nothing recent. The other wounds were clean. You are no doubt wondering if these injuries are connected with his death. It seems not. The schoolmasters said the boy was perfectly healthy. He showed none of the symptoms associated with blood poisoning."

"What about blood loss?"

"All the recent wounds had been dressed. There were no signs of excessive bleeding or dehydration."

Liebermann arranged the photographs in a neat pile and stroked the straight edges.

"Then, it looks like the boy has either been tortured or . . . he has taken part in some bizarre rite of initiation."

"Scars are deemed a sign of honor and distinction among dueling fraternities."

"Yes, but only if those scars were acquired while in pursuit of what is termed satisfaction. This scarring"—Liebermann tapped the photographs—"is of a very different kind." The young doctor lit a cigar and eased back into his chair. "The oldest wounds are to be found on the victim's chest. More recently the boy was cut under his arm and on his upper thigh. The latter two areas seem to have been selected for the purpose of concealment. But if so, why was concealment not a consideration when the first wounds were inflicted?"

Rheinhardt shrugged.

"And why are there three sets of cuts?" Liebermann continued. "Surely, an initiation ritual would take place only once?" Liebermann shook his head, as if annoyed by the number of questions that were crowding his mind. "And what on earth are we to make of those crural lacerations—so conspicuously close to the genitals?"

Rheinhardt twisted the horns of his mustache.

"Strange things happen in military schools. Some boys gain extraordinary power over their peers. I have heard of some cadets ruling over their comrades like tyrants—meting out punishments, extorting levies, devising sadistic games. Perhaps Zelenka was unfortunate enough to have become the victim of one of these juvenile despots."

Liebermann flicked through the photographs and found an image of Zelenka in the infirmary. It was a close-up of his face. Although his features were square and masculine, there was something in his expression that suggested sensitivity, intelligence.

"I abhor bullying," said Liebermann, "and it is most distressing to contemplate the depredations of institutional life—the utter misery that some boys must endure; however, Professor Mathias has concluded that Zelenka died of natural causes. The cuts on his body, whatever they represent, and however they got there, are an irrelevance! All that you can do is notify the school of your findings and trust that they will eventually find and expel the culprit. You cannot proceed with a murder investigation, Oskar, if there has not been a murder."

Rheinhardt sipped his brandy. "But . . ." The inspector shifted uncomfortably. "I have a feeling . . ."

Liebermann rolled his eyes.

Rheinhardt continued worrying his mustache. "There's something about this that doesn't smell right."

"My dear friend, your feelings of unease are very easily explained—and can be attributed to your strong protective instincts. You are resistant to the idea that Zelenka died naturally, because of his youth. If you accept that such a thing can happen to him, you must also accept that it can happen to others: namely, your two daughters. Naturally, this is such an awful consideration that a defensive mechanism has come into play. By denying the existence of latent and fatal pathological processes, you experience less anxiety and preserve a comforting illusion. Moreover, if you can prove that Zelenka was murdered, you will vitiate Professor Mathias's conclusions, making it seem even less likely that the same fate could affect your loved ones. But unfortunately, Oskar—the *Erlkönig* is a reality: a reality not of the spirit world but of the material world. And he comes not in the shape of an elven king but as minute lesions in the brain, and freakish electrical discharges that disturb the beating of a young heart." Liebermann looked at his friend, and compassion creased the skin around his eyes. "Oskar, I wish that it were otherwise."

Rheinhardt sighed. "You are right, of course. I dare say there *is* something in my soul that rages against the death of children—and for the very reasons you so eloquently describe. Be that as it may, I cannot free myself of the gnawing suspicion that there is more to Zelenka's death . . ." His voice trailed off into uncertainty. Then he added: "I will continue with the investigation, in spite of Professor Mathias's findings."

Liebermann offered Rheinhardt another cigar. "I very much hope, Oskar, that when the time comes, you will be able to satisfy Commissioner Brügel. He will want to know why the resources of the security office have been used to discover the identity of a . . . sadistic schoolboy, which I fear may be all that this investigation is destined to reveal."

Rheinhardt took the cigar and repeated: "I have a feeling."

9

IT WAS A DULL MORNING: the sky was layered with massy strips of dense gray cloud. Rheinhardt took care as he negotiated the damp cobbles, which descended at a steep angle toward a scrubby, water-logged field. On either side were squat bungalows, the walls of which were mottled and streaked with an algal slime. In the distance, he could see four gas towers: enormous structures that loomed beyond a misty veil of persistent mizzle.

Rheinhardt found the bungalow he was looking for. It was cleaner than its neighbors but was not in good repair (the gutter was leaking). A lever pump was situated just outside the entrance, and a number of metal buckets were hanging in a neat row under the eaves. An empty birdcage—swinging forlornly—had been suspended in a recessed casement.

The door was opened by a woman. She was wearing a simple black dress, and the flesh around her sharp, intelligent eyes looked swollen. She had been crying.

"Frau Meta Zelenka?" The woman nodded. "I am Inspector Rheinhardt."

"Of course," she said, dabbing her cheeks with a handkerchief. "I'm sorry—please come in."

Rheinhardt stepped across the threshold into a dark room that felt oppressively compressed due to its low ceiling. Sitting at a table was a large man with short reddish hair. He wore a brown jacket over a vest, the top buttons of which were undone. On seeing the inspector, the man rose, but very slowly—an uneasy coming together of body parts—such that the simple act of standing appeared to require monumental effort. Rheinhardt noticed the man's hands. They were laborer's hands—oversize, the white knuckles like eggs, the skin leathery, the veins raised and twisted.

"My husband," said the woman. Her German was nuanced with a Slavic accent. "Fanousek, this is Inspector Rheinhardt."

The man bowed, although the movement seemed to involve nothing more than a pained hunching of his shoulders.

Beyond the table was a sideboard on which stood a devotional candle and a crucifix.

"Forgive me for intruding on your grief," said Rheinhardt.

Fanousek lowered himself back into his chair, and Meta drew up a seat beside him. Her slender hand traveled across the surface of the table until it reached her husband's, whereupon his long fingers opened and closed tightly around hers.

"Thank you for agreeing to see me," said Rheinhardt, sitting opposite the couple. "And please accept my heartfelt condolences."

"What do you want, Inspector?" said Fanousek. Like Meta's, his German was accented; however, the question—although blunt—was not discourteous, merely direct.

"Information. About yourselves—and about Thomas."

"Why?"

"I must complete a report. For the commissioner." It was not the precise truth—but it was true enough. Rheinhardt couldn't very well declare, *I'm here because of a presentiment, a feeling* . . .

Rheinhardt took out his notebook.

"You are both Czech?"

"Yes."

"And how long have you been living in Vienna?"

"Ten years."

Theirs was a typical story—of hardship in rural Bohemia, the promise of prosperity in Vienna, then factory work, and finally disappointment. Fanousek worked in a warehouse. Meta sold cheap rye bread imported from Hungary at a Saturday market.

"With respect," asked Rheinhardt hesitantly, "how could you afford to send your son to Saint Florian's?"

"We couldn't," said Meta. "Thomas was awarded a scholarship."

"Really? How did that happen?"

"Thomas spent a great deal of time in the company of our priest, Father Hanak. He encouraged Thomas, gave him books, even gave him free lessons at the presbytery: Latin, calligraphy, mathematics. . . . Then the good father found out that one of the breweries, one of the Czech breweries, sponsored a place at the *oberrealschule* for a boy born in Bohemia and"—Meta swallowed her pride and continued—"from an impoverished household."

Rheinhardt gestured to indicate that the Zelenkas' pecuniary circumstances, however straitened, were of little consequence as far as he was concerned.

"Was Thomas happy at Saint Florian's?"

"Yes, as far as we know. He enjoyed his studies—particularly the scientific subjects. He did complain once or twice about having to do drill every day, but that was all."

"What about the other boys? Did he say anything about them?"

"No."

"He must have mentioned his friends?"

"Thomas was a quiet boy. Thoughtful. He didn't say much." She glanced at her husband and produced a gentle smile. "Like his father."

Through a square window, Rheinhardt saw sheets of rain blowing across the bleak industrial landscape.

Meta opened a drawer in the table and removed a photograph. She looked at it for a moment and said: "He was so handsome in his uniform." She pushed it across the table. "A fine-looking young man: a soldier."

The photograph had been taken in a studio. The boy was wearing a low shako with a leather peak, a tunic with stiff high collars, trousers, and boots. His right hand rested on the hilt of his sabre. He was standing in front of a painted backdrop of giant fern leaves and exotic creepers. Unfortunately, the photographer's tropical tableau was spoiled somewhat by a strip of patterned carpet in the foreground.

"May I take this?" asked Rheinhardt. Meta's expression became anxious—almost fearful. "I promise to return it later today. I would like to make a copy for submission with my report."

Meta's eyes softened.

"Yes . . . you can take it."

"Thank you," said Rheinhardt. "Thomas appears so . . . so very healthy. Had he suffered from any illnesses in the preceding year?"

"No," said Fanousek. "And he was as strong as an ox. He used to help me down at the warehouse, lifting heavy crates. The men used to comment on it."

Rheinhardt remembered what Nurse Funke had said about Thomas always having colds: he slipped the photograph into his notebook.

"Where did Thomas sleep?"

Fanousek jerked his head back toward a closed door.

"Would you object to me taking a look?"

"No," said Meta. "But we cannot come with you. It is too distressing. We have left things . . . as they were."

"Of course," said Rheinhardt.

The boy's room was very small, with most of the floor space taken up by a low bed, a washstand, and a chest. On the windowsill was an orderly row of books, arranged according to size. Rheinhardt examined some of the titles: Homer's *Odyssey*, Ranke's *History of the Popes*, a Latin primer, and a well-thumbed edition of *Les Tentations de Saint Antoine*. Above the bed was a garish print of Christ on the cross—a close-up portrait, showing the Messiah's anguish in dreadful detail, blood streaming from his wounds.

Rheinhardt knelt down and opened the chest. It contained some old clothes, which he carefully removed and laid out on the bed. Beneath these he discovered a penknife, some old exercise books, a bottle of ink, a pack of playing cards, and two letters. Both were addressed to Thomas Zelenka and were written in the same scrawly hand.

Dear Friend,

The letter had been written the previous summer, and the correspondent was a boy called Isidor Perger. He was, evidently, another pupil at Saint Florian's, who—at the time of writing—was holidaying on the Traunsee with his family.

Thank you for your assistance with the Latin.
I don't know what I would have done without you. . . .

Rheinhardt skipped over a paragraph in which the author lamented his poor mathematics results, and then another in which he described walking along the esplanade at Gmunden.

Suddenly a sentence seemed to resolve itself more sharply against the yellow background.

Needless to say, I do not want to go back.

Rheinhardt peered at the jagged script, trying to decipher its violent oscillations.

I swear, I would run away if you said you would come with me. We could travel the world—go to South America, India, or China. However, I know that you think such talk is foolish. Sometimes I wonder whether I should tell my father what is happening. But what good would that do? He would say I am being unmanly. He doesn't care—no one does.

Rheinhardt stood up.
I care, he thought. *I care very much.*

IO

LIEBERMANN HAD DECIDED TO BUY himself a new fountain pen. He drifted through Alsergrund, inspecting the displays in stationery shop windows, until a distinctive line of town houses came into view. He found himself standing on a corner, looking up a very familiar road—the road where Miss Lydgate lived.

At that moment it occurred to him that, perhaps, he had never *really* intended to a buy a new pen. Indeed, it seemed just as likely that his need to make such a purchase had been a convenient fiction, permitting him to draw ever closer to a woman for whom his complex feelings were becoming increasingly troublesome.

Liebermann's impromptu self-analysis was confirmed when the justification for knocking on the Englishwoman's door presented itself with minimal effort. Miss Lydgate had asked him to recommend a dancing teacher, and he had replied: *Herr Janowsky.* It would be perfectly reasonable for him to call on Miss Lydgate, in order to give her Herr Janowsky's address.

"Dr. Liebermann," said Amelia. Her greeting was accompanied by a transient smile that reminded Liebermann of wind on water—a sudden perturbation, followed by stillness.

"Miss Lydgate, I was just passing . . . and I wondered if you still wanted Herr Janowsky's details?"

"Herr Janowsky?"

"My sister's dancing master? I have his address."

Amelia's face registered mild surprise.

"It is very kind of you to have remembered, Dr. Liebermann. Please, do come in."

While Amelia prepared tea, Liebermann was obliged to pay his respects to Frau Rubenstein—a sweet-natured widow and friend of his father. Liebermann had brought Amelia and Frau Rubenstein together, knowing that both women were in need of what the other possessed: the old woman, companionship, and the younger one, a place to live. After a few polite exchanges, Liebermann ascended several flights of stairs leading to Amelia's rooms on the top floor. He was invited to sit and was subsequently plied with Earl Grey and *wiener vanillekipferl*—sweet crescent biscuits made with ground almonds and vanilla sugar.

Liebermann gave Herr Janowsky's address to Amelia, which prompted her to thank him, once again, for inviting her to the detectives' ball. She then asked how Inspector Rheinhardt had fared after his departure. Liebermann explained that the inspector was investigating the death of a young man at a military school—but he did not elaborate.

On the table was a volume bound in scuffed leather and with a blank spine. Others like it were stacked in a neat pile by the hearth. These were the private journals of Amelia's German grandfather, Dr. Ludwig Buchbinder: confidant of Prince Albert, Physician-in-Ordinary to the queen of England, and scientific visionary.

Liebermann picked up the book and allowed the covers to fall open. The pages released a distinctive, ripe odor—an evocative quintessence of time, scholarship, and decay.

"Do you still intend to edit these journals for publication?" he asked.

"Indeed," said Amelia. "I was only recently considering that very volume—which contains a remarkable section on the history of automata."

"It is not a subject I know very much about," said Liebermann, hoping that she would rectify his ignorance.

"The creation of automata has always been associated with medicine . . . and particularly with doctors who have an interest in blood."

"Really?"

"Yes—my grandfather has written that the first working model of the circulatory system was devised by a German physician, who announced his success in the *Journal des Savants* in 1677."

Amelia halted—suddenly self-conscious.

"Please, do go on . . ."

"Many more doctors embarked on similar projects—and the eighteenth century witnessed the creation of numerous 'blood machines' of increasing sophistication. These 'philosophical toys' caused much consternation among religious thinkers, who were concerned that, by making manikins that actually bled, doctors were engaged in a Promethean labor—and that their real intention was to create artificial life." Amelia's hair caught the light and, for a brief moment, became incandescent—a shimmering haze of red and gold. "Eventually," she continued, "even the most adventurous members of the scientific community were frightened by the implications of their work, and in due course artificial men became an increasing rarity in medical schools. In time, of course, they vanished altogether."

"How very interesting," said Liebermann, still distracted by a residual image of her sudden ignition—a vague, haunting impression of flame and the colors of autumn. "One is reminded of your countrywoman, Mary Shelley—her cautionary tale of Frankenstein, or the modern Prometheus."

"She was—I believe—aware of the work of several German physiologists, which she mentions in her preface."

Amelia's talk of artificial men reminded Liebermann of something he had once heard, about a chess-playing automaton that had been built in Vienna for the amusement of the empress Maria Theresa.

"It might have been the brainchild of Maelzel," he added.

"The inventor of the metronome?"

"Yes. . . . But I can't be sure. I have only the dimmest recollection of what is supposed to have transpired."

Miss Lydgate was extremely interested in this historical vignette; however, she concluded that, even if the story were true, the automaton itself must have been nothing more than a clever deception.

Liebermann always enjoyed such conversations with Miss Lydgate. She was an unconventional woman, yet her peculiarities possessed a certain charm: her pedantic speech, her stiff deportment, and the quite extraordinary intensity of her facial expressions.

He was a psychiatrist, and something inside him—some nameless but essential part of his being—was irresistibly drawn to the unusual.

They continued their conversation until the sky darkened and it was no longer permissible for Liebermann to stay. He rose from his chair, exchanged a few pleasantries, and kissed Amelia's hand. On the landing he insisted that she stay upstairs—he did not expect her to show him out.

As he made his descent, Liebermann became acutely aware of the physical and mechanical properties of his body: locomotion—the movement of joints—his lungs expanding and contracting, his spine resisting gravity. Propriety and apprehension had turned him into an automaton—an artificial man, in every sense. Contrived, inauthentic, affected: a *blood machine*.

II

It was midmorning when Rheinhardt's carriage drew up alongside the wind-scoured statue of Saint Florian. The Gothic façade of the military academy looked much larger than Rheinhardt remembered, and where there had previously been nothing but darkness he now saw wide, flat exercise areas. Ranks of uniformed boys were practicing their rifle drill, responding to the abrupt commands of a burly Tyrolean infantryman.

Rheinhardt passed under the central arch, where he spied Albert—the old soldier—dozing in the cloisters. He shook the veteran's shoulder, gently.

"Permission to report," mumbled Albert before his bloodshot eyes opened. He pulled himself up and croaked: "Ah, Inspector . . . Permission to report: I was asleep."

"And I trust you are now refreshed," said Rheinhardt. "I believe the deputy headmaster is expecting me."

"He is, sir. This way, sir, this way."

The deputy headmaster ushered Rheinhardt into his office and immediately apologized on behalf of Professor Eichmann. The headmaster had been called to an emergency meeting of the board of school governors; Becker hoped, however, that he would be equal to the task of assisting the inspector with his investigation.

Rheinhardt asked Becker to recapitulate the events surrounding the discovery of Zelenka's body. The deputy headmaster's account was entirely consistent—and delivered with calm authority. When pressed for more information about Zelenka's character, he simply repeated what he had said the previous Friday: he had known Zelenka quite well; the boy frequently asked for extra assignments; he was an enthusiastic student. Rheinhardt made a note, more out of politeness than necessity.

"Who else taught Zelenka?"

Becker went through the papers on his desk and consulted a timetable.

"Lieutenant Osterhagen, gymnastics. Herr Lang, drawing and calligraphy. Dr. Kloester, geography. Herr Sommer, mathematics . . ."

There were ten names in total.

A soft knock heralded the arrival of a maid who was carrying a silver tray.

"Your medicine, sir."

She deposited the tray on Becker's desk and made a diffident departure. The deputy headmaster picked up a piece of folded paper and, holding it over a small glass of clear liquid, tapped the side gently. A line of white powder fell out, the tiny grains dissolving as they sank in the liquid. Becker finally stirred the concoction with a spoon.

"Excuse me," he said to Rheinhardt, touching his temple. "I suffer from headaches." He threw his head back and swallowed the liquid as if it were schnapps.

"Are all of these masters here today?" asked Rheinhardt, looking down into his open notebook.

"All of them except Sommer," Becker replied. "He fell down the stairs yesterday and injured his leg." The tone of Becker's voice was unsympathetic, almost dismissive. "He's gone off somewhere to convalesce."

"Do you know where?"

"I'm afraid not. But the headmaster will know."

"I would like to conduct some interviews."

Becker looked at the timetable again and pulled at his forked beard. "You wish to interview *all* of Zelenka's masters?"

"As many as I can, and I would also like to interview one of the boys."

Becker tilted his head. The lenses of his gold-rimmed spectacles became white circles of reflected light.

"Isidor Perger," said Rheinhardt.

"Perger, Perger," repeated the deputy headmaster, straining to put a face to the name. He crossed his legs and drummed the desk with spidery fingers, making his hand crawl forward. Suddenly the drumming stopped and he called out.

"Ah yes, Perger!"

"I have reason to believe that he and Zelenka were close friends."

"Very well. I'm sure that can be arranged. Will you be needing a room in which to conduct these interviews?"

"The provision of a room would be much appreciated."

"There are some disused classrooms upstairs. Not very comfortable, but sufficiently removed from the general hubbub to ensure peace and quiet."

Becker subsequently called for Albert, relieved him of his existing duties, and instructed him to act as Rheinhardt's adjutant for the day. However, when Rheinhardt left the deputy headmaster's office—with the shuffling old soldier at his side—he felt as if he were being indulged rather than assisted.

Rheinhardt followed Albert up a tightly curving spiral staircase, which eventually joined a long corridor with a vaulted ceiling. The space reverberated with the sound of treble voices conjugating a Latin verb by rote. Four boys were walking toward them, all dressed in the uniform with which Rheinhardt was becoming increasingly familiar: low shako, gray tunic, and trousers. Each was equipped with a full-size sabre (one of the boys had his weapon slung too low, and the tip of its scabbard scraped noisily along the floor behind him). Although Rheinhardt knew they must be fifteen or older, their small stature and wide, suspicious eyes suggested a more tender age.

"Good morning," said Rheinhardt.

The boys halted, bowed, clicked their heels—and proceeded in the same tight and disconcertingly silent formation.

Albert ascended yet another staircase—this time wider—and escorted Rheinhardt to a musty, remote corner of the building where a row of half-open doors created wedges of ghostly light among the shadows. The "treasury smell" was particularly strong, having matured, like a piece of ripe cheese, in the undisturbed air.

"You can use any of these, sir," said the old man, struggling to catch his breath.

The classrooms were strangely melancholy: abandoned desks, a waste bin on its side, scattered paper, and a blackboard on which algebraic symbols constituted only half of an incomplete equation. Rheinhardt selected the least cluttered interior and asked Albert to fetch the first master on his list.

Lieutenant Osterhagen was a tall broad-shouldered man with ruggedly handsome features. His blond hair was cropped short, and a deep cleft was visible in the middle of his clean-shaven chin. Remarkably (for a gymnastics master) he walked with a limp. When he sat down, with evident discomfort, he made a passing reference to the "old Transylvanian complaint."

"Transylvanian complaint?" asked Rheinhardt.

"Nationalists," said Osterhagen. "I took one of their bullets when my regiment was sent to deal with a *situation*—if you know what I mean?"

Rheinhardt wasn't sure that he *did* know what the lieutenant meant. Nevertheless, he thought it wise to nod politely and proceed with the interview.

"I'm not surprised he dropped dead," said Osterhagen. "It was obvious there was something wrong with him."

"Why do you say that?"

"He was never well . . . *always* suffering from colds, *always* wrapped up in a scarf and wearing gloves, *always* clutching an exemption certificate from the infirmary."

"He wasn't, then, in your opinion, a very strong boy?"

The lieutenant laughed with savage contempt.

"Good God, *no*. Whatever gave you that idea?"

"I was told that he used to help his father—lifting heavy crates in a warehouse."

"He might have swept the floor, perhaps," said Osterhagen, twisting his mouth to one side in a sarcastic grin. When the inspector did not smile back, Osterhagen added with indifference, "The boy was destined for a career in the civil service. Not the army."

Osterhagen typified a certain type of military man. Blustering, bombastic, and appallingly insensitive. When the interview ended, Rheinhardt was relieved to bid the lieutenant good day.

The next two masters had very little to say about Zelenka. Neither of them had known him very well. Indeed, one of them, Dr. Kloester, confused Zelenka with another Czech boy called Cervenka. Consequently, Rheinhardt had to cross out all Kloester's answers and start the interview again.

Herr Lang—the drawing and calligraphy master—was a more promising informant.

"I was in my rooms when I heard. The headmaster came to the lodges on Saturday morning to tell us all personally. I couldn't believe it . . . such a terrible tragedy. Do you know what happened, Inspector? Do you know how Zelenka died?"

Rheinhardt shook his head.

Lang was in his late twenties. His hair was parted at the side and drawn in thick wavy strands across his head. A wildly undulating forelock occasionally fell forward and had to be pushed back again. His nose was long and straight, and his large, implacable eyes were arresting. The ensemble, however, was mitigated by the lower half of his face, which comprised a thin mustache, an incongruously tight mouth, and a soft, rounded chin. It was these weaker elements, however, that imbued his expressions with an unusual degree of humanity. He was dressed in a navy jacket, the lapels and cuffs of which were decorated with parallel lines of yellow stitching, and pale blue trousers with a prominent pinstripe. His cravat was green and matched a silk handkerchief that burst, rather too abundantly, from his breast pocket.

"He wasn't a talented artist," Lang continued, "but he was an intelligent, attentive boy. I remember showing him some illustrations in *Ver Sacrum*, the periodical of the Secession. He asked me some very astute questions about the artist's purpose—questions concerning symbolism and meaning. I was impressed. One wouldn't have got that kind of response—a mature response—from his comrades. They would simply have smirked and made lewd remarks."

"Why would they do that?"

"Nudity. Even a line drawing of the female form . . ." Lang's sentence trailed off in exasperation.

"I see," said Rheinhardt, inwardly reflecting that the minds of schoolboys had not changed very much since his own youth.

"Zelenka was different," said Lang. "Very self-possessed for his age. A little shy, perhaps, but he was growing out of it. I was very fond of him."

The young master blinked rapidly, and Rheinhardt wondered if he was about to cry.

"Was he happy here, do you think?"

Lang changed position and made a plosive sound that managed to combine incredulity with indignation. His features hardened.

"He was a scholarship boy."

"What of it?"

"I don't think anybody from his background could possibly be happy in a place like Saint Florian's!"

Rheinhardt allowed the subsequent silence to build until Lang felt compelled to justify his expostulation. "Historically, Saint Florian's has always welcomed boys from a particular kind of family. The headmaster doesn't agree with the new egalitarianism that the emperor is trying to promote in our schools and universities."

"Are you suggesting that boys like Zelenka, boys from poor backgrounds, are treated badly?"

Lang got up from his chair and walked to the door. He opened it a fraction and looked through the crack. The sound of Albert's stertorous breathing could be heard outside. Satisfied that there were no eavesdroppers, he closed the door quietly and returned to the table. He did not sit down.

"Look, Inspector." He appeared slightly agitated. "I know that for boys like Zelenka this school is purgatory. I talk to them while they're drawing. I can see it in their eyes—the sadness, the fear. And sometimes they say things."

"What do you mean, 'say things?'"

"I've been to see the headmaster, but, between you and me, Professor Eichmann is only interested in the welfare of boys from *good* families. As for the rest . . ."

"Have you considered discussing your concerns with the board of governors?"

"I have . . . but I won't now. It's too late."

"Why?"

"Because I'm leaving. I intend to hand in my resignation at the end of term."

"Do you have another position to go to?"

"No. I intend to join the Secessionists. You will, I trust, treat what I have said—*all* that I have said—as strictly confidential?"

"Yes, of course."

It was evident from their further discussion that Lang was, and had always been, unhappy at Saint Florian's. He did not enjoy the company of his colleagues, and he found the general atmosphere intolerably oppressive.

"Do you know Isidor Perger?" asked Rheinhardt.

"Yes, he's another scholarship boy."

"I was hoping to interview him this afternoon."

Lang's mouth twisted into a sardonic smile.

"You won't get much out of him." Lang glanced at his watch and edged toward the door. "If you'll excuse me, Inspector, I have a class."

Rheinhardt thanked Lang for his assistance, made a few notes, and walked over to the windows. Peering out of the central lancet, he saw some terraced brick houses (perhaps the "lodges" that Eichmann and Lang had referred to), a stable, and an equestrian enclosure—the outer edge of which was being circumambulated by a troop of boys on horseback. His gaze was drawn upward, toward the fir-covered hills that rolled out into the milky distance.

Rheinhardt felt a curious sense of satisfaction. He was glad that he had come back to the school.

There's something wrong here.

His intuition had been correct.

12

LIEBERMANN HAD LEFT THE HOSPITAL early in order to visit his older sister, Leah. He also expected to see Hannah—their younger sister. Only rarely did the three siblings meet in this way, and such meetings were always planned well in advance, and under a shroud of secrecy. This was necessary in order to stop their parents, Mendel and Rebecca, from taking control of arrangements and turning what would otherwise be a relaxed, informal gathering into a major family event.

Hannah was seated on a sofa, reading a book to Daniel, Leah's son. The little boy was dressed in red lederhosen, a white shirt, long socks, and soft leather shoes. He was also wearing an Alpine hat—which served no real purpose other than to amuse the adults. Occasionally Daniel would laugh, which, in Hannah's company, was a perilous activity. The sound of happy gurgling invariably prompted the youthful aunt to tickle his stomach until his face went red and he was begging for mercy.

Ordinarily, Leah would intervene. But on this occasion, she allowed the mêlée to continue in order to have an intimate word with her brother. She poured him some tea, leaned closer, and said:

"Have you seen Father?"

"Yes, last week. We went for coffee at the Imperial."

"And how was he?"

"Still very angry. Even so, we managed a civil—if rather uncomfortable—conversation."

Relations between Liebermann and his father had become particularly strained since Liebermann had broken his engagement with Clara Weiss—the daughter of one of Mendel's oldest and closest friends.

"Did he mention . . . ?"

"Clara? No."

Leah offered Max a slice of *guglhupf,* which he declined.

"I hear that she's met someone. A cavalry lieutenant."

"Good. I hope they are happy together."

"And you?"

"What about me?"

"Have you met anyone special yet?"

Liebermann paused long enough for his sister to raise her eyebrows.

"Who?"

Liebermann smiled and shook his head. "No one . . . not really."

Leah drew her head back and looked at him askance. It made her appear just like their mother.

Daniel's shrieking became louder. His head was thrown back, only the whites of his eyes were showing, and his cheeks were turning puce.

"That's enough," Leah called. "Really!"

Hannah withdrew her hand and looked up guiltily. "We're only playing."

"You're supposed to be reading!"

Liebermann stood up and walked across the room. He sat down next to Hannah and took Daniel, bouncing him a few times on his knee.

"He's getting so heavy!"

"I know," said Leah, sighing wearily.

"What have you got there?" Liebermann asked Hannah.

"Daniel's klecksography book," Hannah replied.

"Klecksography?"

Hannah opened the book and held it in front of Daniel. The child leaned forward, stretching his hand out toward a striking image—a large symmetrical pattern: as if ink had been spilled on a page, and then the page had been folded along a central vertical crease. It was accompanied by a fanciful verse about a troll, which Hannah read out in a theatrical contralto. The later pages were filled with similar images—symmetrical inkblots, all vaguely resembling the spread wings of a butterfly.

"Are the patterns supposed to represent the characters in the verses?" Liebermann asked.

"Yes," said Hannah. "You look at the shapes . . . and try to see things. Trolls, fairies . . . it's like . . . like a game."

"How very interesting," said Liebermann. "What's it called?"

"Klecksography."

"Leah?" Liebermann's expression became oddly serious. "Where did you get this book from?"

"Oh, I don't know, Max," Leah replied. "But you can get klecksography books anywhere—they're very popular. Why?"

"It's an interesting concept, that's all."

Leah looked at Daniel and shook her head. "Sometimes I wonder whether your uncle has spent too much time with mad people."

13

After leaving Leah's apartment Liebermann traveled into town to collect a long-standing order from Schott's—Schumann's *Twelve Poems by Justinus Kerner*, opus 35, a little-known song cycle that Rheinhardt was keen to try.

On the streetcar home, Liebermann became engrossed in the prefatory notes. He discovered that Justinus Kerner, a physician and poet from Ludwigsburg, was also the author of a posthumous work, *Klecksographien*, which was (by the strangest of coincidences) the progenitor of his nephew's klecksography book and its many variants. Liebermann read that while suffering from depression, Kerner had seen ghosts and monsters in his symmetrical inky creations—and had ascribed for them a place in Hades.

Rheinhardt arrived shortly before eight o'clock, and the two friends began their music-making immediately. They performed Franz Lachner's *Sängerfahrt*, some atmospheric songs by Mendelssohn, and Zelter's *Der König von Thule*. When Liebermann produced the Schumann songs from behind the music stand, Rheinhardt was delighted.

"Excellent, excellent," he cried. "What a pleasant surprise!"

The *Twelve Poems* were a strange cycle—having no unifying theme or coherent key sequence—yet it was their eccentricity that Liebermann found attractive. One of the settings, *Auf das Trinkglas eines verstorbenen Freundes*, was at the same time a lament for a departed friend and a panegyric to German wine. However, it also managed to subsume a meditation on the ineffable bond between the living and the dead.

Rheinhardt clasped his hands in front of his chest and sang the poetry with tender grace:

> *"Doch wird mir klar zu dieser Stund,*
> *"Wie nichts den Freund vom Freund kann trennen."*
> Yet at this hour I realize
> How nothing can part friend from friend.

> *"Leer Steht das Glas! Der heil'ge Klang*
> *"Tönt nach in dem kristall'nen Grunde."*
> The glass stands empty! The sacred sound
> Still echoes in its crystal depths.

As Liebermann played the final cadence, he could see that the deeper meanings of the text had affected Rheinhardt. A detective inspector would appreciate, even more than a physician-poet, perhaps, how the dead—in some sense—are never truly departed. They always leave something of themselves behind.

When Liebermann and Rheinhardt retired to the smoking room, they took their customary places, lit cigars, and contemplated the fire.

"So," said Liebermann, reaching for the brandy. "You are still preoccupied by the death of Thomas Zelenka."

Rheinhardt continued to look at the flames.

"Yesterday I went to Saint Florian's and interviewed—with one exception—all of his masters."

"Why one exception?"

"His mathematics master has had an accident. He fell down the stairs and injured his leg."

"How unfortunate."

Liebermann handed Rheinhardt a glass of brandy.

"When I went to see Zelenka's parents, they said he was a strong, healthy boy. Yet his gymnastics master and Nurse Funke said he was sickly—that he always had colds."

"Perhaps Zelenka feigned illness in order to avoid gymnastics."

"And why would he do that?"

"The boys probably do their physical training bare-chested."

"Which would have necessitated exposure of the cuts?"

"Indeed. He might have wished to keep them concealed."

"But why?"

"Embarrassment, shame ... However, there is a much simpler explanation. He avoided gymnastics because any form of vigorous exercise was painful."

Rheinhardt took Perger's letter from his pocket and pushed it across the table.

"I found this in Zelenka's bedroom—there were two letters, actually, but this is the most interesting."

Liebermann put on his spectacles and unfolded the paper. He read in silence, until he reached the salient passages: *"Needless to say, I do not want to go back. . . . Sometimes I wonder whether I should tell my father what is happening. But what good would that do? . . . He doesn't care—no one does."*

Rheinhardt sipped his brandy, and summarized his encounter with Lang.

"Why didn't you interview Perger?" asked Liebermann.

"I did," Rheinhardt replied. "And Lang was right—he wouldn't cooperate. I told Perger what I thought: that he and other boys—particularly from poor backgrounds—were being persecuted, and that if he told me who was responsible I would see to it that they were punished. He pretended not to know what I was talking about. . . . So then I showed him his own letter to Zelenka. I could see he was shocked, but to his credit the boy managed to sustain his subterfuge. He insisted that I had misunderstood the contents—it meant *nothing*. It was a joke, of course—particularly the part about running away. He said that he and Zelenka were always joking about doing such things."

Liebermann lifted the letter and tilted it in the light.

"At that point—where he mentions running away—it is possible to detect a faint tremor in the script. He was terrified. Whatever he was hoping to escape from, it made his hand shake."

Rheinhardt leaned across the table and looked at the letter more closely.

"It all looks the same to me."

"There is a definite tremor."

Rheinhardt sat back in his chair, a mote of skepticism still glimmering in his eye.

"I thought about interviewing some of the other boys—but there are more than three hundred of them. It would be pointless to select names randomly from the register. Do you think you could persuade Perger to disclose the identity of his persecutors?"

"Perhaps."

"Would you hypnotize him?"

Liebermann shrugged. "Perhaps."

The young doctor's economic response—combined with his arch expression—suggested to Rheinhardt that he had already thought of a possible solution.

Liebermann lit a cigar and exhaled a large nimbus of smoke.

"Of course," he said, "none of this new information shines further light on the death of Thomas Zelenka. Which, I believe, was your original purpose."

"That is true. But in spite of your analysis of my unconscious motives, the defensive denial of premature death, and so forth, I cannot rid myself of a persistent conviction that if I continue with this investigation, *something* relevant, *something* explanatory with regard to Zelenka's death, will eventually arise."

Liebermann took another puff of his cigar.

"Well . . . you might just be right."

"What?" said Rheinhardt, turning his head in disbelief. "Have you changed your mind, then, about policeman's intuition?"

"Not at all." Liebermann tapped his cigar on the ashtray. "However, *if* there is something new to be learned about Zelenka's death—and it is a very substantial *if*—then I am afraid to say, Oskar, that you have failed to interview someone who—in my humble opinion—merits the closest questioning."

"I beg your pardon?"

"The mathematics master."

"What makes you think he's important? I haven't even told you his name. You know nothing about him!"

"I know enough," said Liebermann, smiling into his brandy.

14

DREXLER STUBBED OUT HIS CIGARETTE and immediately lit another. They were a cheap Turkish brand that produced pungent wreaths of fulvous smoke. He had sunk deep into a wicker chair and was hunched over a well-thumbed volume of E.T.A. Hoffmann's short stories, the print of which was illuminated by a candle. His only other source of light was a paraffin lamp, some distance away, suspended from a beam.

"Do you know why you're here, Stojakovic?" It was Kiefer Wolf's voice, emanating from a dark recess on the other side of the room.

Drexler lifted his head. A scrawny Serbian boy was standing between Barend Steininger and Odo Freitag. Steininger was tall, big-boned, and mature enough to sport a downy mustache and fuzzy sideburns. Freitag was much shorter but stocky, possessing a thick, muscular neck and facial features that thrust forward like those of a pit bull terrier.

The Serbian boy peered into the shadows and blinked.

"Come on, Stojakovic," said Steininger, digging his elbow into the boy's side.

"Yes, come on, Stojakovic," Freitag repeated, clapping his hands on his shoulders.

The Serbian boy opened his mouth, but no sound escaped.

"I asked you a question, Stojakovic!" Wolf's disembodied voice grew louder.

"He did," said Steininger, grinning. "Wolf asked you a question."

"Yes, don't be impolite, Stojakovic," said Freitag, tightening his grip. "Be a good fellow and answer Wolf."

The boy glanced at Drexler—but it was a wasted appeal. Drexler shook his head.

"I don't know what passes for good manners in your country, Stojakovic," Wolf barked. "But it is our custom to give an answer when asked a question."

"Very true," said Steininger. "Very true."

The boy's mouth opened again. He produced an unintelligible wavering noise.

"What did you say?" asked Steininger.

"I'm . . . ," the boy croaked. "I'm sorry. . . . What was the question?"

"I don't believe it," said Steininger.

"He wants you to repeat the question, Wolf," said Freitag.

"Are you hard of hearing, Stojakovic?" said Steininger. "A little deaf, perhaps?"

The boy shook his head.

Steininger bent down and looked into the boy's ear. "Then perhaps your ears are dirty?"

Freitag looked into the boy's other ear. "Yes, I believe they are."

"Were you, by any chance, raised on a farm, Stojakovic?" asked Steininger.

"I think he must have been," said Freitag.

"That would explain a great deal," said Steininger.

"Indeed," said Freitag.

"I wonder, do you have soap and water where you come from, Stojakovic?" said Steininger.

They suddenly burst out laughing and looked to Drexler for approval, but his face remained impassive.

"Have you lost your sense of humor, Drexler?" said Freitag.

"Quite the contrary," Drexler replied. "I find Hoffmann *very amusing*."

"Oh, well, if your sense of humor is still intact," said Freitag, "you'll enjoy this—the latest Serbian joke."

"Careful, Freitag," said Drexler. "Some of my ancestors were Serbian."

"Don't worry," said Freitag. "I'll speak very slowly. . . . Now, how do you get a one-armed Serb down from a tree? No idea? All right— you wave at him."

Steininger slapped his thigh and guffawed loudly.

Freitag turned to address their captive: "Why do you Serbians bring a bucket of shit to your weddings?" Before the boy could answer, Freitag added: "To keep the flies off the bride, of course."

Again, Steininger fell about laughing.

"Enough!" Wolf shouted, clapping his hands slowly.

Steininger collected himself and assumed a more serious expression.

"Stojakovic!" Wolf continued. "I will ask you once more. Why have you been brought here?"

"I don't know," said the Serbian boy—his denial sounded like a desperate plea.

"Then I'll tell you," said Wolf. "You have been indiscreet, Stojakovic."

"Now, that is bad," said Steininger.

"Quite unacceptable," murmured Freitag.

"Did you really think," said Wolf, "that you could blab to Lang in the middle of a calligraphy class and not be overheard!"

"I didn't—"

"Speak up!"

"You are mistaken."

"Don't lie, Stojakovic!"

The sound of Wolf's footsteps preceded his appearance. He emerged from the outer darkness between two columns of smoke that turned slowly in the displaced air. His mouth was a horizontal slit—its linearity suggesting boredom. He had a thin, hungry face, and dull gray eyes. However, his hair was bright yellow—like a cap of gold.

Wolf drew on his cigarette and stepped up close to the Serbian boy. They were roughly the same height, and their noses almost touched. Wolf exhaled a cloud of smoke and said, quite calmly: "You have attempted to make trouble for us, and you must be taught a lesson. It is your own fault—you understand? You brought it upon yourself."

The boy could not maintain eye contact, and looked down at the floor. Wolf trod on his cigarette, turned, and marched toward Drexler.

"Get up!"

"Why?"

"Because I want to sit down."

"I'm reading."

"Drexler! I won't tell you again!"

Drexler sighed, got out of the chair, and leaned against the wall.

Wolf reached into the battered suitcase and removed something— an object. The others could not see what it was because Wolf concealed it with his hands.

"Now, Stojakovic," said Wolf, "you will do exactly as I say and no harm will come to you; however, if you choose to disobey me . . ." Wolf raised his arm. He was holding a revolver. "I will shoot you."

Steininger and Freitag looked at each other and laughed.

"Where did you get that from, eh, Wolf?" said Steininger.

Wolf waved the revolver from side to side, indicating that his two lieutenants should withdraw.

"Hey, be careful," said Freitag. "Is it loaded?"

"Of course it's loaded, you fool!"

"Where did you get it from?" Steininger repeated his question.

"I found it."

"Where?"

"Never you mind." Wolf thrust the revolver forward at Stojakovic. "Take your clothes off. Don't just stand there—you heard what I said. Take your clothes off. Hurry up—all of them." His voice had become agitated, and flecks of spittle sprayed out of his mouth.

The Serbian boy undid the buttons of his tunic and fumbled with his belt. His hands were shaking.

He hesitated when he reached his undergarments.

"What are you waiting for?" asked Wolf. "Get on with it!"

The boy peeled off his woolen vest and stepped out of his long johns. He stood, completely naked, in a cone of milky luminescence. He was a thin, pale boy, with alabaster skin and dark hair. His genitals were barely visible, having retreated into a luxuriant tangle of wiry pubic curls. The effect was quite disconcerting. Stojakovic looked feminine, submissive, sexually ambiguous, and the rapidity of his breathing betrayed the magnitude of his terror.

Steininger laughed. It wasn't a comfortable laugh. It had a hysterical quality—ending abruptly, and leaving a tense, uneasy silence in its wake.

"Now what?" said Drexler, snapping his book closed.

Wolf's eyes flashed at Drexler. They were filled with latent fire, an admixture of malevolence and anger. Drexler, who ordinarily experienced the world as if everything in it were somehow removed or distant, felt his sense of privileged detachment slip. It surprised him—like a jolt of electricity. The sinister cast of Wolf's lineaments had reined him in.

Wolf got up and walked purposefully toward the Serbian boy. When he reached his side, he inspected his face.

"Are you crying, Stojakovic?" Wolf asked.

The boy's head moved—a minute, almost imperceptible shake.

Wolf lifted the boy's chin with the barrel of the revolver. Stojakovic's cheeks were streaked with silver.

"Now, what did I tell you about lying, Stojakovic? If you lie to me, you will be punished. It's your own fault—you leave me no choice."

Wolf pulled the revolver hammer back with his thumb. It clicked loudly. Then he pressed the barrel against Stojakovic's temple.

Time stopped.

Drexler tasted metal in his mouth. The silence pulsed in his ears. A seeping, vitrifying cold spread through his limbs. He could not move, and felt that if he tried to, he would shatter.

A loud hissing sound filled the room.

At first, Wolf appeared confused. He looked quizzically at the others, then downward. Urine was flowing in wide yellow rivulets down Stojakovic's legs, feeding an expanding circular puddle, the circumference of which had made contact with the soles of Wolf's shoes.

"You Serbian dog!" Wolf cried, his mouth twisting in disgust. He struck Stojakovic on the head with the butt of his gun. "You animal, you damned animal!"

The boy fell to his knees, blood streaming from a deep gash on his forehead.

Drexler ran across the room and grabbed Wolf's arm, preventing him from delivering a second blow.

"Stop it, Wolf."

"Drexler?" Wolf was no longer angry. Rather, he seemed surprised—as though disorientated after waking from sleep.

"You've made your point," said Drexler. "Now that's enough." Drexler pulled the Serbian boy to his feet. "Pick up your clothes and get out. And no more loose talk in the future, you understand? Get out."

Stojakovic scooped up his clothes and ran into the darkness. They listened to him getting dressed: ragged breathing, the clink of his belt, and, finally, the trapdoor opening and closing.

Drexler looked into Wolf's eyes. The strange light had died, and Wolf's expression was blank. His thin lips were straight again. Slowly, something like a smile began to appear on his face.

"Drexler! You idiot! I wasn't going to kill him. You're losing your nerve!"

Wolf looked over at Steininger and Freitag. It was a collusive look—an invitation. They responded with laughter: fits and starts, encouraged by Wolf's widening smile, mounting, until their lungs and vocal cords were engaged in the production of a continuous asinine braying.

"He wasn't going to kill Stojakovic, Drexler!" Steininger cried, "Whatever were you thinking?"

"Yes, Drexler," Freitag echoed. "Whatever were you thinking?"

It was a good performance. But their relief was palpable.

15

Rʜᴇɪɴʜᴀʀᴅᴛ's ʜᴇᴀᴅ ᴡᴀs ʙᴜʀɪᴇᴅ in his copy of the latest edition of the police journal, which contained an extremely interesting article on the work of Jean Alexandre Eugene Lacassagne—a professor of medicine at the University of Lyon who had made extraordinary advances in the identification of decayed corpses. As he read, Rheinhardt became increasingly aware of piano music: music of incomparable lightness. An innocent, profoundly beautiful melody leaped an octave, before making a modulating descent over a flowing left-hand accompaniment. It charmed him out of the dark, morbid world of mortuaries and rotting cadavers. When the melody climbed again, he lifted his head—as if watching the ascent of a songbird.

His eldest daughter, Therese, was seated at the instrument, her slim fingers negotiating the naïve geography of Mozart's *Sonata in C Major*. On the other side of the parlor, seated at the table, were his wife, Else, and his younger daughter, Mitzi, engaged in some needlepoint. Mitzi was humming along with the tune. None of them were conscious of Rheinhardt's benign scrutiny.

He registered the good-humored curve of Else's mouth, the thickness of Mitzi's hair, and the straightness of Therese's back—the way that something of his own likeness lingered in the lineaments of both his daughters and, by some miracle, did so without diminishing their beauty.

Thomas Zelenka was only one year older than Therese. Although

Zelenka wore a uniform and had been taught to use a sabre, he was still—like Therese—a child.

To die so very young . . .

It was a disturbance in the order of things that Rheinhardt could not—would not—accept as *natural*.

The music suddenly shifted into a minor key, as if responding to his thoughts. He remembered visiting Zelenka's parents—the empty birdcage, the unoccupied bedroom, the void behind Fanousek's eyes: the four gas towers, like massive mausoleums, breaking the line of a bleak horizon, the terrible, suffocating atmosphere of desolation, misery, and loss.

How could any parent survive the loss of a child? How would Rheinhardt ever cope, if the piano playing ceased, the humming subsided, and the parlor was chilled by his daughters' absence? The silence would be intolerable.

Yes, Liebermann was probably right—by denying juvenile mortality he, Rheinhardt, was railing against fate, attempting to safeguard his children. But did that really matter? The existence of such a mechanism did not invalidate his feelings. Perhaps intuition originated in parts of the mind too deep for psychoanalysis to fathom. Moreover, Rheinhardt comforted himself with the thought that even Liebermann was beginning—albeit reluctantly—to accept that there might be something more to Zelenka's death than Professor Mathias's autopsy had revealed.

Rheinhardt looked at his daughters again and was overwhelmed by a force of emotion that made his breath catch. It was not comparable to the comfortable affection he felt for his wife, the companionate closeness that had mellowed and matured over the years. No—it was something quite different. A raw, primitive emotion—a violent, visceral, instinctive attachment combined with a desire to protect, whatever the cost. And yet, at the same time, it was remarkably satisfying and joyful. It defied description, was characterized by contradictions.

The music had recovered the tonic major key, and the principal subject was being recapitulated. The inspector counted his blessings and raised the police journal to conceal his watering eyes and the peculiar shame associated with the expression of uncontrollable, improvident love.

16

Liebermann and his friend Dr. Stefan Kanner were seated in a private windowless dining room. The food they had eaten was traditional fare, simply prepared but deeply satisfying: semolina dumplings in beef broth, Tyrolean knuckle of veal with rice, and *schmalzstrauben*—spirals of sweet batter, fried until golden brown, and sprinkled with sugar and cinnamon. A few *schmalzstrauben* remained, untouched and quite cold, on a metal rack. The wine was unusually good: a local red, the color of garnet, redolent of bonfires, plums, and raspberries. Bleary-eyed, flushed—neckties draped over their shoulders—and gloriously drunk, the two men conversed under an awning of cigar smoke.

"It was a beautiful day," said Kanner, tracing a flamboyant arc with his hand to evoke the cloudless empyrean. "Jeanette and I drove out to Döbling and had dinner, alfresco . . . and the following Sunday we went across the Kahlenberg to Klosterneuburg. On our way home, in the railway compartment, her head fell on my shoulder—and she said that she loved me."

Kanner pushed the box of cigars into the middle of the table, and encouraged Liebermann to take another.

"Go on—help yourself. They're Havanas. A gift from a grateful patient—well, her husband, actually—whom I cured of a zoöpsia accompanied by gastric pains."

"What animals did she hallucinate?"

"Only one: a dancing bear."

"And how did you treat her?"

"Maxim. Just take a cigar and let me finish my story, will you?"

Liebermann muttered an apology and signaled that his friend should proceed.

"Still under the benign influence of the sweet *vin de paille* from the cloister cellar," said Kanner, "I was quite ready to believe her. My customary skepticism vanished, and when our lips met, I was . . ." Kanner's eyes rolled upward. "Transported. The following day, however, my skepticism returned—"

"Which is just as well," Liebermann interjected.

Kanner thrust out his lower lip and blinked at his friend.

"Have I told you this story before?"

"No."

Kanner shrugged and continued. "I spent the afternoon in Café Landtmann . . . and when the streetlights came on, I went for a stroll in the Rathauspark. It was quite dark—but I'm sure it was her."

"Jeanette?"

"In the arms of Spitzer."

"The throat specialist?"

"The very same."

Liebermann threw his head back and directed a jet of smoke at the ceiling. The gaslight flared and made a curious respiratory sound—like a gasp.

"So, she wants to be an actress."

Kanner sat up straight—surprised.

"How did you know that?"

"Throat specialists always have a large number of famous actors and singers among their patients. They are frequently invited to first nights, gala performances, and other glamorous occasions. Among the medical specialities, throat specialists are by far the most well connected with respect to the arts. Subsequently, they are common prey to a particular type of young woman: pretty, intelligent, coquettish, of slender means, and with theatrical ambitions."

"Jeanette."

"*Quod erat demonstrandum.*"

"Yes," said Kanner. "You know, for a psychiatrist, I can be a remarkably poor judge of character." Kanner stared glumly into the ruby bowl of his wineglass before adding: "Shame about old Professor von Krafft-Ebing."

In his inebriated state, Liebermann accepted the sudden change of subject as though it were entirely logical.

"Yes, he will be sadly missed."

"I used to enjoy his public lectures."

"They were very entertaining," said Liebermann, "but I always found them weak, theoretically."

Kanner shrugged again. "People will be reading his *Psychopathia Sexualis* for centuries. What a collection of cases! And what a fine eye for detail! Do you have a favorite? I have always been rather fond of case fifty, Herr Z., the technologist who was only satisfied by women wearing high heels and short jackets, Hungarian fashion."

Liebermann shook his head. "That one escapes me. . . ."

"He was particularly partial to ladies' calves," Kanner continued, "but only when the ladies concerned wore elegant shoes. Nude legs—or nudity in general—did not arouse his interest. I was always amused by Krafft-Ebing's somewhat irregular inclusion of the fact that Herr Z. had a weakness for cats—and that simply looking at a cat could lift him from the deepest depression."

Kanner raised his bloodshot eyes. He scratched his head, leaving a tuft of oiled hair standing on end.

"I too," he said in a distant, somewhat bewildered voice, "am partial to women in short jackets . . . and to be perfectly honest, my spirits have often been lifted by the antics of a cat."

"Well, Stefan," said Liebermann, "perhaps you would benefit from one of the late professor's cures. I would be happy to prescribe regular cold baths and monobromide of camphor, if you wish?"

Kanner made a dismissive gesture.

"Baths are ineffective. When I was a student, I spent a summer in Bad Ischl, where I allowed a retired opera singer to believe she was seducing me. She frequently took a beauty treatment that involved immersion in a tub filled with crushed ice; however, this had no effect on her libido whatsoever. Her sensual appetite was just as keen whether she had had the treatment or not." Kanner swayed in his chair. "Be that as it may"—his delivery had become comically pompous—"it is our duty to honor the memory of a great man." He raised his glass. "To Professor Richard Freiherr von Krafft-Ebing . . . rest in heavenly peace."

"No, no, no," said Liebermann, banging his fist on the table. "May he go to hell. Surely."

"What?"

"The author of *Psychopathia Sexualis* would be bored to tears among the heavenly hosts—angels, seraphim, and cherubim, et cetera, et cetera." Liebermann yawned, patting his open mouth. "Clearly, Krafft-Ebing would prefer hell, where he would find the company much more stimulating—lust murderers, necrophiliacs, and sadists— why, he could start work on the next edition of the *Psychopathia* immediately on arrival!"

Kanner raised his glass again.

"To Professor Richard Freiherr von Krafft-Ebing . . . may you go to hell—and thoroughly enjoy eternal damnation!"

Liebermann reached across the table and touched Kanner's glass with his own, producing a chime that sang with a bell-like clarity. Outside, a woman passed their dining room, laughing loudly. It was a young voice—that of a shop girl, no doubt, who was being entertained by a "respectable" bourgeois husband. The grumble of the man's bass produced a lascivious counterpoint to the girl's contrived gaiety.

"Stefan," said Liebermann, "do you think it would be permissible to have relations with a patient?"

This thought, which had arisen in his mind apropos of nothing, had been translated into speech without conscious effort. Liebermann found himself listening to his own voice as if it belonged to a stranger.

"I beg your pardon?"

"Not a patient in treatment, of course," said Liebermann, now obliged to continue. "But a former patient—assuming that she was fully recovered and that a significant period of time had elapsed since her discharge."

"No. I can't see anything wrong with that. . . . In fact . . ."

"Yes?"

"In fact, I did have a little tryst once, with a former patient." Kanner toyed with his necktie. "We arranged to meet a few times in the Volksgarten, but the erotic frisson that had enlivened our conversations in the hospital was curiously absent. I suspect that it was only because we were forbidden to embrace there that the prospect seemed so alluring. Once the prohibition was lifted, there was nothing left to excite our imaginations. Or perhaps . . ." Kanner swirled the wine and examined the translucent liquid more closely. "Perhaps once removed from the hospital, and deprived of the emblems of power—my black bag, my stethoscope, my potions and elixirs—my imperfections were more readily observed. I was no longer the great healer and became just another philanderer—indistinguishable from all the others, going about their tawdry business behind the bushes."

Liebermann was thinking of Miss Lydgate. Her supine body on a hospital bed: a plain white gown—the rise and fall of her breasts. Her copper hair, pulled back tightly, aflame in a ray of sunlight.

"Why?" said Kanner. "Is there someone at the hospital who has taken your fancy?"

Liebermann shook his head—and as he did so, the room began to rotate. Slowly at first, but then gathering momentum—like the carousel on the Prater.

"Stefan . . . I have drunk far too much."

Kanner picked up the bottle and filled Liebermann's empty glass: "Maxim, we haven't even started!"

17

VON BULOW was immaculately dressed in a dark frock coat, gray striped trousers, and patent leather shoes. A beautifully folded blue cravat was held in place by a diamond tie pin, and his starched cuffs (which protruded from beneath the sleeves of his coat) were fastened with matching studs. Merely looking at von Bulow made Rheinhardt feel slovenly and unkempt.

His old rival was seated opposite the commissioner. Two empty teacups on Manfred Brügel's desk and a shallow bowl containing a solitary *Manner Schnitten* wafer biscuit suggested that the two men had been in conversation for some time.

Although Rheinhardt and von Bulow were both detective inspectors, von Bulow had always been treated as Rheinhardt's superior— largely on account of his privileged background. The practices of preferment and favor were commonplace in Viennese organizations, and the commissioner, being a highly ambitious man, was mindful that von Bulow hailed from an elevated family. The man had relatives in the upper house *and* in the Hofburg. Informed by the notion that goodwill was often reciprocated, the commissioner frequently afforded von Bulow special treatment—usually at Rheinhardt's expense. However, given that this odious situation was entirely unremarkable, and that there was no obvious person to whom a complaint could be directed (other than to the commissioner himself), Rheinhardt had no choice but to tolerate this indignity.

"Come along, Rheinhardt," said the commissioner, beckoning him in with an impatient hand gesture. "Don't just stand there."

Von Bulow stood up—as if in readiness to leave—and then, to Rheinhardt's surprise, sat down again. The commissioner registered Rheinhardt's perplexity and grumbled: "Von Bulow will be staying— there is a matter concerning his current investigation that we need to discuss with you. All will be explained in due course. Now ... where did I put them?" Brügel sifted through the papers scattered on his desk and found a wad of forms under a jug of milk. "I've read your reports, and everything seems to be in order. Although in the future, Rheinhardt, I'd appreciate it if you could do something about the quality of your handwriting."

Rheinhardt squirmed with embarrassment. It was obvious that Commissioner Brügel had only recently compared Rheinhardt's hurried script with von Bulow's elegant copperplate.

"Yes, sir."

The commissioner tossed the reports aside and picked up a photograph of Thomas Zelenka's body in the mortuary. Then he selected another, which showed the lacerations under the boy's arm.

"Peculiar," said the commissioner. "Very strange ... but I see no reason for maintaining security office involvement. Do you?" Brügel lifted his head, and his eyebrows drew closer together: "Well?"

"Sir, we've hardly—"

"These reports are perfectly adequate," said Brügel, allowing his palm to come down heavily on the papers and thereby underscoring the finality of his decision.

"Sir," Rheinhardt protested. "The wounds on Zelenka's body, Perger's letter ..."

"What about them? I'm perfectly satisfied with your explanation ... the persecution of scholarship boys. It's a sorry situation, but there we are. We all know what goes on in military schools. I went to Saint Polten, you know."

"But it's not just a case of bullying, sir. A boy died!"

"Yes, of natural causes."

"Indeed, but I have—" Rheinhardt stopped himself.

"You have what?" asked the commissioner.

There it was again: *I have a feeling ... a feeling, a feeling.*

"I have ... ," Rheinhardt blustered "yet to interview the mathematics master—Herr Sommer. He may have some important information that, I believe, will shine new light on Zelenka's fate." Rheinhardt was playing a perilous game—and he hoped that the commissioner would not press him.

"What makes you think that?"

"It is not my opinion, as such."

"Then whose?"

"Dr. Liebermann's."

Von Bulow shifted in his chair and made a disparaging noise.

"With respect, von Bulow," said Rheinhardt, "may I remind you that Dr. Liebermann's methods have proved very effective in the past—as you well know."

"He's been lucky, that's all," retorted von Bulow.

"No one could possibly be *that* lucky."

"Well," said von Bulow, "there's no other explanation, is there?"

"Psychoanalysis?"

"Jewish psychology! I think not!"

"Gentlemen!" Brügel growled.

The two men fell silent under the commissioner's fierce glare.

Rheinhardt seized the opportunity to continue his appeal. "Sir, I have already arranged for Dr. Liebermann to interview the boy Perger on Saturday. The mathematics master, Herr Sommer, is expected to return to Saint Florian's very soon—"

"Enough, Rheinhardt," said the commissioner, raising his hand. "Enough." Brügel examined the photograph of Zelenka again and mumbled something under his breath. He tapped the photograph and grimaced, as if suffering from acute dyspepsia. "Very well, Rheinhardt," he continued. "You may continue with your investigation."

"Thank you, sir," cried Rheinhardt, glancing triumphantly at von Bulow, whose expression had become fixed in the attitude of a sneer since he'd uttered the words "Jewish psychology."

"But not for long, you understand?" the commissioner interjected. "Another week or so, that's all—and then only if you can get out to Saint Florian's without compromising the success of your new assignment."

"Yes, sir," said Rheinhardt. "I understand."

"Good," said the commissioner. "Now, let us proceed. . . . What I am about to reveal, Rheinhardt, is classified information. You must not breathe a word of it to anyone—not even to your assistant." He paused to emphasize the point, and then continued: "Inspector von Bulow is currently overseeing a special operation—a joint venture with our colleagues from Budapest—the outcome of which is of paramount importance. The very stability of the dual monarchy is at stake. Needless to say, we are directly answerable to the very highest authority."

Brügel leaned back in his chair and tacitly invited Rheinhardt to inspect the portrait hanging on the wall behind his desk: the emperor, Franz Josef, in full military dress.

"What do you want me to do?" asked Rheinhardt.

"We want you to follow someone," said von Bulow.

"Who?"

Von Bulow reached down and picked up a briefcase. He released the hasps and produced a photograph, which he handed to Rheinhardt—a head-and-shoulders portrait of a young man with black curly hair, a long horizontal mustache, and a pronounced five o'clock shadow.

"His name?"

"Lázár Kiss."

It was a brooding, unhappy face, and the young man's eyes had the fiery glow of a zealot's.

"A nationalist?" Rheinhardt ventured.

Von Bulow did not reply. His jaw tightened.

"Rheinhardt," said Brügel, stroking his magnificent muttonchop whiskers. "Given the sensitive nature of this operation, we are not at liberty to disclose any more information than we have to. I must ask you to desist from asking further questions. You will receive your instructions—and you will carry them out. You need not concern yourself with anything more. Is that clear?"

"Yes, sir."

"Do you know the restaurant called Csarda?" said von Bulow.

"On the Prater?"

"It is where Herr Kiss dines. He is a creature of habit, and arrives there shortly after one o'clock, every day. Follow him until late afternoon—then deliver a written report of his movements to my office by six o'clock. You will repeat the exercise on Sunday and Monday, and I will then issue you further instructions on Tuesday morning."

So this was the sorry pass he had come to, thought Rheinhardt—reassigned to do von Bulow's footwork!

"May I ask . . . ," said Rheinhardt, painfully conscious of the prohibition that had just been placed on all forms of nonessential inquiry. "May I ask why it is that I—a detective inspector—have been chosen to undertake this task? Surely, von Bulow's assistant could do just as good a job."

"There must be no mistakes' said Brügel. "You are an experienced officer, Rheinhardt. I know you won't let us down."

The appearance of the commissioner's teeth in a crescent, which Rheinhardt supposed to be a smile, did nothing to ease his discomfort.

"And would I be correct," said Rheinhardt, risking another question, "in assuming that there are some very significant dangers associated with this assignment?"

What other reason could there be for such secretiveness? If they didn't tell him anything, he would have nothing to disclose—even if he were captured and threatened with violence.

"Our work is always associated with significant dangers, Rheinhardt," said the commissioner bluntly.

Rheinhardt passed the photograph of Lázár Kiss back to von Bulow.

"No—you can keep it," said von Bulow. "But do not take it out of the building."

Rheinhardt put the photograph in his pocket and looked up at the wall clock. It was eleven o'clock.

"Csarda," he said.

"Csarda," repeated von Bulow. "I look forward to receiving your report."

Rheinhardt got up, bowed, and made for the door.

"Rheinhardt?" It was von Bulow again. Rheinhardt turned, to see von Bulow inscribing the air with an invisible pen. "Handwriting?"

Rheinhardt forced a smile, the insincerity of which he hoped was unmistakable.

18

PROFESSOR FREUD—enveloped in a haze of billowing cigar smoke—began his third consecutive joke: "An elderly Jew was traveling on the slow train from Moscow to Minsk, and at one of the stops on the way he bought a large salt herring. At the same stop a Russian boy got on the train and started to tease him: 'You Jews,' he said, 'you have a reputation for being clever. How come, eh? How come you are all so clever?' The old man looked up from his herring and said, 'Well, since you are such a well-mannered young man, and have asked me so politely, I'll tell you our secret, but only if you promise not to tell anyone.' The boy suddenly became more serious and swore on his mother's life that he wouldn't tell a soul. 'We Jews,' said the old man, 'are so clever because we eat the head of the salt herring.' The boy was impressed and said, 'In which case, I intend to get clever right away. You still have the head of the herring you've just eaten. Would you sell it to me?' The old Jew was reluctant, but eventually gave in. 'All right, all right,' he said. 'You can have it for a ruble.' The boy couldn't wait to get started and paid. When he was almost finished eating he shouted, 'Wait a minute . . . I saw you buy the whole herring for just ten kopecks—and I paid you ten times more for the head!' The old Jew smiled and said, 'You see, it's beginning to work already.' "

The professor leaned back in his chair, satisfied with the joke's effect on his young disciple: a counterfeit grimace and the ignition of a bright light in Liebermann's eyes.

"Last year, you said you were thinking about writing a book on jokes," said Liebermann. "Is that still your intention?"

"In actual fact," said Freud, "I've been tinkering with the joke book for some time—but progress has been slow. I've been simultaneously engaged on another project: a collection of essays on sexuality, which, I believe, may prove to be of much greater significance. Even so, I keep finding myself returning to the joke book." He paused and puffed on his dying cigar. "Yes, there is much to be learned from a close examination of jokes. Psychoanalysis has demonstrated— beyond doubt—that we should not underestimate small indications. It is by close observation of phenomena that have hitherto been supposed trivial, such as dreams, blunders—and yes, jokes—that we are afforded our greatest insights."

The professor assumed a more serious expression: "The other day, I read something in the *Freie Presse.* . . . One of the mayor's associates had made a joke about Jews who wished to convert. He said that when being baptized, they should be held under water for at least ten minutes." Freud smiled, wryly. "Not a bad joke, all things considered . . . but so very revealing! It would seem that primitive urges— forbidden satisfaction by the prohibitions of civilized society and thus repressed—ultimately find expression in the content of jokes. So it is that our jokes betray us, revealing, as they do, our shameful desires and, in the case of the mayor's associate, a murderous impulse."

Liebermann recognized that this same reasoning could be applied to Freud himself. Such a clear understanding of the dark underpinnings of humor strongly suggested to him that Freud (a Jewish man who had been collecting Jewish jokes for many years—many of which were anti-Semitic) must be ambivalent about his own racial origins. Such ambivalence was not uncommon among assimilated

Jews. Indeed, Liebermann reflected, his own feelings were plainly mixed. He was often embarrassed by the appearance of a caftan on the Ringstrasse, or the Yiddisher pleadings of an impecunious pedlar.

Liebermann noticed that Freud's attention had been captured by the ancient statuettes on his desk, in particular by a small female figure of pale orange clay. She was standing with her weight on her right leg, her head turned to the side, and a mantle was drawn over her loose gown. In her left hand she held a fan, and her hair was drawn back and tied into a bun beneath a conical sun hat.

Freud suddenly looked up. His expression had softened and he had a look that Liebermann had only ever seen on the face of a proud parent—a moist-eyed muted pride.

"Greek," said Freud. "Hellenistic Period—believed to be from Tanagra, 330–250 B.C."

Although Liebermann did not usually share Freud's love of ancient artifacts, being a great enthusiast for all things modern, he did see considerable aesthetic virtue in this particular figure: its poise, its natural and unaffected elegance.

"Charming," said Liebermann. "Quite charming."

Freud broke out of his reverie and offered Liebermann another cigar. The young doctor declined and, seizing the opportunity to change the subject, raised the book that he had been patiently nursing on his lap.

"Have you ever seen one of these?"

He handed the volume to Freud, who, looking rather puzzled, replied, "No. . . . What is it?"

"A klecksography book," said Liebermann. "It's a kind of game, for children."

Freud flicked it open and examined the symmetrical patterns.

"The inkblots," Liebermann continued, "are usually accompanied by verses, which serve to guide the imagination—the idea being to look at the inkblot until what is being described appears. Such books are based on an original by Justinus Kerner—a physician and poet from Ludwigsburg. It occurred to me that this principle might be used to discover the contents of the unconscious. If inkblots are presented without any verses, then whatever the viewer claims to see must reflect—to some extent—a projection from his own mind. After all, there is nothing really there."

Freud hummed and said, "Interesting. . . . It is such a simple task that defenses might be relaxed, resulting in the inadvertent escape of repressed material." He lifted the delightful figurine from her place between a terra-cotta Sphinx and a bronze Egyptian deity and began to stroke the inanimate object as if it were a pet. "Repressed material that might subsequently be subject to a psychoanalytic interpretation."

"Indeed," said Liebermann, enlivened by the positive response of his mentor. "If an observer were to see two wrestling men in an inkblot, rather than an exotic flower, this might indicate the presence of an underlying hostile impulse—not unlike the latent aggression you have identified in jokes. The procedure, however, is not without precedent. I undertook some research at the university library and discovered that Binet has already recommended the use of inkblots to study what he calls involuntary imagination. So I cannot lay claim to having discovered anything original."

"When walking in the Alps," Freud responded dreamily, "I have often lain down and observed the passage of clouds—and in their vague whiteness found the outlines of castles and fantastic creatures. One supposes that from time immemorial mankind has been prone to the imaginative interpretation of natural phenomena—clouds, rock formations, puddles." His voice suddenly became more determined:

"Your discovery—if not wholly original—is still of value. For it demonstrates again the value of the psychoanalytic sensibility. Even in the most trivial phenomena, we can find buried treasure."

Freud turned the page of the book and covered the caption with his hand. Liebermann felt it would be impolite to ask the Professor what he could see, yet, after only a few moments, his curiosity was satisfied.

"How interesting," mumbled Freud. "How very intriguing. I see two herring heads."

"You see?" said Liebermann, unable to resist. "It's beginning to work already."

The professor slowly raised his head. At first, his expression was alarmingly severe, his penetrating eyes showing no signs of amusement. Then, quite suddenly, his face was illuminated by a broad grin.

"Very good," he said, chuckling. "Very good." He pushed the cigar box toward Liebermann. "Now, I absolutely insist!"

19

WOLF WAS SEATED ON a low three-legged stool, trying to concentrate on the book that Professor Gärtner had given him. Again, he read the passage that had stuck in his mind: *"There are no moral phenomena at all, only a moral interpretation of phenomena. . . ."*

Snjezana's room was on the first floor of the inn at Aufkirchen. It was a sorry little place with damp walls, dirty curtains, a rickety bed, and a threadbare screen. Snjezana helped the landlord by day, but in the evenings she read romantic novels, smoked pungent cigarettes, and occasionally received visitors—mostly men from the village or boys from the military school. The rear door of the inn was never locked, and her availability was signaled by a paraffin lamp in her window.

Above her washstand was a photograph of Stari Grad, a Dalmatian town on the island of Hvar. When drunk on schnapps, Snjezana would become melancholic and gaze through her streaming tears at the old seaport. Those who were familiar with Snjezana's habits would, at this juncture, immediately deposit a sum of money under her pillow and leave—because Snjezana's pining was usually followed by a violent eruption of anger during which she would curse all "Germans" and suddenly strike out. Her painted nails were long and sank into flesh with the efficiency of razor blades.

Only a moral interpretation of phenomena . . .

From below, Wolf could hear the sound of an accordion and

raised voices, the hysterical shriek of the barmaid, and raucous laughter. The smell of Snjezana's room was making him feel slightly sick: her overpowering, cloying perfume failed to cover the reek of stale tobacco and the fishy odor that seeped into the atmosphere when she became aroused. He lit one of his own cigarettes—and hoped that its fragrance would neutralize the room's nauseating miasma.

Drexler appeared from behind the screen. He was bare-chested, and was fumbling with the belt of his trousers.

"Your turn," he said.

Wolf closed the book and shook his head.

"No. . . . I think not. Let's go."

"What?"

"I don't feel like it."

The sound of tired bedsprings, relieved of weight, produced a sequence of loud cracking sounds followed by a tremulous hum. Snjezana stepped out from the other side of the screen. She was wearing a long, richly embroidered peasant skirt, and her hair was wrapped up in a black head scarf. Wolf glanced nonchalantly at her breasts—her erect nipples, her coffee-colored areolae.

"You said the two of you." Her voice was accusatory. "That's what you said."

"Don't worry, Snjezana," said Wolf. "You'll get paid."

"For two?"

Wolf sighed. "Yes. For two."

Snjezana sneered—and affected a mocking singsong voice.

"What's the matter with poor Wolf—not feeling well?" She pushed out her lower lip and made circles on her stomach with the palm of her hand. "Is he missing his *mutti*? Does he want her to kiss it and make it better?"

Drexler laughed.

"Be quiet, Drexler—don't encourage her." Wolf tossed some silver coins onto the floor. "I'll see you outside."

Wolf got up abruptly and left the room. The landing was in total darkness, so he had to feel his way down the wooden staircase, his sword striking the banisters as he made his descent. Outside, the air was cool. He leaned up against the wall and looked up at the starry sky. Releasing a cloud of smoke, he watched it rise and dissipate.

"There are no moral phenomena," he whispered. In some peculiar way, the cold impartiality of the heavens seemed to confirm the author's sentiment. He inhaled—and Snjezana's cloying perfume cleared from his nostrils.

20

The Inspector had positioned himself at the back of the classroom—the very same one he had used to conduct his own interviews earlier that week. He had hoped that this would allow him to make discreet observations without distracting Perger.

Rheinhardt was accustomed to Liebermann's preference for oblique methods of inquiry. However, on this occasion the young doctor's behavior seemed so irregular, so incomprehensible, that he was sorely tempted to halt proceedings and demand an explanation. Liebermann had asked the boy if he enjoyed playing chess. He had then produced a chess set from his bag, and a contest of some considerable length ensued. When it was over—and Perger had been declared the winner—Liebermann opened his bag for the second time, and took out a bundle of papers that seemed to have nothing on them except spilled ink.

"And now," said Liebermann, "another game of sorts." Rheinhardt bit his lower lip and stifled the urge to protest. "I would like to show you some inkblots, and I want you to tell me if they remind you of anything."

Liebermann showed the first sheet to Perger.

The boy had a nervous habit of jerking his head upward in small movements—like a rodent testing the air—and when he spoke, his hesitancy threatened to become a stutter.

"No. It . . . it doesn't remind me of anything."

"Come now," said Liebermann, smiling broadly. "You must, at some point, have observed the clouds in the sky and thought they looked like something else? A great galleon, perhaps? The profile of the emperor? Look closely . . . and keep on looking. Eventually you will perceive something familiar. Now tell me, what do you see?"

The boy's eyes suddenly widened. "Yes, yes. . . . Two old men—with long noses."

"Very good. Now here's another. What do you see?"

"A . . . a bat."

"Excellent. And here?"

"The face of a wolf."

And so it went on: Liebermann showing the boy page after page, and the boy responding.

Two dragons . . . a stove . . . sea horses . . . a sad face . . . a skeleton.

Perger was soon finding the task easier—and his descriptions became more detailed.

Duelists—at sunset . . . two bears, dancing . . . another wolf, ready to pounce . . . a cobra—its head pulled back . . . a knight praying by the tomb of his comrade.

When Liebermann had worked through all his inkblots, he said to Perger, "Another game of chess? It is only right that you give me an opportunity to redeem myself."

Rheinhardt was certain that Liebermann had lost the previous game intentionally. He had seen his friend perform respectably against the seasoned enthusiasts who gathered at the rear of the Café Central. It was extremely unlikely that a logician of Liebermann's calibre could be bettered by an adolescent boy.

The new game differed from the first, insofar as it did not take place in silence. Liebermann asked Perger what books he liked to read. What cakes were sold at the Aufkirchen bakery, and whether or not ticks were a problem in the summer months. None of it (as far as Rheinhardt could determine) was of any consequence. Then, after a relatively short period of time had elapsed, Liebermann moved his queen and said "Checkmate." The boy wasn't expecting this sudden defeat and was obviously quite surprised.

"It's a well-known snare developed by the great Wilhelm Steinitz," said Liebermann. "You should have paid closer attention to my knight! But this is a most unsatisfactory outcome, wouldn't you agree? Both of us have now won a game, and I am curious to know which of us is really the better player. Let us have one more game—and that shall be the decider!"

Rheinhardt could sit still no longer. He stood up and clomped over to the window. A single rider was leaping fences in the equestrian enclosure, and beyond, the fir-covered hills were black beneath a taupe sky. Rheinhardt yawned. As he watched the rider repeating his circuit, the classroom began to recede and he gradually slipped into a state of drowsy abstraction. When he finally overcame his torpor, he found himself eavesdropping on a conversation. . . .

Liebermann and Perger were talking about the school: masters, examinations, drill. Occasionally, Liebermann would remind the boy to watch his knight—then proceed with another nonchalant inquiry. Which of the masters taught Latin? Why did Perger find Latin so difficult? Could he speak any other languages? Rheinhardt noticed that the boy's head was no longer jerking upward. He was concentrating on the game, answering Liebermann's questions with an easy, natural fluency.

"Thomas Zelenka was your friend?"

"Yes, he was."

"You must be very lonely now?"

"I have other friends. . . ."

"Of course. . . . Did Thomas have other friends?"

"No, not really: although he was very fond of Frau Becker."

"The deputy headmaster's wife?"

"Yes. He used to go there . . . to the Beckers' house."

"What for?"

"To talk with Frau Becker."

"What about?"

"I don't know . . . but he said she was very kind."

Liebermann leaned forward.

"Careful . . . I fear you haven't been watching my knight."

"On the contrary," the boy replied. "I fear it is you who have not been watching mine." Perger moved his piece two squares forward and one to the side. Then he announced, with a broad, proud grin, "Checkmate."

"Bravo," said Liebermann. "It has been decided, then. You are the superior player. You are free to go."

The boy stood to attention, clicked his heels, and walked toward the door. Just before he passed into the shadowy exterior, he looked back over his shoulder.

"Good luck with your Latin," said Liebermann.

The boy hurried out, his steps fading into silence.

"Well," said Rheinhardt. "Frau Becker! Nobody has mentioned her before. We must pay her a visit." Rheinhardt took out his notebook and scribbled a reminder. "But really, Max, what on earth have you been doing? We've been here for hours. Couldn't you have asked questions about Zelenka earlier?"

"No," replied Liebermann firmly. "To do so would have been a grave mistake."

The young doctor rose from his chair and walked to the blackboard, where he gripped his lapels and adopted a distinctly pedagogic stance.

"You will recall that in his letter to Zelenka," Liebermann continued, "Perger mentions his father in such a way as to suggest a man of unsympathetic character. He worries that his father will think him *unmanly* if he complains or requests help. One can easily imagine what Perger senior is like—a domineering, unapproachable man who was very probably educated at Saint Florian's himself . . . or, at least, a school very much like it. This unhappy father-son relationship would inevitably color Perger's entire perception of authority figures, of which you and I are typical examples. Even under the most benign circumstances, the relationship between father and son is frequently troubled by hostile feelings. They are, after all, rivals who compete for the mother's love. When this already difficult situation is made worse by a tyrannical father, the son's primal anxieties are amplified and he becomes profoundly mistrustful of all manifestations of hegemony. He feels vulnerable, and must protect himself. Now, a child knows that it cannot physically overcome an adult foe; however, it is not entirely powerless. It can still exhibit passive forms of aggression—it can be uncooperative, morose, taciturn. So, you see, Oskar, it was essential that I allow Perger to beat me at chess. The experience gave him a sense of mastery, thus reducing his anxiety and relieving him of the necessity to deploy defenses."

Liebermann turned to the blackboard and, picking up a stub of chalk, wrote *Anxiety, Mastery, Anxiety Reduction* and linked the words with two arrows. He then briefly explained the purpose of the inkblots, emphasizing how involuntary imaginative responses might contain information that a person did not intend to disclose.

"Perger's responses afforded me considerable insight into the boy's mental world—his preoccupations, his sadness, his loneliness, his fear. . . . He is extremely fragile—worryingly so—and these responses also suggested to me how you might proceed, Oskar, with respect to identifying suspects among the boys. You said that there were simply too many pupils to interview. The more or less random selection of names from a list would be utterly pointless—which is of course true. But we are now in a much better position."

"We are?"

"Did you notice how many of Perger's responses referred to predatory creatures? To what extent, I wonder, does this reflect his wretched existence here at Saint Florian's? Must he constantly evade those who might make him their prey? If I were you, I would examine the register and look for names that correspond with the notion of predation: names like Löwe or Wolf—or names that correspond with the notion of hunting, perhaps—like Jäger? I cannot guarantee that this will prove to be a productive avenue of inquiry, but in the absence of any other strategy, you have nothing to lose."

Liebermann turned to the board and wrote "Names suggestive of predation and hunting." He then underlined the phrase, producing a scratching sound that made the inspector wince.

"And the subsequent games of chess?" asked Rheinhardt. "Why were they necessary? If you were attempting to instill in the boy a sense of mastery, why on earth did you allow him to lose the second game? Isn't that a contradiction?"

"By beating Perger, I did indeed run the risk of reviving his anxieties; however, it was a risk I was prepared to take, but only in order to secure a further advantage. After his defeat, I was able to alert him to a specific and deadly maneuver that he was thereafter obliged to watch for. This possibility occupied his thoughts during the third game, to the extent that he was less able to monitor his speech. It was under these conditions that he mentioned Frau Becker, a person whose name has—for some reason—never appeared in connection with Zelenka before."

Liebermann scratched the words "Distraction" and "Less Guarded Replies" on the blackboard. He then tossed the chalk in the air, caught it, and tapped the woodwork.

"I hope you've been listening carefully, Rheinhardt. There will be a test later!"

21

THE BECKER RESIDENCE was a large house occupying the summit of a gentle rise that swept up from Aufkirchen. From the garden gate, looking toward the village, the onion dome and spire of the Romanesque church was just visible over the trees. Rheinhardt and Liebermann paused to admire the view before following the gravel path toward their destination.

Their approach disturbed a sleek fat crow. Flapping its wings, the bird took off, a worm wriggling in its closed beak. Two more crows were circling the chimney, cawing loudly. The combination of their plaintive cries, the moribund garden, and a low, oppressive sky created an atmosphere of sinister melancholy.

The door was answered by a Czech housemaid, who escorted Rheinhardt and Liebermann into a spacious parlor, where they were asked to wait. A few minutes later a striking woman appeared in the doorway. She was young, blond, probably in her early twenties, and extremely attractive: earnest eyes complemented a wide sensual mouth and a petite retroussé nose. At first Rheinhardt thought that there might have been some mistake, and that this woman was, in fact, Becker's daughter; however, her identity was confirmed as soon as she spoke.

"Inspector Rheinhardt, my husband didn't tell me you would be coming here today. Forgive me. . . . You find us unprepared for guests."

If the first surprise was Frau Becker's appearance, then the second was her accent. It was distinctly provincial.

The inspector introduced his colleague and said: "Frau Becker, it is I who must apologize. Your husband did not know that we intended to visit. And please, do not concern yourself with hospitality—a few minutes of your time is all we ask."

"The least I can do is offer you some refreshments, Inspector. Shall I ask Ivana to make some tea?"

"That is most kind—but no, thank you."

"Please—Herr Doctor, Inspector . . ." She indicated some chairs. "Do sit." And she perched herself on the edge of a chaise longue.

"I would like to ask you," said Rheinhardt, "some questions about the boy Zelenka."

Frau Becker required little prompting. She spoke of how the news of Zelenka's death had shocked her; how her thoughts had gone out to his parents, and how she would miss their conversations. The fluency and urgency of her speech declared the authenticity of her feelings—as did the sudden halting pauses, during which her eyes glistened.

"Imagine," she said, shaking her head and dabbing her eyes with a handkerchief. "To lose a son—and only fifteen years old."

"How was it that you became acquainted?" asked Rheinhardt.

"The masters at Saint Florian's—particularly those with wives—often invite boys to their houses. It is encouraged here. Although the boys look like men, in many ways they are still children. They miss their families, ordinary things . . . sitting in a garden, a glass of raspberry juice with soda water, home baking. Zelenka always wanted me to make spiced pretzels. I have a special recipe—given to me by my grandmother."

"How often did you see Zelenka?"

"He used to come at my husband's invitation with other boys, and sometimes he would come on his own. I think he enjoyed my company—felt comfortable. You see, his family is poor, and I . . ." Frau Becker hesitated for a moment, and blushed. "I also come from a poor family. We had this in common."

Rheinhardt found himself glancing down at the young woman's blouse. It was made of black lace and lined with flesh-colored silk, a combination that created a tantalizing illusion of immodesty. A gentleman's eye was automatically drawn down to the transparent webbing, which promised the possibility of indecent revelation.

"What was Zelenka like?" said Rheinhardt, forcing himself to look up, and loosening his collar.

"A kind, intelligent boy. But . . ."

Frau Becker paused, her expression darkening.

"What?" Rheinhardt pressed.

"Unhappy."

"Because of the bullying—the persecution?"

Frau Becker looked surprised. "You know about it?"

"Yes."

"He never told me what happened—what they did to him—but I could tell that it was bad."

"Did he ever mention any names?"

"No. And when I asked, he refused to answer. He said it would only make things worse. He would get called a squealer, a snitch, and other horrible names—they would pick on him even more."

"Did you speak to your husband?"

"Of course."

"And what did he say?"

"He told me that unless boys like Zelenka are prepared to name their tormentors, nothing can be done. The whole school can't be watched every hour of the day. And I suppose that's true—isn't it?"

"May I ask a question?" said Liebermann. Frau Becker assented. "May I ask whether or not you had any dreams last night?"

"I beg your pardon?" Frau Becker looked at the doctor in surprise.

"Did you have any dreams—last night?"

"Yes," she said, tentatively. "Yes, I did."

"Would you be kind enough to tell me what occurred in your dream?"

Frau Becker shrugged. "I could . . . but it's nonsense, Herr Doctor."

"Please." Liebermann urged her to continue.

"Very well," said Frau Becker. "I dreamed that I went to the theater with my husband. . . . One side of the stalls was empty. My husband told me that Marianne and her fiancé had wanted to go too—"

"Marianne?"

"A friend."

"An old friend?"

"Yes, we grew up together. As a matter of fact, I got a letter from her yesterday, which contained some very important news. She has just got engaged to a lieutenant in the uhlans."

"Go on."

"Where was I? Oh yes . . . Marianne and her fiancé had wanted to go too, but only cheap seats—costing eight hellers—were available, so they didn't take them. But I thought it wouldn't have been so bad if they had." Frau Becker looked at Liebermann. She seemed confused, and faintly embarrassed. "That's it. That's all I can remember."

Liebermann leaned back in his chair and allowed his clenched fist to fall against his right cheek. The index finger unfurled and tapped against his temple.

"Did the empty half of the stalls that you saw in your dream remind you of anything?"

Frau Becker paused and gave the question serious consideration. Her lips pursed, and a thin horizontal line appeared on her brow.

"Now that you mention it, yes. Just after Christmas, I wanted to see a play—a comedy—at the Volkstheatre. I had bought tickets for this play very early. So early, in fact, that I had to pay an extra booking fee. When we got to the Volkstheatre, it turned out that I needn't have bothered—one side of the theater was half empty. My husband kept on teasing me for having been in such a hurry."

"And the sum of eight hellers—is that associated with some memory of a real event?"

Frau Becker toyed with her brooch, a thin crescent of garnets.

"Not eight hellers but eight kronen. The maid was recently given a present of eight kronen by an admirer. She immediately rushed off to Vienna in order to buy some jewelry."

"Thank you," said Liebermann. "Thank you," he repeated, nodding his head. "You have been most helpful."

Frau Becker looked from Liebermann to Inspector Rheinhardt, her expression inviting an explanation. But the inspector merely thanked her for being so cooperative.

On leaving the house, Liebermann and Rheinhardt discovered that the garden was no longer empty. A man in muddy overalls and boots was kneeling next to a flower bed, tugging coils of dead creeper from a thorny bush.

"Good afternoon," said Rheinhardt.

The man stood up, drew his sleeve across his nose, and uttered a greeting. Rheinhardt introduced himself and showed the gardener a photograph of Zelenka—the one that he had had copied after visiting the boy's parents.

"Do you recognize him?"

"Yes, I recognize him."

"He came here often?"

"Some would say too often." The man's lips suddenly parted. He began to chuckle, revealing a mouth full of yellow carious teeth.

"What do you mean, 'too often'?"

The gardener made a lewd gesture with his hand, winked, and, without excusing himself, stomped off.

Liebermann and Rheinhardt watched him recede.

"Just a moment," Rheinhardt called.

The man accelerated his step and disappeared behind the house.

"When our great poets versify about the rustic charm of country folk," said Rheinhardt, "what do you think they mean, exactly?"

Liebermann stared out of the carriage window at the passing woodland.

"So," said Rheinhardt. "What did you make of Frau Becker?"

"She is very much regretting her marriage."

"If that really *is* the case, then I'm not surprised—I can't think of a more ill-matched couple. However, given that you have never laid eyes on Herr Becker, I must assume that you have determined this by interpreting her dream."

"Professor Freud has explained that dreams are often a reaction to events that occur on the preceding day. This certainly seems to be the case with Frau Becker, who only yesterday received a letter from Marianne, an old friend, containing news of her engagement to an excellent prospective husband—a *dashing* young officer. A common factor linking much of the material that surfaced in her dream—

albeit in the form of distortions—was haste. You will recall that Frau Becker purchased her theater tickets far too early, and the maid *hurried* into town to spend her eight kronen. Taken together, I would suggest that these elements express the following sentiment: '*It was stupid of me to marry in a hurry. I can now see from Marianne's example that I could have got a better husband if I had waited.*' "

Liebermann raised a hand in the air and then let it drop, as if tired of the sheer predictability of human affairs.

"I suspect that Frau Becker's story," he continued, "is one with which we are all very familiar. An attractive provincial girl, desiring a better life, encounters an older man of means. She beguiles him with her youthful good looks, but after they are married, she discovers that the life of a schoolmaster's wife is not what she'd expected. She is bored, stranded on a lonely eminence in the woods, trapped in a big empty house, miles away from the delightful shops on Kärntner Strasse, Kohlmarkt, and the Graben, where she once imagined herself purchasing beautiful, expensive things for her home and wardrobe. Her erotic instinct is frustrated, and she envies her friend, Marianne, who will almost certainly find satisfaction—if she hasn't already— in the arms of her handsome young cavalryman. Such a woman might well find solace in the company of boys like Zelenka: intelligent, sensitive boys, approaching manhood. And such is her appetite that even the gardener is conscious of her misconduct. I cannot believe that the extraordinary properties of Frau Becker's blouse escaped your attention."

Rheinhardt coughed into his hand and his cheeks became flushed. "I did not know where to look!"

"Do you know something, Oskar?" said Liebermann, rubbing his hands together. "I'm beginning to think that there is something quite odd going on at Saint Florian's."

"Ha!" exclaimed Rheinhardt.

"Zelenka appears to have died naturally . . . but the more your investigations proceed, the more you seem to uncover conditions and circumstances that one would ordinarily associate with murder. Sadistic persecution . . . and now the possibility of an illicit sexual liaison. What if Zelenka had threatened to expose Frau Becker? What if he had asked her for money? The boy was very poor and hated Saint Florian's. It might have been his only way out."

"Well," said Rheinhardt, "our opinions seem to be converging at last. You have a strong sense of something being wrong, but you can't quite put your finger on it. In other words, you have a *feeling*. Isn't that so?" Liebermann raised his chin and looked down his nose at his friend with haughty displeasure. "I only hope," Rheinhardt continued, his voice becoming more reflective, "that I am given an adequate opportunity to get to the bottom of it."

Liebermann caught the change of register. "Why shouldn't you be?"

"Oh," grumbled Rheinhardt, "some business of von Bulow's."

"Ordinarily I would ask you the nature of that business, but I know there is little point. You have been ordered to keep it a secret."

Rheinhardt emitted a cry of surprise and demanded: "How on earth did you know that?"

Liebermann closed his eyes and an enigmatic smile played about his lips. "Perhaps I had a feeling," he said softly.

Rheinhardt burst out laughing. "Sometimes," he said, shaking his head, "you can be quite insufferable!"

22

"You wanted to see me, headmaster?"

"Yes indeed, Wolf. Please sit."

Professor Eichmann was signing and dating documents. On Eichmann's desk was a photograph of himself looking considerably younger and dressed in the uniform of an artillery officer. The headmaster glanced up from his paperwork.

"How is your father?"

"Very well, headmaster."

"You will be kind enough to include my salutations when you next write home."

"Of course, headmaster."

Professor Eichmann signed and dated one more document, and said: "You will be wondering why I wanted to see you today." He did not pause for a reply, but instead made some polite inquiries after Wolf's health. He then congratulated Wolf, first for winning a bronze medal in the school shooting competition, and second for having been invited by Professor Gärtner to join his *special* tutorial group.

"He is very particular about who he accepts," said the headmaster. "Such an invitation is extended to only the most promising pupils—boys with the *right* attitude."

When their gazes met, they did so with mutual understanding. They had had similar discussions in the past.

The headmaster toyed with his pen, and spoke for some time about the values of the school and about how, for generations now, Saint Florian's had been producing soldiers of the highest quality. "Men who appreciated the importance of loyalty, fidelity, and obedience—men of honor."

He put his pen down and made some minor adjustments to its position.

"Of course," continued the headmaster, "lately Saint Florian's has been forced to accept a number of boys who do not share our values. Boys who object to our methods, find fault with our principles—and whose families are not acquainted with our traditions. This saddens me, because if an outside party were to question these boys, I fear they would misrepresent us. They do not seem to appreciate that we are—as it were—a family. Loose talk damages the school's reputation—and what damages the school's reputation damages *all* of us."

Eichmann's voice was persuasive, reasonable—but it was also troubled by a trace of anger. The headmaster sighed, smiled, and said: "I understand that Professor Gärtner has recently introduced you to the writings of Friedrich Nietzsche."

"Yes," said Wolf. "We have been reading *Beyond Good and Evil*."

"A very stimulating work," said Eichmann. "Although when Professor Gärtner introduces you to *Thus Spake Zarathustra*, you will discover even greater riches." The headmaster stood up and walked over to the lancet windows. He reached out his right hand and, resting it against the stone casement, leaned forward, allowing his arm to support his pitched body. The sun had dropped below the horizon, and rivers of darkness had begun to appear between the hills. "The police were here again today." His voice was even.

"I know, headmaster."

"Something must be done."

"Yes, headmaster."

"Something decisive."

"Of course, headmaster."

Part Two

The Devil's Trill

23

LIEBERMANN WAS SITTING at the table of an inauspicious coffee-house in Landstrasse with Signor Barbasetti, his fencing master, and two other pupils with whom he was moderately acquainted: Brod and Lind. They had just taken part in a competition. However, none of the three aspirants had performed very well.

Signor Barbasetti concealed his disappointment with a lengthy and somewhat philosophical disquisition on the art of fencing, the conclusion of which was that much could be learned from the close examination of small errors.

Yes, like psychoanalysis, thought Liebermann.

Unfortunately, Barbasetti chose to demonstrate the truth of this maxim by recounting and itemizing the failings of his students in such detail that any bonhomie slowly ebbed away, leaving in its place an intransigent atmosphere of gloom and despondency. Earlier than anticipated, the men rose from their seats, enacted the requisite courtesies, and parted company.

Liebermann was not familiar with the city's third district—and because his mind was still occupied by his mentor's excoriating critique, it took him some time to register that he had strayed from his intended route and was now hopelessly lost. He had wandered into an area consisting mainly of building sites and decrepit terraces: squat buildings with ruined stucco and rotten window frames. The air smelled damp, tainted with a trace of stagnancy (not unlike sewage). At the end of the road a mangy dog was standing beneath a streetlamp, feeding on something in the gutter. As Liebermann approached, the dog stopped eating and gazed up at him with minatory pale lupine eyes: it emitted a cautionary growl, and then began to gnaw on an object that cracked loudly in its mouth. Liebermann turned the corner, and peered down another poorly lit road.

Even though a few windows showed signs of occupancy, most were dark. Indeed, since leaving the coffeehouse Liebermann had not encountered another human being. It was unnaturally quiet, suggesting abandonment and dereliction. He glanced at his watch—and discovered that it was much later than he had thought.

Liebermann halted to consider his position. If he had been going toward the canal, then he would be able to follow its course into town. If, on the other hand, he had been traveling in the opposite direction, he was sure to come across a train line—which would serve the same purpose.

As he contemplated his options, the oppressive silence was broken by a scream—a woman's voice, crying for help. The volume and shrillness of the sound startled Liebermann, who spun around, trying to determine where it was coming from. He then sprinted toward the source, his footsteps sounding loud on the cobbled street. But he had not gone very far when the cries faded. His pace slackened.

An upstairs window flickered into life, its luminescent rectangle inhabited by the silhouette of a man in his nightshirt. The dog began to bark. Ahead, the road curved into darkness.

Where is she?

Liebermann was breathing hard.

The screams had sounded very close. Yet the arc of doors that lay ahead revealed nothing more than the reflected glimmer of a second streetlamp.

Liebermann had no choice but to continue. He quickened his pace and almost missed an opening between two houses—a narrow alleyway. Skidding to a halt, he wheeled around. He could hear scuffling—movements and a whimper. Treading softly, he ventured into the passage. His foot made contact with something soft and yielding. Reaching down, he discovered a woman's bag.

Suddenly, voices. Rough-edged voices, speaking in a harsh working-class dialect.

Liebermann edged forward, taking great care not to make a sound. The alleyway led to a walled yard, dimly lit by a streetlamp located on the other side of the enclosure. The yard was strewn with crates, bottles, and other detritus. A woman was struggling to free herself from a broad-shouldered man who, standing behind her, had clamped a hand over her mouth and wrapped an arm around her waist. Another two men stood in front of the captive, jeering and making obscene remarks. It was obvious what they intended to do.

Liebermann stepped out of his tenebrous hiding place and called out: "Let her go."

The leering duo turned. It was impossible to see their faces in the half-light.

"Let her go," Liebermann repeated.

One of the men laughed.

"What are *you* gonna do about it?"

"I must insist that you let her go."

A stream of profanities ended in humorless guffaws.

"Leave us alone," the other man said. "Leave us alone, all right? Or you're gonna get hurt. Badly."

"Yeah, run along—college boy." This came from the man who was restraining the woman. She began to wriggle. "Keep still, you Gypsy bitch," he hissed. The woman groaned as the villain tightened his grip.

Liebermann stood firm.

"Right," said the nearest man. Liebermann saw him make a swift movement—and the glint of a blade flashed in the man's hand. He began to move forward. "Let's see if I can change your mind."

"As you wish," Liebermann replied.

The young doctor had been holding his sabre under his arm. Grabbing the hilt, he pulled it from the scabbard—producing as he did a satisfying ring of resonant steel—and held the sword aloft. Its appearance was greeted with a gasp and another stream of profanities. However, the man with the razor continued his approach, and his companion followed.

Liebermann could now see his adversary's features. He was bald, with swollen ears, a snout nose, and a scar that crossed his lips, disfiguring his mouth. It was a brutish countenance, suggesting the haphazard adhesion of lumps of clay. Liebermann searched the eyes for signs of intelligence but found only savage stupidity and an appetite for mindless violence.

The man jumped forward with surprising speed, swiping his razor close to Liebermann's face. But Liebermann had the superior weapon. Before the man could retreat, the young doctor's sabre had slashed through his forearm. The thug cried out, dropping the razor and falling to his knees. His companion, however, had armed himself with a large plank of wood, from which projected several nails. He was taller than the bald man, and more agile. Dodging Liebermann's first lunge, he swung the plank hard against the doctor's side. It was not a painful blow, but had sufficient force to make Liebermann stumble.

While Liebermann was trying to right himself, the tall man landed a second blow on his shoulder. This time it was extremely painful—sharp and searing. A nail had penetrated his skin, and as he pulled away, he heard the sound of ripping.

"Again," the bald man shouted.

His companion raised his makeshift club, but on this third occasion he lifted it too high, exposing his torso and conceding the vital second that Liebermann required. The young doctor swung his sabre horizontally, creating a glimmering semicircle, the edge of which, if it had been displaced by another two inches, might well have proved fatal. The tall man buckled over—a torrent of blood gushing from his abdomen.

Liebermann waited until the tall man's rapidly weakening legs gave way, and then marched over to the woman and her captor.

"Release her," he ordered.

The broad-shouldered man looked over in the direction of his accomplices, both of whom were now cursing and crawling toward the alleyway. He swore, and pushed the woman forward with such force that she crashed into Liebermann, making him reel back. However, the maneuver was not a continuation of the fight. The coward simply ran off, and the wretched trio disappeared, yelling florid imprecations.

"You had better sit down," said Liebermann.

He gestured toward a crate. "Are you hurt?"

The woman shook her head.

Liebermann bent down and examined her face. She pulled back a little, alarmed at the sudden proximity.

"I'm sorry, do forgive me. Your face . . . Your face is grazed. . . . I'm a doctor." Liebermann touched her cheek gently. He could smell her perfume—a distinctive combination of fragrances. "There may be some swelling there tomorrow."

He withdrew and stood up straight.

"Thank you," the woman said. "Thank you, Herr Doctor . . . ?"

"Liebermann."

"Liebermann," she repeated. There was something odd about her intonation, as if she had expected his name to be Liebermann and was satisfied that the expectation had been confirmed.

"My pleasure," said the young doctor, bowing.

She glanced toward the alleyway.

"We shouldn't stay here." She spoke with a slight Magyar accent. "They could come back . . . and with more of their friends."

"But are you recovered?" said Liebermann. "Perhaps a few more minutes—to compose yourself?"

"Herr Doctor, I am perfectly capable of walking."

There was a note of indignation in the woman's voice, a note of pride. It was almost as if she had construed Liebermann's solicitous remarks as a slur—an imputation of weakness. Liebermann also noticed that, for someone who had just survived such a terrible ordeal, she was preternaturally collected.

She stood up, straightened her head scarf, and adjusted her clothing. She was wearing the short jacket favored by Hungarian women and a long, richly embroidered skirt. Liebermann offered her his arm, which she took—naturally and without hesitation.

On entering the alleyway, Liebermann picked up the bag he had discovered earlier. It was remarkably heavy.

"This must be yours."

"Yes, it is. Thank you." She took it, and they proceeded to the street.

"Well, Herr Dr. Liebermann." The woman halted and released his arm. "I am indebted . . . a debt, I fear, that it will be impossible for me to repay. You have shown uncommon courage and kindness." She took a step backward. "Good night."

"A moment, please," said Liebermann. "If you mean to walk these streets unaccompanied, I cannot allow it. I am obliged—as a gentleman—to escort you home."

"That will not be necessary."

Liebermann was dumbfounded. "But . . . but I insist!"

She smiled, and the proud light in her eyes dimmed a little.

"I have already caused you enough trouble." She reached up and gently brushed his shoulder, where a hank of silk lining sprouted from the torn astrakhan.

"Think nothing of it," said Liebermann, crooking his arm. "Now, where do you live?"

"Near the canal."

"Then you must show me the way. I am not familiar with the third district and—to be perfectly honest—I was quite lost when I heard your cries."

She nodded—and *there it was*, again. A curious, fleeting expression, as if his words had merely confirmed something that she knew already.

The woman set off, taking them through a maze of empty backstreets.

"What happened?" asked Liebermann, flicking his head back in the direction from where they had come. "How did you get into that . . ." He paused before adding "Predicament?"

"I had been to visit a friend," said the woman "And was simply walking home. When I passed that alleyway, those . . . animals jumped out and grabbed me."

Liebermann felt her shuddering.

"Did you not know that it is unwise for a woman to walk the streets at this time?"

"I am new to Vienna."

"Well, one should be very careful."

"I will be in the future."

"It was most fortunate that I was carrying my sabre."

"Yes, I was wondering—"

"A fencing competition," Liebermann interjected. "Earlier this evening."

"Did you win?"

"No, I lost. And quite ignominiously."

Liebermann asked the woman a few polite questions about her origins (she was indeed Hungarian) and expressed an earnest hope that the evening's events would not prejudice her opinion of Vienna and its inhabitants. She responded by saying that nowhere could ever displace Budapest in her affections—but that she would make every effort to comply with his request.

"What is your specialty, Herr Doctor?"

"Psychiatry."

The majority of people reacted quite warily to this admission, but the Hungarian woman responded as though she thought his branch of medicine worthy of the utmost respect. "And where do you work?"

"The General Hospital."

She urged him to continue, and he spoke for some time about his duties, the new science of psychoanalysis, and the patients in his care. She was very attentive, and asked him some extremely intelligent questions about the causes of hysteria.

"Yes," said the woman pensively. "To study the human mind—a privilege—and endlessly fascinating."

They arrived at their destination—a small apartment building at the end of a gloomy cul-de-sac. The woman did not have to wake a concierge to gain admittance—the door was standing wide open. A tiled arcade led to a courtyard, on the other side of which was a short iron staircase leading to a sheltered landing. A solitary gas lamp agitated the flagstones with a muted yellow lambency.

The woman stopped and—looking toward the stairs—said, "I think I can manage the remainder of the journey on my own." The statement was nuanced with a hint of dry humor.

Liebermann found himself looking at the woman properly for the first time. She was very beautiful—but not in the sense that her features conformed to a classical ideal. Her beauty was less conventional—less finished, less tame. She had long dark hair tied up loosely in a head scarf. Her mouth was generous, and her long straight nose gave her face unusual strength. The arch of her eyebrows was gentle—the extremities rising rather than falling at the temple. This peculiarity created the illusion of otherworldliness, recalling storybook illustrations of elves and sprites. From her ears dangled two ornate silver earrings, encrusted with black stones. Liebermann remembered the way she had been insulted—*Gypsy bitch*—and there was indeed something Romany, something exotic about her appearance.

Hungarian women were reputed to possess a unique and potent beauty, and in her case the reputation was clearly merited.

Liebermann bowed and pressed his lips against her hand. Rising, he said: "I don't know your name."

"Trezska Novak," she replied.

Liebermann suddenly felt awkward. "Well, Fräulein Novak . . . good night."

"Good night, Herr Dr. Liebermann." She took a few steps, and then stopped and, looking back, added, "I am indebted—truly."

He watched her cross the courtyard, ascend the stairs, and unlock the door of her apartment. Before she entered, she waved. Liebermann returned the gesture, again feeling awkward—as if his arm had become a cumbersome appendage. He heard the sound of a bolt engaging but did not move to leave. Instead, he continued to stare at the empty landing. The gas lamp sputtered.

Quite suddenly, Liebermann was overwhelmed with curiosity: he wanted to know more about Trezska Novak and regretted not having asked her more questions. He had talked too much about himself—the hospital, hysteria, Professor Freud. What was she doing in Vienna? And why was an educated woman living in such a district? Shaking his head, he rebuked himself—it was none of his business. He should be getting home.

Reluctantly, Liebermann made his way back to the street, where he became aware that his shoulder was hurting badly and that he was extremely tired (almost to the point of exhaustion). He set off toward the canal, praying that he would find a cab.

24

"Where have you been, Rheinhardt?"

"Following Herr Kiss, sir—as instructed by Inspector von Bulow. I began my surveillance outside his apartment in Landstrasse at six-thirty this morning and—"

Brügel shook his bovine head. Evidently he did not want to hear about Herr Kiss.

"Have you seen this?" The commissioner was holding a folded newspaper in his hand.

Rheinhardt shook his head.

Brügel handed him the *Arbeiter-Zeitung*.

"Do you know it?"

"Yes, a socialist daily—isn't it?"

"Sit down, Rheinhardt . . . and turn to page ten."

An article had been circled in red ink.

The recent death of a young cadet at Saint Florian's oberrealschule— reported in the Neue Freie Presse on the 19th of January—served to remind me of my own school days, spent at that very same educational establishment. . . .

Rheinhardt read on, his heart accelerating as his eyes were drawn down the page by words that seemed to stand out from the text in bold relief.

Sadism . . . cruelty . . . torture . . .

He made a supreme effort to calm himself, returned to the beginning, and attempted to read the article without skipping.

I was a pupil at Saint Florian's from 1893 to 1896 and can say, without fear of exaggeration, that these were the most unhappy years of my life.

The writer went on to describe a culture of violence, which he claimed was tacitly endorsed by the headmaster and senior members of staff. His most startling assertion, however, was that the suicide of a boy reported in 1894 was, in fact, a case of manslaughter, being the direct result of a heinous practice known as "doing the night watch." This was a form of punishment meted out by older boys, in which the victim was made to stand on a dormitory window ledge from "lights out" until dawn. Sadly for Domokos Pikler a nocturnal cloudburst made the ledge slippery, and he fell to his death.

Rheinhardt drew the paper closer.

I hope that the authorities—such as they are—will be mindful of this, my candid and truthful revelation. Alas, for personal reasons my identity must remain undisclosed. Sincerely, Herr G., Vienna.

When Rheinhardt had finished reading, he placed the newspaper on Brügel's desk.

"Pikler . . . Pikler," said Rheinhardt. "I don't remember the name."

"One of old Schonwandt's cases. He retired the following year . . . not a very competent detective." The commissioner said nothing for a few moments—and his habitual scowl became even darker and heavier than usual. "This afternoon," he continued, "I received a telephone call from one of the education minister's aides. He discoursed—at some length—on the importance of maintaining public confidence in Austria's military schools and hoped that, should the article you have just read come to the emperor's attention, Minister Rellstab will be able to assure His Majesty that the security office treats such accusations very seriously and that any fatalities occurring in military schools are always thoroughly investigated. I explained that you were still in the process of making inquiries . . . and that you would be submitting a final report on the death of Thomas Zelenka in due course."

"But, sir . . . I can't possibly proceed with my pursuit of Herr Kiss *and* continue investigating Zelenka's death. Saint Florian's is situated in the woods: a long drive from the center of Vienna. It would take me—"

"You are no longer operating under Inspector von Bulow's command," the commissioner interrupted.

"I have your permission to return to Saint Florian's?"

Brügel nodded dismissively. He did not have the good grace to articulate an affirmative response.

"Thank you, sir," said Rheinhardt, suppressing the urge to leap from his chair and exclaim with delight.

For once, Rheinhardt left the commissioner's office in a happy mood. He swaggered down the corridor, humming the ebullient victorious theme from the final movement of Beethoven's *Fifth Symphony*.

He rapped on von Bulow's door, waited an inexcusably long time for permission to enter, and found von Bulow hunched over his desk, writing a report with a gold fountain pen. The supercilious inspector did not look up. His bald pate shone like a billiard ball.

"Von Bulow?"

"Ah, Rheinhardt, I'm glad you're here. . . . There's something I need you to do this afternoon."

Von Bulow kept his head bowed and continued with his task.

"I'm afraid," said Rheinhardt, "that you'll have to get your assistant to do it."

The shiny bald pate was suddenly replaced by von Bulow's angry face.

"What did you say?"

"You'll have to get your assistant to do it," Rheinhardt repeated, enunciating each syllable as if he were talking to someone who was partially deaf.

"That isn't possible," said von Bulow coldly. "He's otherwise engaged."

"Then *you*'ll have to do it."

Von Bulow's eyes narrowed as he grasped the significance of Rheinhardt's airy insolence.

"What . . . what's happened?"

"I've been reassigned to the Saint Florian investigation."

"Who has reassigned you?"

"Commissioner Brügel, of course."

"But that's not—"

"Possible?" Rheinhardt smiled. "Perhaps you would be so kind as to collect Herr Kiss's photograph later this morning? I will have no further use for it."

The look of shocked bemusement on von Bulow's face gave Rheinhardt inestimable pleasure.

On returning to his office Rheinhardt sat at his desk, where he found a note from Haussmann: *Fanousek Zelenka would like to see you.*

25

STEININGER, FREITAG, AND DREXLER were playing cards on the floor. They were sitting cross-legged on an old blanket that had been spread out for their comfort. The tableau they created recalled the Middle East: they might have been gamesters at a bazaar. Wolf was lying on some cushions a short distance away, reading *Beyond Good and Evil*. They were all smoking, and the lost room was filled with gently undulating hazy veils of cigarette smoke.

"I'd like to get into the cavalry," said Steininger. "I have a cousin in the cavalry. He wears a very handsome uniform. He told me to join because you get to ride spirited horses and attract the attention of girls."

"My father disapproves," said Freitag.

"What? Of girls?" said Steininger, grinning.

"No, of the cavalry," said Freitag. "He says it's corrupt. Who do you want to join, Drexler?"

Freitag swigged some slivovitz from a bottle and handed it to Steininger.

"I haven't decided yet," Drexler replied.

"You're not thinking of the civil service, are you?" said Freitag indignantly. "I can't think of anything more dull."

Drexler looked over his spectacles. "I haven't decided yet," he repeated calmly.

Steininger belched.

"Must you be so disgusting?" asked Wolf, without taking his eyes from his book.

Steininger shrugged, and, ignoring Wolf, said: "What about the infantry, Freitag?"

"The foot rags?" Freitag replied. "Possibly."

Wolf tutted.

"What?" said Freitag.

"I suppose the infantry are all right," said Wolf sarcastically. "If you want to die an utterly pointless death defending Greeks from Turks and Turks from Greeks."

Steininger and Freitag looked puzzled.

"He's talking about Crete," said Drexler.

"Crete?" said Steininger. "What about Crete?"

"That's where the Eighty-seventh were sent," said Wolf. "The Christians rebelled against the Muslims, and the Greeks landed two thousand soldiers to help them overthrow the Ottoman sultan. The Eighty-seventh were sent over to separate the opponents—and they were given excellent new white uniforms so that they would be especially conspicuous in the bright sun and easy for agitators to pick off! Yes, you two join the infantry. . . . I can't think of anything more noble, can you, than to selflessly lay down one's life for one's Greek and Turkish brothers? Your parents will be most proud."

Steininger pushed out his lower lip. "Well, it's easy for you to criticize us, Wolf. But you haven't told us where you're going."

"Yes, Wolf, where *are* you going?" Freitag repeated, the pitch of his voice raised slightly in irritation.

Wolf sighed and—still without turning to look at them—said in pointedly weary tones: "I do not intend to prance around on a horse in order to attract the attention of witless females. Nor do I intend to waste my life in some garrison town—where the only person who can read without moving his lips is the local doctor. I do not intend to meet a premature end trying to suppress some meaningless peasants' revolt in Transylvania, and I most certainly don't intend to stand between two barbarian races hell-bent on each other's annihilation, thousands of miles away from home. No . . . I have other plans."

"What plans?" asked Freitag.

"Oh, do shut up, Freitag," said Wolf. "Can't you see that I'm trying to read?"

26

IT WAS LATE AFTERNOON when Rheinhardt arrived in Landstrasse. He had not forewarned the Zelenkas of his intention to visit; consequently, he was not surprised to find the bungalow empty. Removing a box of cigars from his coat, he passed the time puffing contentedly and contemplating the gasworks through a trail of rising smoke. Perhaps, on account of his elated state, these bleak edifices no longer looked ugly. They appeared romantic—like the dolmen tombs of mythic warriors, or the watchtowers of Valhalla.

Meta was the first to return. She immediately apologized—for no obvious reason—and ushered Rheinhardt through the door. The cramped living space was just as he remembered it: shadowy and claustrophobic. After offering him a chair, she began making tea.

"Your husband left a message—you wanted to see me?"

"Yes," said Meta. "It's about Thomas's things."

"Things?"

"His possessions. . . . We received a parcel from the school, yesterday morning." She paused, and struggled to control a sudden swell of grief that made her chest heave. "His clothes, a little money . . . his schoolwork and some books. But something was missing. His dictionary."

Meta came to the table and placed a cracked cup in front of the inspector. He thanked her, and indicated that she should continue.

"It was very expensive . . . Hartel and Jacobsen: bound in green leather, with gold lettering. Fanousek worked very hard to get the extra money we needed. We thought Thomas should have something like that—so that he wouldn't stand out so much. We thought the other boys would have such things."

Meta sat down opposite Rheinhardt and searched his face for a response. He felt vaguely disappointed. His expectation had been that the Zelenkas would have something interesting to tell him— something that would help him solve the mystery of their son's premature demise. The loss of the boy's dictionary, however valuable the book might have been, seemed rather trivial under the circumstances.

"Are you suggesting that it has been stolen?"

Meta shrugged. "We just want it back."

Rheinhardt nodded. "I will make some inquiries."

"Thank you, Inspector."

His promise to make *some inquiries* was hollow, disingenuous. He might ask one or two questions, he supposed, but that was all.

Rheinhardt sipped his tea.

There was nothing more to say—and the silence became increasingly brittle. Yet the inspector was reluctant to leave. He did not want to depart under a pall of disappointment, feeling that his earlier high spirits had been dissipated and that he had wasted his time.

"You said that there were other things in the parcel. May I see them?"

"Yes," said Meta. "Everything we received is in Thomas's room. I put the clothes in the chest—the other things are on top of it."

She gestured toward the closed door. As before, she was disinclined to follow.

Rheinhardt entered the boy's room and was struck by its terrible stillness—more so than before. He recalled sitting in his parlor, listening to Therese playing the piano and Mitzi humming, he recalled contemplating the horror of being predeceased by one's own children, and as he recalled these things, he felt as if the back of his neck was being chilled by an icy exhalation. He turned around nervously, half expecting to see the Erlkönig.

The strange presentiment passed, and Rheinhardt was visited by a sad realization. Fanousek and Meta did not want Thomas's dictionary back in order to sell it. They wanted it back because it was Thomas's—and everything that Thomas had owned was here. This was all they had left of their son.

Rheinhardt knelt by the chest and began to flick through the boy's exercise books. The margins were filled with teachers' comments—most were helpful, but a significant number were merely sarcastic. Beneath these exercise books was a much larger volume with hard cloth covers and thick yellow paper. It contained sketches: a vase, naked bodies in various Olympian poses, and a seated woman. They were not very accomplished works of art—the athletic figures in particular were flawed by errors of proportion. However, the seated woman was executed with just enough proficiency to suggest the distinctive lineaments of Frau Becker.

The next exercise book was full of numbers and algebraic equations. Throughout, the left page had been used for rough work and was a chaotic mess of scribbled operators and products. The opposite page, however, was much neater, showing, step by step, the precise method employed to calculate answers.

Something caught Rheinhardt's attention: a systematic regularity among the rough work—number pairs, arranged in neat columns of varying length. Rheinhardt had forgotten most of his school mathematics. Even so, he was reasonably confident that these pairings had nothing to do with Zelenka's calculations. Moreover, although some were in Zelenka's hand, most of them were in someone else's—someone whose numerals were much smaller. Inspection of the marginalia soon established that the additional number pairs had been produced by the mathematics master, Herr Sommer.

What did they mean?

Rheinhardt remembered that Liebermann—for reasons the young doctor had not cared to disclose—was of the opinion that Herr Sommer should be closely questioned. Liebermann's penchant for mystification was extremely irritating, but Rheinhardt could not suppress a smile, impressed as he was by his friend's perspicacity.

27

LIEBERMANN HAD SPENT MUCH of the afternoon conversing with a patient who had once been a distinguished jurist and who now suffered from dementia praecox. One of the symptoms of the old lawyer's illness was incontinence of speech. He had expounded upon a bizarre but entirely cohesive philosophical system that had been revealed to him—so he claimed—by an angelic being (ordinarily resident on Phobos, a satellite of the planet Mars). It was the jurist's intention to record this new doctrine in a volume that he maintained would one day become the scriptural foundation of a new religion.

The old lawyer's speech was ponderous, and after the first hour Liebermann's concentration began to falter. An image of Miss Lydgate insinuated itself into his mind, and, as was usually the case whenever he thought of the Englishwoman, he found himself wanting her company and conversation.

The jurist droned on, speaking of circles of influence, Platonic ideals, and the progress of souls; however, Liebermann had disengaged. The jurist's words carried no meaning and became nothing more than a soporific incantation.

Miss Lydgate.

Amelia . . .

What an extraordinary woman she was. How different from all the other women he had met in his life. Liebermann thought of his adolescent infatuations, the dalliances of his university years—and

Clara Weiss, to whom he had once been engaged: beautiful, amusing, and from a family much like his own. Yet he had not really enjoyed her company. Clara was too superficial, preoccupied as she was with fashion and society gossip. Unable to sustain a meaningful conversation, she was the very opposite of Amelia.

Liebermann whispered her name: the weak syncopation of the A followed by the subtle lilt of the last three syllables. The second of the four, he noticed, required him to bring his lips together—as in a kiss.

Amelia, Amelia . . .

How he wanted to see her, to sit with her in her modest parlor, breathing the subtly scented sweet must of old volumes, drinking tea, and listening to her precise and ever so slightly accented German. Something inside him, something profoundly deep, altered—an inner movement or shifting. The sensation was impossible to describe, but a memory came to his aid that captured—at least in part—the quality of his experience. Once, in the Tyrol, he had watched a great lake thawing. He had listened to the groaning sounds emanating from the frozen-solid surface—a doleful music reminiscent of human lamentation. Then, quite suddenly, the keening had been silenced by a thunderous crack. A jagged black rift had appeared, and two massive ice floes slowly drifted apart. This was how he felt now. As if something locked—something frozen—had suddenly been released.

It was a moment of revelation, every bit as mysterious as those described by the jurist.

He wanted to see Miss Lydgate, not only because her conversation was stimulating, but also—more truthfully—because he was haunted. *Yes, haunted!* By the redness of her hair, the gleaming whiteness of her shoulders, the intensity of her pewter eyes, and the memory of her waist—held close—as they'd danced; by the precious rarity of her smile, the accidental touching of hands, and the ghostly imaginings that anticipate the transformation of sensual dreams into reality. In short, he wanted to see Miss Lydgate because he was in love with her. He had never permitted himself to use *that* word before in relation to Miss Lydgate, but as he did so now, he recognized that it possessed the authority of an indisputable diagnosis.

"Thank you," said Liebermann, interrupting the jurist's disquisition. "Most interesting. We shall continue our discussion tomorrow."

"But I have only just begun to explain the principle of equivalence," protested the jurist.

"Indeed."

"An essential teaching, particularly if you are to appreciate fully the moral implications of the principle of plurality."

"Very true—I'm sure; however, regretfully, I really must draw our meeting to a close."

Liebermann summoned a nurse and instructed her to escort the old jurist back to his bed. He returned to his office, where he made some perfunctory notes. Then, grabbing his new coat (another stylish astrakhan), he departed the hospital with long, purposeful strides.

Unexpectedly, the weather had become more clement. The air was warmer, and carried with it a foretaste of distant spring—the promise of renewal.

Liebermann felt elated, relieved of the onerous burden of pretence and self-deception. He would arrive at Amelia Lydgate's door unencumbered by excuses or insincere justifications. It was not his intention to declare his love, but rather to initiate a process of change. His intercourse with Miss Lydgate had always been formal. This was attributable, in part, to the Englishwoman's character (the famed reserve of that indomitable island race); but it was also due to their shared history, their past roles as doctor and patient, something of which had persisted well beyond the termination of Miss Lydgate's treatment. If their relationship could be placed on a different footing, then perhaps there was hope. . . . She was a thoroughly undemonstrative person, yet he had reason to believe that honesty would now prevail. In the minutiae of her behavior, he had more than once observed—so he flattered himself—evidence of a burgeoning attachment. His love would be reciprocated! And if he was wrong? Well, *so be it!* At least, in Nietzsche's eternally recurring universe, the dissatisfaction, frustration, and pain arising from his inauthentic existence would be short-lived.

The young doctor had become so preoccupied by his racing thoughts that his journey through Alsergrund seemed to take no time at all. Suddenly, Frau Rubenstein's house reared up in front of him. He paused, collected himself, took a deep breath, and raised the knocker. Three decisive strikes announced his arrival.

What should I say to her?

On such occasions, it was usually Liebermann's custom to rehearse a speech of some kind—to decide upon a few ready phrases. But he had been too agitated to discipline his thoughts to this end, and he now found his head filled with a yawning emptiness.

He waited . . . and waited.

Perhaps . . . I shall invite her to the opera—or another ball?

More time passed—and he knocked again.

The door opened, and he drew back in surprise. It was not Miss Lydgate's face that had appeared but the wrinkled visage of Frau Rubenstein.

"Herr Dr. Liebermann."

"Frau Rubenstein." He bowed and took her hand.

"I am afraid that Amelia is not here," said the old woman. "She left about an hour ago." After a slight pause, she added, "With a gentleman." This addendum was colored by a frown and a note of disapproval.

"From the university?"

"No . . . no, I don't think so. His German wasn't very good." Again, Frau Rubenstein hesitated before continuing. "And his English . . . There was something about it. . . . It sounded strange."

But she never receives visitors, thought Liebermann. *She never entertains.*

"Was he a young gentleman?"

"Yes . . . about your age, I imagine." The old woman's eyes narrowed. "Do you know him?"

Liebermann tried to conceal his unease with a smile.

"No." He felt awkward—his arms seemed to stiffen in unnatural positions. "Did she say where they were going?"

"Yes," Frau Rubenstein replied. "Café Segel."

"I see. My apologies for disturbing you, Frau Rubenstein. When Miss Lydgate returns, please tell her that I called. It was not a matter of"—his chest tightened—"importance."

As he prepared to retreat, Liebermann noticed something odd about Frau Rubenstein's expression—a puckering of her lineaments indicative of concern. She seemed about to offer an afterthought, but instead shrank back into herself.

"Frau Rubenstein?" Liebermann enquired. "Are you all right?"

"Yes," said the old woman. "It's just . . ." Liebermann encouraged her to continue with a hand gesture. "Perhaps I am mistaken—but Amelia seemed . . . not herself."

"Not herself?" Liebermann's soft repetition created a flat echo.

"A little upset, perhaps."

Liebermann nodded. "Thank you. I will . . ." His sentence trailed off. What would he do? What *could* he do? "I am sure there is no cause for concern."

He bid Frau Rubenstein good evening and set off down the road—his previously purposeful stride reduced now to a despondent shamble.

Miss Lydgate's visitor was probably a foreign associate of her academic mentor, Landsteiner. In all likelihood, there was nothing to worry about. She had offered to show the gentleman a local coffeehouse, and he had agreed to the plan. Yet, as Liebermann made his way toward his apartment, he could not let the matter rest. He continued to ask himself questions, and in due course became increasingly uneasy. Why had Miss Lydgate appeared upset? Frau Rubenstein was not confident in her judgment, but what if she was correct? What if Miss Lydgate *had* left the house while distressed and in the company of a stranger?

Liebermann changed direction and headed off toward Café Segel.

His route took him across a busy thoroughfare where he dodged between carriages—and earned himself an imprecation from an angry driver. A tram rolled by, delaying him once again, before he reached the other side. Entering a warren of connected backstreets, he finally emerged opposite Café Segel—which occupied a whole corner.

Beneath a striped awning, tables and chairs had been placed outside. At one of these sat Miss Lydgate, with a young man whose dress was somewhat irregular. The cut of his clothes was distinctly foreign—and the broad brim of his hat curled upward at the sides.

Miss Lydgate was smiling at him. They were talking, intimately, with their heads bent forward. The man stood. He offered Miss Lydgate his hand, which she took without hesitation. They were facing each other, and both remained curiously still—as if magically transfixed—staring with wonderment into each other's eyes. The man's arms rose and he embraced Miss Lydgate, pulling her toward him—gathering her in, tenderly. He held her close, and planted kisses in the abundance of her hair. She offered no resistance: her surrender was voluntary—and total.

Liebermann raised the collar of his coat, turned away, and vanished into the shadows, reeling like a drunkard, inebriated by the potency of his own emotions—a heady concoction of disappointment, jealousy, and rage.

28

BERNHARD BECKER HELD HIS GLASS up to the light and stared into the vortex of dissolving crystals. Through the cloudy elixir, he could see the book-lined walls of his study. The entire room seemed to expand and contract in synchrony with his thumping heart. He threw his head back and poured the liquid down his throat, wincing at the astringency of the alcohol. Numbness spread around his mouth and lips.

He found himself thinking of something his wife had said about the young doctor, the one who had accompanied Rheinhardt a few days earlier.

Tall, handsome—with kind eyes. Yes, that was how she had described him. . . .

Becker experienced a flash of anger.

They had knowingly visited his wife behind his back. It was completely unacceptable.

Dishonest, improper, disrespectful!

And why had they asked Leopoldine about her dreams? Why did they want to know about her dreams!

Becker pressed his thumbs against his temples and made small circular movements with them.

His wife had been wearing her lace blouse, the one with the flesh-colored silk lining. He had told her more than once that he did not like this item of clothing—that it did not suit her. In fact, he thought it vulgar, cheap, and immodest. But he could hardly say so (she was oversensitive about such things, quick to take offense). It was typical, absolutely typical, that Leopoldine should have been wearing *that* blouse on the very day when Inspector Rheinhardt chose to call, with his tall, *handsome* colleague.

Becker was seized by the "urge" again—its arrival attended by a vague sense of guilt. A part of his mind, a very small part (no more than a token gossamer conscience) resisted—raising a faintly articulated objection. However, this inner voice of reason was soon silenced by a tidal flood of emotions: hurt, fury, and, most of all, burning, insatiable curiosity. He left his study and tiptoed across the landing, positioning himself next to the banisters. He leaned over the polished wooden handrail, listening intently. The distinctive whisper of a turning page informed him of the whereabouts of his wife. She was sitting in the parlor, reading one of her inane romantic novels. He nodded to himself, emitted a soft grunt of approval, and crossed the landing, before quietly turning the handle of their bedroom door. Once inside, he lit three paraffin lamps.

Becker paused and looked at Leopoldine's dressing table. The surface was littered with circular baskets overflowing with ribbons and hairpins, an assortment of brushes, and numerous unguents and perfumes. A gauzy nightgown was draped over the oval mirror—and an item of underwear had been discarded on the floor.

The word "slattern," declaimed with biblical authority, sounded in Becker's head. He picked up the drawers—and tested the sensuous viscosity of the material with the tips of his fingers. His body trembled with desire and resentment. Throwing the garment aside, he edged toward the bed. He glanced once at the door—anxious not to be discovered. It reminded him of his adolescence, the perpetual stealing away, the fearful intensity of his need—and his immoderate indulgence in the solitary vice. . . .

Was it true? he wondered. *What the doctors said about self-pollution? Did it really unhinge the mind?*

Breathing heavily, he reached for the eiderdown and ripped it back. Then, grabbing a paraffin lamp, he held it over the bedsheet and examined the stretched, taut linen with forensic scrupulosity. He pressed his nose into the fabric and sniffed, with fevered canine excitement.

Nothing different. Nothing strange. Only a familiar muskiness, the barely perceptible olfactory signature of their connubial mattress.

Becker walked around the bed, still swinging the lamp close to the white sheet, his eyes performing watchful oscillations. *No traces. Thank God. No traces.*

He felt relieved, and his shoulders relaxed. But his reprieve was short-lived. At once, he realized his error. Reaching down, he ran his hand across the crisp sheet. It had only recently been changed. Of course there would be no traces on *this* sheet!

He pulled at the tapering points of his beard: he noticed that his hand was trembling. In his head, he could hear the marrowless voice of his insubstantial conscience: *this is madness. This is madness.* Becker silenced it with a clenched fist, brought violently against his heart.

29

"Outrageous," said Eichmann. "Absolutely outrageous! It's shocking that Austerlitz should have consented to printing it. But I suppose it's what we have come to expect from the *Arbeiter-Zeitung* . . . always trying to stir up dissent. They call themselves socialists but really they're just troublemakers!"

The headmaster shook his head with such violence that the artfully placed strands of hair raked across his crown were unsettled, revealing the baldness beneath.

"Do you remember Domokos Pikler?" asked Rheinhardt.

"Of course I do . . . a strange, solitary boy. Hungarian. And wouldn't you know it! They say that Hungarians are a melancholic race—have you heard that?"

"Yes."

"Well, Pikler was a typical Magyar. I don't think I ever saw him smile. He killed himself, Inspector. He killed himself because he was afflicted with a profound constitutional melancholy."

"What about this punishment? 'Doing the night watch?' "

"I've never heard of it. The product of a fevered imagination, as were the author's other wild—and frankly ludicrous—allegations."

"Do you have any idea who this Herr G. might be?"

"No. Pikler's death was almost ten years ago. Long enough for me to forget which pupils were here at that time. I could go through the old registers, if you wish? Seeing the names of former pupils sometimes jogs my memory."

"I saw Frau Becker recently," said Rheinhardt. "On Saturday, in fact." The headmaster raised his eyebrows, inquisitively. "She is of the opinion," Rheinhardt continued, "that Thomas Zelenka was bullied—and that such behavior is commonplace at Saint Florian's."

"Yes . . . Frau Becker," said Eichmann, leaning back in his chair and smiling. "Well, if I may be blunt, Inspector, you shouldn't treat anything she says too seriously." He then adopted a more complicit tone of voice. "I trust you are a discreet man, Inspector? This is a delicate matter, and I would be mortified if my deputy were to discover that I had been less than complimentary about his wife."

Rheinhardt nodded.

"In spite of her . . ." Eichmann searched for a word that might serve as a diplomatic substitute for the several pejoratives that had obviously just occurred to him. But, failing, he was forced to declare, "In spite of *everything* about her"—when he said the word 'everything,' he traced an annulus in the air, implying some vague and disagreeable totality—"my dear wife, Ursula, did all that she could to welcome Frau Becker into our small but vitally important community of masters' wives. However, it was soon evident that Frau Becker did not enjoy the company of her peers. She found Ursula and the other wives . . . old-fashioned. The girl means well—I have no doubt—but her attitude to the boys was hopelessly naïve. She would have believed anything Zelenka told her—and would have lavished sympathy when a reprimand for disloyalty or unmanly conduct would have been much more appropriate."

This last sentence was said with an air of finality. Eichmann picked up a little bell on his desk and rang it loudly. The door opened and Albert entered.

"Permission to report—ready to escort the inspector, sir."

"Thank you, Albert," said the headmaster. Eichmann then turned to Rheinhardt and said: "I am sorry to say that—once again—you will be unable to interview Herr Sommer. He has still not recovered from his accident."

"I see," said Rheinhardt.

"Even so, Herr Sommer has written to me, and I understand that he intends to return by the end of the week." The headmaster reached for a sheet of paper on which were listed several names. "Now . . . the boys you wished to interview. They are all waiting upstairs. I must confess to being more than a little intrigued by this request—and I wonder why, exactly, you believe that these particular pupils will be able to assist you with your investigation?"

Rheinhardt did not respond.

The headmaster continued, "But of course, I understand that it is not for me to question your methods."

Rheinhardt rose from his seat, bowed, and joined Albert by the door.

"Inspector?" Eichmann called out. Rheinhardt stopped and turned to face the headmaster. "How long do you intend to continue this investigation? Another week? Another month?"

Rheinhardt shrugged. "Until I am satisfied."

Eichmann was clearly irritated by Rheinhardt's abstruse answer. Dispensing with any further courtesies, he dropped his gaze, signaling that the audience was now over.

Rheinhardt set off with his guide. The old soldier chose an extremely convoluted route—descending a floor before rising two floors in a different part of the building. Eventually, they began to ascend a familiar-looking staircase that disgorged them in front of the disused classrooms. Rheinhardt could hear youthful voices emanating from one of the half-open doors. He looked in and saw a dozen boys lounging around in an atmosphere of relaxed, carefree disregard. Some were leaning back on chairs with their feet up, others were playing cards; two were arm wrestling, and a few others were standing suspiciously by an open window. Although none of the boys were smoking, the air was hazy and smelled of tobacco. As soon as they noticed the inspector, they all fell silent, put on their shakos, and stood to attention.

"At ease," said Rheinhardt, amused by their reaction.

He introduced himself and explained that he wished to speak to them individually and that in due course he would summon them one at a time. Then, instructing Albert to sit in the corridor (where the old veteran would no doubt fall asleep), he entered the same classroom that he had made use of on his previous visits. Settling himself at the teacher's table, he took out his notebook and examined his list of names, all of which were associated—to a greater or lesser extent—with the idea of hunting or predation.

Jäger, Fuchs, Falke, Wolf . . .

Prior to that moment, Rheinhardt had been excited by the prospect of conducting these interviews. Yet, now that he was sitting there, about to proceed, he felt a certain uneasiness that shaded into despondency. The boys next door had all been selected because of Isidor Perger's responses to Liebermann's inkblots. The young doctor's rationale had sounded very persuasive at the time—his vocabulary carrying with it the imprimatur of scientific authority: *projection, involuntary imagination, the unconscious.* All very impressive; however, in the absence of Liebermann's advocacy, the whole enterprise seemed less certain, its suppositions wanting, the outcome more uncertain.

Thus, when Rheinhardt went to call the first boy, he was feeling far from optimistic and, perhaps, faintly ridiculous.

Rheinhardt's despondency deepened over the course of the first four interviews. The two Fuchses on his list—Ferdinand and Lear—were big, gangly, amiable fellows. They were respectful, quick to smile, and completely devoid of vulpine cunning. Penrod Falke turned out to be a rather small, and frankly effeminate, first-year student, and Moritz Jäger was an unlikely persecutor of scholarship boys—being one himself. None of them had known Zelenka very well, all denied the existence of bullying at Saint Florian's, and all shook their heads—apparently mystified—when Rheinhardt asked them about "doing the night watch."

The fifth boy, Kiefer Wolf, was quite different.

At first he behaved impeccably, but very soon he began to show signs of boredom and impatience—he sighed, toyed with his sabre, and looked around the room in a distracted fashion.

"Did you know Thomas Zelenka?"

"No."

"You must have spoken to him."

"No—I don't think so."

"But he was in your year."

"There are many people in my year whom I don't speak to."

"Why's that?"

"I don't know. I just don't."

"Perhaps there is something about them?"

"Possibly."

"Perhaps you feel that you have nothing in common?"

"Perhaps."

"That they do not come from very good families?"

"Their origins are of no consequence to me."

"Then why don't you speak to them?"

"One cannot be familiar with everyone."

"You don't dislike them, then?"

"Dislike them? I am indifferent to them. . . ."

There was nothing particularly incriminating about the boy's answers, except a general evasiveness; however, his facial expressions were becoming increasingly provocative. An ugly smirk occasionally disturbed the neutrality of his thin mouth, and his declarations of ignorance were delivered in a tone rich with sarcasm. It was an accomplished performance, in which tacit mockery never quite amounted to insult—but came very close.

The boys who were still waiting in the next room had been getting progressively louder. Rheinhardt could hear squeals of delight, the sound of scraping chairs, and running. They seemed to be playing a game of some kind. Strange, thought Rheinhardt, that those same young men (who only an hour before had been smoking and playing cards like hardened campaigners) were now enjoying the infantile pleasures of tag. Such was the peculiarity of their age.

Wolf raised his hand to his mouth as if politely covering a yawn— but his steady gaze and relaxed neck muscles showed that the gesture was pure artifice.

"Are you tired?" asked Rheinhardt.

"Yes," Wolf replied, without inflection. "We were practicing drill—at sunrise."

The boy smiled.

Rheinhardt watched the bloodless lips curl, and, as they twisted, he observed in their convolution, in their counterfeit charm, something unsettling.

Policeman's intuition . . .

He had trusted his instincts before, and he must trust them again.

This was not an ordinary smile. This was a cruel smile, a malignant smile. This was the smile of a sadist.

"You tortured Zelenka, didn't you?" said Rheinhardt softly. "You and your friends. You held that poor boy down, and you cut him."

A peal of good-humored laughter sounded through the walls.

Wolf's smile did not vanish—if anything, it intensified.

"That is a very serious allegation," he said calmly.

"I know," said Rheinhardt.

"The kind of allegation," Wolf continued, "that one should make only when one has sufficient evidence. And I know for a fact, Inspector, that you have nothing of the kind."

Rheinhardt was unnerved by the boy's confidence. By his steady, silky delivery.

"My uncle," added Wolf, "will be most aggrieved when he hears about your conduct."

"Your uncle?"

"Yes. My uncle Manfred."

"What has your uncle got to do with this?"

"A great deal." Wolf's lips parted, showing his even teeth. "He is not only my uncle but your superior. He runs the security office: He is Commissioner Manfred Brügel."

30

LIEBERMANN SAT, HIS CLENCHED FIST against his cheek, his forefinger extended, tapping his temple, while the old jurist again discoursed at length on the principle of plurality as revealed to him by the angelic being from Phobos. But the young doctor was not really listening. His mind was wholly occupied by the events of the preceding evening. A monochrome re-creation of Miss Lydgate repeatedly surrendering herself to the mysterious stranger's embrace flickered in his head like the moving images of a kinetoscope. This harrowing, cruel coup de théâtre was accompanied by an interminable torrent of inner speech: *Why didn't she tell me about him? Why should she? She was not obliged to tell you anything! Her private life is no concern of yours. . . . But she must have known that I . . . that I . . . You were indecisive—you dithered and procrastinated. Unforgivable.* And so it continued throughout the morning—an endless stream of questions, remorse, and self-recrimination.

After the old jurist, Liebermann saw a young woman with a pathological fear of spiders, a civil servant who derived pleasure from dressing in his wife's clothing, and an utterly miserable "comic" actor. The peculiar and ironic condition of the latter would ordinarily have piqued his interest, but Liebermann was completely unable to focus on what the man was saying. Eventually, the young doctor was forced to concede defeat. There was no point in proceeding—he was in no fit state to practice. He fabricated an excuse that would account for his absence, and retired to a nondescript coffeehouse located behind the hospital.

On entering the establishment, he felt somewhat ashamed of his white lie—particularly so on observing that all the other patrons were absconding medical students trying to recover after a night of excessive drinking.

Liebermann stirred his *schwarzer* and sank into a state of ruminative abstraction. In the play of light on the surface of his coffee he saw—once again—a trembling suggestion of Miss Lydgate falling into the arms of her lover.

Although the notion was unjustified, Liebermann could not rid himself of the feeling that he had been deceived, and the longer he sat, ordering *schwarzers*, smoking Trabuco cheroots, and thinking, thinking, thinking, the less unreasonable his position seemed. Miss Lydgate had given him the impression that she was a bookish intellectual: refined, elevated, untroubled by baser instincts, with little or no interest in gentlemen. The young doctor tapped his cigar, and a long cylinder of fragile ash dropped onto the tabletop, creating a starburst of white ash. How could he, the most astute judge of character, have been so wrong! (Like all psychiatrists, he had immense difficulty grasping the fundamental truth that self-understanding is considerably more problematic than understanding others.)

A dark thought, like a black storm cloud, rolled over the flat horizon of his consciousness. Miss Lydgate had once suffered from hysteria . . . and *he* had treated her. He remembered something that Professor Gruner, the former head of department, had said to him— a warning that he had instantly dismissed: *As we all know, the female hysteric is cunning, malicious, and histrionic. She is a consummate seductress. The credulous physician is easy prey.*

At the time, Liebermann had considered Gruner an old fool: unsympathetic, misogynistic, and an advocate of barbaric electrical treatments. Yet now, as Liebermann sank deeper and deeper into a quagmire of unhappy, bitter confusion, he found himself reviewing his opinion.

"No," he said, quite suddenly—surprised and embarrassed to discover that he had spoken the word aloud. An unshaven medical student sitting at the next table raised his head and looked around the room with bleary bloodshot eyes.

I cannot blame her! I cannot think this way!

Annoyed at his own weakness, annoyed at his willingness to entertain a pernicious, morally bankrupt account of hysterical illness, annoyed at the ease with which he had condemned Miss Lydgate (just like the patriarchal women-hating psychiatrists he most despised), Liebermann sprang up from his chair. He tossed some coins onto the table and departed the coffeehouse, eager to put his unsavory descent into self-pity and despair behind him.

Liebermann walked back to the hospital at a brisk pace. He went directly to his office, where he applied himself to revising the wholly inadequate patient notes he had made earlier.

There was a knock on the door.

"Enter," Liebermann called out.

A man appeared, wearing a smart uniform with orange and gold piping, two rows of buttons bearing relief eagles, and a green hooded cloak. The splendor of his appearance (which revealed the typically Viennese fondness for civic grandeur) vastly inflated the importance of his station and function.

"Herr Dr. Liebermann?" he asked, breathlessly.

"Yes."

The telegraph messenger handed Liebermann an envelope and retreated a few steps. He lingered in the doorway. Liebermann dug deep into his pockets but could find the makings of only a sorry tip, having disposed of most of his change in the coffeehouse.

Liebermann opened the envelope and found a note inside, written in an elegant, looping hand.

Dear Dr. Liebermann,

I trust this note will discover your whereabouts—as I have had to improvise your address. We did not speak of music, but I have a strong feeling that it is important to you—that you possess a musical soul. This evening, I will be performing a selection of Tartini's works for violin. (A ticket is enclosed.) I very much hope that you will come. Please accept my apologies for giving such short notice.

Once again, thank you for your most timely assistance.

With fond greetings,
Trezska Novak

So that's why she's in Vienna! She's a violinist!

Liebermann raised the note and passed it under his nose. He recognized the woman's perfume: the upper register, a combination of clementine and mimosa, the lower, white amber and musk.

"Trezska Novak." He said her name out loud, affecting a Hungarian accent. It tripped off his tongue with a jaunty dance rhythm. For the first time that day he smiled. Not a great, radiant smile, but a smile nevertheless.

31

On leaving the hospital, Liebermann walked to Café Landtmann, where he ordered a large plate of Wiener schnitzel followed by two slices of *topfenstollen*. His appetite, which had been notably absent, had suddenly returned. As his fork sliced through the crumbly pastry, the fragrance of lemon zest, cinnamon, and rum intensified. He relished the sharp flavors, which seemed to revive all his senses: the world became more vivid.

By seven o'clock he was on a tram, which took him to the nearby seventh district. He soon found the small concert venue where Trezska was playing. Examining the billboard, he discovered that she was sharing the platform with two other musicians: a pianist, József Kálman, and a cellist called Bertalan Szép. The concert seemed to be part of a cultural initiative and was sponsored by Árpád Arts, a charitable foundation promoting young musicians from Hungary.

Liebermann entered the building, deposited his coat in the cloakroom, and purchased a program. He loitered in the foyer for a few minutes and studied the audience. They were entirely unremarkable, although there were more Hungarians present than might ordinarily have been expected. Capturing an usher's attention, he was guided to a central seat in the fourth row. The auditorium was already quite full, and an obese woman, wearing a feather boa and a floral hat, scowled at him when she had to stand up to let him pass.

As he settled down, Liebermann noticed a group of men advancing up the side aisle. They were dressed in elegant black suits and looked, so Liebermann thought, like representatives of the charitable foundation. One of them sported an award of civil merit: a large cross, hanging from a violet and green ribbon—the Royal Hungarian Order of Saint Stephen. Among their number, Liebermann was surprised to glimpse the white tunic and gold sash of an Austrian general. He did not get a very clear view of the man, but he saw that he was carrying a bouquet of flowers. The dignitaries took their seats—all in the front row—and almost immediately the lights dimmed.

A door at the back of the stage opened, and József Kálman—a thin, sallow man with sunken eyes—marched to the piano. He played some fanciful pieces by Karl Goldmark and a selection of mazurkas, nocturnes, and ballades by Stephen Heller. Liebermann judged Kálman to be technically proficient, but his interpretations were far too literal. Be that as it may, the audience was determined to praise the young artist, and responded with vigorous applause and hearty cries of "Bravo! Bravo!"

The cellist, Bertalan Szép—a stout fellow with comically horripilated hair—was an altogether more accomplished performer. He produced an excellent account of Bach's *Suite Number Six in D major*, managing to make the melancholy voice of his instrument sing with joy. He continued his recital with an amusing transcription of an orchestral interlude by a Russian composer, titled *The Flight of the Bumblebee*—the conceit of the piece being that its curious chromatic melody emulated precisely the frantic buzzing of the busy insect. When Szép took his bow, Liebermann was pleased to bring his hands together with genuine enthusiasm.

Contemplating the vacant platform, Liebermann found that he was peculiarly excited by the prospect of seeing Trezska Novak again. He began to wonder if his recollection of her was accurate: the full mouth, the strong nose, and those striking eyebrows. She had seemed very beautiful—at the time—but they had met under exceptional circumstances. Perhaps his heightened state of emotion had affected his perception of her. He was hoping—rather anxiously—that his memory had not deceived him, and that the woman who was about to occupy the stage would prove to be an exact copy of the woman he had rescued in Landstrasse.

The door at the rear of the stage opened and Trezska Novak materialized out of the shadows. Liebermann was not disappointed. Indeed, so arresting was her appearance that the audience produced an appreciative soughing that preceded their applause. She was wearing a black satin dress, and her hair fell in thick lustrous locks around her shoulders. Above her heart, she had pinned a brooch—shaped like a horned moon—which burned with a fiery white adamantine light. Her expression was serious and purposeful. She curtsied, gripped the violin beneath her chin, and waited for the clapping to subside. Then, closing her eyes, she drew her bow across the strings.

A strange, improvisatory scraping filled the hall: the opening bars of Tartini's G-minor sonata, more popularly known as *The Devil's Trill* (on account of the composer's insistence that it was revealed to him by Satan in a dream). The melody was serpentine, sinister, and creeping, occasionally finding a major key and offering the listener hope, only to dash it again by twisting back into a tonal wasteland of eerie ambiguities.

Liebermann had heard *The Devil's Trill* performed once before, at the Saal Ehrbar, but it had not affected him so deeply. In that concert, the work had been performed with a piano accompaniment, which had only diminished the music's power. The lone voice of the violin was more haunting, more mysterious—imbued with a raw, chilling urgency.

Of course, thought Liebermann. *When the devil played to Tartini, he played alone!*

Trezska did not open her eyes, but communed with her violin, swaying and rolling from side to side. The demonic obliquity of her eyebrows and the rapture of her playing stirred in Liebermann memories of Faust: a capricious notion that this woman might once have gambled with her soul in exchange for greater mastery of her instrument. The sheer spectacle of her performance charmed the audience into forgiving any technical deficiencies. She was like a magician, artfully misleading by means of a carefully choreographed *danse macabre.*

The conservative second movement was followed by the opening bars of the third, a fortissimo howl that might have escaped from the mouth of a doomed Florentine in Dante's hell. Jerking rhythms led to fluid accelerandi and savage down-bowed chords. Then the famous trills: frenzied, dizzying, convulsive, becoming louder and louder—climbing in pitch and volume. Trezska leaned backward, and her tresses tumbled off her shoulders. Her eyes opened. In the sulfurous gaslight they appeared incandescent with infernal rage. When the music finally reached its arpeggiated dissolution into nothingness, almost everyone listening had been persuaded that this extraordinary composition was, indeed, the devil's handiwork.

Trezska completed her recital with a less dramatic piece: Tartini's *Pastorale for violin in scordatura.* Gradually, its gentle rusticity and bucolic breeziness dispelled the stench of brimstone, and visions of eternal torment were replaced by idyllic vales, drones, pipes, and slumbering shepherds.

When the final notes had faded and Trezska had removed the violin from beneath her chin, the audience responded with noisy delight. Several of the dignitaries in the front row jumped to their feet—and others seated behind copied them, clapping and cheering. Through the mass of bodies, Liebermann caught a glimpse of white and gold—and saw Trezska bend to take the bunch of flowers from the Austrian general.

After collecting his coat from the cloakroom, Liebermann left the hall and set off toward the Ringstrasse. He passed a Bosnian hawker, in crimson fez and pointed slippers, who attempted to sell him a kettle and an inlaid snuffbox. The sound of Tartini's diabolical trills still persisted in the young doctor's mind. They had acquired a siren-like quality, exerting a subtle tractive power that slowed his step. Moreover, he had begun to question the propriety of his precipitate departure. Trezska Novak had sent him a personal invitation. Surely it was discourteous to leave without congratulating her. This simple point of etiquette was frequently observed in musical circles, was it not? Such were his justifications.

Liebermann stopped, turned around, and made his way back to the concert hall, slipping down a side alley that led to the artists' entrance. He rapped on the door, which was opened by a porter. Jangling some loose change in his pocket, he asked the functionary to convey his compliments to Fräulein Novak. Some silver coins changed hands and the porter disappeared. A few minutes later the door reopened and Liebermann was admitted into a narrow corridor. A few gentlemen were standing at the far end: one of them was Bertalan Szép. He was smoking a cigar, and his arm was casually slung around the shoulders of his cello case. The porter indicated Trezska's dressing room.

A gentle tap on the paneling produced an invitation to enter.

Trezska was seated in front of a large mirror.

"How good of you to come."

"It was my pleasure."

She did not stand to greet her visitor but remained perfectly still, conversing with Liebermann's reflection.

"I like to sit quietly after a concert." She smiled softly. "I find it . . . necessary."

"Yes. One needs to recover after expending so much emotional energy—and the pieces looked physically taxing, too. It was a very impressive performance: I have never heard the great G-minor sonata played unaccompanied before."

Something like a shadow passed across Trezska's face. "I was pleased—although some would say that I took liberties with the andante . . . and the allegro was somewhat uninspired, don't you think?"

Liebermann understood that a musician of her quality was not seeking a blithe denial.

"The problem lies—at least in part—with the composition itself. The allegro is musically inferior. Even so . . . I enjoyed it immensely."

"You *are* fond of music," said Trezska, her gaze becoming more penetrating. "I was right—wasn't I?"

"Yes."

"What is your instrument?"

"The piano."

Trezska looked satisfied, almost smug, and without uttering a single word managed to communicate something like: *Yes, of course you're a pianist—how could you be anything else?"*

Now that he was close to her, Liebermann noticed that Trezska's cheek was still a little swollen. She had used make-up to disguise her injury.

"How is your graze?"

"Sore . . . but getting better."

"Good."

There was a knock on the door, followed by the appearance of Szép. He acknowledged Liebermann with a bow, and said to Trezska: "We are off to Csarda. . . . Kiss is coming. Count Dohnányi and his guest will be joining us later."

Liebermann noticed that Trezska's eyes flicked toward the bunch of flowers she had been given, now laid on top of her dressing table.

She shook her head.

"I'm going home," said Trezska. "Tell Kiss to get me a cab."

"Going home?" said Szép, evidently surprised.

Trezska touched her head. The gesture was languid and affected, like that of an operatic diva.

"A headache," she said, with unconvincing indifference. "Please tell the count that I am sorry—I know he will be disappointed."

"Very well," said Szép. He shrugged, and left the room.

Trezska's gaze met with Liebermann's reflection again, and her cunning smile invited him to acknowledge the insincerity of her exchange with Szép. She stood up, her dress rustling, and turned to face him. For the first time that evening they looked at each other directly. Her expression changed, switching from mischievous complicity to something more serious. Liebermann stepped forward and took her hand in his. He kissed her long delicate fingers, on which he detected the distinctive fragrance of her perfume: the clementine was particularly sweet.

"Forgive my presumption, but I would . . ." Liebermann hesitated before continuing his sentence. "I would very much like to see you again."

32

"Where are you taking me?"

Wolf punched Perger as hard as he could. His knuckles sank into the soft area of the lower back, just to the right of the spinal column. The boy cried out in agony—and Wolf punched him again. The force of the second blow pushed the boy forward, and he fell to his knees. Wolf's hand closed around his victim's mouth.

"Just shut up! Not another sound. Ask me again—and I swear I'll . . . I'll . . ." Nothing came to mind, and once again Wolf resorted to violence. He brought his knee up into the space between Perger's shoulder blades, which produced simultaneously a sharp crack and a sickening dull thud.

"Now get up!" Wolf grabbed Perger's collar and pulled him to his feet. "And keep going."

They followed the landing until they reached the pitch-black space beneath an ascending staircase. Wolf pushed Perger away and crouched down, feeling for the ridge of the trapdoor.

"Wait here. If you try to run away you'll regret it. Do you understand?" Perger didn't reply. "Do you understand?" repeated Wolf, emphatically.

"Y-y-yes," stuttered Perger.

Wolf lowered himself into the lost room, lit the paraffin lamp, and hung it on the nearest beam.

"Perger?"

A terrified face appeared in the square aperture.

"Get down here—No. Not like that, you fool. Sit on the edge and push yourself off."

The younger boy dropped onto the crate but immediately lost his balance and toppled off. He did not attempt to get up but remained very still, sprawled out on the floor.

"You clumsy idiot."

Wolf trod on Perger's buttocks, using the springiness of the flesh to add lift to his step. He got back onto the crate, reached upward, and pulled the trapdoor closed.

"Now . . . get up."

Perger tried to stand, but before he could get to his feet, Wolf jumped off the crate and delivered a kick to his ribs. Perger rolled over, groaning.

"I said, get up."

Perger looked at his tormentor, his eyes wide with fear.

"W-W-Wolf . . . I can't get up. I c-c-can't—not if you won't let me."

"I swear to God, Perger . . ."

The boy scrambled to his feet while Wolf strolled over to the suitcase and rummaged through the contents. He returned, smoking a cigarette.

"Stand beneath the lamp."

The boy obeyed, and Wolf slumped back in the old wicker chair. He said nothing, but simply watched—and smoked. The thin line of his mouth and the enamel glaze of his stare betrayed no emotion. Only the sound of Perger's heavy breathing broke the cruel and protracted silence.

"Take your clothes off."

"W-what?"

"You heard."

Wolf leaped up and jabbed the burning end of his cigarette at Perger's face. The younger boy jerked back to avoid contact and immediately began to fumble with the buttons of his shirt. When he had finished, he stood naked, his body trembling and his gaze lowered to the floor.

Returning to the wicker chair, Wolf sat down and stubbed out his cigarette beneath the heel of his boot. Without pause, he lit another and resumed his relaxed but attentive attitude. The point at which his foot had made contact with Perger's chest was now marked on the boy's skin by a red circle, which promised to mature into a livid bruise. Wolf found the injury curiously satisfying—not merely because it represented the exercise of power, the making of his own morality, but also because of an elusive aesthetic quality. The expected transformation of hue (through scarlet, yellow, purple, and black) was comparable, in Wolf's estimation, to the seasonal transformation of leaves between summer and autumn—only more exciting. Why did poets make so much of one but not the other? A thought came into his mind, an abridgement of the aphorism from *Beyond Good and Evil* that had made such a deep impression on him: *Perhaps there are no phenomena, only interpretations of phenomena.*

Wolf sucked on his cigarette and blew out a steady stream of smoke.

"What did you tell him?" he asked.

Perger looked up, his features blending confusion with fear.

"Who?"

"The fat policeman—the detective."

Perger shook his head. "Nothing."

"Oh, but you did," said Wolf. "I know you did."

"I didn't," cried Perger. "I didn't tell him anything . . . not the first time. I didn't say a thing. And the s-s-second time, he came with a doctor. . . . He played chess with me—and showed me p-p-patterns . . . inkblots . . . and asked me what I could see in them . . . and he asked me about the bakery . . . and t-t-ticks . . . and . . . and . . ."

"Enough," shouted Wolf, stamping his foot. "Talk sense! You're gibbering like a lunatic!"

Perger emitted an odd whimpering sound, and pulled frantically at his short hair.

"I didn't s-s-say anything, Wolf. I swear . . . I swear on my mother's life."

"Ha!" said Wolf. "Swearing on the life of a Galician whore is hardly a warrant of honor. That won't save you."

"I s-s-swear . . . I didn't say anything."

"Then why did the fat policeman want to speak to me—after he had spoken to you?"

"He didn't speak to me. It was the doctor. He spoke to me, but about chess, and his seeing game. . . . He showed me p-p-patterns, inkblots, and asked me if I could see anything in them . . . and he asked me about Zelenka. . . . I said Thomas was my friend, and that Thomas liked Frau Becker . . . but nothing else."

"That's it. I've had quite enough of your slippery answers, Perger!"

Wolf flicked his cigarette across the floor. It rolled away, trailing orange sparks. Then he stood up and marched over to his victim. He was carrying a revolver. The younger boy cringed as Wolf pressed the gun's barrel against his temple.

"What . . . did . . . you . . . say?"

Wolf pronounced each word emphatically, and underscored each syllable by pushing the gun hard against Perger's head.

"I don't think you understand the gravity of your situation," said

Wolf. Then, letting his tongue moisten his upper lip, he added: "Kneel." He angled the revolver so that it exerted a downward pressure, and pushed Perger to his knees.

"Please . . . I beg you," sobbed Perger. "I'll do anything . . . anything you want. . . . Please don't kill me."

The thrill of prepotency coursed through Wolf's veins, swelling his heart and galvanizing his loins.

I'll do anything . . . anything you want.

Wolf stared down the length of Perger's back, at the pale, unblemished planes of skin sloping away and curving out of sight. His gaze followed the descending vertebrae, and lingered on Perger's tense calf muscles. The soles of the boy's small feet were slightly wrinkled. To his great embarrassment, Wolf found that it was not only his victim who was shaking—he himself had begun to shake too.

"I know what you used to do for Zelenka," he said softly. "He told me. And now . . . now you'll do it for me."

With his free hand, Wolf began to loosen his belt.

33

THE CARRIAGE TURNED OFF the Schottenring at the university and rattled down a long road that took them through the ninth and seventeenth districts.

"Herr G.'s article in the *Arbeiter-Zeitung*," said Rheinhardt, "came to the attention of one of the aides in the education department. He wanted to make sure that if His Majesty got to hear about it, Minister Rellstab could inform him that something was being done, that the matter was being properly dealt with. Brügel—with typical bad grace—performed a volte-face, and I was told, somewhat obliquely, to resume the investigation."

Liebermann polished his fingernails on his coat sleeve and examined them closely.

"How did Eichmann react when you questioned him?"

"He said that it was all nonsense: that Pikler suffered from constitutional melancholy and had obviously killed himself, that he had never heard of the 'night watch' . . . and he said these things with absolute conviction. He didn't look like a worried man—someone trying to keep secrets."

"Are you trying to discover who 'Herr G.' is?"

"I've assigned Haussmann to the task." Rheinhardt squeezed one of the horns of his mustache and checked the revived point for sharpness with his forefinger. "I also asked Eichmann about Frau Becker."

Liebermann looked up, his eyebrows elevated in interest.

"He described her," Rheinhardt continued, "as gullible, naïve, and indulgent—inclined to believe the claims of any boy seeking attention and sympathy. In addition, she seems to have made little or no effort to be accepted by the headmaster's wife and her circle. Indeed, I suspect that Frau Becker might have been quite outspoken—openly criticizing the school and Frau Eichmann's opinions."

The carriage halted in order to let some traffic pass at a crossroads. Looking out of the window, Liebermann observed a Coptic priest standing on a corner. He had a long black beard and was wearing a mitre. A purple waist band was wrapped around his long dark green cassock. The driver cracked his whip, and the priest slowly slipped from view.

"Later the same day," Rheinhardt continued, "I interviewed some of the schoolboys. You know, the ones who had names suggestive of hunting and predation."

"And . . . ?"

"Well, I must be candid with you, Max. At first, I had my doubts. That test of yours, the inkblots you showed Perger . . . The entire enterprise seemed very fanciful." Rheinhardt reached into his pocket and produced a small box of slim cigars. He offered one to his friend, which Liebermann took. "And to make things worse," he continued, "the first few boys were amiable, good-natured, harmless fellows." Rheinhardt struck a vesta and lit Liebermann's cigar, and then his own. "However . . ." Rheinhardt leaned back and exhaled a cloud of smoke. "I then questioned a boy called Kiefer Wolf and . . . well, there was definitely *something* about him."

"What do you mean, 'something'?"

"He was insolent, rude, supercilious . . . but that wasn't it. No . . . it was when he smiled. I thought . . ."

"What?"

The inspector shook his head. "Oh, what's the use! I can't explain—and you are sure to say something disparaging about policeman's intuition."

"Not necessarily. I must confess that I am developing a grudging respect for your clairvoyance!"

"See? I knew it!"

"Oh, Oskar, you are being oversensitive. Please continue."

"All right, then, I'll say it plainly: he gave me a bad *feeling*. In fact, he gave me such a bad feeling that I somewhat rashly accused him of torturing Zelenka. I wanted to see how he would react."

Rheinhardt looked troubled, and drew on his cigar. "He was very calm . . . just sat looking at me with dull gray eyes. He pointed out that I had made a very serious and unsubstantiated allegation. Then he advised me that he was going to tell his uncle."

Liebermann smiled. "Commissioner Brügel?"

Rheinhardt puffed out his cheeks and let the air escape slowly. "How did you know that?"

"A slip of the tongue that you made earlier." Liebermann made a dismissive gesture. "But it is no matter. . . . I wonder why Brügel never mentioned that he had a nephew boarding at Saint Florian's."

"I don't know."

"And has the boy written or spoken to his uncle?"

"It's difficult to say. I haven't seen Brügel since Wednesday."

Liebermann tapped his cigar above the ashtray set in the carriage door.

"But you didn't do anything *very* wrong, Oskar."

"No, that's true. But it complicates matters, doesn't it? Brügel is always irascible. He's hard enough to deal with at the best of times.

When he discovers that I have accused his nephew of torturing Thomas Zelenka . . ." Rheinhardt's sentence trailed off, his head shaking from side to side.

"Perhaps Brügel has some inkling of his nephew's character," continued Liebermann. "Which would explain why he attempted to stop your investigation. . . . Is it possible that he was protecting his family's interests? Their reputation?"

Rheinhardt considered the young doctor's insight—but did not see how it helped him very much.

"I am in a rather difficult position now. Even if Wolf did torture Zelenka, it doesn't get us very much further with respect to explaining the boy's death."

"Well, this is what we find when we follow hunches instead of reasoning things out."

"See?" said Rheinhardt. "You can't stop yourself from mocking me! I have something to show you." Rheinhardt handed Liebermann a mathematics exercise book. "This was Zelenka's—it was returned to his parents with his other effects. Although . . ."

"What?"

"There was one item missing. A dictionary."

"Is that important?"

"I don't think so—but Zelenka's parents do. They said it was very expensive. They had to save up for it. Anyway . . ." Rheinhardt pointed at the exercise book. "You will see that there are columns of paired numbers on the pages designated for rough work. Similar pairs can be found in the marginalia—written in the master's hand."

"Herr Sommer?"

"Herr Sommer. I am no mathematician, but these numbers seem to have nothing to do with the surrounding calculations."

"You think they are . . . what? Coded messages?"

Rheinhardt nodded.

"Oskar," said Liebermann, sitting forward, "may I have your notebook and a pencil?"

His expression was eager.

"Of course."

Liebermann stubbed out his cigar and folded the exercise book so that it would remain open. He then transcribed some of the number pairs into the notebook, and next to these wrote some letters of the alphabet. He repeated the process several times, before flicking over a page and starting again. This time, he constructed an alphanumeric table. He soon became completely engrossed in his task, and Rheinhardt—deprived of conversation—stared out the window.

The rumbling of the carriage wheels on cobblestones was shortly accompanied by noises indicative of frustration. Liebermann shifted his position, tutted, grumbled under his breath, and tapped the pencil against his teeth. His crossings-out became more violent, the flicking of pages more frequent, and eventually he declared: "Impossible . . . nothing works. I thought it was going to be a simple substitution cipher!"

Rheinhardt turned to face his friend.

"I asked Werkner to take a look—he's one of our laboratory technicians at Schottenring. He's usually quite good at this sort of thing. But he didn't get very far either. Indeed, he was of the opinion that I might be mistaken."

Liebermann bit his lower lip, and his brows knitted together.

"I wonder," said Rheinhardt. "Do you think we should consult Miss Lydgate? She is a woman of such remarkable intelligence—and she has helped us before."

The young doctor's posture stiffened.

"She is indeed very gifted . . . but I do not know whether her talents extend to cryptography."

Liebermann handed the notebook and pencil back to Rheinhardt.

"Yes," said the inspector. "But it is permissible—is it not—to request her assistance again?"

Rheinhardt looked at his friend quizzically.

"You may do as you wish," said Liebermann, picking a hair from the fabric of his trousers.

34

BERNHARD BECKER sat behind his desk, gazing uneasily at his two guests. His pupils were enlarged and his fingers were drumming on his blotting paper.

"Inspector," said Becker, "you must understand, my dear wife is a very sensitive woman. She is compassionate and easily moved to sympathy. I believe that Zelenka took advantage of her . . ." He hesitated for a moment and added, "Kind nature." Becker peered over his gold-rimmed spectacles. "Of course bullying takes place at Saint Florian's. I don't deny it. But such behavior is commonplace in military schools, and it is no more a problem for us than it is for Karlstadt or Saint Polten. Zelenka led my wife to believe that terrible things happen here . . . extraordinary things. But this is simply untrue."

"Did you read Herr G.'s article in the *Arbeiter-Zeitung*?"

Becker smiled—a haughty, disparaging smile.

"Yes. The headmaster showed it to me."

"And?"

"It is utterly absurd," said Becker. His tightly compressed lips suggested that he was disinclined to elaborate. For a moment he toyed with a spoon, which was standing in an empty glass on his desk.

"When we spoke last," said Rheinhardt, "you did not mention that Frau Becker had a particular fondness for Thomas Zelenka."

The deputy headmaster's expression became severe.

"Why should I have? It's entirely *relevant*." From the tone of his voice it was clear that Becker had meant to say the exact opposite. He maintained his defiant expression for a few moments, but this gradually softened into doubt as he recognized his error. "Irrelevant!" He blurted out the correction as if emphasis and volume would negate his blunder. "Let me be candid, Inspector," Becker continued. "I knew that Zelenka's death would cause Poldi much distress—and I saw no purpose in bringing her to *your* attention."

"You wished to spare her a police interview?"

"Yes, Inspector, I did. And I believe I was correct to do so. Your *surprise* visit achieved nothing—as far as I can see—save to remind Poldi of Zelenka's demise, which made her tearful all week!"

"I am sorry," said Rheinhardt. "Obviously, this was not our intention."

"Well," said Becker, harrumphing as he stroked his forked beard.

"I trust," interjected Rheinhardt, "that you will convey our sincere regrets to Frau Becker."

Becker grumbled an assent and added: "If you intend to interview my wife again, you would perhaps be courteous enough to request my permission first?"

"Of course," said Rheinhardt.

At that point there was a knock on the door, and Professor Gärtner appeared.

"Ahh," said the old man, with timorous uncertainty. "Deputy Headmaster, Inspector Rheinhardt." He did not acknowledge Liebermann. "I am sorry to interrupt, but could I have a quick word—Deputy Headmaster? It's about my report to the board of governors."

"Excuse me," said Becker, rising from his chair and leaving the room.

As soon as the door closed, Liebermann reached forward and snatched the empty glass from Becker's desk.

"What are you doing?" asked Rheinhardt.

The young doctor did not reply. Instead, he sniffed the contents, and held the glass up to the window. The weak sunlight revealed a viscous puddle of liquid at the bottom. He then ran a finger around the inside of the glass, collecting a patina of white residue, which he licked off.

"Bitter—followed by the slow emergence of aromatic flavors . . ."

"That's his medicine," said Rheinhardt. "He took some when I was here before. He gets headaches."

Liebermann wiped the inside of the glass with his finger again, and rubbed the residue into his lips and gums.

"I know what this is." He replaced the glass and adjusted the spoon so that it was standing in exactly the same position as when Becker had left. "And I certainly wouldn't prescribe it for headaches. It's—"

Liebermann fell silent as the door opened and Becker reentered the room.

"My apologies, gentlemen," said Becker curtly.

Liebermann straightened his necktie and smiled winsomely at Becker as he sank back into his chair.

For reasons not clear to Rheinhardt and Liebermann, the deputy headmaster launched into a tedious homily on fraternity, explaining how it should be considered the most cardinal of virtues. Occasionally he lapsed into ponderous rhetorical German, and Rheinhardt suspected they were listening to a set speech that he had bored many a schoolboy with during countless morning assemblies. In due course, the inspector took out his fob watch and declared that time had positively flown by—and that they were now in great danger of being late for their appointment with Herr Sommer.

"Would you like me to call Albert to escort you?" asked Becker.

"No. I think we can find our own way."

"Good. Herr Sommer lives in the fourth lodge—on the ground floor. You will find his name on the door."

"Thank you," said Rheinhardt.

The two guests got up to leave. However, the inspector hesitated a moment and said, somewhat tentatively, "Might I ask, Deputy Headmaster, where you and your wife met?"

Becker frowned and replied "Styria."

"Indeed?" Rheinhardt prompted.

"I met her while I was on a summer walking holiday. She was . . ." He swallowed before proceeding. "She was a waitress—at one of the guesthouses." A slightly pained expression twisted his mouth.

"Forgive me for asking a delicate question," Rheinhardt continued, "but has Frau Becker asked you for more money recently—in addition to her usual housekeeping?"

The deputy headmaster's cheeks reddened with embarrassment and anger.

"Our domestic arrangements are a private matter."

"I'm sorry," said Rheinhardt. "I did not mean to offend."

Aware that they had now very much overstayed their welcome, Rheinhardt and Liebermann removed themselves from the deputy headmaster's office with unceremonious haste.

35

RHEINHARDT AND LIEBERMANN PAUSED by the statue of Saint Florian. Close by, some cadets were presenting arms, and beyond them more boys could be seen quick marching around a square of tar-grouted macadam. An order from a rifle lieutenant brought the fast-moving column to an abrupt halt. The two friends looked at each other, and their gazes communicated a mutual disquiet—a tacit suspicion of martial virtues.

They walked around the school building, past another parade ground, and found the path that led to the lodges. Two rows of small terraced houses came into view. The final house at the end of the second row had HERR G. SOMMER painted in small white letters on the door. It was sandwiched between the names of two other masters: Herr Paul Lang and Dr. Artur Düriegl. The second of these was barely visible, being much faded and partially scratched out.

Rheinhardt rapped on the door with the plain iron knocker, but there was no response. He tried again, and whistled a snippet of melody from Schubert's *Unfinished Symphony*.

"He's not in," said Liebermann.

Rheinhardt consulted his pocket watch.

"Sommer sent me a telegram yesterday, confirming that he would be here at two o'clock. How very odd. What should we do?"

"I am confident that he will come—but we may have to wait awhile."

"What makes you say that?"

Liebermann shrugged his shoulders and pretended that his remark was nothing more than a superficial off-the-cuff observation.

"Come, Oskar," said Liebermann cheerily. "Let us find somewhere to sit."

Behind the living quarters the two men discovered a bench. It was positioned to afford a picturesque view of the hills. Ominous banks of nimbostratus were gathering in the east; however, the prospect had a certain romantic charm—particularly when the wind became stronger, bending the trees and sweeping flossy tatters of cloud overhead. Rheinhardt and Liebermann made some desultory conversation but soon fell silent, choosing instead to smoke cigars and contemplate the brooding majesty of the landscape.

Once again, Liebermann found himself thinking about Miss Lydgate. The image of her falling into the stranger's embrace flickered into life—accompanied by a flash of anger. He had to remind himself that such feelings were unjustified. She had not misled him. He had not been deceived. However, he soon discovered that his anger could not be extinguished, only diverted. If he wasn't being angry with her, he was being angry with himself. It was most frustrating. He did not want his peace of mind to be hostage to a memory. Besides, there was something to look forward to now. . . . He was taking Trezska Novak to the Prater on Saturday. He should be thinking about *her*—not about Amelia Lydgate!

Almost an hour had passed before Liebermann nudged Rheinhardt, alerting him to the approach of a pitiful figure hopping along with the aid of a crutch, his right leg bent at the knee to keep his bandaged foot from touching the ground.

The two men rose from the bench and introduced themselves.

"Inspector Rheinhardt, Herr Dr. Liebermann," said the man, propping himself up. "Gerold Sommer." In spite of his disability, he accomplished a perfectly respectable bow. "Please . . . this way." He glanced up at the sky. "I think it's about to rain." Stabbing the ground with his crutch, he propelled himself up the path with renewed energy.

The mathematics master led Rheinhardt and Liebermann back to the lodges. As he searched his pockets for the key, he asked: "Have you been waiting long, gentlemen?"

"Since two o'clock," Rheinhardt replied.

"Why so early, Inspector?"

"That was the time you specified, Herr Sommer."

"Good heavens. I could have sworn I'd said three." He unlocked the front door and pushed it open. "If I am mistaken, I do apologize. I usually have a very good head for figures."

Sommer ushered his visitors through a narrow hallway and into his study. The overall impression was one of neglect and untidiness. A table had been pushed up against one of the walls. Its top was covered in exercise books and various calculating instruments: a three-hundred-and-sixty-degree protractor, triangles, compasses, and a very large slide rule. Sommer's library was scattered around the floor, with some volumes being lined up against the baseboard. Beneath the window a row of large tomes supported a precariously balanced second tier.

Sommer limped over to a scuffed leather reading chair and attempted to sit down. He refused Rheinhardt's assistance and managed, in due course, to position himself so that he could fall back safely. He landed heavily on the cushion.

"Please, gentlemen," said Sommer. "There are two stools beneath the table."

Rheinhardt pulled one out for himself, but Liebermann declined the offer. It was his preference to stand.

"Well," said Sommer, staring at Rheinhardt with large, moist eyes. "How can I assist?"

The mathematics master was in his early thirties. His hair was parted in the center and his mustache was neatly trimmed. He was a handsome man; however, the nobility of his face was mercilessly subverted by a pair of protruding ears.

Rheinhardt glanced at Sommer's bandaged foot.

"I fell down some stairs and sprained my ankle," Sommer continued, feeling obliged to explain his condition. "It was extremely painful. The joint became horribly swollen. Like this." He demonstrated with his hands. "I thought I'd done myself a very serious injury; but, fortunately, it turned out to be nothing more than a torn ligament. I've been convalescing near Linz: a small sanatorium run by Professor Baltish." He looked across the room at Liebermann. "Do you know it, Herr Doctor?" Liebermann shook his head. "A very fine establishment," Sommer added, his gaze oscillating nervously from one guest to the other.

"Herr Sommer," said Rheinhardt, detecting the man's discomfort and trying to disarm him with an avuncular smile. "Your accident— when did it happen?"

"A few weeks ago."

"When, exactly?"

"I could hardly forget. It was the day we heard the dreadful news about Zelenka."

"We?"

"Herr Lang and myself . . . The headmaster came to tell us *that* morning." Sommer shook his head. "We were stunned."

Rheinhardt asked the mathematics master about the dead boy.

It transpired that he had known Zelenka very well, choosing to describe him as a *favorite*. However, when he talked about his relationship with the boy, he said nothing that Rheinhardt didn't already know. Indeed, repeated exposure to certain words and phrases—*mature, sensitive, an able student, interested in science, could be shy*—had rendered them almost meaningless.

As Sommer spoke, Liebermann sidled toward the window and surreptitiously examined some of the book titles. The larger volumes were mathematical texts and standard works of reference—a dictionary, an atlas, an encyclopedia—and on top of these were some histories of ancient Greece and a volume titled *The Nude—Photographic Studies.*

"Tell me, Herr Sommer," said Rheinhardt, shifting his plump haunches on the hard wooden stool, "what do you know of Zelenka and the deputy headmaster's wife, Frau Becker?"

Sommer's expression altered, his eyes quickened by curiosity.

"Zelenka was very fond of her. I know that because he told me so. And I believe that fondness was reciprocated . . ." His sentence ended on an imperfect cadence as if he had intended to say more but had changed his mind.

" 'Fondness,' Herr Sommer?"

The mathematics master sighed. "Ordinarily I would be more circumspect, but as this is a police matter . . . I must confess, I have heard things said. It is possible that Frau Becker and Zelenka . . ." He raised his eyebrows and nodded knowingly.

"Frau Becker and Zelenka were, what? Having a sexual relationship?"

"Well, I don't know about *that*," said Sommer, taken aback by Rheinhardt's directness. "I don't know what went on!"

"Then what are you suggesting?"

"That their friendship was not . . . entirely innocent. The boys make jibes at one another. You overhear conversations in class, in the corridors. . . . And Herr Lang—"

"Herr Lang?"

"Look, Inspector, Lang's a decent enough fellow. I don't want to get him into trouble."

"We will treat everything you say confidentially."

"Thank you, thank you. . . . Herr Lang is the art master—he lives upstairs. Sometimes he comes down for a brandy and cigars. Naturally, we talk. . . . I am certain he knew that something was going on."

"What did he say?"

"That the boy had a crush on Frau Becker, that he had made some drawings of her, that they had spoken, and that the boy had said things . . . I don't know what. But, evidently, enough to make Lang suspicious."

"We spoke to Frau Becker about a week ago," said Rheinhardt, producing his notebook and flicking through the pages. "She said that Zelenka and boys like him—that is to say, boys from poor backgrounds—are often bullied and persecuted at Saint Florian's." Rheinhardt leaned forward. "Is that true?"

The muscles around Sommer's jaw relaxed and he smiled faintly. He seemed strangely relieved.

"Yes, that is true. The boys do terrible things to each other—quite terrible."

"What, exactly?"

"In the past, some boys have confided in me—spoken of their torment. Weapons have been used . . . knives, sabres."

"And who is responsible for performing these abominable acts?"

"There are ringleaders, of that I'm sure. But none of the boys I've spoken to would ever disclose their identities. They are simply too fearful."

"Do you know a boy called Wolf? Kiefer Wolf?"

"Yes—I do . . ."

"Is it possible that he is a ringleader?"

"Wolf, Wolf," Sommer repeated the name, and stroked his chin. "It wouldn't surprise me—he is a deeply unpleasant boy."

"And who else do you think might be involved?"

"Steininger, perhaps . . . and Freitag . . . and another boy called Drexler. I've often seen them together, smoking—just outside." Sommer gestured toward the window. "There's a plane tree they stand under."

"Herr Sommer, have you spoken to the headmaster about this?"

"Yes, I have. And Lang has too . . . but . . . This is confidential?"

"Indeed."

"Professor Eichmann has never been very concerned about such behavior. This may be because he thinks that bullying is inevitable and that there is little point in trying to stamp it out. However, I am also of the opinion that he believes bullying serves some educative function. Through bullying, the boys are prepared for the harsher realities of life. . . . It is not a view that I would subscribe to, but I know that there are many masters who would not disagree with Professor Eichmann."

"Who?"

"Osterhagen, Gärtner . . ."

Rheinhardt scribbled their names in his notebook.

"You won't tell them, will you?" said Sommer anxiously. "You won't tell them it was me who—"

"No," Rheinhardt cut in. "Rest assured, you have my word."

"Good," said Sommer, worrying a loose stud on the arm of his chair.

"Are you aware, Herr Sommer, that an anonymous article—extremely critical of Professor Eichmann—has been published in the *Arbeiter-Zeitung*?"

"No, no," said the mathematics master, shaking his head. "I wasn't aware. No."

Rheinhardt summarized Herr G.'s comments and allegations.

"Have you heard anything about this punishment, this so-called 'night watch'?"

"No . . . no, I can't say I have."

"What about the boy who died—Pikler? Do you know anything about him?"

"No, I'm afraid not. I wasn't teaching here then."

Rheinhardt looked up at Liebermann to see if he wished to ask a question. But the young doctor signaled that he was content to observe and listen.

"Do you recognize this?"

Rheinardt handed Sommer Zelenka's exercise book.

"Yes, of course."

"Then could you tell me the significance of these numbers?" Rheinhardt turned some pages. "You see . . . here, and here . . . these number pairs in the margin are in your hand."

"Ah yes," said Sommer, suddenly laughing. But his laugh was far too loud for someone whose eyes appeared so fearful. "Yes, they are a kind of game I used to play with Zelenka. A memory game. I would write some numbers down and he would try to remember them . . . and then *he* would write some numbers down, and I would try to remember them."

"But there are only a few numbers in most of the columns. Look here, for example: 2 24, 106 11, 34 48 . . . It would be no great feat of memory to remember these."

"I know—and I couldn't agree more." Sommer's protruding ears turned red. "It was quite ridiculous."

"Why did you arrange the numbers in pairs?"

"No reason, really. I happened to do so the first time and Zelenka copied thereafter. It became a convention. They are completely random. Just random numbers, that's all."

"And what was the purpose of this . . . this game?"

"Amusement."

"Amusement?" said Rheinhardt, incredulously.

"It amused Zelenka." Again Sommer laughed. "Ridiculous, I know."

Rheinhardt looked at Liebermann.

"Herr Doctor, would you like to ask Herr Sommer any questions?"

"No," said Liebermann.

"Are you *quite* sure?" said Rheinhardt.

"Yes," replied Liebermann. "Quite sure."

36

Wolf and Drexler were sitting on the roof of Saint Florian's, close to the upper stories of an old tower. The lower stories, still intact, were not visible. They were below the roof itself. The tower may once have been freestanding, or part of the old religious foundation that predated the school. But the capricious architecture of Saint Florian's—having an organic quality—had somehow absorbed this ancient edifice. It was now a redundant cylinder of stone that sank through three floors. No one had yet discovered a way of getting inside the tower. Walls closed it off. A doorway in the basement might have been the original entry point, but it too had been sealed off with enormous stone slabs.

Why would one do that? thought Drexler. *To keep people out? Or to keep something inside?*

On a parapet that circled the turret were three winged gargoyles—one of which, Drexler realized, bore a striking resemblance to Professor Gärtner.

"So," said Drexler, "what *are* you going to do?"

Wolf did not react.

"I'm intrigued," Drexler added. "I won't tell anyone." He stood up and pushed his cigarette into the gargoyle's mouth. "If there is a hell, I wonder if such things exist...."

"You should stop reading those stupid Hoffmann stories: you're becoming fanciful."

"Come on," said Drexler, ignoring Wolf's jibe. "What's this plan of yours?"

Wolf blew out two streams of smoke from his nostrils.

"I'm going to get a position at the Hofburg—and in due course join the emperor's personal guard."

"No . . . seriously, Wolf," Drexler said, pressing him.

"I *am* being serious."

Drexler leaned forward to inspect Wolf's face.

"Yes," Drexler said, more to himself than to his companion, "I think you are."

"My uncle is head of the security office," Wolf continued. "He's quite well connected—and can pull a few strings. It wasn't my idea originally. . . . It was my mother's."

Drexler laughed. "Your mother's!"

"Yes. She's overprotective." He permitted himself a crooked grin.

"The Hofburg, eh?" said Drexler. His expression suddenly changed. "But surely you'll need to get better examination results. You've hardly been applying yourself lately."

"I am quietly confident."

"The chances of you mastering trigonometry between now and the final examinations are—in my opinion—vanishingly small. If this is your great plan, Wolf, then I'm afraid I am singularly unimpressed."

"Remember that," said Wolf. "Remember what you just said. And when you're crouching behind a bush, cold, hungry, your boots covered in cow shit, trying to dodge the bullets of the next would-be king of the Carpathians, think of me. Yes, think of me, in my clean uniform with its razor-sharp creases, warm, well fed, accompanying the emperor to state openings and banquets, drinking champagne at the opera, and watching comedies at the Court Theater."

"You are deluding yourself, Wolf."

"Go to hell, Drexler."

"Well—to be frank, I think that's a lot more likely than you going to the Hofburg."

Wolf glanced at his watch. He flicked his cigarette into the air and stood. A powerful gust of wind made him stumble, and he steadied himself by touching the stone arc of a demon's wing.

"Drill," he said.

The two boys set off, climbing over the bizarre terrain: fallen chimneys, a scattering of tiles—and the ruin of a small observatory. Inside the little cabin, Drexler spotted the rusting remains of an antique orrery. He would take a closer look next time.

"Where are you going?" Wolf called as Drexler veered off.

"This way." Drexler gestured. "It's quicker."

"You can't get down that way."

"Yes, you can," said Drexler, indignant.

They came to an area where the surface on which they were walking was interrupted by a deep channel. Water had collected at the bottom. Wolf looked over the edge and saw the reflection of his head, silhouetted against the bilious sky. It was a long way down, and there was no way around. The channel stretched from one side of the roof to the other.

"See?" said Wolf. "I told you we shouldn't have come this way."

"What are you talking about?" said Drexler. "You just have to jump across. Some iron steps are attached to the side of the building—and they lead to a window. It's always open."

"Jump across? Don't be ridiculous. The gap's too wide."

"No, it isn't."

"You'll break your neck."

"I won't."

Drexler took a few steps backward and then ran toward the precipice. He glided through the air and a second later landed safely on the other side. "See? Easy. It's narrower than you think."

Wolf looked at Drexler, and then up at the octahedral spires of the Gothic façade.

"You're not scared, are you, Wolf?" Drexler called.

"Of course not."

Wolf ran—but just before leaping, he pulled up short.

"Come on, Wolf—it's easy."

"Your legs are longer than mine," said Wolf. "You have an unfair advantage."

"*Life's* unfair, Wolf! Now jump, will you?"

Another gust of wind destroyed Wolf's confidence completely.

"No. . . . I can't do it."

"Well, you'll have to go the long way down—and you'll be late."

Drexler raised his hand and loped off.

"Drexler," Wolf fumed.

"What?"

Wolf's anger suddenly subsided. "Make up an excuse for me."

Drexler nodded, found the top of the iron steps, and swung himself over the parapet.

37

Liebermann maintained a pensive silence as the carriage rattled down the hill toward Aufkirchen. He appeared to be wholly occupied by the patterns produced by runnels of rainwater on the window. Raising his hand, he allowed his forefinger to trace the length of a silvery braid that was being blown sideways across the glass.

"Well?" said Rheinhardt.

Liebermann started. "I'm sorry, Oskar. Did you say something?"

"Surely the rain cannot be so very interesting."

"Forgive me," said Liebermann, removing his hand from the glass. "I've been thinking."

"Indeed," said Rheinhardt. He made an interrogatory hand gesture, inviting Liebermann to elaborate.

A gust of wind buffeted the carriage, and the driver cursed loudly. Liebermann, ignoring the string of colorful expletives, made a steeple with his fingers and peered at his friend.

"I believe we can now be certain," he began slowly, "that Zelenka and Frau Becker were lovers."

Rheinhardt nodded. "I had not expected Sommer to be so candid."

"Although, to be frank," Liebermann continued, "with respect to this matter, I found your interview with Becker more revealing—and more compelling—than your interview with Sommer."

Rheinhardt tilted his head.

"But Becker didn't say anything about his wife's liaison with Zelenka!"

"You will recall," said Liebermann, "that he said his wife was compassionate and easily moved to sympathy. He then said that Zelenka had taken advantage of her kind nature. However, he hesitated for a fraction of a second in the middle of the sentence."

"What of it?"

"Well, it sounded like this: '*Zelenka took advantage of her*' . . . and then Becker added, almost as an afterthought . . . '*kind nature.*' Psychoanalysis teaches us that there is much to be learned from a careful study of the subtleties of speech. The truth was too much to hold back. He could not stop himself from telling us what he knew. Moreover, when you asked him why he hadn't mentioned Frau Becker's fondness for Zelenka before, he made a significant verbal blunder. He said: '*Why should I have? It's entirely relevant.*' Of course, what he meant to say was: '*Why should I have? It's entirely irrelevant.*' The more an individual tries to conceal something of importance, the more he betrays himself with such errors! Finally, did you notice that whenever he spoke of his wife, he kept on touching his wedding ring? He was like a patient suffering from an obsessional neurosis, checking to ensure that some valued possession has not been entirely lost."

"Most interesting," said Rheinhardt, twirling his mustache, "Most interesting; however, the principal purpose of our visit to Saint Florian's today was to interview Herr Sommer, a man who you, for reasons still unclear to me, have always insisted would shine some light on the mystery of Zelenka's death. Now, as far as I'm concerned, our investigation has not been furthered greatly. He has simply confirmed what was already suspected: that Zelenka and Frau Becker were having an illicit liaison, that boys like Wolf torment scholarship boys, and that the headmaster turns a blind eye to such behavior."

"I can assure you, Herr Sommer is . . ." Liebermann paused to select an appropriate word. "Involved."

"How do you mean, '*involved*'? I don't understand."

Liebermann tapped his fingers together. "Immediately after Sommer learned of Zelenka's death, he fell down some stairs and sprained his ankle—which gave him an ideal excuse to get away from Saint Florian's."

"But it was an accident, Max! And it must have been a genuine accident or he wouldn't have volunteered the name of his physician, Professor Baltish. We can easily check his story."

"No, Oskar. You misunderstand me. I am sure his sprain *is* real; however, as Professor Freud has explained, if one really examines the context of any accident, one can often see how it might have served some purpose. In other words, accidents are motivated. This motivation is, however, unconscious. The individual does not *plan* to have an accident. As far as he is concerned, it just happens."

"All right, then, what does Herr Sommer's stumble mean?"

"Well, quite obviously, that he did not want to be questioned about Zelenka. He wished to postpone questioning for as long as possible—and he stood to benefit in two ways. First, the police investigation might have been closed before his return, thus he would have succeeded in avoiding questioning altogether. Second, if the police investigation was still in progress on the date of his return, he would have had sufficient time to collect himself and would be better prepared. Of course, it was always possible that you would travel to Linz in order to interview him—but even if you had, he would still have secured himself a period of respite. The fact that he needed time to think things through suggests the existence of a complex situation in which many factors needed to be taken into consideration. I had always suspected Herr Sommer's *involvement*—from the moment you mentioned his accident; however, my suspicions were confirmed beyond doubt when he arrived an hour late. Again, his error speaks volumes. He did not want to be interviewed. He was still attempting to avoid you. And the question you must ask yourself, Oskar, is: why?"

Rheinhardt frowned. "What are you suggesting, Max? That Sommer killed Zelenka?"

"Zelenka died of natural causes."

Rheinhardt rolled his eyes. "According to Professor Mathias, but you have already admitted that the more we probe the world of Saint Florian's, the more we discover conditions and circumstances ordinarily associated with murder."

Liebermann stared at his hands, and continued to tap his fingers together. "He was lying about the article in the *Arbeiter-Zeitung*."

"What?" said Rheinhardt.

"You asked him if he was aware of the article, and he replied: '*No, no . . . I wasn't aware . . . no.*' He denied knowledge of the article four times. A perfect example of overcompensation."

"But people often repeat things."

"Not four times, Oskar," said Liebermann. He paused, and then mischievously drove his point home with a repetition: "Not four times."

"Why on earth would he lie about that?"

"Consistency. I think it highly unlikely that Professor Baltish's sanatorium takes a socialist daily . . . and needless to say, Sommer also lied about the numbers in Zelenka's textbook."

"Did he?"

"Oh yes. Did you see how red his ears went?"

"I attributed that to embarrassment."

"No. His laughter was completely false, and he was far too eager to stress that the numbers were random. His story about the memory game was complete nonsense—although, on reflection, I imagine it was probably the best bogus explanation that he, or anybody else, might fabricate."

"So," said Rheinhardt, his face becoming lined with intense concentration. "What have we surmised? First, Zelenka and Frau Becker were having a sexual liaison. Second, Sommer did not want to be interviewed after Zelenka's death, and third, he is a liar—his most notable lie being that the numbers in Zelenka's exercise book represent nothing more than a silly game. . . . What if . . ." The creases on Rheinhardt's face deepened. "What if Sommer learned of Zelenka's affair with Frau Becker, and conspired with Zelenka to blackmail her? He is clearly not a man of means. Their activities might have necessitated coded communications."

Liebermann frowned, crossed his legs, and brushed a fold from his trousers. He was clearly unimpressed.

"Becker knew that Zelenka was 'taking advantage' of his wife. Therefore, his relationship with the boy must have been strained, difficult . . . and yet there is nothing to suggest that this was the case. In fact, Zelenka appears to have been something of a teacher's pet . . . sucking up to his science master and requesting extra assignments, which Becker was happy to provide."

Rheinhardt suddenly remembered how Liebermann had behaved when Becker had left the room.

"Oh yes. Why did you taste Becker's medicine?"

"I wanted to know what it was."

"And did you recognize it?"

"Yes, I think so—although it was an unusual prescription for headaches."

Liebermann smiled faintly, and turned his face to the window, resuming his inspection of the runnels of rainwater. Rheinhardt, accustomed to his friend's irritating penchant for mystification, managed some halfhearted tutting to communicate his annoyance.

"It is all utterly infuriating," said Liebermann. "Clearly, there is something going on at Saint Florian's . . . but it is almost impossible to ascertain what! I am reminded of the frustrating phenomenon of being unable to recall a familiar name. The name hovers at the periphery of awareness, and the more you try to remember it, the more it seems to evade recollection. Perhaps we should stop thinking about this right now—or Becker won't be the only one with a headache!"

38

THE SPECIAL TUTORIAL GROUP met in Professor Gärtner's rooms. On account of his age and seniority he occupied an entire lodge. It was his custom to spoil his favored pupils, and an impressive selection of pastries had been laid out on the table, ready for consumption when the tutorial was over: cheese and apple strudels, made especially for the professor by the school chef, and an artistically arranged spiral of *ischler gebäck*—fruit-conserve biscuits drizzled with chocolate.

The prospective feast was something of a distraction for most of the boys, who were gathered in a semicircle around their mentor. They stole quick glances at the spread, and their stomachs grumbled in anticipation.

Wolf, however, wasn't in the least troubled by the strudels and the sugary fragrances that sweetened the air. He had been transported by the strange declamatory prose that Professor Gärtner had been reading aloud from a slim cloth-bound volume. Even though the old man's voice was dry and wheezy, the text vibrated in Wolf's memory. Each word possessed a gonglike, resonance.

I teach you the Übermensch . . . the superman . . .
What is the ape to men? A laughing stock or a painful embarrassment.
And just so shall man be to the superman . . .

Where is the lightning to lick you with his tongue? Where is the madness with which you should be cleansed?
Behold, I teach you the superman: he is the lightning, he is the madness . . .

Gärtner sat in a high-backed leather chair. He was wearing his academic gown, and his short silver hair glittered in the lamplight. When he had finished his reading, he began a lengthy exegesis.

"What we *are* must be overcome. Man, as he is, must be destroyed. We must become something more than human . . . *Homo superior.* The philosopher is quite clear as to how this transition can be achieved. Man becomes *Übermensch* by his *will to power*—by abandoning old doctrines and replacing them with new ones, by rejecting societal ideals and so-called morality, by a continual process of overcoming arbitrary self-limitations. . . . The philosopher challenges us, throws down the gauntlet: *Can you furnish yourself with your own good and evil, he asks, and hang up your own will above yourself as a law? Can you be judge of yourself and avenger of your law?*"

The old man raised his head and looked around the room. Some of the boys shifted uncomfortably as his interrogative gaze made them painfully aware that they were not really listening. Wolf, however, leaned forward. He felt excited, but did not really understand why. The professor's gaze locked with his. Wolf was not unnerved by Gärtner's scrutiny: on the contrary, he welcomed it. The boy nodded his head.

Yes, he said silently to himself. *I can be judge of myself—and avenger of my law.*

Professor Gärtner smiled at his most enthusiastic student.

39

LIEBERMANN WAS SITTING OUTSIDE Csarda—the Hungarian restaurant where Trezska had suggested that they should meet. Although the sky was overcast, it was not a particularly cold day. The table was well positioned and offered a clear view of the tree-lined boulevard along which crowds of people—from all walks of life— were making their way toward the amusements, beer-houses, concert hall, and theaters. A Carpathian peasant, wearing a white fur cap, was wandering somewhat aimlessly in front of the restaurant, obviously overwhelmed by the festival atmosphere of the Prater.

When Trezska arrived, Liebermann stood to greet her, bowed, and kissed her hand. Stepping back, he smiled, showing his admiration with tacit but unmistakable pleasure. She was wearing a maroon jacket, cut to accentuate the slimness of her waist. The garment was decorated with black braid and was slightly reminiscent of a soldier's tunic. The folded-back cuffs were threaded with silver. Her gray skirt—which clung tightly to the curve of her hips—was woven with a muted blue check. She had pinned her hair up, and her hat sprouted a plume of exotic feathers. On the lapel of her jacket was the same brooch that she had worn for her concert: a crescent of diamonds. Close up, the glittering stones looked large and very expensive: *More expensive*, thought Liebermann, *than a budding concert violinist should be able to afford.* As soon as this thought had formed, it was followed by a second: *A gift from an admirer, perhaps?*

Ordinarily, Liebermann was not a jealous person but the experience of discovering Miss Lydgate in the arms of her lover had affected him deeply. He had become mistrustful, suspicious. At once, the young doctor was disappointed with himself, annoyed that he had already inferred the existence of a shadowy competitor!

"Is anything wrong?" asked Trezska.

Liebermann was astonished. He had not, as far he was aware, betrayed his inner feelings with a frown.

"No, nothing's wrong." Anxious to conceal his embarrassment, he risked a bold compliment. "You look wonderful."

Trezska did not demur, but returned his smile.

Liebermann was relieved to find that their conversation flowed more naturally than he'd expected. He had judged that she might be, by nature, quite reserved—aloof, even; in fact, he was quite wrong. She was warm, friendly, and quick to laugh. He asked her if she had been to the Prater before, and she replied that she had—but only to eat at Csarda. She was not familiar with the amusements. Liebermann suggested that they should visit the Kaisergarten—to which she again responded with unexpected enthusiasm. From Liebermann's experience, beautiful, fashionably dressed women often allowed their hauteur to harden into a brittle carapace. Trezska's excitement was endearing.

They inspected the menu, and while they did so Trezska extolled the virtues of the head chef. She insisted that Liebermann try his *gulyás*.

"They do it correctly here . . . a traditional recipe, not like the heavy goulashes you might be used to. *Gulyás* was originally a shepherds' dish—the midday meal. It shouldn't be too rich."

As on all Hungarian tables, there were three rather than two condiment shakers: one for salt, one for pepper, and a third for paprika. When the *gulyás* arrived, Liebermann was given a soup, instead of a stew, and at the bottom of his bowl he found large tender chunks of mutton. Trezska offered Liebermann the paprika shaker, which he declined—his *gulyás* having already been seasoned quite enough for his taste.

"Well, what do you think?" asked Trezska.

"Good—very good," he replied. The *gulyás* was just as Trezska had described: wholesome rustic fare, but fragrant with tangy herbs and spices.

From inside the restaurant, a small band consisting of a cimbalom player and two violinists began a mournful waltz. Swooping glissandi and complicated embellishments suggested a Gypsy origin. It caught Liebermann's attention.

"An old folk song," said Trezska, "*Dark Eyes.* It's all about a young hussar who is rejected and throws himself into the Tisza."

A capricious smile played around her lips.

Their conversation turned to more serious music. They discussed the Bach violin and keyboard sonatas, Marie Soldat-Röger's interpretation of the Brahms D-major concerto, a new Russian opera, and the distinctive tone of pianos made in Vienna. After which, Liebermann encouraged his companion to talk about her own musical accomplishments. Trezska had only just begun to build a reputation as a solo artist in Budapest, having spent two years studying in Rome and Paris; however, she had won several scholarships, a competition in Prague, and had even played at a private function in Berlin for her celebrated countryman, the virtuoso Joseph Joachim.

"Do you have any more concerts planned? In Vienna?"

"No, sadly not: next year, perhaps."

"Oh," said Liebermann. "Then, how long will you be staying?" he added hopefully.

"In Vienna? Another month or so. My old violin professor has arranged for me to take some lessons with Arnold Rosé."

Liebermann repeated the name. He was most impressed. Rosé was the concertmaster of the philharmonic.

"What pieces will you be studying with Rosé?"

"Beethoven's spring sonata—and Mozart's E minor."

"I am familiar with the spring sonata, of course, but I'm not sure that I've ever heard the E minor."

"Not a great work, by any means. But it is one for which I have a particular affection. It is the only violin sonata that Mozart wrote in a minor key." Her black eyes flashed at Liebermann. "There! You see? It must be true what they say about Hungarian melancholy."

The *gulyás* was followed by coffee and two enormous slices of *dobostorte*: each wedge was comprised of seven alternating layers of sponge and chocolate cream. The *dobostorte*—named after its creator József Dobos—had become, in just over ten years, the first world-famous Hungarian dessert. *And deservedly so*, thought Liebermann. The chocolate cream was dense, buttery, and exquisitely rich.

After discreetly paying the bill, Liebermann offered Trezska his arm, and they set off in the direction of the amusements. As they got closer, they were absorbed into a bustling, noisy crowd. The air was filled with the babble of several languages: German, Hungarian, Slavic, and even occasional snatches of Arabic. On either side, marquees and little huts began to appear. Fortune-tellers, sausage vendors, a troupe of acrobatic dwarves, strong men, and belly dancers were all plying their trade. The most bizarre attraction was an "electrocution extravaganza"—where a long line of venturesome young men were awaiting their turn to be galvanized.

"Where are we going?" asked Trezska.

"Venice."

Trezska threw Liebermann a puzzled look, but the young doctor simply smiled—as if to say, *You'll see.*

They continued walking until they came to a wide concourse that was dominated by a massive double arch. Capital letters running across the top read: VENEDIG IN WIEN—*Venice in Vienna.* The structure was decorated with ornate moldings, at the center of which was a bas-relief of a winged lion, the symbol of Saint Mark. Two giant planets hovered above the columns at either extremity.

"What on earth?" Trezska's pace slowed.

"A re-creation of Venice," said Liebermann, tracing an arc in the air with his hand. "Here, in Vienna."

"What . . . you've reconstructed the whole of Venice, in one of your parks?"

"Well, not exactly . . . but something very close to it."

Trezska's expression communicated a mixture of amusement and surprise at this astounding demonstration of Viennese hubris.

"Extraordinary," she whispered.

They passed beneath one of the arches and were immediately transported to northern Italy. Renaissance villas overlooked a piazza, on which ladies and gentlemen were milling around—smoking, talking, and sipping champagne—as if they were attending a society function.

"Come on!" Liebermann tugged Trezska's arm. "This way."

They crossed the square, ascended a broad stone staircase, and came to a canal on which black lacquered gondolas were sedately moving in opposite directions.

Trezska leaned over the balustrade and burst out laughing. "Ridiculous."

"Let's get one. There's no better way to see Venice."

Only a short distance away, several empty gondolas were tied to colorful mooring poles. Liebermann hired the services of a gondolier and helped Trezska into the boat. Once she was seated, he said "Just one moment," dashed over to a champagne pavilion, and returned, slightly breathless, carrying a bottle of Moët and two glasses.

The gondolier cast off and guided his vessel through a network of canals. They glided beneath bridges, past grand palazzos and theaters, past old churches, and through gardens of exotic trees. In due course, the illusion overcame Trezska's resistance. She sipped her champagne, suspended disbelief, and succumbed to the romance of the world's most magical city.

Sensitive to the demands of the situation, the gondolier sought out a small, secluded pool, overlooked by a façade whose design recalled the Doge's Palace. The door of a little café opened directly onto the water, and from inside came the jangling of mandolins. The gondolier moored his vessel and, catching Liebermann's eye, winked and vanished into the café.

Immediately, the young doctor and his companion drew closer together. They lowered their voices, and began to speak more intimately. Liebermann told Trezska about his family: his garrulous mother, his disapproving father, his two delightful sisters. He told her about the district where he had grown up, the schools he had attended, and his time at the university. He told her about the cities he had visited and about his fondness for English literature and London. And after a short hiatus, during which they both listened to the delicate, persistent thrumming of the mandolins, Trezska reciprocated. She told Liebermann about her father, who had also been a violinist— but who had died when she'd been very young. She told him about her mother, whose aristocratic family had disowned her when she had married below her station. And she told him about her life in Budapest: of Castle Hill, shrouded in autumn mists, the scent of violets in the spring, and the magnificent, ruthless winters, which froze the Danube, making it possible to walk from Pest to Buda.

The gondolier reappeared, and soon they were off again, drifting through the gently lapping waters. On the floor, the empty bottle of champagne lay on its side, rolling with the gentle movement of the boat. Liebermann leaned back, and felt Trezska's head resting on his shoulder. An easy silence ensued, one that did not require filling. Above Liebermann's head, the strip of sky between the roofs was becoming darker.

When the gondola reached the landing from which they had begun their odyssey, Liebermann helped Trezska out with one hand while tipping the gondolier with the other.

"The champagne has made me feel sleepy," said Trezska. "Shall we go for a walk?"

"If you like."

"Away from all these people . . ."

"Yes, of course."

Liebermann led Trezska out of the make-believe world of Venedig in Wien and off toward the Freudenau. They strolled down the Haupt Allee, talking with less urgency—increasingly more at ease. As they progressed, Liebermann became conscious of a sudden plunge in temperature. It was getting windy, and a few drops of rain had begun to fall.

"Quick," said Liebermann, "let's shelter under there."

A large solitary plane tree was close by, and they dashed to take cover beneath its canopy of tangled branches. The patter of rain became louder, and the Prater was bathed in an eldritch luminescence.

A subtle flickering illuminated the clouds, and a low rumbling followed. Then, quite suddenly, there was a bright white flash, a tremendous clap of thunder, and the skies opened, releasing a torrential downpour.

Liebermann noticed that Trezska looked agitated. Her eyes were wide open and she had begun to pace.

"It's all right," said Liebermann. "It'll soon stop."

His solicitous remark had no effect. She continued to appear uneasy. Liebermann wondered whether she was pathologically frightened of thunderstorms. But the sky had been getting more overcast throughout the day, and she had showed no obvious signs of distress. He dismissed the thought: a brontophobic would have been anxious to get inside hours ago.

"What's the matter?" Liebermann asked.

Trezska attempted a smile, but failed miserably.

"I . . ." She hesitated and lowered her eyes. "I don't like it here."

"Well," said Liebermann, puzzled. "The rain *will* stop—and then we can leave."

"No. I think . . . I think we should go now."

"But we'll get soaked."

"It's only rain. Come, let's go." Trezska looked at the sky and pouted.

"Are you afraid?"

She paused for a moment, and then said: "Yes."

"But it's just—" There was another flash and a boom so loud that the ground shook. "A storm."

"Come," she said. "I'm sorry. We can't stay here."

"But why not?"

"We just can't!" A note of desperation had entered Trezska's voice. While Liebermann was still trying to think of something to say, she added, "I'm going." And with that she marched out into the violent weather.

Stunned, Liebermann watched her, as she held her hat in place while striding determinedly back toward the amusements. Then, realizing that he was not being very gentlemanly, he ran after her.

"Trezska?"

When he caught up with her, he removed his coat and draped it over her shoulders. She did not slow down to make his task any easier.

"We must get away. Now hurry."

They maintained their pace, walking briskly into sheets of cold rain. Liebermann's clothes were soon drenched, his hair was plastered to his scalp, and a continuous flow of water streamed down the back of his neck.

Whatever is the matter with her? thought Liebermann.

There was another flash, but much brighter than its predecessors. The grass seemed to leap up, each blade sharp and distinct in the dazzling coruscation. The rain looked momentarily frozen, becoming rods of crystal suspended in the air, and a fraction of a second later there was an explosion—a great ripping, accompanied by a shower of bark and smoldering splinters. Liebermann swung around and saw flames licking the trunk of the scorched plane tree. They had been standing exactly where the bolt had struck. If they had not moved, they would have been killed.

40

Commissioner Manfred Brügel looked troubled. In his hands he held a letter.

"Well, Rheinhardt, this is all very difficult—very difficult indeed. But let me assure you, I would have wanted to talk to you had I received a complaint from *any* of the Saint Florian pupils. The fact that I am related to Kiefer Wolf is really of little consequence. You understand that, don't you?"

"Yes, sir."

The commissioner was visibly disturbed by the transparency of his own deceit. He coughed into his hand, mumbled something about professionalism, and then concluded his introductory remarks by repeating the word "good" three times.

Rheinhardt was accustomed to feeling a sense of foreboding whenever he entered the commissioner's office. But on this occasion the presentiment of impending doom was fearfully oppressive.

"Now, according to my nephew," said Brügel, "you went to Saint Florian's on Thursday the twenty-ninth of January in order to conduct some interviews. Is that right?"

"Yes, sir."

"You interviewed my nephew—and several other boys."

"Yes, sir."

"Whom I presume you had previously identified as suspects?"

Rheinhardt crossed his legs and shifted uncomfortably. He could see where this line of questioning might lead and sought to divert the conversation elsewhere.

"Prior to interviewing the boys, I had spoken to Professor Eichmann, the headmaster, about the *Arbeiter-Zeitung* article and—"

Brügel waved his hand in the air. "Yes, yes—we can discuss Eichmann later." He glanced down at the letter and continued, "The boys you interviewed—they were suspects?"

"Well, only in a manner of speaking. . . . They were boys who I thought might be able to tell us more about the bullying at Saint Florian's. If the *Arbeiter-Zeitung* article—"

Again, Brügel cut in: "And how did you identify these . . . these *suspects*?"

"With the help of Herr Dr. Liebermann."

The commissioner snorted. "And how did Dr. Liebermann identify them?"

"He used a psychological technique to probe the mind of Isidor Perger, the boy who wrote those letters to Thomas Zelenka."

"And what was this psychological technique?"

Rheinhardt grimaced. "He showed Perger"—Rheinhardt's expression became more pained—"inkblots . . . and asked the boy what he saw in them."

"Inkblots."

"Yes, sir."

"And by inkblots, you mean . . . ?"

"Blots of ink . . . on paper, sir. I am sure Dr. Liebermann would be willing to explain how the procedure works."

"That won't be necessary, Rheinhardt."

The commissioner took a deep breath and was evidently struggling to contain himself. A raised vessel appeared on his temple, in which Rheinhardt detected the pulse of Brügel's fast-beating and furious heart.

"And is it true," said the commissioner, in an uncharacteristically controlled voice, "that you accused my nephew of torturing Thomas Zelenka?"

For a brief moment, Rheinhardt found himself wondering whether it was not *such* a bad idea, at this juncture, to simulate a fainting fit. He could very easily relax his muscles and allow his ample frame to slide off the chair, after which he would be lifted onto a stretcher and conveyed to the infirmary, where he might rest, sleep perhaps, even dream of walking holidays in the Tyrol. On further reflection, he decided that he had better get the ordeal over with.

"Sir," he said resolutely, "you will appreciate, I am sure, how a direct accusation will sometimes unnerve a suspect. That forceful assertions can even produce a confess—"

"It's true, then," Brügel interrupted.

"Yes," Rheinhardt sighed. "Yes, it is true."

"And on what evidence did you base this accusation?" asked Brügel.

Policeman's intuition, thought Rheinhardt. *Your nephew's crooked smile.*

Rheinhardt shook his head and murmured something that barely qualified as language.

"I beg your pardon?" asked Brügel.

"Nothing . . . nothing very firm, sir."

The commissioner folded the letter and placed it in a drawer. He then leaned across his desk and began to lecture Rheinhardt on one of his favorite topics: the importance of maintaining standards. Gradually, Brügel's voice took on a hectoring tone, and in a very short space of time he was thumping the desk with his fists and reprimanding Rheinhardt for running a shoddy, incompetent investigation. His anger, which he had succeeded in suppressing for so long, now boiled over. The commissioner roared and spat out his invective with apoplectic rage.

As Rheinhardt listened to this tirade, he experienced it not intellectually, or even emotionally, but physically. It was like being bludgeoned with a heavy club. The irony of his situation did not escape him. He was being bullied. Bizarrely, he too had become one of Wolf's victims.

When the commissioner was spent, he leaned back in his chair, breathing heavily. His face had turned red, and some foamy spittle had collected in his muttonchop whiskers.

"Please accept my apology, sir," said Rheinhardt.

The commissioner grunted and granted the disgraced inspector permission to leave.

When he reached the door, Brügel called out:

"Rheinhardt."

"Sir?"

The commissoner was suddenly changed. He looked smaller: older, wearier, and perplexed. It was an extraordinary transformation.

"He's my youngest sister's boy," said Brügel. "Her only child. He's no angel, but he would not . . . No, you are quite wrong. And consider yourself lucky. This will go no further. I'll see to that."

Had Liebermann been present, he would have had much to say about the commissioner's sudden transformation, and his curious, incoherent adieu. But Rheinhardt was in no fit state to consider such things. Eager to leave, he bowed, clicked his heels, and left the commissioner's office like a man escaping a fire.

41

Isidor Perger was sitting on a stool, flanked by Steininger and Freitag. In front of him stood Wolf. The blond boy drew his sabre and held it up close to Perger's face.

"Well," he said. "What do you see?"

Perger shrugged. "Nothing. . . . Your sabre, Wolf."

"Are you blind, Perger?" asked Steininger.

"No,"

"Then why can't you see it?"

"See w-what? I can't see anything."

"I'll hold it closer," said Wolf, thrusting the blade forward. Perger flinched. "Does that help?" Wolf added.

"I . . . I can only see the b-blade . . . the b-blade of your sabre."

"Now," said Wolf, "for the last time: I want you to take a long, hard look—and tell me what you see."

Wolf tilted his sabre so that it caught the yellow flame of the paraffin lamp. A scintilla of light traveled around its sharp, curved edge.

Perger squinted. "Yes, there's . . . s-s-something on the blade. A speck of something."

"Good," said Wolf. "And what do you think that might be?"

"R-rust?"

Wolf sheathed his sabre and began to clap. He brought his hands together with slow, exaggerated movements.

"Very good, Perger," interjected Freitag, unable to conceal his mirth.

"Yes, very good indeed," Steininger repeated.

"What a pity, then," continued Wolf, "that this should have eluded your attention."

Steininger and Freitag shook their heads and tutted.

"You should have put more into it," said Steininger.

"More elbow grease," said Freitag, frowning and miming the oscillating action of polishing a sword. Then, unable to resist a cheap joke, he allowed his arm to drop, re-creating the movement in front of his crotch.

Steininger began to guffaw, but Wolf silenced him with his glazed, humorless stare.

"I'm afraid, Perger," said Wolf, "that you *must* be punished. However, I am not sure yet what form this punishment should take. Now, even as I speak, I notice that my boots could do with a good clean. Would you be willing to clean my boots, Perger?"

"Yes, Wolf."

"Would you be happy to lick them clean?"

"Yes, Wolf."

"Including the soles? Although I feel obliged to tell you that I went to the stables today and stupidly trod in some manure."

"Y-yes, Wolf."

"My boots could do with a clean, too," said Freitag.

"And mine," said Steininger.

"Well," continued Wolf. "How about that, Perger? Would you be willing to lick Freitag's and Steininger's boots too?"

"Yes, Wolf."

"And you see," said Wolf, assuming a fatigued expression, "in agreeing so readily, you demonstrate the inadequacy of the punishment. It simply isn't enough. A fellow like you needs more! Something that will leave a lasting impression, something that will remind you to perform your duties more diligently in the future . . . something that has a reasonable chance of countering your extraordinary laziness!"

Wolf produced a revolver from his pocket. He released the cylindrical block and showed Perger that one of the six chambers contained a cartridge. Then, swinging the cylinder back into alignment, he spun it until it halted with a click. He cocked the hammer with his thumb.

"Here," said Wolf, offering the gun to Perger. "Take it."

The boy took the weapon in his shaking hands.

"Put the barrel in your mouth and pull the trigger. The odds are very much in your favor."

"No, Wolf. . . . I c-c-can't."

"Ah, but you c-can, and you w-will!" said Wolf.

Perger's eyes brimmed, and tears began to roll down his cheeks.

"Don't be pathetic, Perger!" Wolf shouted. "Put the barrel in your mouth and pull the trigger. Now!"

Perger raised the gun, but its ascent was slow—as if it had become too heavy to lift. Indeed, Perger's entire body seemed to have become weak and floppy. He began to sway, and his eyelids flickered. Freitag and Steininger gripped his tunic and held him upright.

"Don't swoon like a woman, you—you . . . you Galician whore's son!" He grabbed Perger's wrist and pulled it up, shoving the gun barrel between the boy's lips. Then, covering Perger's hand with his own, he applied a minute amount of pressure to the distraught boy's trigger finger.

"Here, let me help. Come on, Perger, be brave. I'm not going to do it for you."

Perger emitted a strange keening.

Suddenly there was a creaking sound, followed by the thud of feet landing on the floorboards and the *whump* of the trapdoor closing. A few moments later Drexler appeared.

"What's going on?" he asked.

"Perger's playing Russian roulette," Wolf replied.

"Yes," said Steininger. "He's unhappy at Saint Florian's—and has decided to end it all. He's not the first."

"And he won't be the last," said Freitag.

"A tragic waste," said Steininger.

Drexler walked over to Perger and eased the revolver out of his mouth. Perger's hand slowly descended to his lap. He rested the gun on his thigh and bowed his head.

"What on earth do you think you're doing, Drexler!" Wolf shouted.

The other boy didn't reply. He simply shook his head and bit his lower lip.

"Look, Drexler," Wolf continued, "I don't know what's got into you lately, but my patience is running out. You're always spoiling things. And if you carry on like this, well, I am obliged to say—you won't be welcome here for very much longer."

Wolf threw a glance—a silent appeal—in the direction of Steininger and Freitag.

"Yes, Drexler," said Steininger. "This is our place . . . and if you're not going to join in . . ."

"You should stay away," said Freitag.

Drexler ignored the two lieutenants and took a step closer to Wolf.

"Let him go, Wolf. Look at him." He gestured toward the hunched, crumpled figure on the stool. "This is pathetic."

"What did you say?"

"I said, this is pathetic!" It was now Drexler's turn to include Steininger and Freitag. "Can't you see, you two? It's all getting out of hand. These stupid games—"

"You've lost your nerve, Drexler," Wolf cut in. "Go on—admit it."

"It doesn't take very much nerve to pick on Perger!"

"More nerve than you have—evidently."

"It's cowardly, Wolf!"

"What?"

"You heard."

"How dare you call me a coward! How dare you!"

Wolf snatched the revolver from Perger's loose grip and pointed it toward Drexler.

"Go on, then—shoot," said Drexler.

"You think it's a blank cartridge. Don't you?"

Once again, the intensity of Wolf's gaze surprised Drexler, and he was unsettled by a tremor of doubt.

"I'm a coward, am I?" Wolf continued.

Unexpectedly, he released the cylinder, spun it, and cocked the hammer. Then he pressed the barrel against his own temple and grinned: a maniacal rictus.

Behold, I teach you the Übermensch.

The Übermensch balks at nothing. . . . The Übermensch has no fear. . . .

"Wolf?" said Freitag. He could not conceal his anxiety.

Wolf pulled the trigger. A dead click.

"Who's the coward now? Eh, Drexler?" He said, handing over the revolver.

Drexler examined the weapon. His mouth went dry and he became aware of an ethereal whistling in his head. Steininger and Freitag were looking at him—their expressions showed intense concentration rather than their usual brutish insouciance. Drexler gripped the end of the barrel between his teeth and squeezed the trigger.

Another dead click. The whistling stopped.

Without hesitation, Wolf took the weapon back, prepared it for firing, and pointed the muzzle between his own eyes. He was still grinning his deranged grin, but this time his hand was shaking. A film of sweat had appeared on his brow. When his finger finally closed on the trigger and the silence was broken only by the hammer's fall on another empty chamber, he burst out laughing and threw the gun at Drexler. The other boy snatched it out of the air.

"Only three left, Drexler," Wolf said. "Your turn."

Drexler looked at the gun, and then at Wolf. He cocked the hammer. The distance that he usually interposed between himself and the world had suddenly vanished. Reality stormed the ramparts of his senses, and he became acutely aware of the minutiae of existence: the systolic and diastolic components of his pulse, the expansion and contraction of his lungs, the passage of air in his nostrils, the taste of metal in his mouth, and the lost room, with its familiar contents—the suitcase, the wicker chair (and the permanent fragrance of tobacco, fear, and erotic discharge)—this haven of shabby delights—every part of it acquired a vivid immediacy. He was alive and he did not want to die.

"This is absurd," said Drexler. He lifted the revolver and looked into the end of its barrel. Its circularity suggested eternity, and its blackness oblivion. There were other things he could be doing at this moment in time: making love to Snjezana, reading Hoffmann, or simply smoking on the grounds and watching the moon rise. He shook his head.

"Oh, you're all insane," he said contemptuously, tossing the revolver aside. It landed a few feet away. There was a loud report, a bright flash, and a hazy cloud of gunpowder smoke rose up like a spectral apparition.

"My God," said Steininger.

"It . . . it was live!" gasped Freitag.

In their state of shock, the two lieutenants had loosened their grip on Perger's tunic. The prisoner fell forward and sprawled facedown on the floor.

"Get up, Perger," said Wolf.

The boy did not reply.

Wolf nudged him with his foot. The body was inert.

"Get up, Perger," Wolf repeated.

Drexler fell to his knees and rolled the body over.

"Oh no . . . God, *no*." A dark stain had appeared on Perger's tunic.

Silence.

"What shall we do, Wolf?" said Freitag softly.

Steininger took a step back. The color had drained from his face. He was fearful, dismayed.

"Perger?" said Drexler, pushing at the body. "Perger? Can you hear me?"

There was no response. The dark stain was expanding—an almost perfect circle, close to Perger's heart.

"Christ," said Steininger. "He's dead."

"No," said Freitag. "He can't be . . ."

Drexler grasped the fallen boy's hand. "Come on, Perger, wake up!"

"It's no good, Drexler," whispered Wolf. "You've killed him."

"Me?"

"Yes, you! It was *you* who had the gun last."

"But it wasn't my . . . ," cried Drexler, incoherent with desperation. "I didn't . . . I . . ."

"Wolf's right, Drexler," said Steininger. "It *was* you who had the gun last."

"Yes," Freitag agreed. "If you hadn't thrown the gun, Perger would still be alive."

42

Inspector Rheinhardt had copied the number pairs from Zelenka's exercise books onto a single sheet of paper, which he now handed to Amelia Lydgate. The Englishwoman fell silent, and simply stared at the figures. Time passed. She was obviously attempting to decipher them, and Rheinhardt was reluctant to disturb her. He glanced across the room at Haussmann and raised a finger to his lips.

Eventually Amelia looked up.

"Are you absolutely sure that these numbers represent coded messages, Inspector?"

"Well, not absolutely. . . . However, it was Dr. Liebermann's opinion that Herr Sommer did not tell us the truth when he said that these numbers were a memory test, and I am inclined to agree. The commitment of random number pairs to memory is surely an activity from which both pupil and master would derive very limited pleasure. And such an activity would be unlikely to keep them amused over a period of several months. Therefore, if the numbers are not a memory test, then they must be some kind of code."

A vertical crease appeared on Amelia's brow.

"My father—also a schoolmaster—insisted that I learn the value of the mathematical constant pi to fifty decimal places. Successful recitations were the source of considerable pleasure and amusement to both of us. Indeed, my father could barely stop himself from joining in when I reached the final ten digits: six, nine, three, nine, nine, three, seven, five, one, zero. *There!* I can still recall the sequence quite clearly. For those who enjoy mathematics, numbers can be a very satisfying entertainment; however, it is undoubtedly the case that for the nonnumerical such pleasures are as recondite as music is to the tone-deaf."

Rheinhardt did not know how to respond. He glanced at Haussmann, tacitly requesting assistance, only to discover that the young scoundrel was biting his lower lip and that his shoulders were shaking with suppressed laughter.

"Indeed," said Rheinhardt. "Indeed . . ." He twisted the waxed horns of his mustache and said: "Am I to take it, then, that you do not share our view?"

"I am not taking issue with your conclusion, Inspector—merely the reasoning that you employed to reach that conclusion."

"Ah," said Rheinhardt, more encouraged. "Then you accept that the numbers might be a code?"

"Yes," she said, a little hesitantly. "But if they are, the code is not conventional. That much I can determine already."

"I see."

"May I take this with me?" She raised the paper in her gloved hand.

"Yes, of course."

"I will give it careful consideration."

"Once again," said the inspector, "I am much indebted."

Amelia rose, and Rheinhardt kissed her hand.

"How is Dr. Liebermann?" she asked.

"Well."

Unusually for her, the Englishwoman looked a little flustered.

"I have not had the pleasure of his company of late, although the fault is entirely mine. I have been somewhat preoccupied with . . .

matters . . . various matters." Amelia fumbled with her reticule and then added: "Would you be so kind as to convey my best wishes to the good doctor?"

"Consider it done, Miss Lydgate."

"Thank you, Inspector—you are most kind."

"Haussmann," Rheinhardt addressed his assistant. "Please escort Miss Lydgate out of the building and hail her a cab."

"That really won't be necessary," said Amelia. "I am perfectly capable of finding my way out of the security office. Good afternoon, gentlemen."

She looked blankly at the two men, and left the room.

Rheinhardt raised his finger and silently shook it at Haussmann.

The young man blushed, and in an effort to excuse himself whispered: "I'm sorry, sir, but her manner is so peculiar."

The inspector was unable to disagree.

43

TREZSKA STOOD BESIDE LIEBERMANN'S PIANO. Their gazes met—and, simultaneously, they began to play. The opening violin melody was fluid and generous—an outpouring of enchanting sweetness. Although the subtitle "Spring" was added to Beethoven's F-major sonata after his death, it was extraordinarily appropriate, capturing completely the mood of the work. The music was bright and blooming—fresh, bursting with vital energy—but there were depths implied by the poignant changes of harmony that elevated this sonata above the usual conventions of pastoral writing. Beethoven, the most human of composers, never merely observed nature—he engaged with it. Thus, the gamboling of lambs and the blossoming trees—which the music so readily suggested—served to introduce a more profound philosophical program. This was not a sterile description of a season—tuneful meteorology—but an inquiry into that most awe-inspiring of all vernal phenomena: romantic love.

When they reached the adagio molto espressivo, Liebermann took advantage of the slower tempo to steal glances at Trezska. Her eyes were closed and her body arched backward as she drew her bow across the strings of her instrument. She had unpinned her hair, letting it fall to her shoulders. Liebermann marveled at how strands of such midnight-blue blackness could also shine so brightly. His stare dropped—briefly—to her compressed cleavage, and then down to the slim girdle of her waist. In the pianissimo passages he could detect the creaking of her corset. He inhaled her fragrance, not just the clementine and mimosa of her perfume, but her entire olfactory signature. Liebermann knew that the French had a word for this sensuous bouquet—the totality of a woman's smell—but it had slipped from his memory.

After they had finished playing the spring sonata, Trezska wanted to repeat certain passages again. She was unhappy with the scherzo, and wondered whether the rondo had not been played a little too fast. She flicked the pages of the open score back with the tip of her bow.

"Allegro ma non troppo," she said curtly.

They discussed some technical details and she asked Liebermann about the quality of her performance.

"Well," he said, evidently apprehensive, "it was very beautiful . . . a very lyrical reading . . ."

"However?"

"You inserted a few glissandi in the adagio, which is not really how the Viennese like their Beethoven." Not wishing to be harsh, he added, "I am simply pointing this out because Rosé will almost certainly object."

"And . . . ?" Trezska prompted, demonstrating her percipient sensitivity: she had detected another unexpressed caveat in the cast of Liebermann's features.

"The vibrato," said Liebermann. "Again, perhaps a little too much for Viennese tastes."

"I see," she said. Then, tapping the open page with her bow, she indicated that she was ready to repeat the rondo.

As they played, Liebermann thought back to what had happened two days earlier on the Prater: the tree, Trezska's prescient anxiety, and the lightning strike. In the carriage, driving back to Landstrasse,

Trezska had at first been preoccupied, but by the time they had crossed the Danube canal, her spirits had rallied. She had grasped Liebermann's hand, squeezed it affectionately, and thanked him for a wonderful day. It was as though the lightning strike had never happened—and, strangely, they had not spoken about it since. Before they parted, he had invited her to his apartment to practice the spring sonata, so that she might be better prepared for her lessons with Rosé. "Yes," she had said. "If you don't mind—that would be very helpful."

When they had finished the rondo, Trezska tuned her violin, and put more rosin on her bow. She played a few scales and, between these, the fragment of a melody. It was so exotic, so distinct, that it immediately aroused Liebermann's interest.

"What was that?"

"A folk song: did you like it?"

"Yes. It sounded rather . . . unusual."

Trezska played another angular phrase. "I learned it from a peasant woman. It had been taught to her by her mother, who had learned it in turn from *her* mother—the woman's grandmother. The song is called *The Reaper*—and it has been passed down, so she said, from mother to daughter, for countless generations. I asked her how old it was and she replied, 'As old as the world.' "

Trezska drew her bow across the lower strings and produced a primitive, haunting melody. It was based on a simple modal figure—but was executed with excessive and wild ornamentation. The meter was irregular, changing every few bars. It was a sound that conjured an image of people working the land, engaged in perpetual back-breaking toil: it suggested great plains and an overarching sky—the scorching summers and bitter winters of an infinite steppe.

"Quite extraordinary," said Liebermann.

"The *real* music of my country," Trezska said proudly.

"Would you play some more?"

"No, not now. Another time. We have work to do."

"Of course."

They played some more Beethoven, and a few Mozart sonatas—including the little E minor. In due course, Liebermann raised his wrist and pointed to his watch. The law decreed that music-making in Vienna had to cease at eleven—and it had just gone half past ten.

"It is getting late—and, sadly, we must bring our music-making to an end. Besides, you must be tired. Shall we find you a cab?"

Trezska smiled, and shook her head. "That won't be necessary. I have no intention of returning to Landstrasse."

She glanced through the open double doors and across the landing, to what she clearly hoped was Liebermann's bedroom.

44

GEROLD SOMMER PEERED OUT of his window. He was grateful that the sky had cleared and the moon was shining brightly. A lamp at this hour would be conspicuous on the grounds of the school. He put on his coat, picked up a paraffin lamp and a box of matches, and hopped down the corridor on his crutches. Thankfully, Lang was a heavy sleeper. Sommer turned the key carefully and pushed the front door open. The air was freezing. He thought of returning to his room to get some gloves and a hat but decided against it. Too much noise.

The path sparkled with frost and was easy to follow. It took him to the front of the school. He passed the statue of Saint Florian and entered the courtyard. It was much darker beneath the cloisters, and it was at this point that he lit his lamp. He adjusted the wick so that it provided just enough illumination for him to find his way—but no more.

Once inside the school, he progressed to the back of the building and with great difficulty descended a flight of stairs that led to a large damp basement room, one wall of which was covered in lockers. They were arranged in alphabetical order. Sommer lowered the lamp, and read the names: Zehrer, Zeigler, *Zelenka*. He pulled the wooden door open and waved the lamp around, attempting to illuminate the shadowy recess.

Nothing.

He placed the lamp on the floor and thrust his hand inside the locker, frantically exploring the space with his fingertips.

Still nothing.

He cursed under his breath.

"Looking for something?"

It was a young voice—one of the boys.

Sommer started and swung around.

On the other side of the room the speaker struck a match. The flame slowly rose to meet the end of a cigarette and cast a yellow light over the distinctive features of Kiefer Wolf. "It's no good, sir," said the boy, exhaling a cloud of smoke. "All Zelenka's possessions were removed. Well . . . with the exception of one item."

Sommer swallowed.

"What . . . what was it?"

"The only thing that I thought was worth taking: a rather fine dictionary."

"Give it to me."

"Why should I?"

"It's of no use to you."

"True. But it's clearly of considerable use to you!"

As Wolf drew on his cigarette, his face reappeared—infernal, in the red incandescence.

"What do you want, Wolf?"

"Only that you continue to honor our arrangement."

"I've already said that I would. I'll keep my word. . . . You don't need that dictionary as well!"

"Have you read much Nietzsche, sir?"

"What?"

"Nietzsche—the philosopher."

"I know who he is, boy!" said Sommer, suddenly angered.

"According to Nietzsche," said Wolf, "you can never have enough power."

Part Three

Fierce Chemistry

45

Liebermann was unfamiliar with Zielinski's—but it was where Trezska had insisted that they meet: a small, dilapidated coffeehouse, close to her apartment in Landstrasse. He had chosen to sit at the rear of the coffeehouse on one of several quilted benches, arranged in pairs, with an oblong table between: a small velvet drape increased privacy by partitioning the heads of adjacent patrons.

Liebermann looked at his wristwatch. Trezska was late. As time passed, he began to look at his wristwatch with increasing frequency, succumbing by degree to worries about her safety. He was considerably relieved, therefore, when the door opened and she finally appeared. The young doctor waved, capturing her attention. Trezska smiled and rushed over, flushed and a little agitated.

"I'm so sorry. My first lesson with Rosé—it lasted much longer than I'd expected."

Liebermann stood and kissed her on the cheek. Now that she had arrived, the wait that he had endured seemed inconsequential.

"How was it? The lesson?" Liebermann asked.

Trezska pulled a dissatisfied face. "I could have played better." She beckoned a waiter: "Absinthe . . . and some sugared almonds."

Liebermann shifted along the bench and invited Trezska to sit next to him. She slid her violin case under the table and sidled up close.

"Forgive me," said Trezska. "I am exhausted. Rosé is a demanding teacher—and very pedantic. At one point, he even questioned the way I was holding my bow! The Mozart was acceptable but the Beethoven . . ." She shook her head. "Very poor."

"What was wrong with it?"

"I don't know. Perhaps I allowed myself to become overawed. . . . The performance was too timid."

"What did Rosé say?"

"He was polite enough—but clearly unimpressed. He wasn't happy with my phrasing and thought that I was treating certain rhythmic figures too freely; however, if I had been more at ease, I am sure I could have produced a more confident performance. Then he might have been better able to understand what I was trying to achieve and less inclined to seize on what he saw as technical deficiencies."

"Perhaps you will be able to communicate your intentions better next time? You will be more accustomed to Rosé—and less anxious, no doubt."

Trezska took his hand and squeezed it affectionately—an expression of gratitude for his solicitous remarks.

The waiter returned and deposited Trezska's order, along with a carafe of water, on their table. She reached out and turned the bottle so she could examine the label. It showed an eighteenth-century dandy in a striped jacket and Napoleonic hat being approached by a flower girl. The legend read JULES PERNOD, AVIGNON.

Liebermann asked Trezska about Rosé's teaching practices, and then indulged in a little musical gossip.

"Did you see his wife?"

"No."

"She is Director Mahler's sister. They married only last year. In fact, the day after the director himself got married. They say that when Rosé was at Bayreuth, the orchestra lost their way in the middle of *Die Walküre*. He stood up and with great skill managed to get them all playing together again. Mahler was in the audience and is supposed to have exclaimed—'Now, that's what I call a concertmaster!' "

"How is it that you know so much about Rosé?" asked Trezska, a line of perplexity appearing across her forehead.

"This is Vienna," said Liebermann—as if no further explanation were necessary.

Trezska lifted the bottle and poured a small quantity of absinthe into two tall glasses. The liquor shimmered. It was translucent, like melted emeralds.

"Watering absinthe is something of an art," said Trezska. "One must conduct the ritual with the same reverence that the Oriental peoples reserve for their tea ceremonies."

She picked up a miniature perforated trowel and balanced it across the rim of her glass. Taking a lump of sugar from the bowl, she placed it on the pinholes. Then, tilting the carafe, she allowed a weak, twisting trickle of water to douse the sugar. The white crystals dissolved, and opaque droplets fell into the glass, turning the elixir a milky green. After a few moments, the absinthe became magically opalescent. It seemed to emit a pale glow, like the mysterious light of fireflies. The air filled with a redolence that was difficult to describe— a sickly bouquet with coppery traces.

"How long have you been drinking absinthe?" Liebermann asked.

"Oh, for some time now: I first became partial to the *green fairy's* charms while I was studying in Paris."

"Yes, it is something of an institution there, I understand."

"More than that—a religion."

Trezska maintained the steady flow of water.

"You know," said Liebermann, "I once read a monograph by the distinguished Parisian physician Dr. Valentin Magnan, of the asylum of Sainte Anne. In it, he identified a specific neurological condition that he styled 'absinthe epilepsy.' Magnan contends that absinthe can affect the motor centers of the cerebellum and the paracerebellar nuclei, producing convulsions and hallucinations of sight and hearing."

"It is also the inspiration of poets," said Trezska, "the favored spirit of visionaries, and an extremely potent aphrodisiac."

Their eyes met. Liebermann smiled and pushed his glass toward her.

"You doctors," she said, watering the second absinthe. "You seem to find fault with everything. You'll be saying that smoking is bad for you next."

Liebermann drew on his cigar. "Well, I must admit, it has been suggested . . . but that can't be true."

"How is it cured, this absinthe epilepsy?"

"Magnan recommends long cold baths—up to five hours—and purges of Sedlitz water."

"In which case, I would rather suffer from the illness than endure its treatment! *Prost!*"

They lifted their glasses and touched them together. The controlled, gentle collision produced a low-pitched *clunk*. Liebermann took a tentative sip and savored the unusual flavor.

First, a strong impression of anise, but then the arrival of other registers, seeping out slowly, teasing the palate—a suggestion of mint, a tarry undercurrent of licorice. . . . After he had swallowed the absinthe and it had numbed the back of his throat, he became aware of an unpleasant medicinal aftertaste—as if an iron button had been dissolving in the saliva beneath his tongue.

"Well?" asked Trezska. "What do you think?"

"Interesting—"

"Any hallucinations?"

"No, but I can well believe a sufficient quantity might induce them!"

"It happened to me once," said Trezska nonchalantly. "I was sitting in a café on the Place Pigalle. I had been drinking with friends and fell into a kind of stupor.... I felt a summer breeze on my face and heard the sound of a brook. The sun shone down on my closed eyes.... It was all very vivid—and seemed to last forever.... When I was finally roused, I collected my things together and walked toward the door. Yet I could still feel the heavy heads of flowers brushing against my skirt."

She turned to face Liebermann. Her expression was shadowed with dark sensuality. The absinthe glistened on her lips—an enticement that he was simply unable to resist. Liebermann leaned forward and kissed her. When they drew apart, she smiled and, taking his hand, locked her fingers between his.

Liebermann could now see why Trezska had been so insistent that they meet in Zielinski's. It was the kind of establishment where a couple could become quite intimate without attracting much attention.

Trezska asked Liebermann about his work at the hospital, and he told her about the deluded jurist who claimed to be in conversation with an angelic being from Phobos. She listened intently and, after he had finished, said: "But how can you be sure that this old man *is* deluded?" Then they embarked on a philosophical discussion about the nature of reality, a conversation that became less and less coherent as they imbibed larger quantities of absinthe.

Liebermann gazed out into the coffeehouse through a dense pall of cigarette and cigar smoke. The clientele of Zielinski's was comprised of workmen, artists, and a few women whose abundant cleav-

ages and raucous laughter declared their profession. Music was provided by a zither player: an unkempt gentleman with an eye-patch
and wild white hair. He plucked an itinerant melody that at times
became nothing more than a random selection of pitches. Occasionally something recognizable would emerge—a fragment of Strauss or
Lanner, but no more than a musical paring, flotsam on a wash of watery strumming. No one seemed to mind, and indeed, after a while,
Liebermann began to find the abstract ambient qualities of the zither
player's improvisations quite pleasing.

Liebermann stared into the pallid opalescent mixture in his glass.
He took a deep breath and asked:

"What happened . . . that day, on the Prater?"

"Ah," Trezska replied. "I was wondering when you were going to
ask."

"You had what? A premonition?"

She sighed. "You are a doctor . . . a man of science. You do not believe in such things, I am sure."

"I . . ." Liebermann was conscious of his own deceit but could not
stop himself. "I have an open mind."

Trezska did not look convinced.

"There are many respectable scientific societies," Liebermann
continued, "that take a serious interest in paranormal phenomena.
Even Professor Freud, the most ardent of skeptics, has demonstrated a certain willingness to entertain the idea of mind-to-mind
communication—telepathy."

Trezska's features softened, indicating that she had decided to give
her companion the benefit of the doubt.

"Yes, I do get strong feelings sometimes. It is supposed to be in my
blood . . . my mother's side."

"Second sight?"

"Whatever you want to call it."

Liebermann's expression became troubled. "But could it not be that . . . we were walking in an open space and, rather foolishly, chose to stand under the tallest tree. This, of course, would be the tree most likely to attract lightning. If we had discussed our situation, we might have concluded that we were in danger." Liebermann sipped his absinthe. "Now, could a similar process have taken place in your unconscious mind? You were not aware of the process but experienced only its product or consequence—namely, fear. Comparable dissociative processes operate in dreams and serve to disguise their meaning."

Trezska playfully tapped Liebermann's cheek. "Why must you try to explain everything?"

"It is generally better to understand things . . . than not."

Trezska selected a pink sugared almond from the bowl and pressed it between her lips. As she sucked the icing from the nut, she pouted. This repetitive and subtle movement aroused in Liebermann a desperate desire to kiss her again.

"According to my mother," said Trezska, "her side of the family are related to the house of Báthory."

Liebermann's expression became blank.

"You've never heard of Erzsébet Báthory?" Trezska continued. "The vampire countess?"

"What?" Liebermann laughed.

"She was a Transylvanian noblewoman. Legend has it that she first killed and then bathed in the blood of nearly a thousand young maidens—simply to preserve her beauty."

Trezska produced a faint, ambiguous smile. Liebermann could not determine whether she was being serious or joking. He began to feel distinctly odd: woozy, detached. His vision blurred and he moved his head backward and forward to regain his focus.

"Are you all right?" Trezska asked.

The strange jangling of the zither sounded peculiarly loud—a concatenation of gongs and bells.

"I fear," said Liebermann, "that Dr. Magnan's speculations concerning the effects of absinthe on the brain may be correct." His speech was slurring. "Indeed, I would hazard a guess that the active chemical ingredients have just reached my cerebellum and my para-cerebellar nuclei, with predictable consequences."

"Perhaps I should take you home?" said Trezska.

He felt her hand unlock from his, and the heat of her palm on his thigh.

"Yes," Liebermann replied. "Perhaps you should."

46

IT WAS THE DEAD of night. A thick mist had descended into the valley, and the four boys had to consult a compass to find their way. They assiduously avoided footpaths, and as a result their progress was slow. The ground was muddy and treacherous—an adhesive mulch that made each step effortful. Boggy hollows were brimming with ice-cold filthy water that filled their boots and soaked their trousers. Sometimes the trees would grow closer together, and the spaces between would become congested with prickly leafless bushes. Then the boys were unable to move forward, and had to retrace their steps and find some other way.

Wolf led the group. He carried a paraffin lamp, the light of which barely mitigated the darkness. Freitag followed, carrying a shovel, and straggling behind, striving to keep up, were Drexler and Steininger, each grasping the corners of a large, sagging jute sack.

Suddenly, Wolf raised his arm. The others stopped.

"What is it?" whispered Freitag.

Wolf beat the air with his hand, a burst of quick downward movements indicating that the others should be quiet.

The boys froze, and listened intently. Wolf lowered the wick of his lamp, and attempted to peer through the opaque veils of turbid brume. Something scampered away, and Wolf sighed with relief. He consulted the compass again and pointed slightly to the left.

"Wolf," said Steininger. "Wolf, I can't go on."

"Keep your voice down."

"It's too heavy. Let's do it here. . . . There's no need to go any farther, surely."

"Freitag, you take over."

"No, Wolf, I'm exhausted. Drexler can carry it on his own—it's all *his* fault."

"It is *not* my fault!" said Drexler angrily. "If you hadn't insisted on playing your stupid games!"

"I said keep your voices down!" said Wolf.

"Really, Wolf," said Steininger, dropping his end of the sack. It landed with a dull thud. "We've been walking for hours. We don't need to go any farther."

"And we have to get back, remember," said Freitag.

"And what about our uniforms?" said Steininger. "We can't arrive for drill practice looking like this! We'll need time to get them cleaned up."

"I'll wake Stojakovic," said Wolf.

"No," said Drexler. "We can't involve anybody else! Not tonight."

Wolf paced around the circle of trees in which they were standing. He then tested the ground with his foot, kicking up some turf.

"It's not too hard," he said.

"Then let's get started," said Steininger, snatching Freitag's shovel and driving its pointed blade into the earth.

Drexler leaned against the nearest trunk and rested his forehead on his coat sleeve. His moment of repose was at once disturbed when he opened his eyes and observed in the contours of the bark a peculiar arrangement of knots, whorls, and ridges that suggested the lineaments of a human face—an old, deeply lined face, with bushy eyebrows and a long wavy beard. The sad eyes were full of anguish. It was as if some unfortunate soul had been magically incarcerated in the timber. The image reminded Drexler of the fantastic stories of E.T.A. Hoffmann. The boy drew back—and felt a freakish chill that made him shiver.

"How deep should the trench be?" asked Steininger.

"How should I know?" Wolf answered irritably.

"But what if animals . . ."

"Dig him up?"

"Well, yes."

"What animals?"

"I don't know, but it's possible, isn't it?"

"All right," said Wolf, glaring. "Make it deeper!"

Drexler looked over at the abandoned sack and considered its contents. He felt a wave of pity and regret. The swell of emotion that made his eyes burn was only just containable, but his self-control gave him no satisfaction. He knew that this was just the beginning. There would be worse to come: guilt, nightmares, and various forms of mental torture. The terrible millstone of his secret would weigh heavily on his conscience for the rest of his life, and would eventually drag him down to the depths of hell. He had never believed in such a place before, but now it all seemed quite plausible.

He turned away and stared into the darkness.

Steininger's digging was creating a hypnotic rhythm: the crunch of the blade penetrating the soil—a heave of effort—and then the dull rain of soil on leaves. Its regularity was comforting and lulled Drexler into a kind of trance. Once or twice, he noticed discontinuities of consciousness: he was so tired that he must have nodded off. . . .

Freitag gasped: a sudden intake of breath, cut short and invested with the rising pitch of surprise.

Steininger stopped digging.

An owl hooted.

"What is it?"

"I thought . . . I thought I saw something move. Over there."

"What?"

Freitag's voice shook. "It was big, like a bear."

"Don't be so ridiculous," said Wolf. "If it was a bear, we'd soon know about it!"

"I didn't say it was a bear—I said it was *like* a bear. Really, I did see something. Something big."

"Pull yourself together, Freitag," Wolf commanded.

Freitag shook his head. "I'm going. I don't like it here."

Wolf grabbed his arm. "Look, it's just your imagination! There's nothing out there!"

He gestured between the trees and raised his lamp. Nothing was visible, except the restless mist.

Freitag swallowed—subdued by the steel in Wolf's eyes.

"Yes . . ." Freitag smiled—somewhat desperately. "Yes . . . of course. My imagination."

"Don't be a fool, Freitag," said Wolf, releasing his grip.

Drexler said nothing, but his heartbeat was thundering in his ears. He had seen something too—exactly as Freitag had said: something large and lumbering—big—like a bear. He marched over to Steininger.

"Give me the shovel. You're too slow, Steininger. Let's finish this business and get away from this awful place."

47

THE WAITER SWOOPED BY, skilfully replacing Rheinhardt's empty soup bowl with a dish containing dumplings, fried pork chops, a slice of boiled ham, frankfurter sausages, and a steaming mound of cooked sauerkraut. Rheinhardt inhaled the meaty fragrances and dressed his meal with large dollops of bright yellow mustard. Looking over at his companion, he noticed that Liebermann was toying with his food, rather than eating it, fishing noodles out of his broth and watching them slither off his spoon like tiny serpents.

"What's the matter—lost your appetite?"

"Yes. I'm feeling a little fragile, to be honest. Last night I . . ." He massaged his temple and winced. "I drank too much."

"Well, there's no better cure for a hangover than a big, hearty meal. Finish your soup and try the onion steak . . . or the Tyrolean liver. Something substantial!"

Liebermann stirred the contents of his bowl and observed the stringy ballet with glum indifference.

"I saw Miss Lydgate on Tuesday," Rheinhardt added breezily.

Liebermann looked up from his soup. "Did you?"

"Yes. I showed her the number pairs from Zelenka's book."

Liebermann's expression was unusually flat: a peculiarity that Rheinhardt attributed to his friend's intemperance of the night before.

"Was she able to assist?"

"Well, she said that the numbers *might* represent some form of code—but, if so, one of a very unconventional type. She promised to study them and give an opinion in due course."

Liebermann nodded.

Rheinhardt sliced his dumpling and speared a strip of boiled ham.

"This is quite, quite delicious," he said, chewing with more volume than was really permissible according to the standard prescriptions of etiquette. "Oh, and Miss Lydgate said something about not having had the pleasure of your company lately . . . and being otherwise engaged—and that I should convey her best wishes when I next saw you."

Liebermann set his jaw and mumbled something inaudible, which Rheinhardt was perfectly content to accept as a token of gratitude.

The arrival of a pianist was received with restrained applause. The musician adjusted the height of his stool, flicked the tails of his coat, and sat down slowly. When his hands fell on the keyboard, the coffeehouse filled with a mournful dirge. The marchlike accompaniment suggested the trudging feet of a regiment of soldiers, every one of whom yearned to return home. It was an inconsolable song of reminiscence and lamentation.

"Brahms?" asked Rheinhardt tentatively.

"Yes," Liebermann replied. "*Hungarian Dance Number Eleven in D minor*. It's usually heard in a four-hand arrangement . . . and he's playing it very slowly."

"Still . . ."

"It is very affecting, yes."

"I rather like it."

They listened for a few moments, until a subtle modulation in the music suddenly released them from its thrall.

"So tell me," said Liebermann. "What happened with old Brügel? Did the nephew carry out his threat?"

Rheinhardt rolled his eyes to the ceiling.

"Yes. He did write to the commissioner, informing him of my accusation. Subsequently, I was summoned by Brügel and given a complete dressing down. He was furious—I've never seen him so angry."

"His overreaction confirms my earlier speculation. He knows what sort of a boy Wolf is. He is simply trying to safeguard the interests of his family."

Rheinhardt waved a piece of sausage on the end of his fork. "When I was leaving, Brügel became more subdued. He said that Wolf was the only child of his youngest sister. The boy was no angel, he admitted, but he said I was quite wrong about him." Rheinhardt paused, his eyes becoming less focused. "There was something about the way he referred to his sister . . . an uncharacteristic tenderness."

"In most families," said Liebermann knowingly, "the eldest son is often the youngest daughter's special protector—and a mother cannot help but idealize her only child. One does not need to be a very great psychologist to understand Brügel's motive. He loves his sister, and he is trying to stop you from breaking her heart. That is why his anger was so immoderate."

Liebermann sat back in his chair, satisfied with his perspicacity. He noticed with irritation that a wayward spot of broth had landed on the cuff of his jacket. He tutted, reached into his trouser pocket, and pulled out a monogrammed silk handkerchief. As he did so, some pink sugared almonds fell and scattered onto the floor. The young doctor reached down, picked them up, and placed them on the table-cloth.

Rheinhardt stopped chewing.

"Sugared almonds," said Liebermann, with a sheepish half smile.

"Indeed," said Rheinhardt.

"I wasn't expecting them to be there."

"Evidently not," said the inspector, resuming his chewing, and revising his estimate of how much alcohol his friend had imbibed the previous evening.

Liebermann wiped his cuff clean. Trezska must have put the almonds in his pocket while they were both inebriated—or perhaps he had put them there himself; these innocent bonbons aroused in him a peculiar sense of incompletion and imminence. He stared at the almonds and began to play with them on his napkin—as if he might stumble upon an arrangement that would release their mysterious secret.

He remembered something that Trezska had said: she had praised the mind-altering properties of absinthe: *the inspiration of poets . . . the favored spirit of visionaries.* Why was that important? As hard as he tried, he couldn't think why.

"Are you feeling unwell?" Rheinhardt asked.

Liebermann dismissed his solicitous remark with a peremptory hand gesture.

They had returned to his apartment and made love. He could remember *that* well enough. Then, afterward, he had been lying in bed, still feeling very odd—and . . . *That was it!* He had experienced a flash of insight: something to do with almonds, and something very, *very* important.

"Ha!" Liebermann exclaimed.

"Whatever is the matter, Max?" said Rheinhardt, somewhat irritated by his friend's eccentric behavior.

The young doctor suddenly seemed galvanized. His movements acquired a nervous urgency.

"I would like to take another look at those photographs."

"What photographs?"

"The photographs of Zelenka . . . and I would also like to speak to his parents."

"Why?"

Liebermann shook his head. "When you first told me about Zelenka's death, you said—did you not?—that he had been conducting some experiments involving . . . vinegar?"

"Yes, that's right. I did say that."

Liebermann picked up the almonds and rattled them in his closed fist.

"How very interesting. Almonds and vinegar!"

The young doctor's eyes were alight—and he had acquired a slightly fevered look.

"I don't know what you were drinking last night," said Rheinhardt. "And I'm not sure that I want to know; however, whatever it was, I would strongly advise, that—at all costs—you eschew it in future." Before Liebermann could respond, Rheinhardt's expression had changed from dudgeon to despondency. "Oh no, what now?" His assistant, Haussmann, had just walked through the door.

The young man's arrival at their table coincided with the final bars of the Brahms *Hungarian Dance*, and when he spoke, he had to compete with a loud round of applause.

"Instructions from Commissioner Brügel, sir. You must proceed to Herrengasse—immediately. There has been . . ." He looked around to make sure that no one was listening and lowered his voice. "*An incident.*"

"I beg your pardon?" said Rheinhardt, cupping his ear.

"A body, sir," said the assistant, with a hint of impatience. "In Herrengasse—a high-ranking officer in His Majesty's army."

"Who?"

"General von Stoger."

"I see," said Rheinhardt.

"Commisioner Brügel . . . he said that you are to initiate the investigation, but you must expect to be relieved by Inspector von Bulow as soon as he is located."

"Why?"

"Er . . . don't know, sir. Perhaps it's all to do with . . ." He glanced at Liebermann, unsure about whether to continue.

"Yes, yes," said Rheinhardt. "Von Bulow's confounded assignment—whatever it is!"

The inspector pressed on his knees to raise his bulky frame, and looked affectionately at his unfinished meal. "What a dreadful waste," he said. "And I was so looking forward to the chef's *topfenstrudel*." Then, addressing Liebermann, he added: "What are you supposed to be doing this afternoon?"

"Case notes."

"Can it wait?"

"Yes—I could write them up this evening."

"Perhaps you would be kind enough to accompany us?"

"If you wish."

Rheinhardt turned toward the door, but his dynamism was suddenly extinguished. He seemed to be overcome by a curious lassitude. Retrieving his abandoned fork, he impaled an untouched dumpling and stuffed it into his mouth, whole. He then said something quite unintelligible to Haussmann.

"I beg your pardon, sir," said the bemused assistant. "I didn't quite catch that."

"Photographer," he repeated. "Get the photographer . . . and find Professor Mathias."

As they left, a man at an adjacent table turned to watch them go. He had dark curly hair, an impressive mustache, and the fiery eyes of a zealot.

48

Professor Eichmann was seated behind his desk, staring at the photograph of himself as a youthful artillery officer. As a child, he had dreamed of wearing such a uniform, distinguishing himself in battle, and becoming a celebrated general. But in real life his precocious fantasies had come to nothing. His career in the army had not been very remarkable—although this was through no fault of his own. He had been honorably discharged in his early twenties due to ill health. The doctor had attributed his breathlessness to a congenital heart defect. At the time, Eichmann had been devastated; however, he was an intelligent, resourceful young man, and soon turned this misfortune to his advantage. He excelled at university, wrote a modestly succesful history of the Austrian land forces, and won the respect of his academic peer group.

Yet, in spite of his achievements, the disappointment of his early discharge from the artillery lingered.

He had wanted to be a man of action, and academia was—for him—far too distant from the battlefield. In due course, he trained as a teacher and sought a more direct relationship with the world. Although he had been denied glory, he could still influence those destined to take his place.

While still in his thirties, he had written an impressive article on the importance of military schools. It had become commonplace in coffeehouses to hear patrons bemoaning the state of the army. Who could deny that it was underfunded, ill-equipped, and in need of modernization? Eichmann, however, had argued that the significance of these factors had been exaggerated. What really mattered was "character." If the army—and in particular the Austrian army—was going to meet the challenges of the new century, then it should be supplied with soldiers of a certain "type." Thus, military schools had a key role to play in determining the destiny of the dual monarchy. Moreover, Eichmann had proposed that this right sort of character should be modeled on a vision of man described in recent philosophical writings. Such works might introduce teachers to some very useful principles.

It was an argument that had attracted the interest of the headmaster of a military school situated in the Vienna woods. The school was called Saint Florian's. Eichmann was immediately offered a teaching post. Five years later he became deputy headmaster, and three years after that, the headmaster had died and Eichmann had stepped into his shoes.

On the whole, Eichmann's project had been successful. The school now had a fine reputation. In addition, old boys occupied significant positions in the military hierarchy. The survival of the empire was— to a greater or lesser extent—dependent on these men of character whose thinking he had shaped. Thus, in a sense, he had inveigled his way back onto the battlefield. Some of their glory—at least in part— belonged to him.

There was a knock at the door.

Eichmann turned the photograph of his younger self aside.

"Come in." It was the deputy headmaster. "Ah . . . Becker," said the headmaster, gesturing toward a chair. "Well?"

Becker advanced, but did not sit.

"He didn't attend any classes yesterday—and he hasn't been seen all day today. The prefects have undertaken a thorough search of the school, including the outbuildings."

"Have you spoken to any of his friends?"

"Perger doesn't have friends—as such."

"All right, then—classmates?"

"A boy called Schoeps claims to have seen him in the dormitory on Tuesday night. That, I believe, was the last time anyone saw him."

"He must have absconded."

"Yes, sir, that seems to be the most likely explanation."

The headmaster shook his head. "This is all we need."

"Quite. Most inopportune."

"Thank you, Deputy Headmaster," said Eichmann.

Becker bowed and left the room.

The headmaster opened a drawer, took out a sheet of headed notepaper, and began writing.

Dear Herr Perger,

I regret to inform you that your son Isidor appears to have absconded from the school. This is a very serious matter.

The headmaster paused and bit the end of his pen. He recalled his talk with Wolf. For a moment, it crossed his mind that the boy might have misundertsood him.

No, he thought. *Surely not.*

Returning his attention to the letter, he continued to write.

49

Liebermann examined the cracked surface of a large oil painting that depicted the 1683 battle of Vienna. The colors had been dimmed by generations of cigar smoke, but it was still possible to make out the noble figure of the Polish king, Jan Sobieski, confronting the Ottoman commander—Grand Vizier Merzifonlu Kara Mustafa Pasha.

What if Vienna had fallen? thought Liebermann. *What then? Would the cry of the muezzin now be heard, resonating along the banks of the Danube, the Rhine, or even the Seine, calling the faithful to evening prayer?*

He felt a small detonation of pride in his chest.

Vienna.

The peoples of Europe were much indebted to the Viennese—if they but knew it!

Liebermann stepped away from the painting, with its massive carved frame and its jaundiced, barely discernible figures, and surveyed the large gloomy room in which he was standing.

Thick embroidered curtains were drawn across three of the tall rectangular windows. Only the fourth pair of heavy drapes had been pulled back to admit a sour, enervating light. From the high ceiling hung a massive iron chandelier—notable for the complexity of its loops and involutions. Stalactites of congealed wax hung from its six dishes like a macabre merry-go-round of dangling atrophied fingers. The ceiling itself was equally ornate, indented with step-sided coffers. Below the ceiling was a cornice of regularly spaced moldings: rosettes, garlands, and openmouthed lions baring their teeth.

Two suits of armor stood guard on either side of the double doors. Other furniture included assorted chairs, a Japanese lacquered cabinet (shaped like a pagoda), a wall table (on which an antique chess set was displayed), a porcelain stove, some bookshelves, and—rather strangely—a battered leather saddle. Liebermann supposed that this last item must have been of sentimental value to the general, having been of service during some notable campaign. Military men—whose fundamental purpose it was to kill others—could be remarkably sentimental.

The center of the room was dominated by a mahogany desk: behind it was a high-backed wooden chair, and on this chair sat a stout gentleman with a bulbous pockmarked nose. His hair had receded, and, like many men of his generation, he had—in deference to the emperor—chosen to sport a fine set of muttonchop whiskers. He was wearing a quilted smoking jacket, with velvet trimmings, and loose-fitting silk trousers. Liebermann noticed that below the desk the general's big feet occupied a pair of elegant oriental slippers traced with silver thread and with toes that curled upward.

Liebermann could hear Rheinhardt's baritone through the closed double doors. He was interviewing one of the general's servants in the hallway. Although the inspector was speaking in hushed tones, his strong voice carried. It was answered by a muffled and considerably weaker tenor.

The general might have been taking a nap—such was his innocent attitude. His left cheek was pressed against the red leather inlay of the desktop, his arms were sprawled out to either side of his head, and his eyes were closed. However, in his right hand he held a bulky

Borchardt pistol, and a gaping hole had been blasted through his skull—just above the ear.

A pile of books had toppled as the general had fallen forward. Most of the titles were by German theoreticians of warfare—but one volume, on closer inspection, turned out to be a lighthearted collection of military anecdotes. The pale calf bindings of the more academic works were spattered with blood and gelatinous globs of brain tissue. On the corner of the desk was a deep, wide ashtray that contained three cigar stubs.

Liebermann heard the sound of brisk footsteps advancing up the hallway, and then new voices and a brittle exchange. The double doors opened and a tall man entered, followed by a younger man who was evidently his assistant. Although Liebermann had heard a great deal about Rheinhardt's nemesis, Victor von Bulow, they had never been formally introduced. Liebermann remembered von Bulow from the detectives' ball and had seen him once before, the previous year, arguing with Rheinhardt outside Commissioner Brügel's office.

Von Bulow swept into the room and came to an abrupt halt on the other side of the general's desk. He and Liebermann looked at each other—though the *manner* in which the two men observed each other was curiously intense and searching. It did not suggest passive reception but, rather, an active seeking-out. They were *inspecting*. And as is always the case when two well-dressed men meet, the object of their attention was, first and foremost, clothing: value, quality, and provenance.

They recoiled slightly when they both observed—simultaneously— that they were wearing identical astrakhan coats, supplied almost certainly by the very same shop. This resulted in their expressions shifting—in tandem—from mild indignation to what might have been a form of grudging respect. However, their tacit truce was quickly dissolved. In a transparent attempt to assert his sartorial advantage, von Bulow tugged at his shirt cuffs to reveal the glitter of his diamond cuff links. Rheinhardt, who had followed von Bulow in, witnessed this silent but perfectly comprehensible exchange with some amusement.

"Herr Dr. Liebermann?" said von Bulow icily.

"Inspector von Bulow," said Liebermann, inclining his head.

Von Bulow walked around the desk, his stare fixed on the general. "I trust you have not touched the body."

"That is correct. I have not touched the body."

"Good." Von Bulow crouched down to get a better view of the head wound. "Pathology is not your specialty, Herr Doctor . . ."

Von Bulow had subtly stressed his statement so that it sounded a little like a question.

"Indeed," Liebermann confirmed. "I am not a pathologist. I am a psychiatrist."

"You will appreciate, then, I hope," said von Bulow, "that your presence here can serve no purpose."

It was a blunt and discourteous dismissal.

Liebermann retained his composure and acquiesced with a curt nod. As he walked toward the door, von Bulow called out: "Oh, and Dr. Liebermann . . ." The young doctor stopped and turned around. "Inspector Rheinhardt was acting without proper authority when he invited you to accompany him. You must not tell anyone what you have seen here today. Do you understand?"

"With respect," said Rheinhardt, coughing uncomfortably, "that really isn't right. I was instructed by the commissioner to initiate standard investigative procedures until your arrival. And that's exactly what I've done. There is nothing irregular about Dr. Liebermann's attendance. He has been of considerable assistance to the security office on many occasions—as you are well aware. If this investigation is—how shall we say? Sensitive?—then perhaps you should ask Commissioner Brügel why he did not make this absolutely clear vis-à-vis my instructions."

Von Bulow paused and stroked the neat rectangle of silver bristle on his chin. He seemed to be reconsidering his position, weighing up costs and benefits on an internal mental balance. His pale gray eyes—almost entirely devoid of color—stared coldly at Rheinhardt. A sudden reconfiguration of his angular features suggested that his obscure calculations had been successfully completed.

"Thank you, gentlemen," he said softly. "I am *most* grateful for your help." His intonation had become unctuous—oily with sarcasm. "Be that as it may, now that I am here—you may both leave."

Rheinhardt, exasperated, strode over to von Bulow and handed him his notebook.

"You may as well have this. I've just interviewed the head servant. The house staff were all dismissed last night at seven and told not to return until this afternoon."

Von Bulow flicked through the notes.

"Rheinhardt, how can you possibly expect me to understand this scribble? I'll interview him again myself."

Rheinhardt shrugged. "As you wish, von Bulow. You should also know that Professor Mathias has been asked—"

"Professor Mathias!" von Bulow cut in. "Dear God, Rheinhardt, you're not still using that lunatic? I'll be appointing my own pathologist, thank you. Now, gentlemen, the suicide of one of His Majesty's generals is nothing less than a national tragedy. I really must be getting on."

He extended his arm toward the doors.

In readiness to leave, Rheinhardt looked over at his friend; however, Liebermann was hesitant.

"I'm sorry," said Liebermann to von Bulow. "But did you just say . . . *suicide*?"

Von Bulow turned on Liebermann with evident impatience.

"Yes."

"You are of the opinion that General von Stoger took his own life?"

"Well, of course he did!"

"And why do you say that?"

"Because General von Stoger is lying here—quite dead—with a gun in his hand and a very large hole in his head. Now, for the last time, Herr Doctor, would you kindly leave? I have work to do."

Von Bulow's assistant smirked.

"Forgive me," said Liebermann, making his way back to the body. He beckoned to von Bulow, urging him to examine the general's wound more closely. "Observe," Liebermann continued. "There are no powder burns on the general's temple. No grains embedded in the skin. Most people, when they choose to end it all by shooting themselves, place the muzzle of the gun against the epidermis—pressing it in, hard." Liebermann made a gun shape with his hand and pressed the tips of his fingers into his temple. "Presumably," he continued, "to reduce the possibility of making an error. Only rarely—very rarely—will a suicide hold the pistol at a distance. You are correct that I am not a pathologist; however, I *am* a psychiatrist, and it is a sad fact that members of my profession are frequently the first to discover individuals who have committed suicide. I have seen many suicides . . . and one notices certain resemblances between them."

Von Bulow snorted. "It may be very rare—as you suggest—for a suicide to hold the weapon at a distance, but it is not so exceptional as to recommend that we should abandon common sense! Now, Herr Doctor, if you would kindly let me conduct *my* investigation in the manner to which I am accustomed!"

Dispensing with any pretence of courtesy, von Bulow flicked his thumb toward the exit.

"And the absence of a suicide note?" said Liebermann, ignoring von Bulow's rude gesture. "Does that not strike you as being a little odd? Gentlemen of von Stoger's class and rank always leave a suicide note."

"Herr Dr. Liebermann," said von Bulow coldly, "you are testing my patience!"

"I do apologize," Liebermann replied. "I have neglected to mention the most important of my observations. No powder burns, no suicide note . . . these are simply auxiliary to the principal fact, which, if I may be so bold as to declare, is—in my humble judgment—quite compelling."

Von Bulow's arm dropped to his side. He was reluctant to ask the young doctor what this compelling *principal fact* was and so cede his authority. He glared at Liebermann, who had chosen this moment to conduct a minute study of his fingernails. He picked off a cuticle. Rheinhardt, the long-suffering victim of Liebermann's irritating penchant for obscurity and mystification, was, for once, delighted.

The ensuing silence became frigid and intractable.

Von Bulow—finally overcome by curiosity—ungraciously spat out his question: "What are you talking about!"

"Simply this," said Liebermann, smiling. "The general's eyes are closed. This is not remarkable in itself, being commonplace when people die naturally. But when people die suddenly—their eyes remain open. In the anguished state that precedes suicide, we can be quite sure that the eyes are wide open—staring, in fact. And this is how we—us psychiatrists—usually find them." Liebermann paused for just enough time for von Bulow to register von Stoger's heavy, hooded lids. "Inspector, someone closed the general's eyes postmortem. And I strongly suspect that the person who did that was also the person who shot him!"

The blood drained from von Bulow's face. He ran an agitated hand over the silver stubble at the back of his head.

"Good day," said Liebermann, marching briskly to the closed double doors. Before opening them, he looked back into the room and added, "And don't be fooled by that tight grip. A gun can be placed in the hand immediately after death, and then when rigor mortis sets in, it creates the illusion of a holding-fast."

Rheinhardt bowed, and followed his friend out into the hall. The servant whom Rheinhardt had been interviewing was still waiting.

"Sir?" said the servant to Rheinhardt. "May I retire to my quarters now?"

"I'm afraid not," said Rheinhardt. "My colleague Inspector von Bulow wishes to ask you some more questions."

The man acquiesced glumly.

Rheinhardt and Liebermann began walking down the hallway, their footsteps sounding loudly on the shiny, polished ebony.

Unable to restrain himself, Rheinhardt slapped his friend on the back.

"That was truly excellent, Max, excellent. You made von Bulow look like a complete idiot."

In response, the young doctor took a sugared almond from his pocket, tossed it into the air, and caught it in his mouth. He bit through the icing and produced a loud, satisfying crunch. "Let's go back to Schottenring," he said. "I must see those photographs again."

50

WOLF WAS SITTING IN the lost room, alone, smoking his way through a packet of gold-tipped cigarettes. He had acquired them from Bose, a plump and effete baron from Deutsch-Westungarn, whose arm he had twisted until the boy had squealed like a stuck pig. Resting on Wolf's lap was a large book, the cover of which was made of soft green leather and embossed with gold lettering. The endpapers were marbled. Wolf licked his finger and began to turn the pages. The movement of his hand across the spine became faster and faster—each transition was accompanied by a double syllable of friction and release. The sound was not unlike a person gasping for breath. Although he was not reading the text, Wolf's expression was attentive.

The monotony of the task created a void in his mind, which soon filled with recent memories.

Earlier that day Wolf had been summoned to the headmaster's office. The old man had rambled on in his usual way about values, honor, and reputation, but in due course his well-practiced oratory had stalled. He had become somewhat incoherent. Eventually, the headmaster had made an oblique reference to *the matter discussed* on the occasion of their last meeting.

"It appears that Perger has absconded."

"Yes," Wolf had replied.

"This sort of behavior cannot be countenanced. When he is

found, I will have no other option but to expel him. Whatever plea is made on his behalf—and I'm sure that at least one well-meaning but misguided advocate will come forward—nothing, and I mean nothing, can possibly excuse such appalling misconduct."

"No, sir," Wolf had agreed. "It is quite disgraceful."

The headmaster had risen and, as was his habit, had gone to the window.

Wolf recalled the nervous catch in his voice: "I take it we have understood the situation correctly. Eh, Wolf? I mean . . . Perger *has* absconded, hasn't he?"

"Why, yes," Wolf had replied. "There can be no other explanation for his disappearance, surely?"

"Good," the headmaster had muttered, evidently reassured by the boy's steady confidence.

Wolf now turned the final page. None of them had been annotated. He had observed a few inky marks here and there but nothing of any obvious significance. Wolf closed the book and opened it again at the frontispiece, an antique etching of a bearded scholar in a library. At the foot of the title page, in small lettering, he read "Hartel and Jacobsen," beneath which was the publisher's address in Leipzig, and the year of publication: 1900.

As far as Wolf could determine, there was nothing remarkable about the dictionary at all—except, perhaps, its quality. He traced the tooled indentations with his finger.

Why on earth did Herr Sommer want it so badly? He had been desperate, that night in the locker room.

Wolf inspected the inside covers in order to determine if anything incriminating had been slipped beneath the endpapers, but it was obvious that no one had tampered with them. The space between the spine and the binding was also empty.

It was a mystery.

Suddenly irritated by his failure to discover anything there that he could use to his advantage, he threw the dictionary aside and picked up a thinner volume that he had previously laid at his feet. He reverently removed the bookmark and turned the blotchy print toward the paraffin lamp.

Just as the clouds tell us the direction of the wind high above our heads, so the lightest and freest spirits are in their tendencies foretellers of the weather that is coming. The wind in the valley and the opinions of the market place of today indicate nothing of that which is coming but only of that which has been.

The great philosopher's words were like a prophecy—but not just any prophecy. This was a prophecy meant especially for him. Wolf smiled, and a thrill of almost erotic intensity passed through his entire body. He was the future. Tomorrow belonged to him.

51

The Kohlmarkt was bustling with activity. A woman carrying a brightly wrapped parcel smiled at Liebermann as she passed, so delighted with her purchase that she could not suppress her joy. Two splendidly accoutred hussars, standing on the porch of a milliner's, were speaking loudly in Hungarian. On the other side of the street marched three Hasidim wearing long black caftans and wide-brimmed beaver hats. The Michaelertor—the massive green dome that towered above the entrance of the Hofburg Palace—dominated the view ahead. It looked particularly beautiful against the pastel wash of the taupe sky.

Liebermann had sent a note to Trezska earlier in the week, arranging to meet her at Café Demel (the imperial and royal confectioners). He had stated, with some regret, that their rendezvous could be only brief as he had some pressing business (a useful if somewhat overworked euphemism) to which he must attend later in the day. The young doctor had chosen Café Demel not only because of its reputation but for reasons of expediency, as he hoped to get the first of the day's *business* out of the way before Trezska's arrival.

Opening the door of the café, Liebermann stepped inside, and was immediately overcome by the aroma of coffee, cigar smoke, and the mingling of a thousand sweet fragrances. It was a warm, welcoming interior, suffused with a soft amber light. The gilt chandeliers were encrusted with opaque faintly glowing globes, as densely clustered as grapes on the vine. To the right, patrons were seated at round tables in a mirrored dining area, and to the left stood a long counter, dark wooden wall shelves, and numerous display cases. Every available space on this side of the café was occupied by cakes and sweetmeats: candied peel, marzipan animals, fondants and jellies, whole discs of torte—covered with thick dark chocolate—jars of brandy snaps, Turkish delight, *vanillekipferl*, meringues, pots of raspberry cream and apricot sauce, pear compote, artificial coins wrapped in gold and silver paper, *guglhupf, apfelstrudel*, dumplings bursting with glistening conserves, pastry pillows and Carinthian cinnamon buns. In the center of this cornucopia was a rectangular cake that had been made—with the aid of much yellow icing—to look exactly like the Schönbrunn Palace.

A woman who was standing behind the counter came forward.

"Good afternoon," said Liebermann. "Herr Tishlar is expecting me." He glanced at his watch—he was exactly on time.

The woman indicated that he should follow her to the back of the café, where he was instructed to wait by some doors. She returned in the company of a very stout gentleman whose tiny mustache was distinguished by curlicue extremities. He was still dressed in his kitchen clothes.

"Herr Doctor," he exclaimed. "Herr Tishlar, at your service."

The master baker bowed low and performed an unnecessarily baroque flourish with his right hand. Liebermann recognized immediately that he was in the presence of a man who regarded his art as equal to that of Titian or Velázquez. The woman silently withdrew.

"You are most kind," said Liebermann, reaching into his coat pocket and withdrawing a photograph and a magnifying glass. "I promise I will be brief. I wonder . . . would it be possible for you to identify this pastry?"

The image he handed to Tishlar showed Zelenka's notebook and a blurry, untouched wedge of cake.

Peering through the lens, Herr Tishlar answered without hesitation: "Almond tart." He then handed the photograph and magnifying glass back to the young doctor.

"Are you sure?" said Liebermann—taken aback by Herr Tishlar's certainty.

"Quite sure," said the baker. "And—if you will forgive my immodesty—no ordinary almond tart! *That*, Herr Doctor," said the master baker, tapping the photograph and pushing out his chest, "is one of ours. It is a Demel almond tart!"

Herr Tishlar guided Liebermann over to a display case and pointed to a roundel (sprinkled with castor sugar and strewn with striped ribbons) in a wooden box.

"Notice the pleating around the edge," he said with pride. "Unique! It is the work of Herr Hansing—each of our pastries is made by a dedicated specialist who makes nothing else."

Liebermann examined the photograph, and then returned his attention to the pastry. His untutored eye was unable to discern anything particularly distinctive; however, the master baker's confidence was persuasive and Liebermann was happy to accept his expert opinion.

"Thank you," said the young doctor. "You have been most helpful."

"Do you require any further assistance?"

"No . . . that was all I needed to know."

"Then I will bid you good day."

Herr Tishlar bowed and sashayed back to his kitchen.

Liebermann, smiling broadly—perhaps too broadly for a solitary man with no obvious cause of delight—dropped the photograph and magnifying glass into the side pocket of his coat and found a table near the window, where he sat, still smiling.

Trezska was twenty minutes late; however, her tardy arrival did nothing to dampen his spirits. Liebermann dismissed her excuses and urged her to make a close study of the impressive menu. After some deliberation—and two consultations with the head waiter—they both ordered the Salzburger Mozart torte: a sponge cake with layers of marzipan, brushed with chocolate cream and apricot jam, and decorated with large orange-flavored pralines.

They talked mostly about music. Trezska described how she intended to play the spring sonata for Rosé at her next lesson—and the conversation naturally progressed to Beethoven. Liebermann regaled his companion with a musical anecdote concerning Beethoven's mortal remains and the composer Anton Bruckner. Apparently, when Beethoven's bones were being exhumed for skeletal measurement, Bruckner had barged into the chapel of the Währing cemetery, pushed the experts aside, and grasped in both hands Beethoven's skull—which he then began to address. Unmoved by Bruckner's devotion, those present quickly took back the skull and manhandled Bruckner out of the building.

Liebermann then asked Trezska if she would like to go to a concert at the Tonkünstlerverein—a recital including some Hugo Wolf songs and a performance of the Fauré sonata for violin and piano. She agreed instantly, and became quite excited when he told her that Jakob Grün was the soloist.

As they spoke, Liebermann was distracted by Trezska's beauty: the darkness and depth of her eyes, the color of her skin, and the shape of her face. Something of their lovemaking seemed to persist in the lower chambers of his mind: impressions of movement and memories of touch. He desired her—and that desire was predominantly physical; however, his attachment was becoming more complex. He had developed a fondness for her idiosyncrasies: the subtle cadences of her accent, the timbre of her voice, the way she moved her fingers when speaking, and the swift efficiency with which she could make small adjustments to her hair. It was in these little things—and the inordinate pleasure he derived from noticing them—that Liebermann recognized love's progress. Cupid was a cunning archer, and penetrated defenses by choosing to land his arrows in the least obvious places.

The clock struck two, reminding Liebermann of his other engagements.

He paid their bill at the counter and purchased a circular box of sugared almonds, which he presented to Trezska as they emerged from the café.

She grinned: "What are these for?"

"For . . . introducing me to the transcendental properties of absinthe."

"I thought the green fairy made you feel ill."

"She did. However, that did not stop me from appreciating her magic."

Trezska detected some deeper meaning in this remark—but she did not demand an explanation.

"Thank you," she said.

The atmosphere on the Kohlmarkt had become smoky, and a few gaslights had already been lit. In the distance, the Michaelertor had become shrouded in a violet haze.

Liebermann took Trezska's hand, pressed it to his lips, and inhaled the fresh, crisp bouquet of clementine and mimosa. The familiar fragrance aroused in him a curious sentiment—a kind of proprietorial satisfaction.

She turned to move away, but at that very moment a gentleman stepped ahead of the advancing crowd and cried out, "Amélie."

He was smiling at Trezska—and his expression was somewhat excited.

Trezska glanced back at Liebermann, and then at the gentleman.

"I'm sorry . . . but you have mistaken me for someone else."

The man had a handsome, harmonious face, which momentarily appeared shocked before resuming an expression of composed amiability.

"No—surely not. It is you!" He laughed—as if he had just penetrated the meaning of an exclusive joke. "Franz . . . Remember?"

He appeared eager, expectant.

Trezska's brow furrowed. "With the greatest respect, I have no idea who you are."

"But . . ."

The gentleman now looked confused.

Trezska turned to look back at Liebermann—a silent request for assistance. He stepped forward and said simply: "Sir . . . ?"

The gentleman had not noticed the young doctor and now started for the second time. He withdrew slightly.

"Of course," he said, smiling contritely at Trezska. "I must . . . I must be mistaken. Please, dear lady, accept my sincere apologies . . . and to you, sir," he added, making brief eye contact with Liebermann. "Good afternoon." Straightening his hat, he strode off toward the Graben.

"How very peculiar," said Trezska.

"Yes," Liebermann replied.

"He gave me a fright."

They hesitated for a moment, both of them somewhat discomfited by the encounter.

Trezska shook her head. "Never mind. Now you must get going or you will be late."

After leaving Demel's, Liebermann walked to the Volksgarten, where he caught a tram to Ottakring and his next appointment.

Dr. Kessler was a middle-aged man, balding, with rounded cheeks and oval spectacles that perched on his snub nose. "Ah," he said, studying Liebermann's security office documents. "I suppose you want to know more about Thomas Zelenka?"

"No," Liebermann replied. "The boy I need to know more about is Domokos Pikler."

"Ah yes," said Kessler. A line appeared across his otherwise smooth brow. "Pikler."

"Do you remember him?"

"Indeed. I had only just been appointed at the school when . . ." Kessler allowed the sentence to trail off. "I presume," he started again, the tone of his voice more guarded, "your question bears some relation to that reprehensible article in the *Arbeiter-Zeitung.*"

"The article by Herr G., yes."

"I don't know about all the other allegations, but I do know one thing: the correspondent—whoever he is—was completely wrong about Pikler. The boy did not die because of persecution and bad luck. He was not forced to stand on a window ledge, and he did not jump off."

"It was suicide . . ."

"Yes."

"How can you be so sure?"

Kessler looked uneasy. His pate had begun to glisten with a film of perspiration.

"I would like to be frank with you, Herr Doctor. Could we speak, not as investigator and school physician, but rather as two medical men?"

Liebermann understood the nature of this appeal. It was a request for professional confidence—an assurance that discretion would be exercised.

"Of course," said Liebermann.

Kessler pushed the young doctor's security office papers back across the table.

"He was a glum fellow, Pikler. Very glum. He never smiled, never laughed—never responded to banter. He'd just look at you, with a sullen expression on his face. He came to see me on several occasions, complaining of aches and pains, but I couldn't find anything wrong with him—well, not physically. He was a strange boy. . . . In the middle of our consultations he would often ask me questions of a philosophical nature. *What is the meaning of life? What is the point of existence? Why doesn't God intercede to stop the suffering of innocents?* And on one occasion he said something about mortal sin—something like: if atheists are correct, and there is no God, then there is no mortal sin . . . therefore, those who take their own lives might not go to hell, but instead find everlasting peace. Now, you must understand, I had only just taken up my position—and I was not used to dealing with cadets. The headmaster had gone out of his way to stress that the boys could be manipulative—that they might try to get medical exemptions in order to avoid certain onerous duties. I assumed that Pikler was a typical case. A malingerer. Given what happened, I now know that I was horribly mistaken. Some . . ." Kessler winced. "Some might accuse me of negligence. The boy was suffering from melancholia. I suspect that he initially presented with physical symptoms because he found these easier to talk about than his psychological symptoms, and his philosophical questions represented a desperate attempt to make sense of a world that he found perplexing and from which he could derive no pleasure. I should have . . ." Kessler emitted a long sigh that surrendered successive pitches like a descending scale. "Done something. . . . If I had referred Pikler on to a specialist, a psychiatrist—someone like you—then perhaps he would still be with us."

Kessler looked at Liebermann directly. The moistness in his eyes evinced the authenticity of his regret.

"None of us," said Liebermann, "are perfect—and medicine is an inexact science."

An hour later, Liebermann was sitting with Thomas Zelenka's parents in the third district. It was a difficult situation: Liebermann was only there because he wanted to ask one question—a question that he knew would sound utterly absurd without first establishing some sort of context. Thus he set about the formidable task of influencing the flow of conversation such that its end point would be the gustatory preferences of the Zelenkas' dead son.

Although getting the conversation from introductory remarks to the desired topic proved every bit as challenging as he had expected, once the subject had been broached, Meta Zelenka engaged in an extended reminiscence about her son's healthy appetite.

"Did Thomas," said Liebermann—as casually as he could—"have a particular fondness for almond tarts?"

"No . . . not that I can remember."

The young doctor—recognizing that he was perhaps already pushing his luck—changed the subject.

When he was about to leave, Fanousek, who had been eyeing him with some suspicion, said: "I thought you'd come about the dictionary. I thought it might have been found by now."

Liebermann remembered Rheinhardt saying something about such a volume.

"I understand that it was very expensive," said Liebermann.

"Very expensive," said Meta. "More than we could afford."

"Do you remember who published it?" said Liebermann, for want of a better question to ask.

"Yes: Hartel and Jacobsen—of Leipzig. We had to order it directly."

Something stirred in Liebermann's mind—a recollection. Where had he last seen a Hartel and Jacobsen dictionary?

"But why that particular dictionary?" said Liebermann, his curiosity aroused.

"It was recommended."

"By whom?"

"By one of the masters."

"Which one? Can you remember?"

Meta shook her head, and looked at her husband.

"I think it was . . ." Fanousek pulled at his chin. "Herr Sommer. Yes, it was Herr Sommer."

52

DREXLER HAD BEEN EXPECTING NIGHTMARES—but when they came, he was surprised by their power and intensity. They were not like ordinary dreams at all. They were vivid and possessed an extraordinary physicality.

One of them—a macabre re-creation of the night they had journeyed into the woods to bury Perger—was particularly disturbing. Drexler had finished filling the grave and was ready to leave. However, he tarried a moment in order to flatten some loose clods with the blade of his shovel. A pale hand broke through the earth, and the fingers closed tightly around his ankle. He struggled to get free but it was impossible: the hideous grip was like the teeth of a bear trap. He called out: *Help, help . . . Wolf, Freitag, Steininger, help me*—but he had lost his voice. Horrified, he watched them walking away, Wolf's lamp fading until its flickering sentinel light was extinguished by a cloak of darkness. What had really frightened Drexler, however, was what had happened next. On waking, he had discovered that he could not move his leg. He could still feel Perger's bone-crushing hold around his ankle. Panic had threaded through Drexler's body—and his breath had come in short, sharp gulps.

"Not again, Drexler!" Wolf had reprimanded him. Yet the sound of Wolf's heartless voice had been strangely comforting—a reminder that a real world existed in which corpses could be relied upon to stay dead. Sensation had flowed back into Drexler's paralyzed leg, and the ring of pain around his ankle had become first a dull ache, and then nothing—a memory.

Drexler had once overheard one of the masters talking about a doctor in Vienna who could interpret dreams. If so, he did not need his services—he already knew what these dreams meant.

That afternoon, while sitting in the library, he had decided that he must do something.

Drexler crossed the courtyard with his head bowed. The rain was making circles on islands of reflected sky. He entered the chapel and inhaled the familiar fragrance of incense and candle wax. Dipping his hand in the font, he anointed himself with holy water, genuflected, and found a place on a pew with the other boys who were waiting to make their confessions.

In due course he entered the confessional box, knelt down, and observed the shadowy figure of the priest crossing the air through the window grille.

"Bless me, Father, for I have sinned . . ."

He had disobeyed his mother and father, he had deceived others, he had shown disrespect to his elders, he had failed to attend Mass. His confession flowed fluently and easily, but his resolve faltered when he attempted to unburden his conscience of the single sin that—in his estimation, at least—would consign him to hell.

"Father . . ." He hesitated.

"Yes, my son?"

"I . . . I have . . . I have . . ." He could not do it. "I have been to see the whore in Aufkirchen."

The priest, who had been perfectly still, shifted—as if suddenly interested.

"Ahh . . . the whore in Aufkirchen, you say?"

"Yes."

"And what—exactly—was the nature of your sinful act?"

"Father . . . we had relations."

"Relations . . . I see, I see. Did she perform impure acts about your person?"

"She . . ."

"Come now, my son . . ."

"We had relations."

"You penetrated her?"

"I did."

The priest took a deep breath, and exhaled slowly.

"And did she . . . perform any unseemly acts with her mouth?"

"We kissed."

"Yes . . . but did she degrade herself using your person?"

The inquisition went on for some time. When the priest was finally satisfied that he had a complete and thorough understanding of Drexler's transgressions, he offered him counsel with respect to the temptations of the flesh, and warned him that he should not replace one vice with another—especially the vice of *self-pollution*—which would have grave physical and spiritual consequences. The priest then gave Drexler absolution and a penance of prayer.

Drexler did not do his penance. Instead, he marched straight out of the chapel, across the courtyard, and sat in the cloisters, fuming. It was all such nonsense! The priest had clearly been titillated by Drexler's erotic adventures in Aufkirchen: how could such a pathetic individual mediate between him and God? This was not what he wanted. He wanted to be truly absolved. He wanted to be absolved to the extent that he could sleep peacefully again and be free of his terrible, terrible guilt, the sheer magnitude of which made the rest of life seem an empty, hollow, meaningless charade by comparison.

To atone fully, Drexler realized that he would have to pay a forfeit more costly than a few prayers. Such mumblings were not a penance, and would do nothing to ease his pain.

53

THE LECTURE THEATER was almost empty—in fact, there were only five attendees including Liebermann. Professor Freud pointed to a small semicircle of chairs in front of the tiered auditorium and said: "Please, won't you come nearer, gentlemen." He smiled, and beckoned—wiggling his clenched fingers as one might to encourage a shy child. The tone of his voice was exceptionally polite, but his penetrating gaze was determined. The audience, which comprised professional men in their middle years, accepted his invitation and made their way down the central aisle.

Liebermann was already sitting in one of the chairs at the front. He had attended many of Freud's Saturday evening lectures and knew that a request for greater proximity would be issued sooner or later. The professor did not like straining his voice and tried to create an intimate and informal atmosphere when addressing small groups.

Whereas other faculty members might have appeared clutching a thick wad of foolscap, dense with inky hieroglyphs, Freud arrived empty-handed. He always preferred to extemporize.

Once, just before Freud had been about to speak, Liebermann had asked him: "What are you going to talk about?" "We shall see," Freud had replied. "I am sure my unconscious has something planned."

The professor consulted the auditorium clock, which showed seven o'clock exactly. He coughed into his hand and stood erect, as if startled by the occurrence of an unusually arresting idea.

"Gentlemen," he began. "One would certainly have supposed that there could be no doubt about what is to be understood as 'sexual.' First and foremost, what is sexual is something improper, something one ought not to talk about. I have been told that the pupils of a celebrated psychiatrist once made an attempt to convince their teacher how frequently the symptoms of hysterical patients represent sexual things. For this purpose they took him to the bedside of a female hysteric, whose attacks were an unmistakable imitation of the process of childbirth. But with a shake of his head he remarked, 'Well, there's nothing sexual about childbirth.' Quite right. Childbirth need not in every case be something improper."

Liebermann was the only member of the audience who smiled.

"I see that you take offense at my joking about serious things," Freud continued. "But it is not altogether a joke—for it is not easy to decide what is covered by the concept 'sexual.' "

And so he went on, improvising with extraordinary fluency, exploring a range of subjects relating to human sexuality (many of which he chose to illustrate with clinical examples drawn from his own practice). Liebermann was particularly interested in a case of sexual jealousy. . . .

When the lecture ended, at a quarter to nine, Freud took some questions from the audience. They were not very searching, but the professor managed to answer them in such a way as to make the questioners appear more perceptive than they actually were. It was a display of good grace rarely encountered in academic circles.

Liebermann lingered as the auditorium emptied. He approached the lecturer's table. The professor shook Liebermann's hand, thanked him for coming, and remarked that he would not be going on to Königstein's house to play taroc, as his good friend had caught a bad head cold. Moreover, as it was his custom to socialize on Saturday nights—and he was nothing if not a creature of habit—he wondered whether Liebermann would be interested in joining him for coffee and a slice of *guglhupf* at Café Landtmann. The young doctor—always eager to spend time with his mentor—accepted the honor readily.

They made their way to the Ringstrasse while talking somewhat superficially about the attendees. Two of the gentlemen, Freud believed, were general practitioners—but he had no idea as to the identity of the other two. It was truly astonishing, Liebermann reflected, how Freud's public lectures rarely attracted more than half a dozen people. The professor commented, as if responding telepathically to Liebermann's private thoughts, that resistance to psychoanalytic ideas merely confirmed their veracity.

A red and white tram rolled by, its interior lit by a row of electric lights. The passengers, staring out of the windows, seemed peculiarly careworn and cheerless.

Liebermann asked the professor some technical questions about the case material he had discussed in his talk—and, more specifically, about the patient he was treating who suffered from sexual jealousy.

"Yes," said Freud. "Sane in every respect, other than an absolute conviction that when he leaves Vienna, his saintly wife enjoys assignations with his brother—a celebrated religious in their community. The man reminds me of Pozdnyshev in Tolstoy's *The Kreutzer Sonata*. Have you read it?"

"I have."

"You will recall then how Pozdnyshev suspects that the musical evenings his wife enjoys with the violinist Trukhachevsky are merely an artful deceit. So it is with my patient, who has come to believe that when his brother and wife are supposedly praying together, they are in fact enjoying the forbidden pleasures of an illicit union."

"In the end, Pozdnyshev kills his wife—does he not?"

"Indeed . . . Tolstoy understood that jealousy is the most danger-ous of passions. The doctor who takes such a patient into his care can assuredly expect his nights to be much disturbed by fearful imag-inings."

The professor proceeded to make some distinctions between different forms of jealousy, namely neurotic and pathological—the latter being more severe than the former. Then he suddenly seemed to lose confidence in his delineations.

"The problem is," he continued, stroking his neatly trimmed beard, "that one cannot love without experiencing jealousy. It is one of the many common forms of unhappiness that we might ascribe to the *human condition*. In matters of the heart, the boundary that sepa-rates that which is normal from that which is abnormal all but dis-solves. Possessed of this knowledge, the physician must be extremely wary with respect to what he identifies as an illness."

"Surely," Liebermann ventured, "in cases of sexual jealousy where there is insufficient evidence to substantiate an allegation of infi-delity, we can reasonably describe the symptoms as delusional."

Freud shrugged and stopped to light a cigar. He offered one to Liebermann, but the young doctor declined.

"I remember," Freud said, "many years ago, when I was only re-cently engaged to be married . . ." He paused, sighed, and whispered almost incredulously, "A situation arose that caused me much mental turmoil." The professor began walking again. He was looking straight ahead, but his gaze had lost some of its characteristic probing inten-sity.

"I once had a dear friend," he continued. "Wahle was his name. He was an artist of considerable talent. . . . He had also been, for a long time, a brotherly friend of my beloved Martha—and, naturally, they corresponded. I should mention that Wahle was already engaged himself—in fact, to Martha's cousin. So . . . there was never any reason for . . ." He hesitated, drew on his cigar, and exhaled, uttering as he did so the word "suspicion." He nodded grimly. "However, one day, I came across some of their letters, and detected in their content certain *meanings*. . . . I discussed my discovery with Schönberg, a mutual acquaintance, who confirmed my fears. He said that Wahle was behaving strangely, that he had burst into tears when he had heard of my engagement to Martha. Clearly, I could not allow this situation to continue—a sentiment that Schönberg appreciated. He subsequently organized a meeting in a café, where he hoped we would be able to resolve matters civilly.

"Unfortunately, the meeting did not go well. Wahle behaved like a madman. He threatened to shoot me and then himself if I did not make Martha happy. I thought it was some kind of joke. I actually laughed . . . and then he said that it was in his power to destroy my happiness. He could—and would—instruct Martha to end our engagement, and she would obey. It was an insane claim and I couldn't take it seriously. So he called for a pen and paper and began to write the letter there and then. Schönberg and I were both shocked—it contained the same inappropriately familiar terms of endearment that I had seen in his other letters. He referred to his 'beloved Martha' and his 'undying love.' I was outraged, and tore the letter to pieces. Wahle stormed out, and we followed him, trying to bring him to his senses, but he only broke down in tears. I seized his arm and—close to tears myself—escorted him home."

Freud paused for a moment. A beggar, huddled in a doorway, extended his hand. The professor dug deep into his pocket and tossed a coin in the man's direction.

"But the next morning," he continued, "my heart hardened. I felt that I had been weak. Wahle was now my enemy, and I should have been ruthless. He was clearly in love with Martha. I wrote to her, explaining this—but she would have none of it! She sprang to his defense. They were friends, nothing more, like brother and sister! Her refusal to condemn his behavior played on my mind. I began to think about Wahle's threat: perhaps he *did* have some hold over her. Perhaps he *could* make her give me up. I experienced an attack of appalling dread. It drove me quite frantic. I wandered the streets for hours, every night: thinking, thinking, thinking. . . . What had *really* passed between them? Why had she not taken my side—as she so obviously should have done? In the end, I could stand it no longer. I had to see her. I borrowed enough money to travel to Wandsbeck, and we met—for the sake of propriety—in secret. We talked and reached . . . an understanding.

"I returned to Vienna much calmer. But only a week later, that appalling dread returned. I was tormented by the slightest notion that Wahle might be—in any way—dear to her. Something took possession of my senses . . . something demonic. I gave Martha an ultimatum. I demanded that she renounce their friendship completely, and stated that if she failed to do this, I would . . . I would settle the affair with him—finally."

"Finally? You intended to . . ." Liebermann dared not finish the sentence.

Freud shook his head.

"Thinking about it now, I'm not sure what I meant. These events were such a long time ago." As though surfacing from a dream, Freud blinked and turned to look at Liebermann. His eyes seemed to contract—recovering their piercing vitality. "Fortunately, for all of us, Martha agreed. Wahle vanished from our lives, but the wound that he inflicted took many years to heal. So you see—even the most rational of men . . ."

It was an extraordinary confession, but not unprecedented. Liebermann had known the professor to disclose personal details of his life before: his openness was not so remarkable, given that his masterpiece *The Interpretation of Dreams* contained much that would ordinarily be described as autobiographical—and not all of it flattering, by any means. Freud had included in the section on somatic sources an account of one of his own dreams, which he attributed ultimately to an apple-size boil that had risen at the base of his scrotum.

"Indeed," Liebermann responded. "You *are* the most rational of men. So much so that I wonder whether the disturbed mental state that you describe might require a more compelling explanation than simply the *human condition*."

"A more compelling explanation?" Freud repeated, a trail of pungent cigar smoke escaping from his mouth.

"Did these events take place when you were conducting your research into cocaine?"

"Why, yes. . . . I used to take it as an antidepressant. To relieve my despair."

"Isn't cocaine—taken in large doses—associated with insomnia, restlessness, nervous agitation?" Freud's pace slowed as he considered Liebermann's conjecture. He appeared quite self-absorbed, and again pulled at his beard. In a different register, Liebermann added casually: "Cocaine has never been used for headaches—has it?"

Freud started. "I beg your pardon?"

"Cocaine . . . has it ever been used for headaches?"

"No . . . no, not to my knowledge." The professor seemed to gather himself together—although the lines that appeared on his forehead demonstrated that this was only accomplished with much effort. "I had always thought," he continued, "that it might be useful primarily as a treatment for depression and anxiety. For a time, it was administered as a tonic for the German army: and a small amount of cocaine added to salicylate of soda is good for indigestion. But it has had strictly limited application in the sphere of pain relief. You know, perhaps, that Koller's discovery of cocaine as an anesthetic for use during eye surgery owed something to my original research?"

"No, I'm afraid I didn't."

Freud pulled a face that suggested moderate pique—and then, recovering his natural mien, added: "Headaches? No. Never for headaches."

54

THE CARRIAGE HAD NOT yet reached the outskirts of Vienna.

"So," said Liebermann. "It was Gärtner who actually discovered Zelenka's body?"

"Yes," Rheinhardt replied, consulting his notebook. "After which, he rushed upstairs to inform the headmaster—who had just begun a meeting with Becker."

"And did anyone else enter the laboratory?"

Rheinhardt turned a page. "The old soldier, Albert, and two prefects: they were the ones who carried Zelenka's body to the infirmary."

"I see," said Liebermann, adjusting his necktie and quietly whistling a fragment of Bach.

Haussmann turned toward the window, concealing a half smile.

"You know, Max," said Rheinhardt, "I really do wish you were more forthcoming! On our return I will be expected to justify this excursion, and if I am unable to, Commissioner Brügel will be particularly aggrieved. Two days ago he circulated a memorandum to all senior officers, requesting that we make every effort to remain close to the Schottenring station. He intimated that an unusual circumstance had arisen that might require our participation in a special operation at very short notice."

"This 'unusual circumstance,'" said Liebermann, "is it something to do with von Bulow's special assignment?"

Rheinhardt caught his assistant's eye.

"Oh, confound it, Haussmann, I'm going to tell him!" Rheinhardt leaned forward. "Young Haussmann here—"

"What are you whispering for?" Liebermann asked. The inspector pointed toward the carriage box. "Oh, don't be ridiculous, Oskar. The driver can't hear! He's outside!"

"I'm not taking any chances," Rheinhardt replied, resting his elbows on his knees and leaning even closer. "Young Haussmann here was delivering some papers to the commissioner's office. He was about to knock, but held back when he heard raised voices. The commissioner was giving von Bulow—and *yes*, I *did* say von Bulow—a serious verbal drubbing. General von Stoger's name was mentioned . . . and there was talk of something having been stolen from his safe. A document that they called . . ." Rheinhardt's cheeks reddened.

"*Studie U*," said Haussmann, gallantly coming to his superior's aid.

"Did you hear anything else?" asked Liebermann.

"Nothing of consequence," Haussmann replied—but then added: "Well, there *was* one other thing. They kept on referring to the Liderc."

"The Liderc. What does that mean?" Liebermann flashed a look at Rheinhardt.

"I really have no idea."

"Liderc. Are you sure you heard that correctly?" Liebermann asked the assistant detective.

"Yes, Herr Doctor. It was definitely the Liderc," said Haussmann.

"So," Rheinhardt continued, "I strongly suspect that the commissioner is contemplating a large operation, the purpose of which will be to retrieve *Studie U*. As to the factors that will influence his decision to proceed with the operation—or not—we can only speculate."

"Interesting," said Liebermann.

"Needless to say," Rheinhardt added, "I am praying that the commissioner decides against briefing his senior detectives this afternoon." Reminded once again of the matter in hand, the inspector leaned back and spoke now in his usual resonant baritone. "I've sent a telegram to the headmaster and I've made sure that Herr Sommer knows exactly what time we intend to arrive."

"Herr Sommer?"

"Yes, Herr Sommer."

"Why ever did you do that?"

"You said he was trying to avoid us . . . that he was a liar. I assumed—"

"He *did* try to avoid us, and he *is* a liar!"

"Then why don't you—"

"Want to speak to him?"

"Yes."

"Because it isn't necessary: he's not as significant as I once thought."

"Well, you might have said! What on earth made you change your mind?"

"Do you really want to know?"

"Of course I want to know."

"Sugared almonds!"

Haussmann turned again to look out of the window, his half smile now widening to become an embarrassingly conspicuous grin.

On arriving at Saint Florian's, Rheinardt instructed his assistant to wait outside with the driver. He then ushered Liebermann through the stone arch and into the courtyard of the school. The old soldier, Albert, was seated on a bench, his chin buried in his chest. His stertorous breathing—amplified by the cloisters—sounded curiously mechanical: a repetitive grating and grinding. Rheinhardt approached and touched his shoulder, but did not shake him. The veteran's expression spoke too eloquently of blissful release from the heavy yoke of corporeality. Moved to pity, Rheinhardt slowly withdrew his hand.

"I know how to get to Professor Eichmann's office," he whispered. "We'll let this old fellow enjoy his beauty sleep, eh? You can question him later."

Liebermann smiled, recognizing in Rheinhardt's small act of charity a justification for hope. Being a psychoanalyst, he saw the salvation of humanity not in great ideologies, religion, or political reforms but in everyday, barely perceptible deeds of kindness. He found this thought consoling, a counterbalance to his certain knowledge that they were about to find out how easily man becomes a thing of darkness—how easily civilized values blacken and curl in the heat of primitive passions.

Professor Eichmann greeted them with frigid condescension.

"You will forgive me, gentlemen, but I am extremely busy and cannot spare you much time."

Liebermann promised the headmaster that he would be brief.

"Tell me, headmaster," he said softly, "when you entered the laboratory on the evening that Thomas Zelenka's body was discovered, did you smell anything?"

The headmaster wrinkled his nose—as if the mere mention of smell had triggered some form of malodorous olfactory hallucination.

"The laboratory always smells a little unpleasant."

"Nothing struck you as unusual?"

"No."

"Could you describe how it smelled?"

"Herr Doctor, I cannot see how this line of questioning can possibly prove helpful. As I have already explained—"

Liebermann raised his hands, arresting the headmaster's flow with an expression that begged indulgence.

"Headmaster, I have said that I will be brief, and I promise you I will keep my word. With respect, could you please answer the question: what did the laboratory smell of?"

Eichmann shook his head, tutted, and said: "A little like bad eggs."

Liebermann stared at the headmaster—an inquisitorial, ingressive stare that owed much to his acquaintance with Professor Freud. Then, quite suddenly, he said, "Thank you," and stood to leave.

The headmaster looked first at Rheinhardt and then back at Liebermann.

"Is that all you wanted to know?" Eichmann asked.

"Yes," said Liebermann. "I have no further questions. I trust you will concede that we have respected your convenience."

The headmaster did not appear satisfied—only suspicious.

"Where is Professor Gärtner?" asked Rheinhardt.

"In the staff common room," said the headmaster.

He observed their departure with eyes that radiated contempt.

Liebermann and Rheinhardt found Professor Gärtner sitting alone, ensconced in a fustian armchair and sipping brandy from a metal hip flask. The book on his lap was Thucydides's great *History of the Peloponnesian War*. After some introductory civilities—to which the professor responded with considerably more courtesy than the headmaster—Liebermann repeated his question: "Tell me, Professor Gärtner, when you discovered Thomas Zelenka's body, did you smell anything unusual?"

"Unusual?" repeated Gärtner.

"Yes."

"I don't think so. To be honest, I don't have a very acute sense of smell. It's never been the same since the storming of Brescia back in '49. I was serving under Haynau—with the first battalion, no less—and fell very badly ill. The regimental doctor didn't know what it was. He was mystified. I was sick and very weak for more than a month. When I recovered, I felt well enough. All my body parts were working—just as they did before—with the exception of my nose! The sensation of smell was dulled, blunted. In order to detect the fragrance of a flower, I would have to hold it directly under my nostrils, inhaling deeply, and only then would I catch a hint of its bouquet. My sense of taste was affected, too. Subsequently, I've only ever enjoyed foods with very strong flavors. A good spicy goulash, for example."

Liebermann attempted to interrupt the garrulous professor, but he failed.

"I once met a neurologist from Paris," Gärtner continued, "who said that he'd heard of such things happening, and he spoke at some length about the bulbs that project from beneath the brain. A clever fellow if ever there was one. He had studied with Charcot and knew his Virgil as well as his anatomies. Apparently, there are some infectious organisms that attack nerve tissue, causing permanent damage; however, I *should* say—if my memory serves me correctly—he associated such cases with tropical rather than Mediterranean diseases." Professor Gärtner took a swig from his hip flask, hummed pensively, and added: "I'm sorry, Herr Doctor. I seem to have forgotten your question. What was it you wanted to know?"

Liebermann and Rheinhardt made their excuses and left.

"Well," said Rheinhardt, as they made their way down the stairs. "This isn't going very well, is it?"

Liebermann shook his head. "No, it isn't; however, at the same time, the science of hereditary constitution gives me good reason to remain optimistic."

"Max, what are you talking about?"

"I will explain in due course. Now, let us return to the courtyard."

Albert was still sitting in the same place, although the movement of his head suggested that he was now not sleeping but observing the spiraling of dead leaves in a vortex.

When Rheinhardt and Liebermann arrived, he rose to greet them—saluting and clicking his heels together to produce a hollow knock.

"Ah, my dear fellow," said Rheinhardt. "There you are. Allow me to introduce a colleague of mine, Herr Dr. Liebermann. He would like to ask you some questions."

Albert smacked his lips.

"A doctor . . ."

"Yes."

"Permission to report—I'm as fit as a fiddle, sir. Haven't had a day's illness in years."

"Well," said Rheinhardt, "I'm very glad to hear it; however, the good doctor has not come to inquire about your health. He wants to ask you about the recent tragedy."

Rheinhardt glanced at his friend.

"Do you remember the boy Thomas Zelenka?" asked Liebermann.

"Permission to report: yes, sir. The boy who died."

"Do you remember the evening when his body was discovered?"

"I do, sir. He was found in the laboratory, sir."

"Now, I want you to think back to that evening. I want you to try to remember something for me." Liebermann extended his hand, and touched the old soldier's arm gently. "When you entered the laboratory . . . what did it smell like?"

Albert's rheumy-eyed gaze met Liebermann's clearer one. His tongue slipped out of his mouth and proceeded to swing from side to side, coating his lower lip and bristly chin with saliva.

Rheinhardt was about to repeat the question, but Liebermann silenced him with a hand gesture.

They waited. The sound of gunfire could be heard in the distance.

"Permission to report," said Albert. "A peculiar smell, sir . . . like almonds."

55

Rheinhardt knocked on the laboratory door. The muffled sound of Becker's voice came from within: "Enter."

Inside, the deputy headmaster was seated at a table covered with exercise books. His expression was bored and slightly irritated. Becker stood to greet them, but his face was impassive and the absence of chairs (other than his own) seemed sufficient reason to justify the discourtesy of not inviting the policeman and the young doctor to sit.

Liebermann surveyed the room and, in spite of its ugliness, its exposed pipes, and stained walls, he smiled.

"This takes me back," said Liebermann, nostalgically. "It reminds me of the lab in my old school. I was very fond of chemistry."

Becker showed no sign of sympathetic interest. Instead, he waved his hand over the table and said: "Gentlemen, I have much to do today."

This plea for brevity resonated with the headmaster's: Liebermann supposed that the two men had convened earlier, resolving to obstruct the investigators with a show of churlishness and bad manners.

Liebermann sidled up to the deputy headmaster and examined the book he was in the middle of marking. The boy's work was barely visible beneath a descending curtain of red ink.

"Ahh," said Liebermann recognizing a distinctive illustration from his youth. "The Liebig condenser. You know, I was once told that it wasn't Baron von Liebig who invented the condenser at all but someone else entirely. Is that true, Dr. Becker?"

The deputy headmaster straightened his back and adjusted his gown. Having been presented with an opportunity to demonstrate the depth of his knowledge, he was unable to feign indifference.

"The earliest condenser—to my knowledge—was described by Christian Ehrenfried Weigel in 1771."

"Is that so?" Liebermann responded. "Extraordinary."

Rheinhardt had walked over to the geological exhibits, where he renewed his acquaintance with the shiny black trilobite.

"Inspector," Becker called out, "I would be most grateful if we could proceed expeditiously. I am certain that you and your colleague"—he threw a contemptuous look at Liebermann—"must have many matters awaiting your urgent attention in Vienna."

Rheinhardt rolled back on his heels. "Indeed."

"Then shall we begin?" said Becker, talking across Liebermann.

Rheinhardt inclined his head in Liebermann's direction. "Please continue, Herr Doctor."

"Thank you, Inspector," said Liebermann.

Becker tossed the pen he was holding onto the table. It rolled away, declaring his hostility with each clattering revolution. In the ensuing stillness, the hissing of leaking pipes filled the air with an unnerving, serpentine sibilance.

"I trust your wife is well?" said Liebermann.

"Well enough," Becker replied.

"She is fully recovered?"

"Recovered, Herr Doctor? She was never ill."

"You said that she had been tearful . . . after our visit?"

"She *was* tearful . . . but that is no longer the case."

"Good, I'm glad to hear it. Inspector Rheinhardt and I clearly misjudged the degree to which she had been affected by Zelenka's death." Then, stepping back and looking out over the benches, Liebermann added: "So, this is where the unfortunate boy was discovered. Could you tell me where exactly?"

"There," Becker pointed to the front bench.

Liebermann gazed at the empty floor space between two high stools.

"It is interesting, is it not," said Liebermann, imitating the manner in which he had seen Professor Freud begin his lecture the previous evening, "that we often appropriate the word 'chemistry' when language fails to furnish us with terms adequate to the task of describing the mysteries of love. We are often unable to say why it is that one relationship works and another doesn't. We say that the *chemistry* is right, or the *chemistry* is wrong, or perhaps that the *chemistry* is absent! This instinctive appropriation acknowledges that love is a very physical experience: it quickens the pulse and the breath . . . tears fall. Ironically, love—the most transcendent of all emotions—reminds us that we are mortal. I am of the opinion that our deepest passions are animated by a fierce chemistry, the reactions of which—by virtue of their association with corporeal processes—bring us inexorably closer to death."

Becker tilted his head, and his spectacles became circles of opaque brilliance. "I am sorry, Dr. Liebermann," said Becker. "But I really haven't a clue what you're talking about."

"Do you believe that there is a chemistry of love, Herr Doctor Becker? There is certainly a chemistry of death." Liebermann positioned himself between the first two benches and leaned forward, supporting his weight on outstretched arms. "We are—as yet—

ignorant of the substances that create bonds of affection, but we are not so ignorant of those that extinguish life."

Becker glared at Liebermann, but said nothing.

"How, I wonder," Liebermann continued, "would you describe the bond of affection that existed between Frau Becker and Thomas Zelenka? Is it enough to say that they were fond of each other? That they were friends? Or do you think we would do better to borrow once again the most potent of scientific metaphors. I am disposed to believe that they shared a *chemical affinity*."

The deputy headmaster suddenly turned around and faced the wall.

"Frau Becker and Thomas Zelenka," Liebermann continued. "They were lovers, weren't they?"

"Yes, they were lovers!" Becker exploded. "Are you satisfied now, Dr. Liebermann? Are you satisfied, now that I have admitted it? Now that I am shamed?"

Liebermann's reply was delivered with clinical neutrality. "It was never my purpose to derive any pleasure from your misfortune. I merely desired to establish some important facts."

"Well, there you are! You've succeeded! And what of it?"

Liebermann did not respond. He simply waited. With every passing second a subtle pressure mounted—a tacit demand for explanation. It seemed to weigh down on Becker until resistance was no longer possible. The deputy headmaster raised his hands, and then let them fall—a gesture that suggested both defeat and anger.

"Poldi was never happy here," he blurted out. "Right from the beginning. I could do nothing to raise her spirits. She spent half my monthly salary in the shops on Kärntner Strasse—and she was still inconsolable. She expected too much—from me, and from Saint Florian's. We became more and more estranged, and as we did so, she became more and more obsessed with the boys—the bullying, the persecution. She made a complete fool of herself in front of the other masters' wives—attempting to foment some kind of women's revolt! It was utterly absurd. She came perilously close to losing me my position! Had I not remonstrated with her in the strongest possible terms . . ." Becker hesitated, and the shadow that passed across his face intimated violence. "My prospects at Saint Florian's would have been irrevocably damaged! Zelenka exploited her sympathy—and he did so at a time when our marital relations were at their worst. His presence at the house became an embarrassment. Even the staff made jokes about it. Can you imagine what that is like, Herr Doctor? To have the gardener, the cook, the maid sniggering behind your back—enjoying the spectacle of your humiliation."

"Then why didn't you put a stop to it?" asked Liebermann gently. "Why didn't you prohibit Zelenka's visits?"

"To what end? By the time I had discovered their secret, it was too late. What good would it have done, Herr Doctor, had I acted in such a way as to draw even more attention to my predicament? What good? I am a rational man—a civilized man. I decided to conduct myself in a dignified fashion. Zelenka intended to join the civil service in the summer. I knew that Poldi would follow him. . . . It was simply a question of biding my time until then." Becker glanced back at Liebermann. "Well, there it is, Herr Doctor. You've had it out of me." His gaze took in Rheinhardt, and he added, "I trust you will both say *nothing* of this to anyone."

"And what of your marriage now?" asked Liebermann.

"I don't know. Poldi and I do not talk . . . not as a husband and wife should; however . . ."

"You still nurse a hope that—notwithstanding what has transpired—your marriage might yet survive?"

"I am not so naïve, Dr. Liebermann, as to think that just because Zelenka is dead all will be well again. Zelenka was a consequence, not a cause. Our estrangement had begun long before Poldi and Zelenka discovered their . . . *chemical affinity*; however, since Zelenka's death, I believe Poldi has changed—a little. We have—of late—been more civil with each other. Perhaps Zelenka's death has made her realize that life is precious and that we are sometimes obliged to make the most of what little we are given. And if I can find it within myself to forgive her . . . then, yes, it might not be so foolish to hope for some form of reconciliation."

Liebermann sighed, joined his hands together, and allowed his fingers to bounce on his lips.

"And there we might leave it," he said, his sentence—like an imperfect cadence—failing to find a satisfactory resolution. "Were it not," he then continued, "for the almond tart."

Becker started. "I beg your pardon?"

"The almond tart that you instructed your wife to purchase on one of her many trips into town. You may not know this, but she bought it at the Royal and Imperial Bakers. If you had eaten it, I dare say you would have recognized its very superior qualities—the lightness of the pastry, the moistness of the sponge, the subtle lemon and anise flavorings, and the burnished, sweet caramelized almonds. But, of course, you didn't eat it. Instead, you placed it next to Zelenka's dead body—right here"—Liebermann rapped the bench top—"before rushing upstairs to meet with the headmaster. Is that not so?"

Becker stumbled forward, as if his legs had suddenly lost all their strength. He clutched the handles of a glass-fronted cupboard for support and raised his head as if appealing to heaven for mercy. The effect was vaguely religious, iconic. With his forked beard, long hair, and black gown, Becker seemed to be re-creating the passion of an obscure old saint, as might be depicted among the illuminations on a thirteenth-century altar panel. Inside the cupboard the contents rattled, producing a delicate tintinnabulation.

"Perhaps," Liebermann pressed, "you would care to explain why you did this?"

The deputy headmaster held his fixed attitude and said nothing. It was as if his private torment excused him from any further obligation to speak.

"Dr. Becker?" Rheinhardt took a few steps toward the deputy headmaster. "Are you . . . well?"

Becker's head slumped forward. "Stay away from me, Inspector," he cried. "I don't want your pity! Do you hear? Stay away from me. I will not be humiliated. I have been humiliated enough. Enough, I say, enough!"

The cupboard was suddenly open, and two bottles fell from the deputy headmaster's hands. They smashed on the floor, throwing up shards of colored glass. Liebermann and Rheinhardt watched in dumb amazement as Becker dashed out of the room, slamming the door behind him. A key, turning in the lock, filled the laboratory with the sound of percussive engagement, its grim reverberations evoking the closure of a vault.

Liebermann leaped into the aisle, intercepting Rheinhardt as the inspector instinctively began his pursuit. They collided and both of them almost fell.

"What in God's name!" Rheinhardt gasped. "He'll get away—"

"Hold your breath," Liebermann commanded, grabbing Rheinhardt's arm and dragging him to the back of the laboratory. "Or you'll die!"

Liebermann tried to open one of the windows, banging the frame furiously—but it held fast. He then tried another, which, after repeated blows, gradually yielded. Throwing the window open, he clambered onto the sill and pulled himself up. Grasping the frame for support, he offered Rheinhardt his hand. The inspector was difficult to lift; however, drawing on some inner reserve, Liebermann heaved, and Rheinhardt scrambled out.

When the inspector became fully conscious of their precarious situation, he clutched at a projecting mullion and, looking down at the ground, was moved once again to invoke the deity: "God in heaven!"

Liebermann eased the window down and shut it with the heel of his shoe.

"You can breathe now," he said.

"Max! Why . . . what . . ." There were simply too many questions to articulate. Liebermann rested a calming hand on his friend's shoulder.

"The two bottles Becker threw to the floor contained cyanide and an acid of some description. When the two combine, hydrocyanic gas is produced: freshly created, one sniff can be fatal."

"That's how he killed Zelenka?"

"Yes," said Liebermann. "Potassium cyanide looks like sugar. Vinegar is an acid. The chemistry assignment that he set the boy was fatal. Zelenka would have followed Becker's instructions and—"

"Monstrous," Rheinhardt interrupted, shaking his head.

Beyond the hem of his trousers and the welting of his shoes, the inspector could see their carriage and the statue of Saint Florian. This unusual perspective made him feel quite unsteady, and he pulled back.

"Perhaps you had better not look down," said Liebermann.

"Haussmann?" Rheinhardt bellowed. "Haussmann?"

The door of the carriage did not open.

"Haussmann?" he cried again—inquiry turning into irritation.

In the distance, swaths of fir were turning olive-black in the failing afternoon light.

"The driver seems to have vanished too," said Liebermann.

"That foolish boy!" said Rheinhardt desperately. "Where on earth has he gone!"

"Let's try calling together," said Liebermann. "After three: one, two, three."

"*Haussmann.*"

Liebermann shifted slightly, and a small wedge of masonry broke from the ledge. It plummeted through the air and landed on the gravel, far below, with a barely perceptible whisper. On closer inspection, Liebermann noticed that the stonework around his feet was webbed with numerous tiny cracks. He did not draw the parlous state of the ledge to Rheinhardt's attention. Instead, he counted to three, and they both called out again:

"*Haussmann . . .*"

"*Haussmann . . .*"

"*Haussmann!*"

56

HAUSSMANN AND THE DRIVER were standing in the courtyard listening to Albert, whose rambling speech concerned his involvement with what the young men assumed must be a famous military campaign.

They had been waiting by the carriage, smoking and discussing the driver's intention to marry a flower girl called Fännchen in the spring, when the old soldier had appeared under the archway. He'd beckoned them into the courtyard and suggested that they might continue their conversation in the cloisters, where they could escape the wind and derive more pleasure from their tobacco. The two young men had been touched by the old man's thoughtfulness and, not wishing to offend him, had accepted his hospitable suggestion. Albert had lowered himself onto his favorite bench, hawked a soapy pellet of chartreuse phlegm onto a flagstone, and touched his medals with shaky liver-spotted fingers. The sensation of silk and metal between his thumb and forefinger had evoked memories of his youth and he had subsequently embarked on an epic (and seemingly interminable) tale of martial folly and eventual salvation.

The old soldier's reminiscences were incoherent and digressive, but the two young men listened politely. He spoke of the Austrian occupation of Buda and Pest, a dreaded Hungarian general called Görgey, a bloody siege, a meeting with the czar, and the arrival of two hundred thousand Russian troops.

"We would have been in trouble without them," said Albert, gazing across the courtyard at the chapel but obviously seeing something quite different—a host of ghostly Cossacks, perhaps, heaving into view over a flat steppe. "We were overconfident," he continued. "We underestimated Görgey! A terrible misjudgment, that's what it was—a terrible misjudgment. Thank God for the old czar! God bless him! Although—it has to be said—he was only helping out because of the Poles. See, they'd sided with the revolutionaries, and that had him worried—"

A door suddenly opened with considerable violence, banging against the wall. The deputy headmaster appeared, looking harried and overwrought. He tripped, recovered his balance, and came to an undignified, stumbling halt. Looking anxiously from side to side, he caught sight of Haussmann's group and froze. The attitude that he struck was unnatural, as if balancing on the tips of his toes in readiness to jump. Becker's elbows were crooked at an acute angle and held away from his torso, extending his gown transversely like the wings of a bat: these peculiarities of posture and dress created an illusion of supernatural visitation—something hellish preparing for flight.

The deputy headmaster, however, did not make a vertical ascent. Instead, he composed himself and marched purposefully toward the small gathering.

As he approached, the old soldier stood to attention.

"Permission to report . . . invited these security office gentlemen inside, sir, because of the wind. And then I—"

"Very good, Albert, very good," said Becker brusquely, holding his hand up to show that he did not require further enlightenment. Then, turning toward Haussmann, he said, "If I am not mistaken, you are the inspector's assistant?"

"Haussmann, sir."

"Yes, that's right, Haussmann. . . . I remember you, of course. Inspector Rheinhardt wishes to see you immediately. Albert, take these young men to the infirmary, please."

Haussmann's companion looked somewhat embarrassed.

"Not me, sir. I'm just the driver."

"No," said Becker. "You are to go too."

"Me?" said the driver, touching his chest in disbelief.

"Yes. That is what Inspector Rheinhardt said: 'Tell my men to come up here at once.' "

"Has someone been injured, sir?" Haussmann asked.

"No."

"Then what is he doing in the infirmary?"

"At this precise moment, I believe he is conversing with Nurse Funke. Now, I trust you will excuse me, gentlemen. Albert, the infirmary, please."

Becker bowed, turned sharply on his heels, and walked off toward the courtyard entrance. Albert muttered something under his breath. It sounded like an obscenity, but was rendered unintelligible by the abrasive grinding of a persistent cough.

"Permission to report," he uttered between rasps. "This way, sir."

Haussmann did not follow the old soldier but stood quite still, watching the receding figure of the deputy headmaster. He felt uneasy, troubled. Why did the inspector want the driver? Did he need to lift something heavy? And there was something about that message . . . "Tell my men to come up here at once." It wasn't the sort of thing that Rheinhardt would say. Rheinhardt almost always phrased his orders as if he were simply making a polite request: "Would you be so kind . . . I would be most grateful if . . ."

"Are you coming?" It was the driver.

Haussmann did not reply. His gaze remained fixed on the deputy headmaster, whose pace seemed to be quickening. Once he was through the archway, the wind caught his gown and it rose up, billowing and flapping. Haussmann cocked his head to one side. He thought he could hear something—a tonal inflection—that dropped with the soughing. At first he wondered whether he was imagining things, but then it came again, this time more clearly: voices—a faint cry.

"*Haussmann . . .*"

"*Haussmann . . .*"

"Deputy headmaster! Dr. Becker!"

Through the archway, only the sky and hills were visible. The bellying sail of the deputy headmaster's gown was gone.

Haussmann ran.

"Dr. Becker . . ."

He could hear the jangling of the horses' bridles, the distinctive clop of restive hooves. He ran beneath the arch, and cursed as he saw Becker climbing up onto the driver's box. A whip cracked, and the carriage began to move. Haussmann rounded the statue of Saint Florian and reached out, his fingers almost touching the back of the escaping carriage. But it was too late. The horses were gathering speed and the gap widened.

"Dr. Becker," he called out, helplessly.

The carriage pulled away—and Haussmann reluctantly abandoned his pursuit. Bending forward, with his hands resting on his thighs, he tried to catch his breath. He was immediately startled by the sound of Inspector Rheinhardt calling his name.

"Haussmann!"

The assistant detective stood up and spun around. But there was no one there.

"Haussmann!"

He looked up—and gasped in disbelief.

57

As Haussmann made his way back to the statue of Saint Florian, Rheinhardt and Liebermann watched Becker's progress. The deputy headmaster was whipping the horses with pitiless ferocity. Tracing a wide arc, the carriage careened as it rumbled toward the school gates. Rheinhardt turned away and sighed: a loud, operatic sigh that demonstrated the magnitude of his frustration.

"Never mind," said Liebermann. "He won't get far. I doubt he is carrying very much money, and as soon as we're back on terra firma, you can use the headmaster's telephone and notify the security office."

"I fear that you have forgotten the commissioner's memorandum," said Rheinhardt bitterly. "Brügel will be disinclined to spare me any men *this* weekend."

"What? Not even to assist with the apprehension of a murderer?"

Haussmann arrived back at the statue of Saint Florian as the driver and Albert emerged from beneath the stone arch. The inspector cupped his hand around his mouth and shouted down: "Dr. Becker has filled the laboratory with a poisonous gas. He has locked the door, but he might not have removed the key. Ensure that no one can enter. Albert will guide you to the laboratory. Leave him there to stand guard. No one must be admitted—do you understand? No one. Please notify the headmaster of our . . . situation. Then return with a ladder."

Haussmann's face was a pale oval.

"It was Dr. Becker? He did it?"

"Yes."

"I'm sorry, sir. I'm sorry I let him get away."

The young man expected his apology to be answered with a strongly worded reprimand; however, the inspector, studying Haussmann's pitiful expression from his godlike vantage, merely shrugged and replied: "Better luck next time, eh, Haussmann?"

"Yes, sir," said the assistant detective, humbled—once again—by his superior's humanity. The young man took Albert by the arm and, lending him robust locomotor assistance, set off for the laboratory.

A gaggle of boys appeared over the crest of a nearby hill. They were trudging across open country and were led by a man with a limp. The man had taken his cap off, and even from a distance it was easy to make out the color of his cropped blond hair.

"I think that's Lieutenant Osterhagen," said Rheinhardt. "The gymnastics master."

The boys were not marching in an orderly fashion but following their leader in a loose band, with a few stragglers trailing behind. They had clearly been on some kind of exercise, and their uniforms were covered in mud. It was not long before one of the more observant youths noticed Liebermann and Rheinhardt. Several boys started waving, pointing, and gesticulating, and Osterhagen stopped to raise his field glasses.

In due course, the bedraggled troop arrived, and Osterhagen stepped forward.

"What are you doing up there?" he demanded.

This remark was bluntly delivered and caused considerable amusement among the boys. Osterhagen glared at the worst offenders, silencing their laughter.

"All will be explained," Rheinhardt shouted, "but now is not the time. Lieutenant Osterhagen, would you be so kind as to get a ladder so that my colleague and I can get down."

"Why don't you just smash the window if it's stuck."

"The window is *not* stuck," said Rheinhardt, impatience creeping into his voice. "With respect, would you *please* get a ladder."

"That may not be easy," said Osterhagen. "I don't know where the ladders—if we possess any at all—are kept."

"Then might I suggest," Rheinhardt returned, "that you start looking."

At this point, a section of the ledge—directly beneath Rheinhardt's left foot—gave way. His arms flailed around as he desperately sought to recover his balance. The rotations became more frantic—but he was unable to achieve the necessary redistribution of weight. Slowly, he began to lean into the void. Liebermann—reacting with reflexive speed—grabbed Rheinhardt's coat and pulled him back, steadying his wild movements in a tight embrace.

"It's all right, Oskar. I have you."

Rheinhardt took a deep breath and emptied his lungs slowly, producing as he did so an attenuated whistle.

"Dear God," he expostulated. "That was close!"

Liebermann looked down and saw Lieutenant Osterhagen contemplating the fallen masonry. It had landed perilously close to where he was standing.

"The ledge won't hold for much longer," Liebermann cried. "Please hurry."

Osterhagen—roused from an impromptu meditation on the contingent nature of fate and his own mortality—issued various instructions to the boys, who then began to disperse in pairs. He looked up and said: "I'll be back shortly."

The lieutenant vanished from sight, his asymmetric stride creating a hissing sound on the gravel as he dragged the weaker of his two legs behind him. Only the driver remained, his gaze oscillating between the shattered block of stone and the crumbling ledge.

"Well, Max," said Rheinhardt, "I am indebted. You might have gone over with me. You saved my life."

"But it remains to be seen how much of your life I have actually saved," said Liebermann. "Unless we get down soon, your gratitude may prove excessive."

"Then perhaps we should get back inside?"

"The gas *will* dissipate over time—but hydrocyanic gas is deadly. I think we had better take our chances out here."

Rheinhardt shook his head. "Max," he said with great solemnity, "why did you ever let me eat so many cakes? If I were a more lissome fellow, then perhaps this ledge might hold a little longer." Liebermann smiled at his comrade, who was penitently contemplating the curvature of his stomach. "If we survive this, I swear to you, I'm going on a diet."

Another piece of stone—about the size of an apple—fell to the ground. The sound of its impact startled the driver. His worried face showed that he had already calculated the effect of such a drop on the human body.

Rheinhardt reached into his coat pocket and took out his notebook and pencil. Leaning back against the window, he began scribbling furiously.

"Oskar?" asked Liebermann. "What *are* you doing?"

Rheinhardt held out the notebook so that Liebermann could read what he had written:

My dearest Else,

I love you. Kiss Therese and Mitzi for me—and tell them how much I love them too. My heart, my all, my everything! You have given me so much more than I ever deserved.

Eternally yours,
Oskar

"Do you think it's enough?" asked Rheinhardt.

"If you had time enough to write a whole book," Liebermann replied, "you could not say more."

"Perhaps you would like to . . ."

Rheinhardt offered Liebermann the notebook—but the young doctor did not take it. What could he write, and to whom? There was no obvious recipient. Trezska was his lover—but were they really *in love*? His relationship with his father had never been very good. His mother adored him, but he always experienced her presence as vaguely suffocating. He was very fond of his youngest sister . . . but he could hardly write to her alone.

The imminence of death exposed an uncomfortable truth: there was no one *special* in his life. In his firmament, there were no stars that constellated true happiness, no bright lights to compare with Rheinhardt's wife and daughters. For a brief moment, he found himself thinking of Miss Lydgate, of the times they had spent in her rooms discussing medicine and philosophy, of the companionate closeness they had shared.

Another piece of masonry fell.

"Hurry, Max," Rheinhardt urged.

Attempting to conceal his embarrassment, Liebermann said,

somewhat presumptuously: "Put the notebook away, Oskar—we're not going to die!"

"What makes you say that?"

"Oh, just a *feeling!*"

"Max, you are an exceptionally contrary fellow." Rheinhardt put the notebook and pencil back into his pocket, adding softly: "But I hope you are right."

"Look!" said Liebermann, pointing down.

Osterhagen had reappeared, followed by a column of boys who were bearing the weight of a long flagpole on their shoulders. They came to a halt by the statue and, guided by the lieutenant's stentorian directions, raised the pole up. Then, releasing it from the vertical, they allowed it to lean toward the ledge.

"Don't let it fall," Osterhagen barked. "Gently . . . gently . . ."

Rheinhardt and Liebermann reached out and, grabbing the shaft, lodged the tip firmly against the central mullion.

"We're saved," said the inspector, smiling.

Liebermann watched as Rheinhardt slid down. His landing was accompanied by cheers and boyish laughter. The young doctor followed, making an equally swift descent. Within seconds of his feet touching the ground, Liebermann was startled by a loud crash. The ledge had finally worked itself loose, and lay in pieces on the ground.

58

THE WOODMAN RELEASED THE CATCH and pulled the carcass from the metal trap. He was about to add the animal to his carrying strap when he heard the sound of an approaching carriage. Its low rumbling rapidly increased in volume, until the air reverberated with the skipping beat of galloping horses. Through the trees, he could see the vehicle hurtling down the road at breakneck speed. The driver was half-standing, lashing his geldings, a black cloak flying out horizontally from his shoulders. The incline was steep, and the carriage veered from side to side. It was a reckless, uncontrolled descent. The din diminished as the carriage passed behind the hillside; however, within seconds there was a sickening crash—augmented by an unholy chorus of terrified equine voices. This dreadful cacophony was suddenly extinguished, leaving in its wake an eerie, hollow silence.

Attaching the carcass to his strap, the woodman reset his trap and set off down the hill. He walked to the muddy road and followed the deep ruts that widened where the carriage had skidded. The ground was pitted with hoof marks and littered with ripped-up clods of black earth. The woodman trudged around the bend and saw that the parallel furrows terminated abruptly at the edge of the road.

At the bottom of a ravine was the carriage, its rear wheel still turning slowly. The horses were lying on top of each other, their heads projecting from their bodies at unnatural angles. Some distance away was the crumpled body of the driver.

The woodman continued along the road until he found a point where he could make a scrambling descent. Once he was on the floor of the ravine, he walked back and inspected the driver's body. The man wasn't breathing, and blood was oozing out of a gash at the back of his head. Working quickly, the woodman removed the gown and slung it over his shoulder. He then paused, contemplating the corpse. He tested the man's weight with one enormous hand.

Yes, he could manage it, of course he could. But it was not quite dark, and *they* would soon be out looking for this man—the people from the village, the people from the school.

It was unwise—an unnecessary risk.

Even so, he thought. *Zhenechka will still be pleased with the black cloak.*

He set off into the undergrowth, clutching his booty, and feeling somewhat regretful:

It was a shame to leave all that horse meat.

59

FRAU BECKER WAS SEATED on her chaise longue, a handkerchief clutched in her left hand. She was wearing a black blouse decorated with printed roses—each blossoming from a green stem with two leaves. The collar was fastened with a large oval brooch, on which raised ivory figures promenaded against a terra-cotta background. Her dress was made of satin and ended a little short of her soft doeskin boots, revealing a sliver of her maroon stockings.

Rheinhardt and Liebermann were seated opposite, while Haussmann stood by the door.

"As he poured the vinegar," said Liebermann, "Zelenka thought that he would be observing the effect of a weak acid on a range of innocuous compounds—sugars and salts. He did not know that your husband had replaced one of the test substances with cyanide, probably potassium cyanide. When vinegar and cyanide react, they produce hydrocyanic gas—one of the most poisonous gases known to man. Zelenka would have been killed instantly—and afterward the gas would have dissipated in the atmosphere."

Frau Becker held the handkerchief to her nose and sniffed.

"Zelenka's body was discovered by Professor Gärtner, who immediately rushed to inform the headmaster. Professor Eichmann was at that moment engaged in a meeting with your husband. Some attempts to revive Zelenka were made—but these proved unsuccessful. Professor Gärtner was very distressed, and the headmaster subsequently went to summon the school doctor. Your husband would have had ample opportunity to remove the cyanide—which he then disposed of on his way to Nurse Funke's lodge. Hydrocyanic gas was an inspired choice of poison. It is virtually undetectable at autopsy— apart from a little congestion in the lungs, perhaps, but nothing more. Dr. Becker had assumed that in the absence of any alternative explanation, the pathologist would conclude that Zelenka had died from an unspecified *natural* cause. And this—of course—is exactly what happened. However, your husband is clearly a very fastidious gentleman. Even though his plan was exceedingly clever, it was not perfect. He detected one minor flaw. Hydrocyanic gas leaves a smell in the air—a faint bitter almondlike odor—that might serve as a clue."

Liebermann paused, and allowed the fingers of both hands to touch, each digit finding its twin in a serial sequence.

"Unfortunately, perfectionism—when taken to its extreme—is always self-defeating. You may recall that just before Zelenka's death, your husband asked you to buy him an almond tart."

Frau Becker looked puzzled.

"Which you purchased," Liebermann continued undeterred, "from Demel's."

The young woman's eyes suddenly opened wide.

"How did you . . . ," she whispered.

"The smell of almonds in the laboratory," Liebermann went on, "might have aroused suspicion; however, your husband reasoned that if there was an obvious source of such a smell, it would seem less conspicuous. He kept the almond tart concealed in his desk, and, while he was removing the cyanide, he deposited the pastry next to Zelenka's body."

"But, Max," said Rheinhardt, "Professor Eichmann didn't smell anything."

"Not everyone can, Oskar," said Liebermann, turning to his friend and adopting a more confidential tone. "An inherited factor determines whether an individual can detect the residual odor of hydrocyanic gas. If that constitutional factor is absent, the individual cannot smell it."

The young doctor crossed his legs and returned his attention to Frau Becker.

"Your husband was aware that Zelenka intended to leave Saint Florian's in the summer. Dr. Becker did not want to lose you."

The woman's expression suddenly changed. Her features hardened and the blood drained from her face. She was no longer crying. Indeed, she seemed to have been overcome by a strange, almost sinister calm. When she finally spoke, her words shattered the silence like stones falling through panes of glass.

"I killed Zelenka."

"What?" Rheinhardt cried.

Liebermann gestured to his friend to remain silent. The young doctor put on his spectacles, leaned forward, and observed Frau Becker very closely.

"I killed Zelenka," she said again.

Psychoanalysis had taught Liebermann to respect silences. They were never merely the absence of speech. They could be many things: a tool, a consequence, a protest. Liebermann allowed the silence to consolidate. Undisturbed, Frau Becker's thoughts would clarify. When she was ready to speak, she *would*.

Outside, in the hallway, a grandfather clock was ticking loudly.

Frau Becker twisted a coil of blond hair around her finger. Her stare remained fixed on the floor.

"I have done a terrible thing . . . or should I say we—yes, *we* have done a terrible thing . . . but you must understand, *we* never meant this to happen. If I . . . if *we* had known . . ."

She stopped, released her hair, and lowered her hand. Its descent was slow, and mannered, like an object sinking in water. Her breast heaved—but no more tears came.

"*We?*" said Liebermann softly.

Frau Becker looked up, and her gaze met Liebermann's.

"Myself and Herr Lang."

"The art master," interjected Rheinhardt, discreetly reminding his friend of Herr Lang's identity.

"Since September last year, Herr Lang and I, we have . . ." Frau Becker's resolve faltered. "We have been . . ."

"Lovers?"

She nodded.

Liebermann was unable to maintain his clinical reserve. He craned forward, his eyebrows ascending above the rim of his spectacles.

"My husband was not the man that I believed him to be . . . and this is an awful place, Herr Doctor. A place where someone like me can never fit in. The masters' wives are narrow-minded, and thought bad things about me from the start. I knew what they were thinking, of course. They regarded me as a stupid girl from the country, a gold digger . . . and a lot worse. I tried to get to know them, but it was useless. They didn't want to know me—they didn't accept me. And when I talked to them about the plight of some of the boys—the bullying, the persecution—they weren't interested. It made things worse. They thought I was being ridiculous. One of them called me . . . hyshystorical?"

"Hysterical," said Liebermann, quite unable to resist making this particular correction.

The pale skin around Frau Becker's eyes had reddened. The flesh looked sore, grazed—flecked with tiny raised welts. Liebermann noticed the unusual length and brightness of her lashes, which glinted in the lamplight.

"I *did* love Bernhard," she said, her voice rising in pitch as if she were responding to an accusation of falsehood. "I did. I had never met anyone like him before—an educated man—a distinguished man—a generous man. But he changed. He started to complain about how much money I was spending. He was always in a foul temper. He became angry with me if I didn't understand what he was talking about. I felt neglected, lonely—and Herr Lang . . . Herr Lang was kind to me. He's an artist. He *appreciated* me, accepted me . . . and he cared about all the bad things happening up at the school."

The young woman suddenly stopped, and tugged at her blouse, her expression suggesting utter contempt.

"I have a large wardrobe full of beautiful clothes, but I have never been interested in fashion. I used to tell Bernhard that I needed a new dress every time I wanted to get away. I used shopping as an excuse, so that I could go to Vienna. Sometimes it was possible for me to meet Herr Lang there. He knew places where . . ." Her cheeks flushed like a beacon. Modesty prevented her from disclosing the intimate details of their assignation, but Liebermann and Rheinhardt knew exactly where Lang would have taken Frau Becker. The city was full of private dining rooms—in Leopoldstadt, Neubau, and Mariahilf—where couples could conduct their illicit liaisons without fear of discovery.

"We made our arrangements," Frau Becker continued, "through Zelenka. He delivered our notes to each other—he was our *go-between*, our messenger. I *was* very fond of him . . . very fond. But our relationship was innocent. I knew that my husband suspected that something was going on; however, God forgive me, I did nothing to

F r a n k   T a l l i s

make him think otherwise. In fact, I encouraged his mistrust. On the days that Zelenka came, I always wore something special. And all the time, I knew that whatever inquiries Bernhard made would ultimately come to nothing. The more my husband worried about Zelenka, the better—it put him off, helped to conceal the truth, misdirected his attention. Herr Lang thought I was being very clever—and said that he would do something too. He knew that Herr Sommer was a dreadful gossip, and told him things . . . made suggestions about Zelenka and me, knowing full well that Sommer would be indiscreet. It worked. Soon the whole school was talking—but about the wrong affair! An affair that wasn't happening! You look shocked, Herr Doctor. And I know what you are thinking: '*What sort of woman would do such a thing? What sort of woman would knowingly destroy her own reputation?*' But you see, I had no reputation to protect. People said horrible things about me whatever I did, and at least this way the slander was serving some purpose. Besides, I would only have to endure it for a short time. Herr Lang is leaving Saint Florian's soon. He intends to join a commune of artists living in the Tenth District. I was going to join him, and may still do so. I've been told that such people do not make a habit of judging others."

Frau Becker paused and looked from Liebermann to Rheinhardt, then to Haussmann and back again. Her chin was raised and there was something defiant in the set of her jaw; but the challenge was short-lived. She brought her hands together, nestling the closed fist of her right hand in the palm of her left—and bowed her head.

"If I had known . . . ," Frau Becker continued. "If *we* had known that Bernhard was capable of such insane jealousy, we would never have done this . . . but we did. And because of that, we must now share his guilt."

Liebermann leaned back in his chair.

"I don't think so. You could never have foreseen your husband's actions."

"I'm his wife. I should have—"

"Not in this instance, Frau Becker," Liebermann interrupted. "The man you fell in love with no longer exists. You said earlier that your husband *changed*. I believe that this alteration in his personality had a very specific cause."

"I don't understand."

"Are you aware that your husband took medicine—a white powder which he dissolved in alcohol?"

"Yes. He took it for his headaches."

"Frau Becker, your husband never suffered from headaches. He was deceiving you. The *medication* he took was an extract of the South American coca plant—cocaine. It is a substance once thought to improve mood and increase . . . stamina."

A carriage drew up outside, and Liebermann was momentarily distracted.

"Forgive me for being forthright, Frau Becker," Liebermann continued. "But it is my belief that your husband—being considerably older than you—doubted his ability to *satisfy* a healthy young wife. He started taking cocaine, having probably heard of its use as a tonic by the German army. However, cocaine is a highly addictive substance that, taken in large quantities, can disturb the mind's delicate balance. It can cause various forms of paranoia, a particularly disturbing example of which is pathological or morbid jealousy." A loud knock resounded through the house. "Men are particularly prone to jealous feelings—but these can be grotesquely exaggerated under the influence of such a potent chemical agent. If Dr. Becker had not been addicted to cocaine, I very much doubt whether he would have behaved so irrationally—and with such tragic consequences."

There was the sound of movement in the hallway, and a gentle tap on the door.

"Come in," said Frau Becker.

The maid entered.

"What is it, Ivana?"

"Frau Becker, a police constable has arrived. He would like to speak with you."

"You had better show him in."

Liebermann looked at Rheinhardt quizzically, but the inspector was only able to respond with a shrug.

Haussmann stepped out of the way to let in the constable—a large youth with ruddy cheeks and a forelock of orange hair that peeped out from beneath his spiked helmet. He looked around the room, observing the gathering, but seemed quite unable to explain his presence. Indeed, his expression suggested confusion—complicated by anxiety.

Rheinhardt stood up and introduced himself, which did not seem to help matters. Indeed, the constable now seemed even more nervous and shifted the weight of his body from one foot to the other.

"Well, man," said Rheinhardt, becoming impatient. "What is it?"

"Sir," said the constable. Then, looking toward Frau Becker, he said, "Madam . . . there's been an accident. A carriage left the road and the driver was thrown off! The landlord of the inn at Aufkirchen was passing—and he has identified the body. I am sorry, madam. Your husband . . . he's dead."

Through the window Liebermann could see the city lights: rings of increasing intensity contracting around a central luminescent hub. This pool of stardust was home to nearly two million people. Germans, Italians, Slovaks, Poles, Ruthenians, Slovenians, Romanians,

Gypsies, Catholics, Jews, Muslims, princes, archdukes, shop girls, and paupers. Liebermann fancied that each glimmering lamp was a human soul—a unique life, illuminated by hopes, fears, and aspirations. Such a vast collection of humanity was humbling. Yet he felt an odd, vainglorious compulsion to raise his arm and eclipse the great metropolis with his hand.

Would it be there forever? he wondered. After all, archaeologists had found the ruins of entire civilizations buried beneath the sand.

Liebermann opened his fingers and allowed the lights to reappear. Their constancy was mildly reassuring.

The mood in the carriage was subdued. None of the three men had spoken much since leaving Aufkirchen. They had passed the time, somewhat self-absorbed, smoking Haussmann's French cigarettes. The black Syrian tobacco produced an intransigent fug that smelled unmistakably of burning tar; however, the pungency and excoriating consequence of each draw had not deterred them, and the box—illustrated with a camel and a palm tree—was now completely empty.

Rheinhardt caught sight of his reflection in the window and squeezed the horns of his mustache.

"He could so easily have got away with it."

The sentence was not addressed to Liebermann or Haussmann but to himself.

"Yes," said Liebermann, "and I am struck by a certain irony. If it wasn't for the school bullies, Becker might have succeeded. I doubt very much that you would have been so tenacious had there not been signs of torture on Zelenka's body. In this instance at least, cruelty has served some greater purpose."

"Indeed, but it is a twist of fate from which I will derive little consolation." Rheinhardt turned and peered through the smoke at his friend. "Max, there is something I don't understand." Liebermann invited the inspector to proceed. "What alerted you to the significance of the almond tart in the first place? You never said."

"Have you ever tasted absinthe, Oskar?"

"No."

"Nor had I until last week. I was given some to drink by a friend—and I found that it had an extraordinary effect on the workings of my brain. My thinking seemed to loosen up—suddenly, I was capable of making bold associations. Some of them were complete nonsense . . . but others . . . My companion had been eating sugared almonds, and it occurred to me, apropos of nothing, that almonds contain traces of cyanide. . . . Then I remembered that hydrocyanic gas is deadly—but difficult to isolate postmortem. The photographs of the murder scene came into my mind, and I was troubled by the presence of the pastry. Why was it there? And why wasn't it eaten? After all, adolescent boys are not renowned for their ability to delay gratification. Hydrocyanic gas taints the air with the smell of almonds. The rest—as I have already explained—followed."

"And in order to achieve this . . . this . . . emancipation of the mind, how much absinthe did you drink, exactly?"

Liebermann took off his spectacles and dropped them into the pocket of his coat.

"Not a great deal," he said innocently.

Rheinhardt turned to his assistant and, raising his eyebrows, asked, "Well, Haussmann?"

The young man shook his head.

"See, Max?" Rheinhardt continued. "Even Haussmann doesn't believe you."

60

"I suppose I should congratulate you, Rheinhardt," said Commissioner Brügel, "but I cannot do so without first raising the issue of your absence. You received my memorandum, didn't you?"

"I did, sir."

"And yet you chose to ignore it."

"With respect, sir, you requested that officers should make every effort to remain close to the Schottenring station."

"The meaning of which was quite clear—or at least it was to everybody else."

"I'm sorry, sir. I misunderstood." Brügel's eyes narrowed. "Was the operation successful, sir?"

"No," said Brügel. "It wasn't."

"I heard that some arrests were made."

"Two gentlemen were detained for questioning—but they were released early this morning. Mistaken identity."

"I'm sorry, sir."

Brügel emitted a low growl that rose from the pit of his stomach. "Well, Rheinhardt, I trust there will be no *misunderstandings* of this kind in future."

His knowing emphasis made Rheinhardt feel ashamed.

"Indeed, sir."

"Good." The commissioner shuffled some papers. "I would like you to submit a complete account of the Saint Florian affair by tomorrow evening, after which you will report to Inspector von Bulow for further instruction. There is a pianist, József Kálman, who—"

Rheinhardt felt a stab of resentment. He did not want to report to von Bulow. They were of the same rank—and it was not right that he should be treated as if he were nothing more than von Bulow's assistant.

"Sir?" Rheinhardt interposed.

"What is it, Rheinhardt?"

"I have not completed my investigation . . . at Saint Florian's."

Brügel's head swung forward. "What *are* you talking about, Rheinhardt? We know who killed Zelenka—and why. There is nothing more to investigate."

"The cuts on the boy's body, sir. The bullying . . ."

"Don't be ridiculous, Rheinhardt! The case is closed!" Brügel's hand came down on his desk, creating a hollow thud—the quality of which suggested the snapping shut of a great tome. "Now," Brügel resumed, "Kálman breakfasts at a disreputable coffeehouse in the third district—a place called Zielinski's. . . ."

61

LIEBERMANN RAN HIS FINGER down Trezska's back, tracing the flowing contour of her spine. As he did, he admired the smoothness of her olive skin—its depth and lustre. He stroked her buttocks and allowed his hand to fall between her thighs.

On the bedside cabinet was an absinthe bottle and the trappings of Trezska's habit—a sugar bowl, a miniature trowel, and a carafe of water. Two tall glasses stood in front of the bottle, one of them three-quarters full. Through its pallid contents the candle shone like a burning emerald.

The bouquet of their lovemaking still permeated the atmosphere. Liebermann inhaled and registered a hint of perfume amid a blend of darker fragrances—musk-orchid, attar, and oysters.

His perceptual universe was strangely altered. Everything seemed removed, distant, and dreamlike. Yet, paradoxically, minute phenomena acquired unnatural prominence. A mote—floating upward on the air—commanded his attention as if it were an entire world. Its inconsequential ascent was majestic and beguiling.

Liebermann became aware of Trezska's voice. It was muffled, and her speech was slurred. She was talking into the pillow, her face concealed beneath a shock of black hair. She was extolling the virtues of the Hungarian nobility.

"They have real charm . . . style, panache. The Telekis and Károlyis. The late empress appreciated their company—as did her son . . . poor Rudolf. But that's another matter. There was once a peasants' revolt in the sixteenth century. They caught the leader—and do you know what they did with him? They made him sit on a red-hot throne. They pressed a red-hot crown on his head . . . and made him hold a red-hot scepter. His retinue were made to eat his flesh—while it was still sizzling."

"Where did you hear such a story?" Liebermann asked.

"It's not a story—it's true."

"Like the vampire countess. What was she called?"

"Báthory—Erzsébet Báthory."

Liebermann leaned forward and let his lips touch the nape of Trezska's neck. She shivered with pleasure and rolled back onto her side.

"That man," said Liebermann. "The one who stopped you outside Demel's."

"What?"

"The man who called you Amélie—Franz . . ."

"Oh yes. Strange, wasn't it?"

Trezska brushed her hair away, but it sprang forward again—hanging across her face like a curtain.

"You knew him, really, didn't you?"

Trezska's eyes flashed and her full lips widened into a smile. She began to laugh. "Are you jealous?"

"He seemed so certain . . . so sure."

"You *are* jealous!"

Trezska threw her arms around Liebermann's shoulders and raised herself up, pressing her breasts against his chest. She kissed him, forcing her tongue between his teeth and taking possession of his senses. She tasted of anise, mint, and licorice. When Trezska finally released him, she grinned, and kissed him once more, gently on the nose—a comic peck.

"Don't be jealous," she whispered. "Don't be jealous."

The candle flickered and the glasses filled with green lightning.

O! beware, my lord, of jealousy;

It is the green-ey'd monster . . .

"Othello," he said.

Trezska drew back. "What?"

"A play by Shakespeare. If the green fairy doesn't get me, then the green-eyed monster will."

"You are very drunk," said Trezska gently. "Lie down, my love."

Trezska tugged at his arm, and Liebermann was surprised by his own lack of resistance. He fell, and when his head hit the mattress, he closed his eyes—it was like being knocked out. He was dimly conscious of Trezska's limbs, wrapping around his hips and shoulders. She pulled him close, smothering him with her flesh.

"Sleep," she whispered. "Sleep . . ."

Liebermann could hear her heart beating.

Too fast, he thought. *Too fast.*

He wanted to say something else. But words failed him, and seconds later he was asleep.

Part Four

The Opera Fountain

62

Liebermann had arrived at the Schottenring police station late in the afternoon, having spent a tiring day listening to—among others—the old jurist (who was still expounding upon his unique metaphysical system), a milliner with an irrational fear of horses, and an accountant who suffered from impotence—but only in rooms hung with yellow flock wallpaper. He had agreed to help Rheinhardt with the Saint Florian report, which was, at that exact moment, distributed in several incomplete parts over the top of the inspector's desk. They had reached a problematic juncture, and Rheinhardt was gazing gloomily at a page, the lower half of which was conspicuously devoid of his hieroglyphic scrawl.

"What am I supposed to say here?" said Rheinhardt, tapping the empty space. "That my esteemed colleague—Herr Dr. Liebermann—was inspired to link the presence of the pastry in the laboratory with cyanide poisoning due to the effect of absinthe on the . . . What did you just say?"

"The paracerebellar nuclei."

"My dear fellow," said Rheinhardt, "no matter how many anatomical terms you employ, the fact remains that you were—not to put too fine a point on it—drunk."

"I'm afraid I can't agree with you. The action of absinthe on the cerebrum merits special consideration. It engenders a unique mental state. To say that I was merely *drunk* hardly does justice to its mind-altering properties. It is—after all—the favored spirit of artists and visionaries."

The crescents of loose flesh beneath Rheinhardt's eyes seemed to sag a little farther.

"Although such an appeal might be received sympathetically by the chief of the Sûreté," said the inspector, "I can assure you that Commissioner Brügel will be singularly unimpressed."

"Then write that my suspicions were aroused when I interviewed Perger and discovered that almond tarts were not sold at the Aufkirchen bakery."

"But that would imply that you had already identified the pastry in the photograph as an almond tart. In fact, you didn't go to Demel's until . . ." Rheinhardt thumbed through his papers and recovered a particular sheet. "Until Saturday the seventh of February."

"Couldn't you just omit the date?"

"Absolutely not." Rheinhardt scowled. However, before he had exploited the full dramatic effect of his exaggerated expression, he added in a lighter, conversational tone: "He's disappeared, you know."

"Who?"

"Perger. He seems to have absconded. You will recall, perhaps, that he had wanted to run away with Zelenka."

"Where do you think he's gone?"

"If his letters are anything to go by, he's probably hiding in the hold of an Italian cargo vessel, heading for South America!" Rheinhardt sighed, shook his head, and laid down his pen. "This is supposed to be a final report," he continued, waving his hand over the chaotic spread of papers. "Yet there are still unanswered questions. The number pairs in Zelenka's exercise book, the cuts on his body. I received a note from Miss Lydgate yesterday morning. She said that she had tried all kinds of substitutions and transformations—but without success. She concluded that if the number pairs *are* a code, it is one that can be broken only with the aid of a unique formula or 'key.' Alternatively, the number pairs may have been simply chosen at random and have no special meaning."

"Which would, of course, be entirely consistent with Sommer's story . . . the memory game." Liebermann leaned back in his chair and tapped his temple gently. "Yet everything about him suggested to me that he was trying to hide something."

"What, though? And how could it have been connected with Zelenka?"

Liebermann pursed his lips, and after a lengthy pause said: "I have absolutely no idea."

Rheinhardt picked up his pen again. "Brügel has reassigned me to von Bulow's team. As far as the commissioner is concerned, once this report is submitted, the Saint Florian's case will be consigned to the archive."

"Where he will want it to remain, gathering dust."

"Exactly. I keep on thinking of that dreadful nephew of his. I have no solid evidence to support the allegation, but I am convinced that Kiefer Wolf was torturing Zelenka . . . and he is probably torturing others right now—as we speak. It weighs heavily on my conscience."

Liebermann remembered the boy Perger: his stutter, his timidity, his respectful compliance—the innocent happiness that illuminated his features as he moved his knight forward. *Checkmate.* The excitement in his treble voice had been touching. It was sad that this poor, sensitive boy was now bound for some distant shore where God only knew what fate might befall him.

"If only there were someone willing to speak out against Wolf,"

Rheinhardt continued. "But of course, there never is . . . and so it goes on. I dread to think what kind of officer he will make."

Liebermann pulled at his lower lip. "If none of the boys can be relied on to give evidence against him, then logically there is only one other way by which he could ever be exposed. Confession. He must make a confession."

The inspector looked disappointed. "Well, that's hardly going to happen—is it?"

"Persecution is as much about exercising control as it is about deriving sadistic pleasure. Therefore we might ask ourselves what kind of person desires absolute control?" Rheinhardt gestured for Liebermann to continue. "A simple answer—surely—suggests itself: one who fears *loss of control*. I am reminded of some of Adler's ideas. . . ."

"Max," said Rheinhardt, "what are you thinking?"

Liebermann smiled. "Allow me to explain."

63

They were seated in the disused classroom.

"Does my uncle know that you are here?" said Kiefer Wolf to Rheinhardt.

The inspector did not reply.

"I doubt that he does," Wolf continued. "In which case, I can assure you that I shall be writing to him again."

"Just answer my question."

"The investigation is over. Uncle Manfred told me so. Inspector Rheinhardt, I believe you are acting without authority."

"That is an extremely insolent remark."

"No, Inspector, it is merely an accurate one."

The boy folded his arms and leaned back in his chair. The line of his thin lips twisted slightly, suggesting modest satisfaction.

"There were cuts on Zelenka's body," Rheinhardt persevered. "How did they get there?"

"I don't know," said Wolf.

"I think you do."

"Then you are mistaken." Wolf made a languid movement with his hand and added, "Inspector, I would very much like to present myself for rifle practice. A Tyroler Kaiserjäger is coming this afternoon to give us special instruction. I have been selected to represent Saint Florian's at the end-of-year shooting tournament against Saint Polten and the headmaster was anxious that I should attend."

"I am afraid that you will have to stay here until I am satisfied that you are telling me the truth."

"The headmaster will be very displeased."

"For the last time, Wolf, what do you know about those cuts?"

"Nothing, Inspector."

The boy's complexion was clear and his skin as smooth as alabaster. He seemed preternaturally calm.

"Very well," said Rheinhardt. Turning to his friend, he called out, "Herr Doctor?"

Liebermann, who had been patiently waiting by the window, picked up his black leather bag and crossed the room. He sat in front of Wolf and smiled.

"Do you study botany here?" he asked.

The boy's eyes narrowed with suspicion.

"Yes . . . we have had a few classes."

"And what did you learn about?"

"The structure of plants . . . the different families."

"Then perhaps you were introduced to the perennials of the Solanaceae family? They can be found in the local woods and meadows."

"I am afraid I cannot remember," said Wolf. "It is not a subject that interests me."

"Even so, I suspect that you would recognize the name of at least one of the Solanaceae." Liebermann inserted a dramatic pause before proclaiming: "Belladonna!"

The young doctor raised his eyebrows, encouraging a response.

"Yes," said Wolf. "Of course I recognize that name. But what of it?"

"The plant grows from a thick fleshy root—about this high." Liebermann sliced a horizontal plane through the air. "It has a dingy purple-brown bell-shaped flower, and smooth black berries that ripen in September."

The neutrality of Wolf's expression was interrupted by a series of brief, flickering emotional responses that oscillated between perplexity and amusement. He was about to speak, but Liebermann silenced him by wagging an admonitory finger.

"I understand," Liebermann continued, "that belladonna acquired its appellation in the Middle Ages, when young women employed the plant's extracts to dilate their pupils." Liebermann observed Wolf's blank visage and added for clarification: "So they would seem more beautiful."

"Herr Doctor," said Wolf, "as I have already said, I am not very interested in botany."

"I promise you, my purpose will soon become clear." Again, Liebermann smiled. "Now, where was I? Oh yes . . . it was not only a favorite of young women—it was also valued by men of dubious morality whose intention it was to seduce them." Wolf rocked his head to one side, and a scintilla of interest nuanced the vacancy of his steady gaze. Liebermann continued. "You see, it was soon discovered that if belladonna was secreted into a young woman's drink, she would become remarkably compliant, forgetting virtue and agreeing readily to suggestions of an improper nature. She would become— as it were—less inhibited. Belladonna was also found to have medical applications. The great tenth-century Persian physician Avicenna recommended belladonna as an anesthetic—and it has been intermittently used by surgeons ever since. For example, only a few years ago some colleagues of mine at the university published a fascinating paper on the development of a new pre-anesthetic. By combining one of the alkaloids of Japanese belladonna with morphine, they were able to induce a somnolent state in their patients, which they designated 'twilight sleep.' Now, while undertaking this research, my colleagues noticed something very interesting: patients in twilight sleep would often mumble. However, if asked questions, they were able to reply—and these replies were perfectly coherent. Moreover, all answers to questions were somewhat literal—and invariably honest."

Liebermann made a steeple with his fingers and added: "This finding has led many to speculate as to the wider uses of Japanese belladonna and morphine. For example, this new pre-anesthetic might be of immense value to the police, who, on encountering reluctant witnesses, would be able to administer it as a kind of truth serum."

Liebermann leaned forward, undid the hasps of his leather bag, and pulled out a long narrow box. It had an attractive polished walnut finish and brass fittings. Turning a small key, Liebermann lifted the lid and turned it toward Wolf so that he could examine the contents. Inside, resting in a molded depression lined with green velvet, was a large metal-barreled syringe with an unusually long needle. Next to it was a small bottle, filled with a grayish liquid.

Liebermann removed the bottle, lifted it up, and swirled the contents.

"Japanese belladonna and morphine," he said softly.

Wolf swallowed.

"If you would be so kind as to remove your tunic and roll up your shirtsleeve," Liebermann said. "Then we can begin."

Wolf tried to stand, but as he did so his shoulders met resistance. Rheinhardt had positioned himself behind Wolf's chair and immediately forced the boy back down again. Wolf's head spun around.

"You can't do this!"

Rheinhardt's grip tightened.

"Take off your tunic and roll up your shirtsleeve. . . . You heard what the good doctor said, Wolf."

Liebermann made a great show of taking the syringe from its case and drawing off the contents of the bottle.

"You must keep very still," said Liebermann calmly. "Or—I'm sorry to say—this will be quite painful. Now, your tunic, please."

"No," said Wolf, his face contorting with horror. "No. . . . You can't."

"Come now," Liebermann interrupted. "Don't be alarmed. The experience of *twilight sleep* is not unpleasant—so I am told. Patients describe a warm, floating sensation . . . liberation from earthly concerns."

Again Wolf attempted to get up, but Rheinhardt held him fast.

"Very well," said Liebermann. "If you won't remove your tunic, I'll just have to proceed without your cooperation."

The young doctor aimed the syringe at Wolf's upper arm. He moved the shiny cylinder forward along a horizontal trajectory. Its progress was slow and stately—like a silver airship gliding over the Prater.

Wolf's eyes became fixed on the sharp point of the advancing needle.

"For God's sake, stop!" the boy cried. "I'll tell you. I'll tell you everything." Beads of perspiration had appeared on his forehead. "But you're wrong about Zelenka. I swear it. You must believe me. . . . I never . . ." He hesitated before adding, "Touched Zelenka."

"Then who did?" Rheinhardt asked.

"If you want to know more about Zelenka," said Wolf, "then you should talk to Herr Sommer."

Liebermann lowered the syringe.

Wolf's expression was pained, as if this revelation had cost him dearly. He fell silent—and the silence became protracted.

Liebermann noticed a subtle change in the boy's expression. The fear in his eyes was diminishing, like the steady trickle of sand vacating the upper chamber of an hourglass, and was being replaced by what could only be described as a look of *calculation*. Liebermann jabbed the syringe back into Wolf's view, and was reassured when the boy started.

"No," said Wolf. "That won't be necessary."

"Why Herr Sommer?" Rheinhardt pressed.

"They were lovers," said Wolf.

"*What?*" said Rheinhardt, his voice rising an octave.

"Zelenka and Herr Sommer . . . They . . ." Wolf hesitated, failing to complete his sentence.

"How do you know that?" Liebermann asked.

"They were seen together last summer. By Freitag."

"Who?"

"Freitag. Another cadet. He saw them walking together up the Kahlenberg."

"Couldn't it have been a chance encounter?" said Liebermann.

"No. You see, they were being intimate . . . in the little cemetery."

"I see," said Liebermann.

The young doctor opened the walnut box and placed the syringe carefully inside. He let the lid fall, allowing it to make a loud thud.

"You have been remarkably discreet, Wolf," said Liebermann.

The boy looked at him quizzically.

"What I mean is," Liebermann continued, "had you chosen to make this revelation earlier, Inspector Rheinhardt would have transferred his attentions—at least in part—from you to Herr Sommer. Yet you didn't say a word. If it *wasn't* you who inflicted those wounds on Zelenka—and you believe that Herr Sommer is party to such knowledge—why didn't you make this revelation before?"

"I didn't want Herr Sommer to get into trouble."

"Why not?"

"Because he is useful."

"How is he useful?"

"We have . . . an arrangement."

"What kind of arrangement?"

"I had promised to keep his relationship with Zelenka a secret, and in return he agreed to falsify my examination results."

"Your examination results!"

"Why are your examination results so important to you?" Rheinhardt interjected. "So important that you are prepared to blackmail one of your masters!"

"I'm no good at mathematics, and I'll need a good pass to gain admission into preferred branches of the military."

Rheinhardt let go of Wolf's shoulders and slumped down on an adjacent chair. He looked tired—and somewhat bewildered by the boy's cunning.

"I am prepared to accept," said Rheinhardt, "pending an interview with Herr Sommer, that you were not responsible for Zelenka's injuries. However, what about Perger? What did you do to him?"

Wolf breathed in sharply. "It wasn't that bad. . . ."

"What did you do?" Rheinhardt repeated.

"I threatened him. That's all."

"Why?"

"Perger knew all about Zelenka and Herr Sommer. Perger and Zelenka were as thick as thieves. I knew that you would eventually get Perger to talk . . . so I pushed him around a bit. If Herr Sommer was disgraced, I wouldn't get what I wanted."

"Do you know where he went—Perger?"

"No," said Wolf. "No . . . no, I don't."

Rain had begun to fall, and the windows resonated with its gentle drumming.

"Apart from Perger and Freitag," Rheinhardt continued, "did anyone else know about Herr Sommer's . . ." The Inspector hesitated. "Herr Sommer's *relationship* with Zelenka?"

"No."

"We have no proof, then, other than your word—and Freitag's, of course."

"I am telling the truth," said Wolf, darting a nervous glance toward the walnut box on Liebermann's lap.

"What if Herr Sommer denies your allegation?" said Rheinhardt.

"I have something in my possession that once belonged to Zelenka," said Wolf. "Herr Sommer was very keen to get hold of it— very keen."

"A dictionary?" said Liebermann.

"Yes," said Wolf, surprised.

"A Hartel and Jacobsen dictionary?"

"Yes. I thought there might be something incriminating written inside—but there isn't. I've checked."

"Where is it?" said Rheinhardt.

"I've hidden it," Wolf replied.

"Somewhere in the school?"

"Yes."

"Then you had better go and get it," said Rheinhardt. "Immediately."

64

"Well?" said Rheinhardt. "Do you think he's telling the truth?"

"On the whole, yes," Liebermann replied. "I am confident that his revelation concerning Herr Sommer's homosexuality is true—and that Herr Sommer had become intimate with Zelenka; however, my confidence in Wolf's testimony faltered at two junctures. When Wolf denied harming Zelenka, he said that he had never touched him. Yet I noticed a slight hesitation before he said the word 'touched'—as though he had met some unconscious resistance."

"Then you do think he was lying. He *did* harm Zelenka."

"No," said Liebermann, shaking his head. "Quite the contrary."

"I'm sorry, Max, you will have to speak more plainly."

"I am of the opinion that Wolf did *touch* Zelenka. . . . And it was the memory of that *touching*, erotic *touching*, that impeded the fluency of his denial."

Rheinhardt blew out his cheeks and exhaled, allowing his lips to interrupt the airflow so as to produce a series of plosions. When he had finished, he said, "And the second thing?"

"When Wolf claimed that he did not know Perger's whereabouts, I thought his denial was too insistent."

"Then perhaps we should administer our truth serum, after all."

Liebermann smiled coyly. "No. There wouldn't be any point." Rheinhardt's brow furrowed. Liebermann tapped the walnut box and continued: "The bottle contains a saline solution and a harmless stain. I would be very uncomfortable injecting a young man with belladonna and morphine."

Rheinhardt's mouth worked soundlessly for a few moments before he spluttered, "I . . . I . . . I don't believe it! Why on earth didn't you tell me!"

"Authenticity! We needed to play our parts with utter conviction."

"But all those things you said about belladonna—did you make it all up?"

"No, it's all true—and we might well have used twilight sleep to loosen Wolf's tongue; however, that would have been such an inelegant solution to our problem. The use of psychological devices is considerably more satisfying, don't you think? More subtle. And my ruse has been successful enough. I have not tampered with Wolf's brain chemistry, yet he has told us a great deal."

Rheinhardt shook his head from side to side. "Sometimes, Max, you test my patience to the very limit."

"Indeed," said Liebermann. "But never without reason."

The young doctor turned the key of the walnut box, and dropped it into the dark, gaping maw of his leather bag.

"What a sorry and sordid state of affairs," said Rheinhardt. "Frau Becker allowed others to believe that she was having an improper relationship with Zelenka so that she might better conceal her assignations with Lang, and at the very same time Herr Sommer's indiscretions were serving an identical purpose, concealing his assignations with the boy himself! It is a pity that none of them stopped to consider the possible consequences of their mutually advantageous lies—particularly on the all too fragile mind of Dr. Becker."

"But who could have really foreseen that these machinations would result in the murder of Thomas Zalenka?"

"That," said Rheinhardt gruffly, "is not the point!"

The two men eschewed further conversation, settling instead for private thoughts and silence. Outside, the rain continued to fall, its persistent pitter-pattering unrelieved and softly insistent. Eventually, Rheinhardt stirred and said, "He will come back—won't he?"

"Yes," said Liebermann.

A few minutes later, the rapid crescendo of Wolf's footsteps heralded his appearance in the doorway. He looked disheveled, and his breathing was labored, suggesting that he had expended a considerable amount of energy recovering the large green volume that he now held against his chest.

"Ah, there you are, Wolf," said Rheinhardt. "I was beginning to wonder where you'd got to."

The boy marched across the room and handed the book to Rheinhardt.

"Zelenka's dictionary," he said.

Rheinhardt stroked the green binding. "How did you get this?"

"I found it."

"What do you mean, 'found it?' "

"It was under Zelenka's bed."

"You took it, then?"

Wolf shrugged.

"You said that Herr Sommer wanted Zelenka's dictionary," Rheinhardt continued. "That he was keen to get hold of it. How do you know that?"

"I discovered him looking for it in Zelenka's locker."

"When?"

"As soon as he got back . . . after his fall."

"Thank you. That will be all, Wolf. Perhaps you would be kind enough to wait next door."

Wolf bowed, clicked his heels, and left the room, closing the door quietly behind him.

Rheinhardt opened the dictionary and examined the antique etching of the bearded scholar. His eyes dropped to the foot of the page.

"Hartel and Jacobsen, Leipzig, 1900. Well, this is certainly the missing dictionary." He then flicked through the pages, toyed with the edges of the marbled endpapers, and poked his finger down the spine. "Wolf seems to be correct. Nothing remarkable or incriminating here."

Rheinhardt handed the dictionary to Liebermann, who ran his fingers across the gold-embossed leather.

"What did Miss Lydgate say . . ."

"I beg your pardon?"

"Something about a key?"

"You mean with respect to the number pairs?"

"Yes."

"She said that the numbers were nonsensical—but they might be made intelligible with a key."

"What if the number pairs . . . ," said Liebermann, playing a five-finger exercise on the binding. "What if the number pairs are coordinates?"

"But this is a dictionary, not a map. Besides, what possible—"

"The position of every single word in the German language," Liebermann interrupted, "can be expressed by using two numbers. The first representing a particular page, and the second representing a specific location on that page. First, second, third . . . and so on. If two people possess the same dictionary, they can communicate any message at all using number pairs. Oskar—did you record some of Zelenka's number pairs in your notebook?"

"Yes, I did," said Rheinhardt.

The inspector dug deep into his coat pocket.

"Read them to me."

"Five hundred and seventy-four—and fourteen."

Liebermann found the correct page and counted down to the fourteenth word.

"Drink."

"One thousand two hundred and fifty—paired with thirty-nine."

Repeating the procedure, Liebermann answered: "My."

"One hundred and ninety-seven—and two."

Liebermann licked his finger and turned the flimsy pages with the speed of a bank teller counting cash.

"Extraordinary," he whispered.

"For heaven's sake, Max—what does it say?"

" 'Blood!' Drink my blood! Now everything makes sense."

"Does it?"

"Oh yes." Liebermann snapped the dictionary closed. "Perfect sense!"

65

"I am sorry to disturb you, Herr Sommer," said Rheinhardt. "But a matter has arisen that requires clarification—and I believe you will be able to assist us."

The mathematics master peeped out from behind the door. His bloodshot eyes shifted from one visitor to the other. Liebermann inclined his head.

"I trust," Rheinhardt continued, "that we have not arrived at an inconvenient time."

"Did you send me a telegram, Inspector?" said Sommer. "If so, it was never delivered."

His breath smelled of alcohol.

"Unfortunately," said Rheinhardt, "circumstances did not permit me—on this occasion—to extend such a courtesy."

"Well," said Sommer. "Since you ask, Inspector, I am rather busy at present. I wonder whether we could postpone our—"

"No," interrupted Rheinhardt, extending his hand to stop the insidious progress of the door toward closure. "That will not be possible."

The firmness with which Rheinhardt spoke made Sommer flinch.

"I see," said Sommer, taking a step back. "In which case, you had better come in."

Sommer limped down the hall and guided them into his study. He pulled two stools from under the table and offered his guests some schnapps; however, his hospitality was politely declined. Liebermann noticed that the schnapps bottle was almost empty, and a little shot glass was already out on the table. There was nothing in the room to suggest—as Sommer had asserted—that he was in the middle of a task requiring sustained attention.

The mathematics master sat down in his leather reading chair and immediately started talking.

"Allow me to congratulate you, Inspector. None of us would have imagined Dr. Becker capable of such a heinous crime. What an extraordinary turn of events. And yet—you know—I have to say—if I am honest—I never really liked the man. I accept that one should never speak ill of the dead, but the fact of the matter is that Becker was a cold, unapproachable fellow, and quick to express disapproval. He once reprimanded me for gossiping, when I was merely sharing a humorous anecdote with Lang about an old master called Spivakov." Sommer watched nervously as Liebermann approached the window. "I am not sure," Sommer continued, "that I can tell you very much more about him—but I will endeavor to do my best. Now, you said something needs to be cleared up—or was it clarified?"

Liebermann reached down and picked up a book from the floor. He opened it and examined the frontispiece.

"I notice, Herr Sommer, that you have purchased a new dictionary," said the young doctor.

"Why, yes," Sommer replied. "My other one was getting old."

"Not *so* old, surely. It was—I believe—a Hartel and Jacobsen . . . and was published only three years ago."

"You are most observant, Herr Doctor," said Sommer. "Yes, I did have a Hartel and Jacobsen, but . . ." He swallowed, and his Adam's apple bobbed up and down. "It wasn't very good on technical terms. Not enough detail. My new dictionary is much better suited to my purposes."

Liebermann turned and walked back across the room. He sat on a stool, opened his bag, and pulled out a large green volume.

"Then why, Herr Sommer," said Liebermann, "were you so anxious to acquire this?"

The color drained from the mathematics master's face.

"What . . . what is it?" The hollowness of Sommer's voice betrayed the insincerity of his question.

"Thomas Zelenka's Hartel and Jacobsen dictionary."

For several seconds the mathematics master presented a blank visage—as if the efferent nerves supplying his face with emotional expressivity had suddenly been severed with a cheese wire. Then, quite suddenly, a burst of galvanic twitches preceded a loud exclamation.

"Ah yes—of course," cried Sommer, clapping his hands together. "You must have heard something or other from that boy Wolf!"

"Indeed," said Rheinhardt.

"Yes. . . . you see, it's a rather expensive dictionary and one that—I'm ashamed to say—I recommended to Zelenka. I should have given the matter more thought, particularly given Zelenka's enthusiasm for the sciences. As you know, Zelenka came from a poor family, so, on my return from Linz, I naturally wanted to make sure that this very valuable item had been safely returned—with the rest of his effects—to his parents. I made some inquiries and discovered that the dictionary had gone missing. I suspected that Wolf was the culprit—and subsequently challenged him. He protested his innocence and made some idle threats." Sommer paused to shake his head.

"Such a disagreeable boy. Now it seems that you have succeeded where I failed. How did you know that Wolf had it? I'm intrigued."

Liebermann leaned forward and dropped the dictionary on Sommer's lap.

"The number pairs that appeared in the marginalia of Zelenka's exercise books—written in your hand, and his—correspond with the location of certain words in this dictionary. The first number refers to the page; the second number refers to the precise position of a particular word. Herr Sommer, we know what you were writing to each other. We now understand the . . . *nature* of your relationship."

Sommer looked up at the young doctor. A faint smile flickered across his face, and a sound escaped from his mouth—an incomplete, forceful exhalation that carried within it a musical note of surprise. In spite of its brevity, this small vocalization was curiously dramatic, communicating both shock and resignation. The smile faded, and Sommer's features crumpled. He buried his head in his hands and began to sob.

"You knew that an autopsy would take place," Liebermann continued, "and that the cuts on Zelenka's body would be discovered. However, you reasoned that these wounds would most probably be attributed to bullying, persecution, or torture—rather than to an *erotic predilection*. To reinforce this misconception, you wrote to the *Arbeiter-Zeitung*, in the guise of a former—and disaffected—pupil, Herr G. In this article, you denounced the culture of cruelty at Saint Florian's, and made reference to an invented punishment—'doing the night watch'—which had supposedly caused the accidental death of an unfortunate Hungarian boy called Domokos Pikler. In fact, Pikler did not fall to his death—he jumped. He suffered from suicidal melancholia. Your ruse was extremely effective. You did not fail to observe the cardinal rule of successful dissimulation: the inclusion of at least some of the truth."

The mathematics master looked up and pulled the sleeve of his quilted jacket across his nose, leaving a trail of mucus on the faded silk. On his eyelashes, the remnants of tears caught the fading light.

"What did I do wrong?" Sommer asked Liebermann. "I did not coerce Zelenka. I did not force him. He wanted to do those things. He was a young man—but not so young as to be unconscious of his own actions, and insensible of their consequences. . . . I did not *corrupt* him. Our physical intimacies—however repugnant you might find them—created bonds of affection. Deep bonds. I know you will recoil if I claim that we knew love. You have opinions, no doubt, concerning the degree to which love can exist under such circumstances. We inverts are disqualified, on medical grounds, from admission into the higher realms of emotional life . . . although greater men have disagreed with that view in the past. Have you read the *Erotes* by Lucian, Herr Doctor?"

"No."

"Two men debate the merits of loving boys compared to loving women. The defender of love for women argues that such love serves procreation, and is therefore more natural—a superior love. But his opponent reverses the argument. He agrees that love for boys is indeed a cultural rather than a *natural* phenomenon. But this shows that those who practice love for boys—or who have the imagination to derive pleasure from unusual acts—rise above nature. Love for boys is not yoked to primitive, animal passions. When the *imaginative* lover makes love, he does so with his aesthetic sensibilities fully engaged. When he makes love, he is—in a way—creating a work of art. He rises above the carnal. When the dialogue of the *Erotes* reaches its final pages, an adjudicator concludes that love for boys is the natural predilection of philosophers. It is the highest love...."

Sommer clenched his fist.

"What did I do wrong?" He repeated his question. "You are a doctor and will describe me as a degenerate, an invert, a deviant. But may I remind you that it was Becker who killed Zelenka, not me! Respectable Dr. Becker, who would never have attracted such degrading appellations. And is it so very wrong to try to preserve one's position, one's livelihood? Had I been candid, I would have lost everything. You are fortunate, Herr Doctor, that your erotic instincts are directed toward socially acceptable aims. You did not make that choice—as I did not choose to be as I am. We are simply what we are—and what I am was not always judged to be bad. That is only the opinion of doctors in these modern times, and one day, opinions may change again. Therefore, do not judge me so unkindly.... The moral heights that you occupy are not so elevated as you think."

Liebermann did not respond. Instead, he stood up and addressed Rheinhardt.

"I'll wait for you outside."

66

LIEBERMANN GAZED OUT OF the carriage window.

The day was at its end and the hills had become shadowy and indistinct. He noticed the light of a fire—a speck of orange in a sea of darkness—and wondered who might be out there at this time. The temperature had dropped, and the landscape was looking particularly inhospitable.

"Cigar?"

Rheinhardt leaned across and offered him a Trabuco.

"Thank you," said Liebermann. The young doctor struck a vesta and bent forward, allowing the end of his cheroot to touch the flame. "I still can't believe I was so slow-witted," he said out of the side of his mouth. "I should have realized the significance of Zelenka's injuries as soon as you showed me the mortuary photographs—particularly those crural lacerations!"

"I must confess," Rheinhardt responded, "I did not know that people did such things."

"Then you should read the late Professor Krafft-Ebing's *Psychopathia Sexualis*. It contains several cases of a similar type. For example, number forty-eight details the circumstances of an unfortunate gentleman whose young wife could only achieve sexual satisfaction if permitted to suck blood from a cut made on his forearm. The *Psychopathia* also contains numerous accounts of vampiric lust-murder."

"Vampiric lust-murder?" Rheinhardt repeated slowly.

"Oh, yes . . . case nineteen: Leger—a vine dresser. He wandered in a forest for eight days until he came across a twelve-year-old girl. He violated her, tore out her heart, ate it, drank her blood, and buried her remains."

Rheinhardt shook his head. It was remarkable how medical men— when confronted with the worst excesses of human behavior— could describe such horrors in the same impassive tone that they also employed when enumerating the symptoms of pleurisy or indigestion.

"What would make a man do such a thing?" Rheinhardt asked.

"A postmortem conducted by the great Esquirol," Liebermann replied, "found morbid adhesions between the murderer's cerebral membranes and the brain."

"Could Sommer suffer from similar adhesions?"

"I very much doubt it—he is no murderer. His predilection for blood is probably best construed as a kind of fetish . . . posing no more of a threat to society than another man's insistence that his mistress should always wear a short jacket." Liebermann drew on his cigar and became pensive. "I cannot recall whether Krafft-Ebing ever reported hemo-erotic tendencies in an individual whose sexual orientation was already inverted. If not, then a thorough study of Herr Sommer might make an original and instructive contribution to the literature. What will happen to Herr Sommer now?"

"His final words to you were very powerful—and I could see that you were moved by his appeal. However, the fact remains that the man abused his position. He assaulted a pupil—for that is how the authorities will view his degeneracy. He spread malicious rumors about Zelenka and Frau Becker—which had fatal consequences. He was prepared to falsify Wolf's examination results, and he submitted an article to the *Arbeiter-Zeitung*, the sole purpose of which was to confuse a police inquiry. I would say, without fear of exaggeration, that Herr Sommer's prospects are not good. Incidentally," Rheinhardt continued, tilting his head to one side, "how did you discover that the *Arbeiter-Zeitung* article was written by Sommer?"

"When we first visited Herr Sommer, I observed his name—Herr G. Sommer—painted by the door. The article in the *Arbeiter-Zeitung* was by Herr G. This coincidence did not escape my notice. Perhaps Herr Sommer was unable to stop himself from signing the article with his own initial because of some strange compulsion—or perhaps he just made a thoughtless error, a slip." Liebermann rested his cigar in the ashtray, which was positioned in the carriage door. "Or perhaps," he continued, "Herr Sommer reasoned that no one would expect a man intent on deceit to implicate himself by employing his real initial—and he therefore acted counterintuitively as a subtle ruse. Whatever the psychic mechanism underlying his action, he succeeded in rousing my curiosity. Human beings are always revealing their secrets in the little things that they do."

The young doctor shrugged and recovered his cigar. He then held up the cheroot and smiled, as if to say, *There will even be a reason why I put this down only to pick it up again!*

"Had Herr Sommer not written his article," Liebermann continued, "things might have turned out very differently. After all, it was Herr Sommer's article that resulted in your reassignment to the Saint Florian case."

"Indeed," Rheinhardt replied. "Zelenka's death would have been attributed to natural causes, and the investigation would have ended quite prematurely."

Rheinhardt twirled his mustache and emitted a pensive growl.

"What?" Liebermann asked.

"I was just thinking. It's odd, isn't it, that my reluctance to abandon this case was due—at least initially—to Zelenka's youth? I found it difficult to accept the death of a . . ." He hesitated before saying "child." Then, pronouncing the words with bitter irony, he added: "The death of an innocent! And yet . . . This same angelic-looking boy . . ." His sentence trailed off into an exasperated silence.

"Professor Freud," said Liebermann softly, "does not believe that we humans ever enjoy a state of grace—a period of infantile purity. He is of the opinion that we can observe presentiments of adulthood even in the nursery. The toddler's tantrum prefigures murderous rage . . . and even the contented sucking of a thumb may provide the infant with something alarmingly close to sensual comfort and pleasure."

"I find that hard to accept," said Rheinhardt.

"Well—you are not alone," said Liebermann, grinning.

When Liebermann entered his apartment, he discovered that his serving man—Ernst—had left an envelope for him, conspicuously placed on the hall stand. Liebermann opened it and discovered a note inside. He recognized the small, precise handwriting immediately. It was from Miss Amelia Lydgate: an apology—and an invitation.

67

Gerold Sommer sat at his table next to a pile of exercise books. He had already finished marking most of them, but there were a few that he hadn't yet looked at. Given his predicament, he had been surprised to find that his thoughts had kept returning to this unfinished task. The sense of incompletion had been so persistent, so troubling, that in due course he had dragged himself from his reading chair where he had sat brooding, and repositioned himself at the table where he was now working.

The work he had set concerned triangles. In his most recent class, he had shown the boys how to calculate the area of a triangle using the method attributed to Heron of Alexandria. Sommer remembered standing by the blackboard, chalk in hand, looking at their bored faces, and saying in a conversational manner: *This attribution is probably incorrect, as Archimedes almost certainly knew the formula, and it may have been employed by many anonymous mathematicians before him. . . .*

This nugget of information had not made the subject any more interesting for the boys. Indeed, one of them—a scrawny fellow with greasy hair—had covered his mouth to disguise a yawn.

It was extraordinary, Sommer pondered, how so many people— boys and men alike—found mathematics tedious. It was such an elegant subject. *In any right-angled triangle, the square of the hypotenuse is equal to the sum of the squares of the other two sides.* Where else could you find such universal certainty, such indisputable truth, such perfection?

Sommer opened the first exercise book, which belonged to Stojakovic. He was gratified to find that the Serbian boy was deserving of a good mark. He liked Stojakovic. The other exercise books contained work of varying quality, but Sommer was a conscientious teacher. He made an effort to write something helpful or encouraging whenever he could—even if he knew the boy concerned to be innumerate and uninterested.

Triangles . . .

Herr Lang, Frau Becker, Zelenka . . .

Dr. Becker, Zelenka, Frau Becker . . .

Frau Becker, Zelenka . . . myself.

Sommer dismissed these intrusive triangulations from his mind. He did not want to think about such things.

When he had finished marking the exercise books, the mathematics master unwrapped some bread and cheese (which he had collected from the kitchen earlier) and opened a bottle of Côte de Brouilly. The wine had been a gift from his uncle Alfred, and Sommer had been saving it for a special occasion. It was dark, full-bodied, and left a fruity aftertaste. After drinking only two glasses, the mathematics master collected his personal papers together and examined them to make sure that his affairs were in order. He then wrote a brief note addressed to his mother, apologizing for his conduct, and another addressed to a friend in Salzburg, which made reference to an outstanding financial debt that he wished to be settled. He then pressed the muzzle of a pistol firmly against his temple and pulled the trigger.

His eyes remained open.

68

As Liebermann marched through the streets of Alsergrund, his thoughts took the form of questions and doubts: moreover, his general disquietude was exacerbated by an unpleasant fluttering sensation in his chest. It made him feel light-headed and breathless. He put his hand in his pocket and touched Miss Lydgate's note.

He wondered why he had accepted her invitation, when he might just as well have replied with a polite refusal. Even though it had been his intention to decline, Liebermann had found himself writing courteous phrases that moved—inexorably—toward a bald statement that she should expect him at the appointed time.

What was Miss Lydgate's purpose? Would she give him some indication, however small, of her changed circumstance, or would she eschew mention of her romantic involvement altogether, choosing instead to pour tea, offer biscuits, and share with him her latest philosophical enthusiasm. He was not sure he could tolerate such a conversation. The temptation to press her for some revelation—or even a complete confession—might be too powerful to resist.

Liebermann was surprised by the strength of his feelings—and shamefully aware of their proprietorial nature. He thought of Professor Freud, the most rational of men, driven to the very brink of demanding satisfaction—because of jealousy. He thought of Dr. Becker, motivated to kill another human being—because of jealousy. And he thought of himself, reeling away from the Café Segel, delirious with disappointment and rage—because of jealousy.

It was an ugly, destructive emotion, and as a civilized man he felt obliged to overcome his primitive urges. Yet the desire to possess a woman exclusively was an indelible feature of the male psyche, and to repress such feelings would simply promote—according to Professor Freud—the development of hysterical and neurotic symptoms. Modern man must either wallow in the mire of his animal instincts or deny them and become mentally ill.

A fragment of conversation:

That man . . . The one who stopped you outside Demel's.

What?

The man who called you Amélie—Franz . . .

Oh yes. Strange, wasn't it?

You knew him, really, didn't you?

Are you jealous?

Liebermann didn't want to be jealous. But there was one thing he didn't want to be even more, and that was mentally ill.

In due course, Liebermann arrived outside Frau Rubenstein's house. He rapped the knocker three times and waited. A few moments later, the door opened and Amelia Lydgate was standing in front of him. She was wearing a simple white dress and her hair fell in blazing tresses to her shoulders. Her eyes—which never failed to astonish him—seemed to be reflecting a bright blue light: the harsh blue of an Alpine lake or glacier. Unusually, she smiled—a broad, uninhibited smile. Its radiance imbued her face with beatific qualities. Indeed, there was something about her appearance that reminded Liebermann of religious iconography: she might easily have replaced the angel in a Renaissance Annunciation.

"Dr. Liebermann." Her voice floated over the traffic. "I am delighted you could come. Please, do come in."

As was his custom, Liebermann spent a few minutes with Frau Rubenstein before following Amelia up the stairs to her apartment. Although Frau Rubenstein's conversation had been unremarkable, he thought he had detected a certain wry amusement in her tone—a certain knowingness. He might even have commented on this had he not had other things on his mind.

"It must be nearly a month since you last visited us," said Amelia. "I believe it was shortly after the detectives' ball."

"Yes," Liebermann replied. "Mid-January, I think."

She glanced over her shoulder at him: "How time flies. . . . Unfortunately, I have not had sufficient opportunity to organize dancing lessons with Herr Janowsky . . . but I still intend to do so."

"You have been busy . . . at the university?"

"Yes," she replied. "And there have been other matters. . . ."

Again she looked over her shoulder and smiled.

When they reached the top landing, Amelia Lydgate ushered Liebermann into her small parlor. As soon as he crossed the threshold, he came to an abrupt halt. There, sitting at the gateleg table, on the chair that *he* had so frequently occupied, sat the gentleman in whose arms Miss Lydgate had swooned outside the Café Segel. The man looked relaxed. His legs were crossed, revealing one of his boots, which was stitched with an ornate and somewhat garish pattern. His wide-brimmed hat was hanging off the back of his chair, and he sported a curious necktie that seemed to be no wider than a shoelace.

The gentleman stood up and extended his hand.

"You will forgive me for addressing you in my native language, Herr Dr. Liebermann, but I have a strong suspicion that your English will be very much superior to my German—which is lamentably poor. It is a great honor to meet a man of whom I have heard such good report." He grasped Liebermann's hand, and squeezed it hard. The man's English was peculiarly inflected. Indeed, it was very different from the English that Liebermann remembered from the time he'd spent in London. Nor was the man's clothing particularly British-looking.

"Permit me to introduce myself," the man continued. "Randall Pelletier-Lydgate—at your service, sir."

"You are Miss Lydgate's . . . cousin?"

Amelia came forward. "No. Randall is my brother."

"But . . ." Liebermann looked at the woman standing beside him. She was glowing with pride. "It was my understanding that you do not have—"

"A brother . . . Indeed." Amelia interrupted him. "That was my understanding too, but apparently I was mistaken."

Liebermann was thrown into a state of confusion. He experienced a sense of intense relief—almost joy—but was then immediately alarmed by his reaction. He was in love with Trezska—wasn't he?

"I think," said Liebermann. "I think . . . you had better explain."

"With great pleasure," Amelia replied. "However, before we proceed, you will no doubt require refreshment—so I must first make some tea."

"Many years before making the acquaintance of Greta Buchbinder— that is to say Amelia's mother—our father, Samuel Lydgate, had enjoyed a brief but intimate dalliance with an actress: Constance Vaughn." Randall's voice was mellow, and his narrative flowed like the song of a lyric tenor. "Their acquaintance was prematurely ended when the English Shakespeare Company—with whom Constance played as a principal—boarded the White Star vessel *Oceanic*, bound for New York. The company was embarked upon a tour of America that would take them through the southern states. Although Constance had promised to write to Samuel Lydgate, he never heard from her again—and so he never learned that she had departed from Liverpool pregnant, carrying his child. Constance—my mother— was an unconventional woman. She was impulsive, prone to violent passions, and—I fear—in her youth might reasonably have been described as a little . . . cranky."

"I'm sorry?" Liebermann said.

"Mentally unstable," Amelia interjected in German.

"Ah, of course. Please continue."

Randall took a sip of Earl Grey.

"In New Orleans, the English Shakespeare Company performed two tragedies and a comedy. One of these tragedies was *Romeo and Juliet*—and my mother played the lead. In the audience was a local businessman called George Pelletier. So impressed was he by the young actress that he sent her flowers and showered her with gifts. A single dinner engagement sufficed to convince him that she was the love of his life, and he proposed that they should be married. My mother, being an indefatigable romantic—her senses assailed by the exotic sights and sounds of New Orleans, drunk with the prospect of adventure and excitement—agreed to the proposal immediately, and one week later when the English Shakespeare Company left town, they did so with one less actress in their troupe.

"I do not know whether my mother and her new husband discussed my paternity—but what I do know is that I was raised in the belief that George Pelletier was my father, and he accordingly treated me like a son. Indeed, a boy could not have wished for a more devoted parent. . . . He died five years ago, and if grief is a measure of affection, then the depth of my sorrow confirmed the strength of our bond. He was a kind, generous man, and I continue to miss his counsel and laughter. Alas, this great loss was soon to be compounded by another. Last year my mother succumbed to a tubercular infection, and on her deathbed—for reasons that I still can only guess at—she decided that the time had come to reveal the truth concerning my provenance. I discovered the name, occupation, and nationality of my real father: a revelation the effect of which—I trust you will appreciate—cannot be overestimated.

"Lydgate is not so common a name in the British Isles, and, having resolved to begin my inquiries among the better educational establishments of London, I was soon rewarded with success. However, I was reluctant to approach Samuel directly. I did not know what manner of man he was—or how he might respond if I presented myself at his door.

"I am accustomed to uncovering facts—it is, indeed, what constitutes the greater part of my work. I decided that I should discover a little more about Samuel's circumstances before alerting him to my existence. I wanted to know more about him in order to better judge whether or not my appearance would be welcome. My agent in London later informed me that Samuel Lydgate had a daughter—Amelia—who was currently studying at the University of Vienna. . . .

"Dr. Liebermann, you cannot imagine how this intelligence affected me. A sister. I had a younger sister!" Randall looked at Amelia, and his expression, Liebermann noticed, was still—in spite of the passage of time—incandescent with joyful disbelief. "I do not know why I was so profoundly moved—but *moved* I most certainly was. Further, it occurred to me that there might be certain advantages if I took the trouble to contact my sister before I approached my father: a younger person might be less rigid—better equipped to assimilate such dramatic news. She might even be prepared to act as a kind of intermediary. So I resolved to travel to Vienna . . . and here I am."

"A remarkable story," said Liebermann. "Truly remarkable."

The subsequent discussion was somewhat circular, returning again and again to reiterations of the fact that Randall Lydgate's history was—without doubt—*remarkable!* Indeed, it seemed to Liebermann that repetitions of this nature were something of a necessity and an unspecified number were required before the conversation was free to proceed beyond general expressions of amazement. Eventually, however, a turning point was reached and the issue of how best to inform Samuel Lydgate of Randall's appearance was given careful and sensitive consideration.

Liebermann's curiosity had been aroused by something that Randall had said earlier, and at an appropriate juncture he said:

"I trust that you will not consider my question impertinent. But you mentioned in passing that your work involves . . . uncovering facts? What is it that you do?"

"I am an archaeologist," said Randall.

"And a respected authority," said Amelia, "on the ancient civilizations of Mexico and Peru."

"Please . . . Amelia," said Randall, embarrassed by his sister's advocacy. "Most of my work takes place in old libraries—poring over ancient maps and mythologies. But on occasion it is my privilege to visit the holy places of the Toltecs, where it is still possible to find—and save—examples of their sublime artistry."

"The Toltecs?"

"A race alluded to in a migration myth as the first Nahua immigrants to the region of Mexico. The name 'Toltec' came to be regarded by the surrounding peoples as synonymous with 'artist,' and as a kind of hallmark that guaranteed the superiority of any

Toltec workmanship." As Randall spoke, his voice acquired a mellifluous, dreamy quality, and his eyes seemed to search out a far horizon. "Everything in and about their city was redolent of the taste and artistry of its founders. The very walls were encrusted with rare stones, and their masonry was so beautifully chiseled and laid as to resemble the choicest mosaic."

It transpired that Randall had clearly inherited some of his mother's appetite for adventure. For he often accepted commissions from North American universities and museums to journey south— into sometimes remote and dangerous territories—in order to recover lost treasures, the existence of which he ascertained from close readings of native legends (recorded by historians with exotic names such as Zumarraga and Ixtlilxochitl).

As the evening progressed, the conversation ranged over an extraordinarily broad range of topics: Amelia's research under the supervision of Landsteiner, King Acxitl, dream interpretation, the hallucinatory properties of certain desert mushrooms (an example of which, curiously, Randall happened to have in his pocket), Nietzsche's concept of eternal recurrence, and the syncopated music of the black people of New Orleans (which Randall obligingly whistled while tapping his foot).

Discussion of rags and ragtime led, by some oblique conversational maneuvering, to the waltz, which prompted Amelia to enthuse— at some length—about the ball she had attended with Liebermann. Randall—to Liebermann's surprise—expressed much interest (perhaps anthropological) in Fasching, and the young doctor found himself offering to take both brother and sister to the clock makers' ball, which was scheduled to take place the following week.

When Liebermann finally took his leave, he felt quite dazed. It had turned out to be an evening very different from the one he had expected. He walked the streets for some time—smoking and thinking—before returning home. When Miss Lydgate had said goodbye, she had reached out and gently touched his hand. After taking a few steps he had looked back, and the image of her standing in the doorway had impressed itself on his memory. Her white dress had billowed in the breeze, and strands of her spun copper hair had streamed across her face. She had pushed them aside, revealing those arresting eyes. The smile that had been fleetingly present throughout the entire evening was gone, and her expression was intense, penetrating—as if she were looking directly into his soul. Liebermann identified the thought as fanciful, but nevertheless felt a shiver of unease.

He had been so very wrong about Miss Lydgate. Indeed, on reflection, Liebermann concluded that in matters of the heart he had something of a gift for being wrong....

69

THE SILENCE THAT PREVAILED in the commissioner's office was absolute. It was the kind of stillness that Rheinhardt associated with mortuaries and provincial churches in winter: an icy, unyielding soundlessness—as obstinate as frozen loam. He wanted to speak, but whenever he tried, his courage failed. This silence demanded the utmost care—and if he broke it carelessly, the consequences would be catastrophic.

The commissioner had not moved for some time. His eyes were fixed on a folder occupying the pool of light beneath his desk lamp. It contained Rheinhardt's supplementary report on the murder of Thomas Zelenka. Brügel's hand crept into the illuminated circle like a grotesque insect emerging from beneath a stone, the first and second fingers raised and testing the air like feelers. Sustaining a convincing illusion of self-determination, Brügel's hand halted before touching the folder—as if it had detected something repellent or dangerous therein. The commissioner's profound, contemplative silence seemed to presage alarming possibilities: not only the prospect of punishment, but actual *expulsion* from the security office.

Rheinhardt had always been a policeman and could imagine no other life. What else could he do? He tried to console himself with the thought that he had acted conscientiously. But, in truth, he knew that he had been impulsive, naïve, and somewhat vainglorious. Now he would suffer the consequences.

Brügel's hand moved forward and his raised fingers dropped down on the folder. The inconsequential beat this movement produced sounded—to Rheinhardt—like the boom of a ceremonial drum: an invitation in some ancient rite to ritual slaughter.

"You disobeyed my orders," said the commissioner, in a low, gravelly voice. "I distinctly recall telling you that as far as I was concerned the Saint Florian's case was closed."

"Yes, sir," said Rheinhardt. "You did. However, with the greatest respect . . ." *I have nothing to lose, now,* he thought. *I might as well defend myself.* Rheinhardt took a deep breath. "Sir, I hold the rank of detective inspector. Although it is my duty to obey *you*—my commanding officer—it is also my duty to serve the Justizpalast, the people of Vienna, and, ultimately, His Majesty the emperor."

Rheinhardt glanced up at the portrait of Franz Josef—only just visible in the reflected lamplight—and fancied that he saw a glimmer of approval in the old man's expression. "I believe," he continued, "that I acted correctly and in accordance with the obligations and necessities of my office."

The commissioner's eyes narrowed and his hand clenched into a tight fist—the knuckles rising up beneath his leathery skin to form a bloodless ridge. On his temple a knotty blood vessel pulsed with febrile malevolence. The commissioner seemed to be on the brink of exploding with rage when—quite suddenly—his expression changed. He sighed, his shoulders fell, and his clenched fist slowly opened.

"My nephew," said Brügel hoarsely, "has been disgraced." Rheinhardt did not know how to respond. Their gazes met, and the commissioner continued. "His mother was so proud of him. This will break her heart." As on the previous occasion when Brügel had mentioned his sister, tender sentiments seemed to diminish him.

"I am very sorry, sir," said Rheinhardt sincerely.

The commisioner opened his drawer and removed a letter, which he placed carefully on the folder containing Rheinhardt's report.

"From Kiefer," he said softly. "It does not exonerate him . . . but it may go some way toward helping us to understand his conduct. You see, the boy claims to have been influenced by certain teachings promulgated by the masters—Eichmann, Gärtner, Osterhagen—a philosophy of power. Young minds, Rheinhardt. They are so malleable—so easily corrupted. . . . I have already spoken to the minister of education—who has promised to attend the next meeting of the board of governors."

The commissioner fell silent again.

"Sir," said Rheinhardt, "am I to be disciplined?"

The commissioner grunted and shook his head.

"Thank you, sir," said Rheinhardt. Not wishing to tempt fate, he stood up and clicked his heels. "Should I report to Inspector von Bulow tomorrow morning?"

"No," said the commissioner. "He doesn't need *your* assistance anymore." Brügel succeeded in investing the possessive pronoun with utter contempt.

"Very good, sir," said Rheinhardt. He bowed—and walked briskly to the door.

70

LIEBERMANN HAD FIRST MET OPPENHEIM in one of the coffee-houses close to the hospital. Although the young man was studying classics at the university, he was a keen amateur psychologist and was always willing to discuss—in his words—*the life of the soul*. He was an enthusiastic, open-minded fellow, and much more at ease with topics such as sexuality and the conflicts arising between nature and culture than most of Liebermann's colleagues. Their friendship was sustained—as it had begun—by occasional, unplanned encounters in the coffeehouses of the ninth district.

Liebermann had risen early and, on his way to the hospital, was pleasantly surprised to discover Oppenheim sitting outside the Café Segel, warming his hands around a steaming, frothy *mélange* and reading a volume of Greek.

They greeted each other cordially, and Oppenheim invited Liebermann to join him for breakfast. Glancing at his wristwatch, Liebermann saw that he had plenty of time to spare and seated himself beside the student.

"What are you reading?" asked Liebermann.

"A *True Story*—by Lucian of Samosata," Oppenheim replied. "An extraordinary piece of writing about a group of adventuring heroes who travel to the moon. It is—at one and the same time—a very early example of fantastic literature and a criticism of ancient authorities that describes mythical events as though they are real."

This weighty gambit was typical of Oppenheim, whose appetite for intellectual stimulation was not very much affected by the hour of the day. Liebermann—prematurely aged by the youth's indecent vitality—ordered a *very* strong *schwarzer*, two *kaisersemmel* rolls, and some plum conserve.

Their conversation ranged up and down the narrow isthmus that connected classical literature and psychiatry, and touched upon Aristotle's *De Anima*, Hippocrates' essay on epilepsy, and sundry poetical works that took melancholia as their principal theme. After they had been talking for a while, Liebermann began to wonder whether the young scholar might know the answer to a certain question that had been annoying him like the minor but persistent presence of a small stone in a shoe.

"Tell me," Liebermann asked, "do you have any idea what a Liderc is?"

"A what?"

"A Liderc."

"Is it a Hungarian word?"

"I believe it is."

Oppenheim stroked his short beard.

"It sounds vaguely familiar . . . and I think I may have come across it in a book of folklore. But I can't quite remember. Will you be at the hospital today?"

"Yes."

"Then I'll look it up and let you know if I find anything."

The sound of church bells reminded Liebermann that he should be on his way. He rose and deposited a pile of coins on the table: more than enough to cover his own and Oppenheim's breakfast. Before Oppenheim could object—as he usually did—Liebermann declared: "You can pay next time."

It was of course what Liebermann always said on such occasions.

Later in the day Liebermann received a short note from Oppenheim.

Dear Friend,

Have just been to the library and managed to run your Liderc to ground in Kóbor's Myths and Legends of the Transylvanian Peoples. The Liderc is a kind of satanic lover—ördögszereto in Hungarian—and is similar to an incubus or a succubus. Victims often die of exhaustion on account of the Liderc's stamina and enthusiasm. Well, I should be so lucky! What on earth do you want to know this for? Did one of your patients mention it—and if so, in what context? Until the next time— when you will allow me to buy you breakfast.

Oppenheim

Liebermann placed the note on his desk and stared at it. For once in his life, he desperately wanted to be wrong.

71

A N O B S E R V E R U N A C C U S T O M E D T O life at Saint Florian's might have described the prevailing mood of the school as subdued. Drexler, however, knew otherwise. He could read the signs like a haruspex: signs that were no less vivid or portentous, as far as he was concerned, than the hot entrails of a freshly slaughtered goat—the whispering, the sidelong glances, the sudden silences, the pursed lips of the masters, the canceled classes. The school was not subdued at all, but seething with nervous excitement.

Drexler was sitting on his own in the dining room, toying with his *bruckfleisch*—a stew consisting largely of innards, blood, and sweetbreads. A pallid piece of offal surfaced among the slices of heart, liver, and spleen, making him feel slightly nauseous. He was thinking about what had happened that morning. He had been standing in the washroom, waiting his turn to use one of the tin sinks.

A line of hunched white backs—goose-pimpled and shivering—the relentless hammering of the old pipes . . .

Drexler had rushed over to claim a vacant basin. While he was splashing tepid water onto his face, he overheard the two boys next to him speaking in hushed tones.

"Murdered . . . in the lodges . . . there for a whole day before they found him."

"What did you say?" Drexler had asked.

The boy next to him had been about to reply, but was silenced by a prefect who struck his calves with a riding crop (carried especially for this purpose).

"Shut up," the prefect had shouted. "You're worse than a bunch of fishwives!"

By midmorning Drexler had been able to establish that there hadn't been a murder at all but a suicide—and that the dead master was Herr Sommer.

This news saddened Drexler, as he had been rather fond of Herr Sommer. When, in the previous year, Drexler had been experiencing difficulties understanding algebra, Herr Sommer had invited him to his rooms and given him extra tuition. Away from the classroom the mathematics master was much more relaxed—much more amusing. He had once told Drexler an extremely risqué joke about a priest and a choirboy. "Our secret," he had said confidentially. Toward the end of that year, Sommer's invitations became less frequent. He seemed to have found a new favorite—Thomas Zelenka. Drexler hadn't minded very much. In truth, he had begun to find Herr Sommer's company less diverting—especially after he'd made the acquaintance of Snjezana.

Drexler tried to swallow a kidney but didn't have the stomach for it. He pushed it back onto the spoon with his tongue and decided he wasn't hungry.

Everything was beginning to unravel.

Zelenka, Becker, Sommer . . .

Even Wolf hadn't been himself lately. He had been summoned to the headmaster's office on Thursday and had refused to say why.

"Did he ask about Perger?"

"Just forget Perger, will you!" Wolf had replied angrily, "He *ran away*, for God's sake! And no one gives a shit where he's gone!"

Drexler was no longer sure whether he could trust Wolf. Greater leniency was shown in courts of law to criminals who confessed their misdeeds and showed remorse. Was that what Wolf was up to?

Before Drexler left the dining hall he went over to another boy and said: "I'm not feeling well. If Osterhagen asks where I am, tell him I've gone to the infirmary."

It was not difficult to leave the school unnoticed at that time of day, and soon he was walking eastward, cross-country toward Vienna. He gave Aufkirchen a wide berth, but could still see the onion dome and spire of the Romanesque church. For a moment he was tempted to change direction. Snjezana would probably be lying on her bed, smoking, and reading one of her novels. He could see her one last time. What harm would it do?

"No," Drexler said out loud, lengthening his stride. "I must get this over with."

He continued walking for more than an hour and eventually came to a tiny hamlet—no more than a cluster of ramshackle dwellings huddled together on a rough track. Drexler followed the path around the base of a hillock, and in due course it took him to a much wider road. He paused in order to get his bearings.

A low, weak sun hovered above the horizon. It was suspended in the sky like a communion wafer: a perfect, lustreless white circle. All around, crows were either taking off or landing, and the air reverberated with their raucous laughter.

Drexler stepped onto the road and continued his descent. Soon he came to another village. He had been to this place several times before but had never stayed very long. Although larger than Aufkirchen, it offered little in the way of entertainment. The inn was fairly respectable and a frequent destination for well-heeled patrons. His parents had taken rooms there once when they'd visited the school.

Opposite the inn was an impressive baroque church, painted

bright yellow, and next to this was the police station. It was not a very auspicious building. Indeed, it might have been described more accurately as an outpost—or guardhouse.

When Drexler opened the door, he was struck by the modesty of the interior: roughcast walls, a single paraffin lamp, and a battered table—behind which sat a big-boned constable with orange hair. He was staring glumly at a silent telephone.

Drexler's appearance seemed to raise his spirits.

"Hello," he said cheerfully. "Are you from the school?"

"Yes," Drexler replied.

"You've come a fair way—lost, are you?"

"No. I've come to report something."

"What's that, then?"

"A murder."

The constable's expression changed. "A murder?"

"Yes," said Drexler. "I shot a boy called Perger. I want to confess. . . . I want to make a statement."

72

LIEBERMANN WATCHED THE LATE-AFTERNOON traffic rolling by: fiacres, omnibuses, trams, and an impressive four-horse carriage with a gold crest emblazoned on its black lacquered door. The occupant—a visiting royal of some description—could just be discerned inside, a shadowy figure craning to get a better view of the opera house.

It was a grand building, constructed in the neo-Renaissance style. However, when it had been completed, the emperor had been overheard agreeing with one of his aides concerning the appearance of the new opera house: it looked . . . *a trifle low, perhaps?* The architect dutifully hanged himself, and two months later his collaborator died of a heart attack. Thereafter, Franz Josef only praised the work of civic artists. "Beautiful, beautiful . . ." became his unvarying response.

Inside the opera house, the orchestra and singers were rehearsing *Siegfried.* Liebermann had discovered this by talking to the doorman, who—for two kronen—was easily persuaded to give him advance notice of the musicians' imminent departure.

The young doctor had stationed himself by one of the two stone fountains that flanked the loggia. He had stood by this particular fountain on numerous occasions but had never troubled to examine it closely. The female figure seated at the summit was the legendary siren Lorelei, and below the elegant bowl were three sentries representing love, grief, and vengeance. Liebermann laughed bitterly. The themes dramatized his circumstance perfectly.

He had fallen in love with Trezska: he had been beguiled by her beauty, virtuosity, and mystery. In the virid halo of an absinthe stupor, she was as irresistible and strange as Lorelei. Yet there was a natural order of things, a universal logic, which insisted that love must always—at some point—be associated with grief. Small partings—which pained the heart—were a mere prelude to the great sundering that awaits all lovers. Deceit, calamity, death—grief could not be postponed indefinitely. Liebermann had already started to grieve—even though the outcome of his inquiries was still uncertain. It did not feel premature. He was not psychic, but he wasn't stupid either. Love had been followed by grief, and he wondered whether vengeance was now waiting in the wings. Presumably, vengeance could come only at *his* behest. Would he summon that dark spirit, and become acquainted with all three personifications of the operatic triumvirate?

Liebermann was familiar with the legend of Lorelei through Liszt's setting of an eponymous poem by Heine. He recollected the opening bars: yearning, ambiguous harmonies, falling for a moment into silence—and then the voice, entering:

> *"Ich weiß nicht, was soll es bedeuten,*
> *Daß ich so traurig bin."*
> I do not know what it means
> That I should feel so sad.

It was a romantic tale of men fatally fascinated by beauty. Liebermann looked up at the Rhine maiden. She was seated on a decorated pedestal, her body half-turned—carelessly exposing her breasts. She was slim—her arms delicately poised—and her corrugated hair flowed off her shoulders. Her expression was wickedly indifferent to masculine worship.

The sound of a voice floated above the traffic. The doorman had come out from beneath the loggia and was waving his hands in the air. Liebermann acknowledged his presence and walked toward the lobby. When he arrived, two men were emerging. The first was taller than the second. His thick dark hair was combed to the side and his beard was neatly trimmed. He wore spectacles, a fine gray suit, and a necktie loosely set to produce a wide knot. The second man was small and wiry, but his face was distinguished by an exceptionally high forehead and a strong, square chin. His hair—which was thinning a little—was brushed back and slightly bristled. He wore spectacles similar to the first man's, a dark jacket, and a white bow tie. Liebermann noticed that his gait was rather unusual: somewhat jerky and uneven.

The first man was Alfred Rosé. The second was Rosé's brother-in-law, Director Mahler. Although Liebermann had been waiting to address the first, the mere presence of the second made his step falter. For Liebermann, Director Mahler was only slightly less than a god.

"Concertmaster?" Liebermann called hoarsely. Rosé didn't hear him, and the young doctor had to call again. "Concertmaster?"

The violinist stopped and turned. "Yes?"

"Herr Rosé, I have a message . . . from one of your pupils."

Rosé didn't respond, but simply looked at his interlocutor inquisitively. Liebermann noticed that Mahler's right leg was twitching. This movement suggested impatience, but his expression was perfectly calm. The director finally stamped the ground lightly, and the twitching stopped.

"Fräulein Novak?" Liebermann added.

"Who did you say?"

"Fräulein Novak."

"I'm sorry," said the concert master, shaking his head. "You must have been misinformed. I have no pupil called Novak."

It was the answer that Liebermann had expected: but he wanted to make absolutely sure that later there would be no room for doubt in his mind.

"A Hungarian lady," he persisted. "She recently sought your advice on the spring sonata?"

Rosé shook his head again—this time more vigorously. "No, my friend. You *really do* have the wrong person."

"So it seems. . . . Forgive me."

Liebermann bowed, and the two men walked on. Mahler immediately began talking.

"I've agreed to the guest engagements—and Salter has confirmed that at least one of my works is to be included in every program." In spite of his severe features, the director spoke cheerily.

"And the fee?" asked Rosé.

"I said I wouldn't accept less than two thousand kronen."

"Two thousand," repeated Rosé, impressed.

As they receded, their voices faded beneath the clatter and thrum of the Ringstrasse traffic.

Liebermann's attention was drawn upward. A dark cloud was floating over the roof of the opera house.

73

EICHMANN PLACED THE LETTER in front of him—a carefully executed, fastidious movement. He took care to ensure that the upper horizontal line of the paper was exactly parallel with the edge of his desk, let his finger run over the embossed seal, and took a deep breath.

"From the minister of education."

Gärtner took a swig from his hip flask. "I see."

"He is going to attend the next meeting of the board of governors. He wishes to raise a number of issues."

"Issues?"

"The minister makes several allusions to the emperor's desire to create a more *inclusive* military—and he writes of the moral obligation incumbent upon educational institutions to respect His Majesty's wishes. The implications, I'm afraid, are all too clear."

"Headmaster? Are you suggesting that . . ."

"I will almost certainly be asked to tender my resignation. And so—I am sorry to say—will my closest allies."

"We must fight them!" said Gärtner. "We must argue our case."

Eichmann leaned forward and ran his finger down the margin of the letter.

"Listen to this: *Young minds are easily misguided, and great care must be taken to ensure that any philosophical instruction given in military schools is concordant with the emperor's vision.* It is over, my friend."

Gärtner took another swig. "The ingratitude, headmaster."

"I have given the best years of my life to this school."

Gärtner pulled his gown around his shoulders, as though he had suddenly felt the temperature drop in his old bones.

"Was it Wolf?"

"He wrote a letter to his uncle—the commissioner of the security office."

"And have you spoken with him? The boy?"

"He sat where you are now, straight-faced, explaining to me how he felt he had been manipulated, corrupted. How he had been mesmerized in your special tutorial group—made to believe things through relentless repetition—that he now understands were disloyal to the emperor . . . not in sympathy with the spirit of an empire comprised of so many great and proud nations."

"Disgraceful. And he seemed such a receptive boy—so full of promise. Did we teach him nothing?"

Eichmann smiled: a humorless display of teeth.

"No. You are mistaken, old friend," said the headmaster. "I fear we taught him too much."

74

THE CIRCLE OF TREES looked different by daylight, and Drexler was uncertain whether he had brought the constable to the right place.

"Just a moment," he said, pausing to consider the landscape.

Drexler went over to a large gnarled trunk, and ran his fingers over the rough surface.

"What are you doing?" the constable called out.

"Looking for something."

The face was less distinct than Drexler had remembered—but it was there nevertheless. An old graybeard, trapped in the timber: two knotty projections serving to create the illusion of a pair of weary, anguished eyes.

"Here," said Drexler, pointing at the ground. "I buried him here."

The constable marched over, swinging the shovel off his shoulder. He stamped the blade into the ground and angled it back, raising a wedge of turf. The ease with which the soil came up was conspicuous, suggesting recent disturbance. The constable grunted, and set about his task with renewed conviction. He was a strong, big-boned youth, and he tossed the earth aside with mechanical efficiency.

"Why did you do it?" he asked Drexler.

"It was an accident," Drexler replied. "We were playing with a revolver . . . and it just went off. I didn't mean to do it."

"If it was an accident, why didn't you tell the headmaster? Accidents happen . . ."

"I don't know. I panicked, I suppose."

"And you carried him—the dead boy—all this way on your own?"

"No. I stole a horse and trap and got as far as the road."

"That's odd. None of the locals reported a theft."

"It belonged to the school. I returned the trap before anyone noticed it was missing."

The constable shrugged, took off his spiked helmet, and handed it to Drexler. Then he wiped his brow and continued to dig. Gravid clouds had begun to gather overhead, and Drexler felt the first faint chill of rain on his cheeks. The hole deepened—but there was no sign of Perger's jute shroud.

"How far down did you bury him?"

"Not *that* far," said Drexler, perplexed. "You must have just missed him. . . . Try here." He pointed to another spot.

The constable sighed, moved a little closer to the tree, and began to dig again. He interrupted his task to look up at the malignant sky.

"We're going to get soaked," he said, swearing softly under his breath.

The shovel's blade met some resistance, and the constable caught Drexler's eye. However, the next downward thrust produced a loud clang that identified the obstruction as nothing more than a rock. Soon the constable had dug another hole, equal in depth to the first.

"I'm sorry," said Drexler. "It was dark. It's difficult to judge distances when it's dark. But I can assure you, I buried him somewhere around here. I remember this tree. You see, it has a face in it . . . an old man."

"An old man, eh?"

"Please, try here." Drexler took two paces away from the tree and stamped his feet.

"I tell you what," said the constable, handing Drexler the shovel. "Why don't *you* dig for a while?"

The young man recovered his helmet and stomped off to seek shelter under the thickest bough he could find.

Drexler began to dig frantically.

Nothing.

Clay, earthworms, stones, roots . . .

He started to dig another hole. Nothing. And another . . .

The drizzle had been succeeded by a persistent saturating downpour.

"All right," the constable called out. "You've had your fun. . . . I suppose you and your friends think this sort of thing is very funny. Well, you won't be laughing after I've given you the good hiding you deserve."

"What?" said Drexler.

"Come here," said the constable, beckoning with a crooked finger. "This isn't a joke. . . . This isn't a joke, you . . . you . . ."

Drexler threw the shovel to the ground and fell to his knees. He thrust his hands into the hole he had dug and clawed at the mud. His tears were invisible on his rain-soaked face.

"Perger!" he cried. "Perger?"

The constable's expression altered. He no longer looked angry, more startled and confused. A little shocked, even. Drexler tried to wipe the tears from his eyes, but only succeeded in smearing his face with mud.

"Perger?" he shouted. When Drexler raised his hands, the constable could see that his fingers were bleeding. His eyes were shining with a terrible urgency.

"Take it easy," said the constable, taking a cautious step forward. *What was it the boy had said? An old man in the tree . . .*

Maybe this wasn't a joke—maybe the boy wasn't right in the head. He certainly didn't look very well.

"I think we'd better get back to the station," said the constable. "We'll have some tea, eh? Warm you up a bit? And then I think we'd better call a doctor."

75

LIEBERMANN PAID THE CAB DRIVER and braced himself against the teeming rain. The carriage rattled away and he walked slowly toward the end of the cul-de-sac. Water was flowing in fast rivulets down the cobbled street and the wind was gathering strength. Low clouds, descending from the west, had created an eldritch twilight.

The battered door—toward which Liebermann was making steady progress—was swinging on its hinges, occasionally crashing loudly against the wall. The fact that nobody had bothered to secure it reinforced the general atmosphere of neglect and desolation.

Liebermann stepped over the threshold and into the tiled arcade. He paused for a moment and pushed a hank of sopping hair out of his eyes. A stream of icy water trickled down the back of his neck. From his shadowy vantage he could see across the courtyard. A man was standing at the foot of the iron stairs. He was facing away from Liebermann and wore a wide-brimmed hat and a long coat. Beyond the stranger, and positioned above him on the covered landing, stood Trezska. She was dressed in readiness to travel, and carried—in addition to her shoulder bag—a small valise. Her violin was in its case at her feet. Yet there had been no sign of a cab waiting for her outside, and the man at the foot of the stairs was clearly making no effort to assist her. Indeed, there was something altogether strange about his situation. He had not chosen to climb the few steps that would have afforded him shelter. Instead, he was standing rather awkwardly, fully exposed to the elements.

Trezska was talking, but Liebermann could not hear her. He was too distant, and the deluge was becoming symphonic. Close by, the rain was drumming on a tin roof and an overflowing gutter was splashing loudly.

A blast of wind threatened to remove the stranger's hat, and the man had to grab quickly at the top of his head to hold it down. Again, Liebermann noted a conspicuous awkwardness—the maneuver had been executed clumsily with the left hand.

Liebermann crept down the passageway, keeping his back close to the wall. When he reached the opposite end, he discovered why it was that the stranger's posture had appeared somewhat unnatural. The man was holding a pistol, the barrel of which was pointed upward, toward Trezska.

The young doctor's response was automatic and unreasoning. He wanted to protect her, even though she had deceived him and even though he suspected that her capacity for deceit was boundless. Such was his disposition that a romantic obligation to a woman would always supersede a *political* obligation. Besides, he now had *so* many questions he wanted to ask her—questions that might never be answered if she were shot dead—that no other course of action seemed possible.

Liebermann ventured out into the driving rain and moved toward the stranger. He approached with great care, ensuring that the soles of his shoes landed gently on the cobbles. He held his breath as he had in early childhood when he used to sneak out of his room after his mother had put him to bed. Strange, he thought, how easily the mind supplies correspondent memories from infancy. Professor Freud was right: much of adult behavior had its origins in the nursery.

The rain was streaming down his face, blurring his vision; however, he was satisfied that Trezska had not reacted to his appearance. If she had, the man would have almost certainly turned to see what she was looking at. As Liebermann drew closer, he could hear Trezska's voice.

"I am sure we can come to some arrangement. After all, we are not entirely without common interests. I have in my possession information which might prove very useful."

Closer—one step at a time . . .

"But," she continued, "you cannot expect me to embark upon such an arrangement without some promise of security."

It was remarkable how calm she sounded, given her predicament, and her German was more fluent and mannered. "You will accept, I hope, that this is not an unreasonable request."

Liebermann observed a crescent of silver stubble beneath the man's hat. A middle-aged man, perhaps? Not too robust, he hoped.

Closer . . .

"Of course, you are at liberty to dismiss everything I have said," Trezska added. "Why should you believe me? But I can assure you that I am speaking the absolute truth."

Liebermann drew back his arm, clenched his fist, and thumped the man as hard as he could in the region of the occipital bone. The man fell forward on the stairs, unconscious, his pistol skittering away. His hat had become dislodged, revealing a bald pate and a pair of slightly tapering ears. Liebermann knelt down, checked the man's pulse, and turned him over. It was Inspector Victor von Bulow.

76

DREXLER WAS LYING IN the infirmary, thinking over the day's events. It had been a miracle, surely. God had interceded in order to give him a second chance. He must use the rest of his life wisely, as the deity rarely acted without purpose.

Dr. Kessler had left more than an hour ago. He was a kindly old fellow and meant well but, in Drexler's estimation, had spoken a lot of nonsense: *You were perhaps very . . . close to Perger? He was your friend? It is indeed upsetting when we lose the company of one for whom we have developed a bond of deep and sincere affection . . .*

Drexler had listened patiently. As far as he could gather, it seemed that the good doctor was proposing that Perger's precipitate *departure* had had the effect of placing his mind in a state of disequilibrium. Drexler was willing to concede that this was true, in one sense, but also recognized that it was entirely inaccurate in another. He had subsequently agreed to take some pills that were supposed to calm his agitation, but as time passed he was forced to conclude that they were largely ineffective.

Now he was bored.

He wanted to read something, and the book of military anecdotes provided for him by Nurse Funke was decidedly dull. He remembered that he had left his volume of E.T.A. Hoffmann short stories in the lost room, and considered that there would be no great risk associated with retrieving it.

"Nurse Funke?" he called.

The nurse appeared at the door and rested her hand against the jamb.

"Nurse Funke, may I collect a book from the dormitory? Some Hoffmann?"

"Dr. Kessler said you should sleep."

"But it's too early for me to sleep. And I find it easier to sleep if I read first."

"What about the book I brought you?"

"I do not wish to seem ungrateful; however, to be perfectly honest, Nurse Funke, I've already read it."

"Very well," said the nurse. "You can go. But you must come back immediately."

"Of course."

Drexler put on his uniform and set off on a circuitous tour of the school that took him—unseen—to the trapdoor.

When he dropped down into the lost room, he discovered that it was already occupied. Steininger was sitting in the wicker chair, smoking a cigarette, with his feet up on a stool. The Serbian boy, Stojakovic, was kneeling before him, vigorously cleaning his shoes. Freitag and another stocky boy called Gruber were standing close by.

When Drexler landed, Stojakovic stopped brushing. Steininger immediately lashed out and delivered a blow to the side of his head.

"Who told you to stop?" Steininger barked.

Stojakovic reapplied the polish and resumed his Sisyphean labor.

"Where's Wolf?" asked Drexler.

"Gone," said Steininger, stroking his downy mustache. "His parents came and collected him today. I don't think he'll be coming back."

"Poor Wolf," said Freitag. "An excellent fellow—but prone to getting big ideas. *Too* big, eh? He was bound to overstretch himself one day."

"What did he do?" said Drexler.

"I managed to speak to him just before he left, while he was packing his bags," Steininger replied. "Apparently he was blackmailing Sommer and the police found out!"

"Is that why Sommer killed himself?"

"Who knows?" Steininger nonchalantly flicked some ash onto Stojakovic's hair. "So . . . where the hell have you been?"

"In the infirmary."

"What! We'd heard that someone had gone mad and the headmaster had called Kessler. My God, it wasn't *you*, was it?"

Freitag and Gruber were amused by the jibe and burst out laughing.

"Yes—it was," Drexler replied calmly.

The laughing died down and Steininger glanced uneasily at Freitag.

"Get up, Stojakovic," said Drexler. He reached down and pulled the boy to his feet. "Go on . . ." He jerked his head toward the trapdoor.

"What in God's name do you think you're doing, Drexler?" Steininger cried. "Can't you see? I'm in command now! I'm giving the orders!" He jabbed his finger at the Serbian boy. "Stojakovic—you try to leave and you'll regret it!"

Drexler pushed Stojakovic, who stumbled away from Steininger.

"Take no notice of him. Go."

The boy was too frightened to leave. He stood, rooted to the spot where he had come to rest.

Steininger caught Freitag's eye and nodded.

"You really have gone mad, Drexler," said Freitag.

"Yes, quite mad," echoed Gruber.

The two lieutenants moved forward.

"Don't you understand?" continued Freitag, pushing his unfin-ished canine face into Drexler's. "We're tired of all your nonsense."

"And I'm tired of *you!*" said Drexler.

Without warning, he brought his knee up sharply into Freitag's groin. As the boy buckled over in pain, Drexler delivered an upper-cut to his heavy chin, which sent him reeling over onto the floor. Drexler then thrust his elbow back into Gruber's face, knocking out several teeth. Steininger attempted to jump up, but Drexler placed both hands against his chest and pushed him back down.

Gruber retreated, his hand over his mouth, blood streaming through his fingers and splashing onto the floor. Freitag was rolling from side to side, moaning and clutching his genitals.

"Stojakovic," said Drexler calmly, "if any of these imbeciles pick on you again, let me know. Now, for the last time, will you please go."

The Serbian boy jumped up onto the box and pulled himself up through the trapdoor. His accelerating footsteps could be heard crossing the floor above.

Drexler went to the old suitcase, opened the lid, and took out his volume of E.T.A. Hoffmann short stories. He slowed as he passed Steininger.

"Now that Wolf's gone, things are going to change around here," he said.

77

"WELL, HERR DOCTOR," said Trezska. The impersonal term of address was employed knowingly, and Liebermann detected in its use a purposeful distancing. "Once again I am indebted. You know, I really think he was about to pull the trigger."

Liebermann reached for von Bulow's hat and slipped it beneath his head. The insensible inspector's breathing was shallow, but not so shallow as to cause the young doctor alarm. Von Bulow would probably wake with blurred vision, dizziness, and nausea: nothing that twenty-four hours' bed rest wouldn't put right.

"You're a spy—aren't you?" said Liebermann.

Trezska observed him without emotion. He grabbed the stair rail and pulled himself up.

"They call you . . . the Liderc?"

Trezska raised one of her eyebrows, indicating that she was impressed.

"And I presume," Liebermann continued, "that this name was chosen because of your willingness to use your feminine *charms* in the service of your cause?"

"You have many flaws, Herr Doctor, but I had never, till this moment, counted prudery among them."

Liebermann ignored her barbed riposte.

"Your mission," he continued, "was to steal a document from General von Stoger—a top secret document called *Studie U*. The unwitting general was encouraged to expect your favors and invited you to his apartment. I wonder, did you always plan to kill him? Or did something go wrong that necessitated his murder?"

"I was supposed to keep the old man *occupied*," Trezska responded euphemistically, "while a comrade opened his safe. The fool made so much noise that von Stoger picked up a poker and went to see what was going on. My comrade panicked. It was most unfortunate."

"And what about me?" said Liebermann. "Was I part of your mission too?"

"You flatter yourself, Herr Doctor. We met by chance."

"In which case . . . you swiftly calculated that I might have some other use: the provision of an alibi, perhaps?"

"If this is to be a frank exchange of views," said Trezska, "then I must admit, the idea *did* cross my mind; however, that was all. I sought your further acquaintance because I felt indebted to you. We Hungarians are nothing if not appreciative. Moreover, I found you very . . ." she paused before adding, ". . . desirable."

A gust of wind lashed the side of Liebermann's face. A fresh cascade of water tumbled from the second story, contributing yet more volume to the existing downpour.

"I see from your expression," said Trezska, "that you find my candid admission distasteful—unbecoming of a lady? Of course, if I were a man, you would think nothing of it. You are not nearly so enlightened as you suppose, Herr Doctor. Now, before I take my leave—which I really must—tell me, what are you doing here? I cannot recall issuing you with an invitation."

"I came here to confront you."

"Why? For what purpose?"

"To see if my deductions were correct."

Trezska laughed. "Another of your flaws, Herr Doctor: intellectual vanity! Well, at the risk of aggravating your conceit, I must applaud you! Your deductions were indeed correct. Which brings me to my next question: How ever did you become so well informed? There are aides in the Hofburg who have never heard of *Studie U*. And as for my code name . . . If you hadn't rendered our poor friend here unconscious"—she gestured toward von Bulow—"I would be considering whether or not you had been recruited by the secret service."

"And what if I was?" said Liebermann.

Before she could answer, a male voice resounded across the courtyard: "Don't move."

Liebermann turned. Coming out of the arcade was a swarthy-looking young man. He was holding a gun and walking straight toward him.

78

THE FOREST WAS VIRTUALLY IMPENETRABLE; however, the woodman was able to find his way by following a series of marks he had made on the tree trunks with his knife: gouges, gashes, and occasionally a rough cross. His furs were heavy with rain, and the sack he was carrying had become burdensome.

No one ever passed this way. Even the local people kept a safe distance. It wasn't only that the little forest was remote and inhospitable. There were stories: of wild animals, of murderous Gypsies—and of children who had entered and never come out again.

It was true that Gypsies were unaccountably fond of parking their brightly painted caravans close by. Moreover, they traveled immense distances to get there—from Russia, Galicia, and the Carpathians. They rarely stayed for more than a day.

Once, the woodman had overheard some men in the Aufkirchen inn gossiping about the forest. Someone had said that the king of the Ruthenian Gypsies had buried a hoard of stolen treasure in the middle of it. A young man who was staying at the inn had insisted that they should saddle up their horses at once. They should ride out to this forest, equipped with lamps and shovels, and they might return the very same night, fabulously rich. But the older men laughed uneasily. It was only a legend—and they plied the young man with so much drink that he fell off his stool and had to be carried to his room.

The woodman emerged in a small clearing. In the center was an ancient stone well and a tumbledown shack. Thick smoke was coming from the chimney, and the air was filled with an acrid odor. He lumbered over to the entrance and knocked gently.

"Come in." The voice was old and cracked.

The woodman pulled the door open and went inside.

In the center of the room was an open fire over which a black cauldron was suspended. Only a few tongues of flame danced around the steaming logs, but they supplied enough light to reveal the squalid surroundings: a dirty pallet bed, bottles, a shelf of earthenware pots, and several cages on the floor. The cages were occupied, and green eyes flashed behind the chicken wire.

Next to the cauldron an old woman sat on a low bench. She had a schoolmaster's black cloak wrapped around her shoulders, and she wore a necklace made from the bones of animals. Her hair was long and gray, and when she smiled, her lips receded to reveal a row of blackened teeth. The upper central incisors were missing.

"Is it him?" she croaked.

The woodman nodded and dropped the jute sack next to the cauldron. Zhenechka got up and hobbled over. Reaching into a worn leather pouch, she produced a silver coin, which she pressed into the woodman's hand.

"Good," she said. "Very good."

She was delighted with the woodman's find—and could put it to many irregular uses.

79

"Put your hands above your head."

The man was wearing a shabby coat, a floppy hat tilted at an acute angle, and a long embroidered scarf. Black curly hair fell from behind his exposed ear, and his mustache was so well waxed that the wind and rain hadn't displaced a single hair. It projected out from his face, defiantly horizontal.

Liebermann obeyed.

"Don't look at me—turn back round," the man continued.

"This is quite unnecessary, Lázár," said Trezska. "Herr Dr. Liebermann is a friend. Had he not come to my assistance"—she gestured toward the supine body of von Bulow—"everything would now be over."

Liebermann felt the barrel of the gun dig into the back of his neck.

"No," said the man. "He's not *our* friend: he's a friend of the fat detective—the one who was following me. I told you not to mess around—not with so much at stake. Now look what's happened."

Trezska looked down at Liebermann. "Ah, now I see why you are so well informed."

"Well informed?" asked the man. "What does he know?"

"He knows about *Studie U.*"

"Then we must kill him."

"I have no idea what *Studie U* is!" Liebermann protested. "I am *very* well acquainted with Inspector Rheinhardt—the person whom

I think you just referred to as the *fat detective*—and I sometimes help him with his inquiries. His assistant overheard a conversation between *this* gentleman—Inspector von Bulow—and the commissioner. *Studie* U and the Liderc were discussed." The gunman took a sharp intake of breath. "Neither Inspector Rheinhardt nor I," Liebermann continued, "have the slightest idea what *Studie* U is, beyond the obvious—that it is a document that must contain some highly sensitive information. As for your code name . . ." Liebermann appealed to Trezska. "You will allow, I hope, that you gave me certain reasons for suspicion on the Kohlmarkt, and I am not an absolute fool."

Before Trezska could respond, the man interjected, "He's lying."

The gunman's intention to fire his weapon was reflected in Trezska's horrified expression.

"No," she shouted. "Wait!"

"What for?"

"If he's lying, why did he knock out von Bulow?"

"Maybe he didn't—maybe it's all a ruse and von Bulow is just pretending to be unconscious, waiting for his moment!"

"Lázár, that's absurd."

"Look, I don't know what's happening here—and neither do you. But we do know that *this* man"—Liebermann felt the gun's muzzle being lodged under the bony arch at the base of his skull—"knows far more than he should, and if you let him live, it will threaten the success of the operation—everything we've worked for! If you don't want to watch, go and wait for me at the Südbahnhof. I'll deal with them both."

The ensuing hiatus was filled with the noise of the roaring deluge: the slop and spatter, the splash and spill—unrelenting, indifferent, merciless.

Trezska threw her arms up in the air, as if she were beseeching a higher authority for assistance. When she let them drop, her bag slipped from her shoulder. It landed on the ironwork with a resonant clang. She crouched down to pick it up.

There was a loud report.

The pressure of the gun barrel at the back of Liebermann's neck was suddenly relieved. Then there was a dull thud, followed by the clatter of Lázár Kiss's revolver hitting the ground.

Trezska was clutching a small smoking pistol.

Liebermann remembered that first night, when he had lifted her bag in the alley and found it unusually heavy. Now he knew why.

He wheeled around. Lázár was sprawled out on the cobbles, blood leaking from a neat circular hole in his forehead.

"You've killed him," whispered Liebermann.

"Yes," said Trezska. "You were telling the truth." She smiled at him, and her distinctive features took on a diabolic cast. "I had a . . . *feeling*. And, as you know, I trust my feelings."

"Who is he?" said Liebermann, extending a trembling hand to the stair rail for support.

"Lázár Kiss—a fellow nationalist. But I have long suspected him of being a collaborator—a double agent. Now, you will forgive me, I have a train to catch. I trust you won't experience a sudden surge of patriotism and try to stop me." Trezska pointed her gun at Liebermann. "I hope you will agree that I have now redeemed my debt—and I have no further obligation to you."

"Would you really shoot me?" Liebermann glanced at the pistol. It was a beautiful weapon, chased with filigree. The handgrip was inlaid with mother-of-pearl.

"What do you think?"

"I think you would."

"Then you would think right."

"Is it in your valise—*Studie U*?"

"Yes."

"What is it? What can be *so* valuable . . ."

Trezska paused. Her expression suggested inner conflict—a struggle of conscience that finally resolved itself in a sigh.

"The emperor's plans to invade Hungary."

"What?" said Liebermann, drawing back in disbelief. "But that's impossible!"

"Before you condemn me, just think how many lives would be lost if the old fool and his senile generals decided to march on Budapest. At least with *Studie U* in our possession we can attempt to avert such a catastrophe."

She picked up her violin case and descended the staircase. As she passed him, she pressed the gun against his chest and kissed him on the lips. When she withdrew, he was dizzy with the sweet fragrance of clementine.

"Until the next time, Herr Doctor."

After taking only a few steps she stopped.

"Oh—and one last thing. If I were you, I would pretend this didn't happen. You know nothing—do you understand? Nothing. If certain individuals suspected that you had been informed of the content of *Studie U*, you would be in great danger. You can, of course, depend on me to exercise the utmost discretion."

She walked to the arcade—and did not look back.

Liebermann checked von Bulow's pulse again and ran across the courtyard. When he came out the other side of the vaulted passageway, the cul-de-sac was empty.

The Liderc.

It was an appropriate name.

80

LIEBERMANN PLAYED THE GENTLE introduction and raised his gaze to meet Rheinhardt's. The inspector rested his hand on the side of the Bösendorfer and began to sing—a sweet melody that possessed the transparent simplicity of a lullaby. It was Schubert's setting of Wilhelm Müller's *Des Müllers Blumen*—*The Miller's Flowers*.

Rheinhardt rocked gently from side to side, conjuring with his lyric baritone a dewy morning of sunlight and rolling hills.

> *"Der Bach der ist des Müllers Freund,*
> *"Und hellblau Liebchens Auge scheint."*
> The brooklet is the miller's friend,
> And my sweetheart's eyes are brightest blue.

Schubert's writing was deceptive. The sweet melody, while retaining its mellifluous charm, was suddenly imbued with painful, inconsolable yearning.

> *"Drum sind es meine Blumen . . ."*
> Therefore they are my flowers . . .

Liebermann scrutinized the notes on the page and marveled at Schubert's genius. Somehow he had managed to conceal in an arc of seemingly harmless values and pitches the absolute anguish of unrequited love. As the song progressed, the phrase was repeated, and with each repetition the listener was obliged to conclude that the young miller's heart would inevitably be broken. The bright blue eyes that he had laid claim to would never be his. Liebermann experienced this realization viscerally, as though he were hearing the song for the first time, and he found his chest tightening—until the constrictive feeling was relieved by a sigh.

When the final chord was reached, the young doctor bowed his head and allowed the notes to fade into a prolonged, respectful silence.

In due course, the two men retired to the smoking room, where they assumed their customary places. Liebermann's serving man had laid out the brandy and cigars, and the fire was already blazing. Rheinhardt noticed that Liebermann's old ashtray had been replaced by a new one—a metal box with a hinged lid.

The young doctor observed Rheinardt's nose wrinkling.

"You don't like it?"

"Well . . . it's a little plain, don't you think?"

"That's the point. It's by Josef Hoffmann."

"Hoffmann?"

"Yes, Hoffmann. Surely you've heard of Hoffmann! He's a designer—and a very gifted one."

"It doesn't take such a great talent to design a featureless box."

"It isn't featureless. If you look closely, you'll see that the surface has been hammered."

Rheinhardt peered at the ashtray and pushed out his lower lip.

"How much did you pay for this?"

"Clearly too much in your opinion; however, the exterior is silver-plated, and it came with a mirrored candle-stand and a cigarette case. One day, Oskar, Hoffmann's designs"—Liebermann flicked the metal so that it made a ringing sound—"will be exhibited in museums of art."

Rheinhardt smiled indulgently, but it was perfectly clear that he thought this unlikely.

The brandy was promptly decanted, the cigars were lit, and soon the room was filled with a pungent haze. Their conversation became fluid and agreeable—touching upon some amusing articles they had both read in *Die Fackel*. Eventually, however, their mood changed, becoming more subdued, and an extended silence signaled their readiness to discuss matters of greater importance.

The inspector tapped his cigar over the new Hoffmann ashtray and addressed his friend:

"Did you hear about Sommer?"

"Yes," said Libermann. "It was reported in the *Neue Freie Presse*."

"A sorry business."

"Indeed."

"And something else—something rather odd—happened up at Saint Florian's last week."

"Oh?"

"One of the boys—a lad called Martin Drexler—presented himself at a local police station, claiming to have killed Isidor Perger in a shooting accident. The boy said that he had buried Perger's body in the woods. He led a constable to the spot—but there was nothing there. Subsequently, Drexler became very distressed and the constable began to have doubts about his sanity. The boy was returned to the school and attended by Dr. Kessler, who prescribed some sedative medication."

"Do you want me to examine him?"

"No—that won't be necessary. I spoke to Dr. Kessler this morning, and apparently the boy is doing well. I mention it only because it struck me as a peculiar . . . codetta to the events with which we have been so closely involved." Rheinhardt directed his gaze into the fire. "Even more curious events have transpired concerning von Bulow and his special assignment."

Liebermann's heart skipped a beat. "Really?" he said, feigning nonchalance.

"Once again, Max," said Rheinhardt, turning toward his friend, "I am obliged to remind you that what I am about to say must be treated in the strictest confidence."

Liebermann nodded and began an unusually thorough examination of the pattern on his brandy glass.

"I was called to the commissioner's office and knew as soon as I arrived that something significant had happened. His attitude was completely different. I wouldn't say that he was being polite . . . but he was certainly being a lot less rude. I could see that he was finding this *act* quite difficult to sustain, agreeableness not being one of his natural endowments. After some preliminary and somewhat strained courtesies, he announced that von Bulow's assignment had ended rather badly—and that von Bulow was currently indisposed and receiving medical care at a sanitarium. It seems that my esteemed colleague was engaged in the pursuit of a Hungarian spy—a woman, known in nationalist circles as the *Liderc*."

"If my memory serves me correctly," Liebermann interjected, "that is the name that Haussmann overheard, is it not?"

"Precisely. Well, von Bulow managed to find her hideaway—at an address in Landstrasse—and actually had the woman at gunpoint when someone came up behind him and struck him on the head. He lost consciousness instantly, and when he woke up, his bird had flown . . . However, next to him he discovered the body of a gentleman known as Lázár Kiss—a man connected with the nationalists and whom Brügel and von Bulow had asked me to follow, when I had wanted to continue the investigation at Saint Florian's. Well, since von Bulow's debacle in Landstrasse, the commissioner has received some extremely discomfiting intelligence. Kiss was indeed a very high-ranking agent. Not one of theirs, however, but one of ours! He was in the Austrian secret service and had infiltrated a nationalist cell. He was on the brink of finding out the identities of several spymasters. As you can imagine, all this places Brügel in a very difficult position: he authorized von Bulow's assignment, and this may have resulted, ultimately, in the failure of Kiss's mission."

"So Brügel fears an investigation?"

"Without a doubt—which is why he is being so civil. I am sure that when the time comes he will expect me to answer questions in such a way as to deflect blame from himself. The old rogue actually had the audacity to say that he had always considered von Bulow a headstrong fellow and wasn't I inclined to agree?"

Liebermann turned his glass. "What actually happened in Land-strasse? Who shot Lázár Kiss?"

"How ever did you know he was shot?" asked Rheinhardt. "Was it something I said? Another of your *Freudian slips*?"

"Never mind," said Liebermann nervously. "Please continue."

"It might have been *her*—the Liderc—or it might have been someone else who arrived at the scene after her departure. And as for who struck von Bulow, who can say? It might have been Kiss—or, again, it could have been someone else entirely. . . . We simply don't know."

Liebermann swallowed. His mouth had gone quite dry.

"Tell me . . . was any attempt made to collect any forensic evidence? Dust particles, hairs, footprints?"

"Yes, of course," Rheinhardt replied. "But nothing of any significance was found. On Friday, you will recall, there was a storm. Everything got washed away."

The young doctor sipped his brandy and settled more comfortably into his chair. "Do you know anything more about this . . . Liderc woman? She sounds fascinating."

"Fascinating but extremely dangerous," said Rheinhardt, throwing his head back and expelling a column of roiling smoke. "The commissioner mentioned that she is a very competent violinist and had begun a modest concert career. She traveled widely under the auspices of a respectable cultural initiative, which—can you believe—received state sponsorship with the emperor's approval! Such brazenness!"

"Where do you think she is now?"

"I suspect that she has gone south. Italy, perhaps. But she will return—when she thinks she can journey home in safety."

Liebermann set his glass aside. "But how does all this relate to von Stoger?"

"Good heavens, Max, isn't it obvious? It was the Liderc who stole the documents from the general's safe—and it must have been her too who murdered him in cold blood."

"She might have had an accomplice?"

"Well, that's possible . . . but what does it matter now? She got away. . . . There will be no trial. She will not be called to account."

"What do you think was in those stolen documents? Did the commissioner give you any idea—any clue?"

"Military secrets, I imagine. But if Brügel knew more, he wasn't very forthcoming." Rheinhardt paused, twisted the horns of his mustache thoughtfully, and continued: "Of course, it is possible that the Austrian secret service intended the Liderc to acquire von Stoger's documents so that she would, in the fullness of time, lead Kiss to her masters. Thus, von Stoger's death might have been the result of misadventure—an accident. Whatever, one thing is certain: their plans went horribly wrong—and most probably because of von Bulow's meddling."

Liebermann allowed himself a half smile. "You must be quite satisfied with the way things have turned out."

Rheinhardt appeared flustered for a moment. He coughed and produced an embarrassed mumble.

"Von Bulow wasn't entirely at fault. I'm sure that some of the confusion must have arisen because of bureaucracy. I suppose the various departments concerned were simply too occupied filling in forms and registering reports to talk to each other. Von Bulow should have been better informed about Kiss. Even so, if—after his recovery—von Bulow is not invited to resume his duties at the security office, you are quite correct: I will not spend very much time lamenting his professional demise."

The inspector lit another cigar—and he looked, that instant, more like a man at a wedding or some other grand celebratory occasion. Seeing his friend so happy went at least some way toward mitigating Liebermann's feelings of guilt. Von Bulow had been the bane of Rheinhardt's life at the security office. And now, at last, he was gone.

"It is truly remarkable," Rheinhardt continued, "how close we came to the perilous world of espionage and counterespionage; still, I am glad that we were not drawn in any further. Indeed, I would go so far as to say that I am grateful for von Bulow's vanity, grateful that he excluded us from the von Stoger investigation. Otherwise we might have strayed onto some very treacherous and dangerous ground. I must say, I am uncomfortable with *that* world—the world of spies—

with its deceptions, double deceptions, feints, and ruses—its fatal lies. It is a world where nothing is as it seems, and nobody can be trusted."

Liebermann stared into the flames and felt a stab of shame.

His friend was so much wiser than his modest exterior ever betrayed.

"Oskar," Liebermann whispered, "I have a confession to make. Something has been weighing heavily on my conscience the whole evening."

"Oh?" Rheinhardt's face filled with concern.

"I promised to get some tickets for the Zemlinsky concert next Saturday . . . but, what with one thing and another, it completely slipped my mind—and it's sold out."

Rheinhardt laughed: a generous, booming laugh.

"God in heaven," he cried. "Is that all? You had me worried! I thought you were going to say something of consequence!"

81

THE CLOCK MAKERS' BALL was a grand affair and was attended by a diverse group of patrons. There were boulevardiers whose glazed eyes, ruddy cheeks, and uncertain feet declared that they were attending their second or even third ball of the evening. There were debutantes in radiant white, and various representatives of the imperial army: infantrymen in blue, artillerymen in chocolate-brown tunics and red collar flashes, and hussars—their short fur-trimmed and golden-braided coats slung casually over one shoulder. A distinguished gentleman with a mane of silvery curls who was surrounded by laughing ladies was identified very quickly as the Dutch ambassador, and it was rumoured that a striking woman wearing a glimmering *peau de soie* gown was a member of the Italian aristocracy.

As soon as Liebermann took Amelia into his arms, he was aware of a difference. She was more confident and followed his lead with less effort.

"Have you been to see Herr Janowsky for a lesson?" he asked.

"No," she replied. "Although I still intend to, once my brother leaves."

"Well, I have to say," Liebermann remarked, "your dancing is much improved."

"I think," said Amelia, "that I understand—although 'understand' is not really the correct word—I think I now *appreciate* the value of your initial advice: to listen to the music with greater care.

To . . ." She hesitated, and the ghost of a smile crossed her face. "Feel it?"

She was dressed in the same clothes that she had worn for the detectives' ball: a skirted décolleté gown of green velvet. Yet she appeared to Liebermann more elegant than he remembered. As they passed beneath a massive crystal chandelier, the light fell on her pewter eyes and he experienced momentarily a sensation like falling. It was not the same feeling as a physical descent but something more profound.

"My brother seems to have made a friend," said Amelia, and, once again, a fleeting smile illuminated her face.

Randall was talking to a dark-haired lady who was wearing an exquisite creation of red silk, black lace, and pearls. She was holding a feathered carnival mask on a long handle and made extravagant use of her free hand while speaking. Liebermann guessed that she was French.

Just before Randall slipped from view they saw him produce a rose from behind his back.

The orchestra was playing with sparkling virtuosity—a great, carousing, fortissimo waltz in which extraordinary liberties were being taken with meter. The melody was held back by the introduction of subtle hesitations, which made the music hover for the briefest moment before each reprieve of the principal theme.

Liebermann recalled a passage from von Saar's *Marianne*: a waltz could melt away years of repression, fanning flirtation into passion. The rapid motion, the relentless turning, the dizzy euphoria, the heat of a woman's back felt in the palm of one's hand . . .

Amelia looked up at him, and her eyes had never appeared more beautiful. He rediscovered the shock of when he had first noticed their inimitable color, neither blue nor gray but something in between: their depth enhanced by a darkening at the edges of each iris.

Liebermann drew her closer, and his lips brushed the silver ribbons in her flaming hair.

The impetuous élan of the orchestra was contagious.

Is this the time?

He had asked himself this question before—on so many occasions.

Is this the time?

Suddenly the tension dissipated, and he whirled Amelia around with such enthusiasm that she briefly achieved flight.

"Dr. Liebermann?"

He laughed, and the vertical crease with which he had become so very familiar appeared on her forehead.

"What is it?" she asked.

How appropriate, thought Liebermann, *that we are attending the clock makers' ball.*

There would be time enough . . .

Even if Nietzsche was right and there was such a thing as eternal recurrence and every man and woman was destined to revisit the lost opportunities of the past in perpetuity—he no longer cared. Psychoanalysis had taught him the importance of little things, and perhaps it was these little things that made human beings human: the mistakes, the blunders, the qualms, the petty vacillations and doubting. Liebermann understood—better than most—that there were hidden virtues in human frailty.

Yes, there was time enough: the promise of days and months and years to come.

Amelia was still looking at him quizzically—waiting for an answer. When it came, it was intellectually disingenuous but emotionally sincere. It *felt* right.

"There's no place like Vienna!" Liebermann cried. And, once again, Amelia's feet parted company with the ground.

Acknowledgments and Sources

I WOULD LIKE TO THANK: Hannah Black, Clare Alexander, Nick Austin, and Steve Mathews—once again—for invaluable editorial and critical assistance; Paul Taunton, Jennifer Rodriguez, and Bara MacNeill for their assistance in preparing the U.S. edition. Professor Ignaz Hammerer and Dr W. Etschmann (Militärgeschichtliche Forschungsabteilung des Heeresgeschichtlichen Museum) for information concerning Austrian military academies; Mirko Herzog (Technisches Museum Wien) for erudite answers with respect to the media and postal services in turn-of-the-century Vienna; Professor Thomas Olechowski (University of Vienna) for advising me on press censorship under the Habsburg monarchy and recommending the *Arbeiter-Zeitung* for the puposes of my plot; Clive Baldwin for alerting me to the existence of Erzsébet Báthory; Luitgaard Hammerer for acting as my unpaid translator, research assistant, and city guide in Vienna (and for finding out about the employment of specialist pastry cooks in Demel); Simon Dalgleish for checking my German and correcting several linguistic errors; and Nicola Fox for continuing to put up with it all.

Saint Florian's military school owes an enormous debt to the *oberrealschule* described in Musil's *The Confusions of Young Torless*. I have unashamedly raided this masterpiece for useful detail, atmosphere, specific settings, and even the odd character. Other books that were informative on the subject of education in fin de siècle Vienna were Arthur Schnitzler's *My Youth in Vienna* and *The World of Yesterday* by Stefan Zweig. Quotations from Nietzsche are mostly from *A Nietzsche Reader* (selected and translated with an introduction by R. J. Hollingdale). Translations of songs were by William Mann, Lionel Salter, and Richard Stokes. *Studie U* was a real document—and is referred to in chapter four ("Politics and Powers") of *Budapest 1900: A Historical Portrait of a City and Its Culture* by John Lukacs. Descriptions of "Venice in Vienna" were based on photographs in *Blickfänge einer Reise nach Wien* published by the Historisches Museum der Stadt Wien.

Information on the history of the inkblot test (before Rorschach) can be found in "The Origins of Inkblots" by John T. R. Richardson, an article published in *The Psychologist* in June 2004. Biographical details on Justinus Kerner can be found in *The Discovery of the Unconscious*, by Henri F. Ellenberger. Frau Becker's dream is based on case material reported by Freud in *Introductory Lectures on Psychoanalysis*, lecture 7. The opening of Freud's university lecture is a transcription of lecture 20 from the same work. Freud's episode of jealousy is exactly as described by Ernest Jones in *The Life and Work of Sigmund Freud*. The description of Mahler's "funny walk" and leg movements can be found in *Gustav Mahler: Letters to His Wife* (edited by Henry-Louis de La Grange and Günther Weiss in collaboration with Knud Martner). Randall Lydgate's description of Toltec civilization is taken from *The Myths of Mexico and Peru* by Lewis Spence, published in 1913 by George C. Harrap and Co. The absinthe ritual (as performed by Trezska Novak) is described in Barnaby Conrad's *Absinthe: History in a Bottle.* The *Erotes*—translated into English as *Affairs of the Heart*—was once attributed to Lucian but is now thought to be the work of an unknown author referred to as Pseudo-Lucian. I took a few liberties with my interpretation of what Pseudo-Lucian wrote—but Herr Sommer's fundamental arguments based on this work are accurate. Liebermann's advice to Amelia Lydgate on waltzing is adapted from a description of the waltz that can be found at http://www.vienneseball.org.

Frank Tallis
London, 2007

DOSSIER

Fatal Lies

FRANK TALLIS

MORTALIS

The Banality of Evil

THE INSPIRATION FOR ONE BOOK often comes from reading another—and for *Fatal Lies* that other book was *The Confusions of Young Torless* by Robert Musil (1880–1942). It is not particularly well-known among English and American readers, but it is regarded as a classic in Austria and Germany.

Musil was born in Klagenfurt and attended military school from the age of eleven but eventually decided on a career in engineering. After a short stint writing technical papers, he resumed his studies in Berlin, where his subjects were philosophy and psychology. *The Confusions of Young Torless* was completed in 1905, several years before he was awarded his doctorate.

Musil's most celebrated work is the monumental *The Man Without Qualities*—still unfinished at the time of his death. It is often linked with James Joyce's *Ulysees* and Marcel Proust's *Remembrance of Things Past*, and together these three books are said to represent the apogee of twentieth-century modernist fiction.

As you might expect, *The Man Without Qualities* is not an easy read; however, *The Confusions of Young Torless* is very accessible. It is fewer than two hundred pages long, is set in a military academy (just like the one Musil attended), and catalogues the psychological development of a young man as he struggles to make sense of a world in which bullying and ritual humiliation are commonplace. Musil's novel is much more ambitious than it first appears. It is a chilling exploration of the origins of fascism.

At one point, a bully provides a justification for violence that owes a debt to Friedrich Nietszche (1844–1900), the philosopher who suggested that the Übermensch or superman, does not respect moral constraints. The idea of making a new morality—beyond conventional notions of good and evil—was one endorsed by the Nazi party for obvious reasons. The conceptual leap required to construe genocide as a reasonable goal is a very considerable one and required new intellectual tools that Nietszche unwittingly provided.

In *Fatal Lies*, I named the headmaster of the military academy Eichmann, in order to raise the spectre of Adolf Eichmann—the Nazi who proposed "the final solution to the Jewish question." It was Eichmann who inspired Hannah Arendt to coin a phrase that has since found its way into numerous works of history and social commentary: "the banality of evil."

Arendt attended the trial of Eichmann in Jerusalem in 1961 and was amazed by his ordinariness. He was more like a petty functionary than a monster. He had become totally preoccupied by the organizational problems and technical details of genocide, at the expense of any moral concerns. He was a simple man who was just obeying orders. Arendt responded poetically, asserting that Eichmann demonstrated the "fearsome, word-and-thought defying banality of evil."

During WWII, "normal" German citizens—when in uniform—were able to commit appalling acts of violence. This phenomenon was so perplexing to postwar social psychologists that they conducted numerous experiments in order to elucidate the factors and processes that might transform teachers, accountants, and doctors into mass murderers. This tradition began with Solomon Asch's studies of conformity, continued through Stanley Milgram's studies of obedience—and culminated with Philip Zimbardo's Stanford prison experiment. Collectively, this body of work yielded results that were entirely consistent with Arendt's notion of "the banality of evil." It seemed that ordinary experimental subjects could be persuaded to inflict pain on others with remarkable ease. Under the right circumstances, almost anyone can become a monster.

This conclusion became received wisdom in the social psychology literature, and was seen as such for more than thirty years; however, in a recent article that appeared in *The Psychologist* (published by the British Psychological Society), Professor S. Alexander Haslam and Professor Stephen D. Reicher have raised significant questions concerning the legitimacy of this long-held view.

It is a surprising fact that Hannah Arendt never saw the end of Eichmann's trial. If she had, her conclusions would have been very different. Early on, Eichmann made efforts to present himself as an innocent "pen-pusher"—only doing his job. But in due course, the mask began to slip, revealing a Nazi ideologue and committed anti-Semite. He appeared, to later observers, as an individual who'd set about his work with visionary zeal and who was proud of his "achievements."

Eichmann and his fellow Nazis were capable of atrocities not because they were ordinary decent folk in uniforms but because they believed passionately in their cause.

Recently, a number of revisionist books have been published highlighting this point. In addition, the validity of the classic experimental studies of conformity and obedience—which supported the banality-of-evil hypothesis—have since been challenged on several counts (including methodological weaknesses).

Professors Haslam and Reicher assert:

> . . . *from Stanford, as from the obedience studies, it is not valid to conclude that people mindlessly and helplessly succumb to brutality. Rather both studies (and also the historical evidence) suggest that brutality occurs when people identify strongly with brutal groups that have a brutal ideology.*

According to this new view, people commit atrocities because they believe what they are doing is right. Ordinary people are not closet monsters after all; however, they can become monsters if they subscribe to certain beliefs. Today, social psychologists should no longer be asking the question: How is it that ordinary people can be persuaded to do terrible things? A better question would be: What are the factors that cause ordinary people to identify with brutal belief systems? In the modern world, the answer to this question is needed with some urgency.

The wide appeal of fundamentalist ideologies—of which national socialism is an example—reveals a flaw in our intellectual and emotional apparatus. The world is a complex place, and we yearn for the comforting solidity of absolute truths. Freud posited that human beings have an infantile wish to experience again the certainty of parental declarations, the tidy polarities of good and bad, wrong and right. Such answers keep the chaos at bay—the complexities of reality, our insignificance, and our likely appointment with oblivion.

The first of our existential crises probably coincides with the onset of adolescence—a fact that provides us with a further reason to admire Robert Musil. He sets *The Confusions of Young Torless* in a military academy—not only to exploit the obvious resonances relating to nationalism and war, but also because such institutions are full of adolescents. Brutality is one of the things that human beings employ to make the world a simpler place—and the generation of Austrians depicted in Musil's masterpiece chose to simplify the world with devastating consequences.

Frank Tallis
London, 2008

Sources

"Questioning the Banality of Evil." S. Alexander Haslam and Stephen D. Reicher. In *The Psychologist*, vol. 21, no. 1, January 2008. Published by the British Psychological Society.

"Introduction." J. M. Coetzee. In *The Confusions of Young Törless* (2001) by Robert Musil. London: Penguin Harmondsworth.

The Death of Sigmund Freud: Fascism, Psychoanalysis and the Rise of Fundamentalism (2007). Mark Edmundson. London: Bloomsbury.

Frank Tallis is a practicing clinical psychologist and an expert in obsessional states. He is the author of *A Death in Vienna*, *Vienna Blood*, and *Fatal Lies*, as well as seven nonfiction books on psychology and two previous novels, *Killing Time* and *Sensing Others*. He is the recipient of a Writers' Award from the Arts Council England and the New London Writers Award from the London Arts Board. *A Death in Vienna* was short-listed for the 2005 Crime Writers' Association Historical Dagger Award. Tallis lives in London.